The Sister Diaries

Karen Quinn

W F HOWES LTD

This large print edition published in 2009 by
W F Howes Ltd
Unit 4, Rearsby Business Park, Gaddesby Lane,
Rearsby, Leicester LE7 4YH

1 3 5 7 9 10 8 6 4 2

First published in the United Kingdom in 2009
by Pocket Books

A CIP catalogue record for this book is available
from the British Library

ISBN 978 1 40744 165 8

Typeset by Palimpsest Book Production Limited,
Grangemouth, Stirlingshire
Printed and bound in Great Britain
by MPG Books Ltd, Bodmin, Cornwall

*To my daughter, Schuyler, who would
never put me in a nursing home.*

To my son, Sam, who would.

LAURA

If you don't understand how a woman could both love her sister dearly and want to wring her neck at the same time, then you were probably an only child.

—Linda Sunshine

When the lawyer read the will, Laura Moon was stunned. Simply, utterly, immutably stunned.

She and her two sisters were seated at the walnut conference table with Sam Hermann, a lawyer with a forehead so large you could watch a movie on it. Laura, twenty-six, twirled a shock of blond curls around her ring finger as she reviewed her to-do list before tomorrow's concert at Golden Manor Nursing Home. Serena, thirty, released her efficient knot of brown hair from its tortoiseshell clip and, having just pumped milk for Valentina, adjusted her bra strap. Amanda, a month shy of forty, frowned as she clacked her manicured thumbs furiously over her BlackBerry, responding to a client's urgent text.

1

Laura knew what was coming. Time and time again, Sunny, their mother, had gone over it with her; that is, until she no longer recognized Laura as her daughter. 'Equal treatment,' she had promised. The house in Tribeca where they grew up and now each had an apartment would go to the three sisters. The Lassiter sketch would also be shared among them. Her mother's only other possessions were a few pieces of jewelry, a mish-mash of furniture, and a wardrobe of well-worn clothes, mostly sweats, nightgowns, and dresses that had seen better days. That was it, the entire estate.

Given the valuable home and artwork to be divided after Sunny's death, one might surmise that the Moons were a family of means. One would be wrong. Mrs Moon had bought the building in the late 1970s for forty thousand dollars after selling a Daniel Lassiter painting. That turned out to be their real estate lottery ticket.

In those days, the triangle below Canal Street wasn't called Tribeca. It was just lower Manhattan, an industrial area filled with factories, warehouses, and print shops. Robert De Niro did not own a restaurant or hip hotel there. There were no restaurants or hip hotels. There were no film festivals. In fact, the name 'Tribeca' had not yet been invented. It would be years before JFK, Jr. bought his loft on North Moore Street and the edgier fashionables followed suit. It wasn't that the Moons were pioneers imbued with great real estate foresight.

No, like the potato farmers of the Hamptons whose fields became their fortune, the Moon millions were made through an accident of urban development.

The building, once a showroom for those clunky Earth Shoes, was located on Duane Park, at the intersection of Duane and West Broadway. It was five stories tall, with three windows across, white painted brick in front, and red brick on the side. The red side abutted a narrow cobblestone street, which gave the place light from three directions, very unusual for a space in the heart of Tribeca.

For years, the family lived in the top two floors and rented the bottom three back to the Earth Shoe Company. About the time Serena was married, the company moved its showroom to New Jersey and Sunny divided the building into three separate units. Recently, a one-floor apartment in the townhouse next door had sold for $2.5 million. Let's see, Laura thought, two-point-five times five stories, that's twelve-point-five million. One third of that is more than four million dollars. Last week I had to borrow grocery money from Serena. Never again.

Laura glanced at Serena, who sat primly at the conference table gazing out the floor to ceiling windows overlooking Park Avenue. At 5'2" and a hundred pounds dripping wet, she went to great lengths to stand as tall as her sisters. Today, Serena wore her last season Narcisco Rodriquez pencil skirt and a vintage sweater along with six-inch heels, bringing her up to 5'8", matching Laura and towering an inch over Amanda. Pathologically neat, she had a habit of twisting her straight mahogany hair into a tight bun and then releasing it. Serena had a perfectly symmetrical face, bee-stung lips, an upturned nose, and arched eyebrows on either side of a thin but deepening line that reflected her life's discontent. Her catlike ebony eyes were framed by lashes coated with thick mascara – jet black, the only color of clothing she ever wore, even in the sizzling August sun.

The Lassiter painting that made the Duane Street house possible was a gift from the artist himself. In 1979, before Serena and Laura were born, their mother, with Amanda in tow, spent a summer in the Hamptons working for Daniel Lassiter while Mr Moon toiled away in the city. The Hamptons are a series of beach communities about a hundred miles from Manhattan along the south shore of Long Island. Set between idyllic ponds and bays on one side and the vast Atlantic Ocean on the other, the area's legendary beauty inspired some of the most important American painters of the last two centuries to work there – Jackson Pollock, Willem de Kooning, and Daniel Lassiter, to name a few. The free play of water, light, sky, and color on the astonishing landscape provided endless possibilities for painters from all schools.

Sunny was hired to be Daniel Lassiter's cook. Like Serena, she was tiny – just shy of five feet –

The Sister Diaries

ALSO BY KAREN QUINN
FROM CLIPPER LARGE PRINT

The Ivy Chronicles
Wife in the Fast Lane
Holly Would Dream

with dark delicate features, intelligent brown eyes, and a short, wavy Clara Bow bob – a petite dynamo that everyone fell in love with the instant she flashed her warm smile and irresistible dimples. She was always flitting about like a fairy, delighting people with her naturally adorable personality.

It was Emma Lassiter who hired Sunny. Emma was a painter herself and had not a stitch of interest in housekeeping. According to family lore, Sunny was supposed to tread quietly into each of their studios at noon every day to deliver lunch – a tuna sandwich with celery for Daniel, egg salad without celery for Emma. On one such occasion, Daniel was having an allergy attack when Sunny happened to tiptoe in. He asked her for some tissues. When she brought them to him, he struck up a conversation and found her thoroughly enchanting. After that, he invited her to eat lunch with him every day. Then he asked her to assist him. It was rumored that she modeled for him as well, but that could not be confirmed because his paintings were too impressionistic.

Emma Lassiter famously resented her husband's extracurricular friendships. In August, she sent Amanda and her mother packing without paying Sunny the wages she was owed. Sunny, furious at being dismissed in such shabby fashion, banged on the door of Daniel's white clapboard studio and appealed to him for relief. To appease her, he rifled his storage cabinet and pulled out two small studies he had painted for his Goddess series. One was a graphite sketch, the other an oil. It was the proceeds from the sale of the oil that paid for the house on Duane Street. Mrs Moon held on to the sketch, which depicted a high-heeled nude with a hulking belly, massive breasts, pointy nails, and bulging eyes. Laura always thought of the woman as Mother Earth, ancient goddess, and modern-day whore all mixed together. It had hung in the family living room for as long as she could remember.

Ten summers later, Mr Moon drove Serena to East Hampton and tried to dump her on Lassiter's doorstep. Serena told of an angry confrontation and harsh accusations between her pale, balding father and a handsome white-haired man in a hangar-like studio. Mr Moon accused Lassiter of fathering Serena, charges the artist vehemently denied. Lassiter then rolled up a massive oil painting on canvas, wrapped it in brown paper, and thrust it into Mr Moon's hands as he ushered him out the door, telling him this should satisfy whatever debt he might owe and never to contact him again.

Mr Moon drove Serena to the beach and left her digging in the sand as he walked into the sea and disappeared forever. The police and Coast Guard searched for him, and his body was recovered three days later. The oversized oil that Lassiter gave Mr Moon that day vanished amidst the confusion. The sisters were devastated by their father's death, especially Serena, who suffered for years from nightmares about being taken to a scary place and abandoned by her own family. She was certain the famous artist was her real father, but her sisters and mother always pooh-poohed that idea lest Serena become even more insufferable than she already was.

The Lassiter sketch still hung in the bedroom where Sunny Moon took her last breath. Laura tried to remember if she had locked the door that morning. She reached into her back pocket to feel for her house key. All her clothes came from flea markets and secondhand shops, but she had a way of creating combinations that always looked downtown-chic. Today, she wore jeans, a white cotton button-down shirt, and ballet flats, the perfect ensemble for showcasing her slender figure, endless legs, and petite breasts. Unlike Serena, Laura never wore black, choosing instead blues, greens, and golds – the colors of abundance. Curly blond hair shimmering with platinum highlights floated cloudlike around her face and loosely down her back. There was something ethereal about Laura, who positively glowed with kindness. Today, her dreamy turquoise eyes betrayed the anxiety she felt; her normally dazzling smile was closed for business.

In a few moments, a mere two weeks after her funeral, the spoils of Sunny's life would be divided among her daughters. In her heart, Laura felt she deserved a bigger share. For the last six years, she had devoted herself to caring for their mother as she sunk deeper into an Alzheimer's fog. Serena had been too busy with her own family to do more than send down a few Fresh Direct prepared meals and 'watch' Sunny at night via a baby monitor. Amanda hadn't had time to physically pitch in, real estate wunderkind that she was, but she paid the grocery and medical bills and handled their mother's financial affairs without complaint. When Sunny first got sick, Laura set aside her career ambitions and tended to her mother's every need, making ends meet by doing whatever came along – modeling, delivering singing telegrams, walking dogs, performing in dive bars and retirement homes. She decided not to make a fuss over the distribution. The last thing she wanted was to fight with her sisters over money.

Sam Hermann sat on the edge of the table, cleared his throat, and pushed his wire-rimmed glasses toward the tip of his nose. 'Okay, I've made copies of the will for each of you,' he said, offering one to Amanda.

Amanda waved it away. 'I need to be uptown in an hour. Let's just get to the punch line.' There was a hoarse timbre to her voice that made her sound like Demi Moore. Today Amanda was her indestructively professional self, in a three-piece navy suit from St John Knit, the only designer she ever wore-because their fabrics never wrinkled and their pieces were interchangeable from season to season. At 5'7" and as slim as a credit card,

Amanda exuded 'real estate hot-shot,' with her almond-shaped yellow-green eyes that lit up when she discussed deals, blood-red Chanel-laquered lips, and corkscrew curly hair the color of apricot jam. Amanda invested a great deal of money and time to get her hair that precise shade of orange, a signature look for the brand she strived to embody – the flame-haired broker of Manhattan's hottest properties.

Sam wiped his brows with a monogrammed handkerchief and then flipped through the pages of the will. 'There are two main assets to be distributed,' he said, stopping to read the crucial passage. 'The house on Duane Street, which was purchased from the sale of my Daniel Lassiter painting, a gift from the artist, is hereby bequeathed solely and exclusively to my middle daughter, Serena. My oldest and youngest daughters, Amanda and Laura, shall be given a lease to live in the home rent-free for one year. In the event that Serena chooses to sell the house, she shall give each of her sisters fifty thousand dollars from the proceeds.'

'Huh?' Amanda said, her brow crinkling in confusion. 'What are you saying? The house goes to Serena and we live there for a year?'

'And collect fifty grand if she sells it?' Laura added.

'That's about it in a nutshell,' Sam said.

Laura was baffled. 'That's not what Mom said. We're supposed to get equal shares. Why would she change her mind?'

Serena's eyes widened to protest her innocence. 'Don't look at me. I don't understand it either.'

Amanda turned to Sam. 'What about the sketch?'

Sam perused the will until he came to the applicable paragraph. He cleared his throat. 'I hereby bequeath the Daniel Lassiter sketch, which was a gift to me from the artist, solely and exclusively to my middle daughter, Serena.'

Amanda shot out of her leather conference chair like a bottle rocket. 'Christ on a fucking cracker! Laura, we've been disinherited.'

Laura clapped her hand over her mouth. The color drained from her face and she could barely breathe. This could not be happening. After six excruciating years of watching Sunny deteriorate, changing her diapers, pureeing her food, feeding her like a baby, struggling to pay bills, Laura was mentally and physically exhausted. She had been counting on the inheritance to allow her to take time off and think about her future, maybe go on one of those *Eat, Pray, Love* journeys. But there was no chance of that now. Sunny had made sure of it.

AMANDA

'Where there's a will – there's a relative.'
                                    —Ricky Gervais

Serena fanned herself. 'My God, I get every-thing. Do you know what that must mean? Could it be? Oh, but Amanda, Laura, how terrible you must feel. Don't worry,' she said in her most concerned voice, 'I'll be a fair landlord.'

Amanda whipped around to confront her. '"A fair landlord"? Could you *be* any more insensitive?'

Serena's jaw dropped. 'Me insensitive? Hello! I give change to homeless people no matter how much they stink.'

Amanda was seething. If Mom wanted to be unfair, she thought, she should have given every-thing to *me*, not Serena. If anyone deserves the bulk of the estate, I do. For years I supported the family, paid for upkeep on the house, and made sure Sunny had the best medical care money could buy. Serena doesn't need the inheritance. Her life is perfect – a TV-director husband, two beautiful kids, no money worries. I'll be a fair landlord

11

indeed. 'Earth to Serena! Laura and I have just been dissed by Mom, in case you hadn't noticed.'

'No,' Sam said, sifting through pages. 'You haven't been dissed. Amanda, your mother left *you* her jewelry. Laura, you're getting her furniture, clothing, and personal effects. Here.' He handed Amanda and Laura each a sealed envelope. 'These are inventories of what you're to receive. Didn't Sunny tell you what she was planning?'

Amanda's eyes flashed. 'No, she did not!'

Sam rubbed his chin thoughtfully. 'Ah, well, my father represented your mother in making this will the year before he died. Personally, I always advise clients who make unequal bequests to be up-front with their children as to why. Otherwise, the kids'll turn their anger on the favored child.'

'Deservedly so,' Amanda said, throwing words at Serena like stones. 'Obviously you exercised undue influence over Mom behind our backs. How *could* you?'

'I was with Mom when she signed her will,' Laura said. 'This is *not* what she signed.'

Sam checked the date on the will. 'This is from six years ago, September. Did she execute one more recently?'

Laura glanced at her sisters, who regarded her expectantly. 'No, the one I witnessed was from eight years ago. Mom's copy is in the safety deposit box.'

'Six years ago September is about when she was diagnosed. She was pretty lucid then, remember?'

Serena said. 'Maybe she decided to write this new one while she still could. I can't believe she left me everything.' She was turning a cigarette over and over in her hand. 'Mom must have known something about my lineage that the rest of us didn't.'

'You're delusional,' Amanda said. 'You look more like Dad than *any* of us.'

'I look more like Dad than any of us?' Serena said. She repeated people's words when she got upset. 'First of all, that's not true. And second, he always loved you two and never loved me, and third, he tried to abandon me, and when he couldn't, he killed himself. Can you fathom how much I've suffered over that? Maybe Mom thought I deserved extra consideration.'

'What? The whole fucking estate?' Amanda said. 'When are you going to stop playing the I-was-there-when-Dad-committed-suicide card?'

'That's right. You weren't the *only* one affected,' Laura said.

'Maybe not, but *I* was hurt the most,' Serena said. '*You* were only six. I'll bet you don't even remember Dad.'

'Yes, I do. Barely,' Laura said, her voice wobbling. 'You two have hundreds of photos and home movies of you and Dad together. I have a half-finished baby book with ten pictures of us. Ten!'

Serena flicked her cigarette lighter and lit up. 'That's because you were such an ugly baby.'

Tears prickled in Laura's eyes. 'Stop it,' she said, biting her lip.

'I had just started college when he died,' Amanda said, thumping Serena hard on the shoulder. 'To think I dropped out to help Mom raise you. I paid for your leukemia treatment, for you to go to the Fashion Institute, for your wedding. If I'd known how ungrateful you'd be . . .'

'Enough,' Serena said. 'How many times do I have to be reminded of how much you've done for this family? And if you're so successful that you can take such good care of everyone, why do you even need Mom's money?'

'It's the principle,' Amanda said. But it was more than the principle. Unbeknownst to her sisters, Amanda was in deep financial trouble. She had been counting on this inheritance to bail her out. Inside, she felt like a ball of tangled Christmas lights. Breathe. Breathe, she thought. Pull yourself together. 'It's not over,' she said. 'This won't hold up in court. We are going to challenge the bequest, right Laura?'

'I don't know,' Laura said. 'We're family. A court fight will tear us apart.'

Sam stood. In fact, everyone was standing except Serena, who sat scrunched in a chair puffing furiously on a cigarette. 'I have to advise you that there's an *in terrorem* clause in this will,' he said. 'Serena, you can't smoke in this office.'

'Oh, for God's sake.' Serena stubbed out her cigarette.

Sam reached over to his mini-fridge, pulled out four bottles of Evian, and handed three of them around. 'Everyone sit. Let's all calm down.'

'A what clause, did you say?' Laura said, taking a chair.

'*In terrorem*. Latin for "in fear." If anyone challenges the will and loses, they inherit one dollar, that's it. No one-year lease, no fifty thousand dollars on the sale of the property. Amanda, you'd lose your mom's jewelry. Laura, you'd lose the clothes and furniture. It's intended to discourage beneficiaries from fighting over bequests.'

'So?' Amanda said. 'It's not like a year lease, fifty grand, some costume jewelry and flea-market furniture mean anything.'

'Maybe not to you,' Laura said. 'Fifty thousand dollars is a fortune to me.'

'It's not about the money,' Amanda argued. 'You took care of Mom for six years. I quit college to help raise the two of you *and* paid for whatever anyone ever needed because Mom couldn't. This is a slap in the face. How can it *not* infuriate you?'

'Of course I'm disappointed,' Laura admitted. 'But Mom must have had her reasons.' Laura professed to believe that everything that transpired in life was perfect. Her soul coach had counseled her on this tenet. Eva Stein was a former Jewish Princess from Miami turned spiritual advisor after an image of the Messiah appeared on one of her matzo balls, or so she claimed. According to Eva, what seems like life's worst disasters usually offer

15

its greatest gifts. It is only through time that you can see the perfection in the stinking pile of crap the universe throws your way.

'I for one am in shock,' Serena said. 'This is completely unexpected.' Red blotches had erupted on her neck and face.

'What I don't understand,' Laura said, 'is how Mom could have let me be her caretaker, knowing that *you* were the primary beneficiary. If that was her plan, why didn't she move in with *you*?'

'And she had me manage her money and bills. Why did she let me do all that work if she planned to screw me?' Amanda groused.

'Maybe she thought Laura would have more time because she's single,' Serena argued. 'Amanda, she knew you understood legal and financial stuff better than any of us. It's not like she wasn't good to you. For all these years, she let us live in the house rent-free.'

'Still, why would she hand the keys to *you*, who didn't do anything for her?' Amanda said.

'Excuse me, hello-oh! I babysat for her every night while Laura went out on the town to party.'

'Serena, you turned on the baby monitor after she took an Ambien and fell asleep,' Laura said, her nostrils flaring. 'You never had to check on her. And I wasn't partying. I was working, *singing*, and it was hardly every night.'

'I don't know why you don't give up that silly quartet of yours,' Serena said. 'Who wants to listen to a bunch of octogenarians and their parents?

16

What's the average age of your band members? Ninety-five?'

Laura glared at Serena. 'Excuse me! It's their age that makes us unique. My guys are world-class musicians. You have no appreciation . . .'

'Okay, fine, whatever,' Serena said, waving her hand dismissively. 'Can we not argue? These were Mom's final wishes. I for one respect them.'

'And I for one don't trust you. You're a liar and thief,' Amanda said. 'First you stole Elliott from me, and now you've stolen our inheritance.'

'I did not steal Elliott!' Serena protested.

Laura's eyes widened and she slapped her forehead. 'And don't forget, she stole all my Barbie dolls and shaved their heads.'

'Just what are you two insinuating?' Serena demanded. 'You know I don't like insinuations.'

'Do we have to spell it out?' Amanda said, leering at Serena. 'T-H-I-E-F.'

SERENA

S erena couldn't believe what her sisters were accusing her of. Haven't we always been there for each other? she thought. I've never given them reason to mistrust me. They're being completely unfair. 'Stop it,' she shouted. 'Both of you. I didn't ask for this inheritance. It was Mom's decision. Why are you so mean? You're always criticizing, never nice to me.'

'That's not true,' Laura said. 'Who's the one who always says you're, you're . . .' She paused. 'You're photogenic.'

'Oh please, photogenic? That's the best you can do? You both hate me. I can't count on either of you. I'm the one with kids. What if, God forbid, something happens to Elliott? I need to be able to support them on my own. And what if, God forbid, my leukemia comes back? I'd need the money to pay for nannies to watch the kids while

18

I'm having treatments and private nurses to watch me. Maybe *that's* what Mom was thinking.'

Amanda got in Serena's face. 'I highly doubt it, since you didn't have kids when she wrote this will.'

'Hey, how can you say you can't count on me after I gave you my bone marrow?' Laura said, looking offended.

'Oh, puh-lease,' Serena said, rolling her eyes. 'Mom *made* you.' If Serena's sense of impending doom was born on the East Hampton beach where her father left her, the cloud of dread that followed her to this day was darkened by her crushing bout with leukemia.

'No one made me give you anything. And don't forget my eggs,' Laura cried. 'Do you have any idea how much those Pergenol shots hurt? You sure as heck counted on me then.'

Well, Laura had her there. The chemo and radiation treatments Serena took when she'd had leukemia left her infertile. Though she could carry a child, she needed donor eggs, and Laura had offered to give Serena hers. Without them, Sebastian and Valentina would never have been born. 'You're right. I counted on you for the eggs.'

'Thank you,' Laura said.

But you only gave them to me out of guilt for not wanting to share your bone marrow, Serena thought.

Why are Amanda and Laura so angry? she wondered. If anyone deserves the house and

19

painting, it's me. Mom wouldn't have had them if not for Daniel Lassiter. He's my real father. I should inherit what was given to Mom by my own flesh and blood.

Suddenly, Sam cleared his throat. Serena had forgotten he was in the room, he'd been so quiet. 'Let's take a step back,' he said. 'Serena, if you agree with Amanda that the bequest is unfair, you can change it. It's called making a variation. You have two years to do it.'

'If you want to stay on speaking terms with us, you'd better make one of those,' Amanda said, poking Serena's arm. 'And I'm not waiting two years.'

'Of course I'll make it right,' Serena muttered. 'Jeez, what kind of sister do you take me for?' Damn Sam Hermann for bringing this up without asking me first in private, she thought indignantly. What am I supposed to say in front of Amanda and Laura? That I *won't* make it right? Now I'm *really* screwed. This is going to cost me.

'I'll believe it when I see it,' Amanda said. 'Laura, get your coat. This meeting is over.'

LAURA

*'Our siblings push buttons that cast us in roles
we felt sure we had let go of long ago – the
baby, the peacekeeper, the caretaker, the
avoider. It doesn't seem to matter how much
time has elapsed or how far we've traveled.'*
　　　　　　　　　　　　—Jane Mersky Leder

The year Serena and Elliott were married,
Sunny invited them to live in the fourth
and fifth floors of the building on Duane
Park. Their first renovation was to add a spectacular
living room, encased in a box of steel and glass, on
the roof. Bordering it on three sides was a two-
thousand-square-foot landscaped terrace with real
grass and a recirculating stream. Half the yard was
populated with potted trees, while the other half
contained an outdoor kitchen and barbecue, theater
seating, and a movie screen. The apartment was
exquisitely furnished, although attached to each
piece was a white card with black letters spelling
'chair', 'couch', 'table', and so on, for Sebastian's
and Valentina's benefit. These were temporarily

21

removed when the apartment was photographed for the Home section of the *New York Times*. Serena's only complaint was that it had been in the Thursday and not the more prestigious Sunday edition.

With Serena and Elliott living in the top two stories, Sunny offered Amanda the second and third. Since Amanda was covering upkeep and property taxes, Sunny wanted her to have the extra space. Amanda decorated the place in a sparse, Zenlike fashion using modern furnishings in a beige, white and cream palette. The windows were dressed with sheer drapes that pooled gracefully onto the bleached-wood floors. Antique Buddhas of all shapes and sizes were placed throughout the apartment, not because Amanda was religious but because their presence comforted her.

From the time they subdivided the building and until Sunny died, she and Laura lived together on the bottom floor. It was filled with a mish-mash of furnishings from the original family home, most of which had been acquired at the Sixth Avenue flea markets. Laura's windows were barred for safety's sake, but she did have direct access to the backyard, which was perpetually over-grown with weeds. For years, she had been too busy taking care of their mother to spend time gardening. Then, after Sunny passed on, she was too grief-stricken to tend to the grass. Serena nagged her endlessly about her yard delinquency, which she said reflected badly on the family as a whole. Laura finally told her to take care of the outside space herself if it bothered her so much. 'Thank you, I will,' Serena said. She hired one of the city's top park and recreation consultants and turned it into a flower-filled playground for her two children, which had just been completed.

Though it had been almost six months since her mother died and the will was read, Laura had yet to smooth the indentation Sunny's head had left on her pillow the night her body was taken to the morgue. It was Laura's nature to move slowly, but this was different. The wound from her mother's death was too raw. Closets and bureaus were filled with her clothes. The small third bedroom in their apartment had become a storage space for her 'personal effects' – furniture, books, racks of dresses, and family photos. Whenever Laura felt stressed, she would go into that room and smell her mother's clothes, try on her red pillbox hat, or just sit quietly amongst the artifacts of Sunny's life. It calmed her right down.

A week after the will was read, Serena promised her sisters she would contact Sam Hermann and make the variation to the bequest. She agreed to set it up so the three of them would share the Lassiter sketch equally, but she insisted on a bigger percentage of the house for herself. After all, she was married with children and needed more space. Laura and Amanda would be given one floor each that they would own outright. Amanda could keep Mom's jewelry and Laura could have her personal effects. Since Laura already lived on one story, she didn't care. Amanda would have to give up a floor of her duplex. She had no choice but to go along with Serena's terms.

Even though Serena hadn't gotten around to changing the will as she agreed, Amanda consolidated her apartment on the second floor as a show of good faith. Serena relocated the children's bedrooms and their home office into Amanda's old living area. As a peace offering, Serena let Amanda be the first sister to hang the Lassiter sketch in her apartment with the proviso that they would rotate it between them every year. Amanda begged her to sell it and split the proceeds, but Serena refused to let it out of the family. 'It's all I have left of my possible father,' she said.

'When are you calling Sam?' Amanda asked Serena on a regular basis. 'You promised to make everything legal.'

'I'm busy now, but I'll get to it,' she would say. 'Relax.'

Over the next few months, an uneasy truce was struck between the sisters and they did their best to get along despite hurt feelings. Laura decided that life was too short to fight with the only family she had left. Eva, her friend and soul coach, used hypnosis to regress her to a time before Mom's illness. A middle-aged woman with spiky hair in shades of orange, gold, and red, Eva had a bartering agreement with Laura: spiritual coaching for singing telegrams. While Laura lay on a lime green La-Z-Boy recliner, surrounded by dozens of flickering candles, Eva prompted her to tell her mother how upset she was to have been disinherited.

'I'm furious with you, Mom,' Laura said. 'I gave up everything to take care of you, everything! No, of course I didn't do it for the money, but you should have treated us equally like you promised. Why didn't you? You created a terrible rift, especially between Amanda and Serena. It was wrong. I don't understand it and I never will.'

'Dahling, even though you don't understand your mother's actions, is there some way you can get into agreement with them, find the perfection in what she did?' Eva said. 'If so, you should thank her for it.'

Laura's eyes fluttered as she tried to see the gift in being disinherited. 'I guess . . . Amanda makes a good living, so she doesn't need the money. I don't make much but my expenses are low. Serena is psychologically fragile. At least now she'll always have a home and we'll never have to worry about taking care of her. So thank you for that.'

'Can you forgive your mother, honey?'

Laura nodded. 'Yes, I forgive you. Knowing you, you had your reasons. I'm letting go and moving on.' In her mind's eye, Laura kissed her mother and said good-bye. After her session with Eva, the heaviness she felt over Sunny's actions lifted and she bore her no ill will.

For her twenty-seventh birthday, Laura asked Serena to throw a little party – just family. 'Please,' she begged her sisters, 'I want us to get along like we used to. That's the best present you can give me.'

Serena said she was happy to do it. She decorated her dining room with colorful balloons, streamers, and a 'Happy Birthday, Laura' banner that Sebastian helped her make.

In the kitchen, nine-month-old Valentina lay on her back kicking and swatting the famous-women-in-herstory mobile that hung over her playpen while four-year-old Sebastian downed a plate of fresh spinach, 'brain food,' his mother called it. The sisters sat around Serena's dining-room table gabbing like old times.

'So I'm evaluating this Upper East Side apartment and I see this door and it's locked,' Amanda said, as she carefully draped her turquoise St John Knit button-tab jacket over the back of her chair. 'I'm dying to know what's behind it, right?'

'I would be,' Serena said. She was wearing an Audrey Hepburn – inspired little black dress with six-inch heels. Her mahogany hair was pulled back into a tight ponytail.

'Well, it was the owner's *dungeon*,' Amanda said, flipping her apricot mane back for dramatic effect. 'They're sadomasochists.'

'No way,' Laura said, slapping Serena's knee.

'Ouch,' she yelped, playfully swatting Laura back. 'I'm sorry but that's sick.'

'They're consenting adults,' Laura said. 'And anyway, didn't you tell me that you and Elliott like to act out . . .'

'Ah-ah-ah,' Serena shouted over her. 'That's ancient history. We're parents now.'

'So what was it like?' Laura said as she unbuttoned the cuffs on her blue tailored shirt and pushed up her sleeves.

Amanda shrugged. 'Your typical dungeon, I suppose. Built-in racks and stocks, a cage big enough for a grown man, whips, chains, ropes, paddles, restraining devices. When I show the place, I'll suggest they knock down the wall and expand the master bathroom. The plumbing is all there, for enemas I suppose.'

'Eeeaw,' Serena said, making a face.

'Do you let people see it when you show the apartment?' Laura asked.

'I have to,' Amanda said. 'It's four hundred square feet!'

'Frankly, I'm shocked that that sort of thing takes place on the Upper East Side,' Serena said. 'All the best families live there.' She stole over to the window and lit a cigarette. Even though it violated every organic and vegetarian belief she had, she snuck in two a day. It was a vice she'd picked up while working in the fashion industry and hadn't been able to shake. But she *never* lit up around the children, and in keeping with her recent decision to go green, she only smoked American Spirits, which used 100-percent-organic tobacco and no additives.

'Don't tell anyone, but the owner is Winston Bullock, from the pharmaceutical family; wife's a socialite, two little kids,' Amanda said. 'And this was right on Mayor Bloomberg's block.'

'That's a beautiful block,' Serena said, blowing

two lines of white smoke out her nostrils like a dragon. 'The Rudolf Steiner School is on that block.'

'Are you applying Sebastian there?' Laura asked. Whenever she said her nephew's name, she felt a tinge of resentment. All her life, she told her sisters that when she had children, she was going to name her son Sebastian and her daughter Valentina. After Serena had her first two children, what did she name them? Sebastian and Valentina. It was typical Serena.

'Rudolf Steiner?' Serena said. 'Oh God, no. They're too diverse for me. A mother at the park told me they have a take-your-gay-friend-to-school day. None of Sebastian's friends are gay, except for Pepe, of course.'

'Five-year-old Pepe-from-next-door?' Laura said. 'How can you tell?'

'When you worked in fashion as long as I did, you *know*,' Serena proclaimed. 'The point is, Rudolf Steiner's not for us,' Serena said. 'We're going for Madison Prep. It's the feeder kindergarten to Harvard.'

'Oh God!' Amanda groaned. 'That school's idea of diversity candidates are families without private jets.'

Laura didn't know whether to be amused or disgusted. 'And what are his chances of getting into this feeder school?'

Serena groaned. 'Who knows? I told them about his genius IQ, but all they cared about was whether he was potty-trained. Can you imagine? He has an IQ two points below Einstein's and all they

28

want to know is, can he deposit his feces into a toilet? I lied and said he could so they'd interview us. If he doesn't get accepted, I'll die. It's the best Baby Ivy in town.'

'I thought he *was* potty-trained,' Laura said.

'He regressed after Valentina was born,' Serena whispered, as though embarrassed. 'The toilet-training consultant we're working with says defecating disabilities are common in situations like this.'

'You do know that they pat 'em down to see if they're wearing those paper training pants,' Amanda said.

'You mean Pull-Ups?' Serena said. 'I know. Sebastian wears them now. For the interview, I'll send him in his Calvins and pray.'

'Why don't you forget Madison Prep and just apply him to Harvard now?' Amanda said. 'If he's such a genius, they might let him in on early, early, early admissions. I'll bet they don't ask about toilet training.'

Laura smiled contentedly at the easy banter between her sisters. It reminded her of how close they became after the endless months Serena spent at Manhattan Methodist Hospital when she had leukemia.

Thankfully, Laura had been a suitable donor for her sister's transplant.

'Is this going to hurt?' she asked her mother as she lay on the gurney. Not that she was scared – she wasn't. She was never one to rush headlong into new situations. All she wanted was to know what to expect. Amanda was outside talking to the doctor. Sunny was holding Serena's hand.

'How can you worry about yourself?' Serena moaned, her voice thick from painkillers. 'Think of what I've been through. You better not change your mind. They already suppressed my immune system. Without your bone marrow, I'll die. But you don't care, do you?'

Laura regarded her sister. With no hair, eyelashes, or eyebrows, she resembled a plucked chicken. A single tear spilled down Laura's cheek. How can she think I don't care? 'Serena, please. I'd slide down a razor into a pool of alcohol if that's what it took to save your life.'

'I'm proud of you, Laura,' Sunny said. 'You're so brave. Serena, we all love you. Whatever it takes to cure you, honey, we'll do it.'

Between Serena's illness and Sunny's long decline, the sisters had become one another's closest friends. The reading of the will changed all that. But today, at the birthday party, it felt like old times. Thank goodness we're moving past all that inheritance drama, Laura thought.

The sound of keys jingling came from the door as Elliott let himself in. Serena flicked her cigarette out the window to the pavement and quickly folded a stick of gum into her mouth.

Laura was impressed. Elliott never left work early, not even the time Serena had the flu and could barely manage the kids on her own.

'Da-deee,' yelled four-year-old Sebastian, running into his father's arms. The boy was small, with flaxen blond hair, curious emerald eyes, and a mischievous smile. His face was peppered with light-brown freckles despite Serena's smearing SPF70 on his skin every morning, noon, and even night because 'it's just a matter of time before doctors discover that moonlight contains cancer-causing rays.'

'Sebastian!' Elliott cried, twirling his lovable little turnip in the air while the boy giggled with delight.

Serena checked her watch. 'Where have you been?'

'I'm sorry,' said Elliott as he gave Amanda and Laura pecks on the cheek. 'You didn't wait for me, did you?'

'We were about to cut the cake,' Amanda said. 'Come on, everyone.'

'No,' Sebastian said. 'Have to move my bowels.' His tan corduroy pants were already halfway down and his face was turning purple.

'He says "move his bowels,"' Laura whispered to Amanda. 'What happened to "poop"?'

Amanda made a 'we're-talking-about-Serena-here' shrug. 'I'll be in the kitchen if you need me to congratulate him when he's done.'

'Elliott, can you take him to the bathroom so I can serve the cake?' Serena said.

Elliott was punching a number on his BlackBerry. 'When I finish this call,' he said, gliding up the stairs.

Serena rolled her eyes and did it herself, as was the pattern in her marriage. She would ask Elliott for

31

help and he'd be too busy or he'd agree and then do it wrong. Serena whisked the boy to the bathroom.

Soon she poked her head out. 'He did it. Yay!' She started clapping. Everyone joined in for the obligatory round of applause.

Sebastian emerged bottomless and beaming. 'Who wants to see what I made?' he said.

'Laura? Care to take a peek?' Serena asked expectantly.

For some months now, Laura felt that her sister was turning into one of those whack-job Manhattan momzillas. For one thing, she made Sebastian walk with a chest harness and leash whenever they were out. 'God forbid he dashes into the street and gets hit by a marauding taxi. I'd never forgive myself.' Then there was the feeder-school-to-Harvard business, and now turd inspections. 'No thanks,' Laura said. 'I'll catch it next time.'

Serena appeared deeply disappointed.

'Do I get a toy, Mommy?' Sebastian asked.

'Of course you do, my little man,' Serena said. 'Come, let's wash your hands.'

Soon Sebastian came skipping into the room with a pacifier in his mouth. Serena followed, holding nine-month-old Valentina, her chubby daughter. Serena had been worried about the pleated rolls of baby fat on her arms and legs, but the nutritionist assured her it was perfectly normal.

'Elliott has to call L.A. He said go ahead without him,' Serena said. She sat down with Valentina in her lap, brushing back the thin wisps of brown

32

hair on her head. 'Sebastian, take that dummy out of your mouth. You know you're not supposed to have that. It causes speech delays, ear infections, and Sudden Infant Death Syndrome. You don't want to die, do you?'

Sebastian removed the nipple of death from his mouth, curling his lips in protest.

'Don't give me that look, young man,' Serena said, 'or I'll call the pacifier consultant and you can tell it to her.' She shook her head. 'I swear, I rue the day my lactation advisor told me to use a dummy to wean him off the breast.'

Amanda waltzed in carrying a homemade chocolate cake with blue candles aflame. 'Happy birthday to you . . .'

Laura's face turned red as everyone sang. 'Only ten candles?' she said. 'I'm twenty-seven.'

'How many more candles *should* there be, Sebastian?' Serena asked.

'Seventeen!' Sebastian screamed.

'Is he a genius or what?' Serena said. 'Does anyone want to hear him sing "Happy Birthday" in Chinese? Anybody? Anybody?'

Laura, since there were no takers, shut her eyes. I wish that Amanda, Serena and I could be close again, she thought, as she blew out the flames.

'I made it from scratch,' Serena said. 'It's from Jessica Seinfeld's cookbook. There's spinach-and-carrot puree in it.'

'You shouldn't have,' Laura said. She meant it. It sounded disgusting.

33

'The icing's made with beets,' Serena added. 'But you can hardly taste it.'

'Open the presents!' Sebastian shouted.

'First let's cut the cake, silly,' Amanda said, dabbing a dollop of chocolate-and-beet icing on his nose.

'Cut an honorary piece for Mom,' Serena said. 'It's her birthday tomorrow.'

'I know. God, I miss her,' Amanda said, her eyes misting.

'Remember last year?' Laura said. 'She was so excited when we sang "Happy Birthday."'

'She clapped when we put the cake in front of her,' Serena said. 'Like a kid.'

'It was downhill from there,' Laura murmured, putting a piece of cake at the empty place at the head of the table. 'Here's looking at you, Mom.'

Amanda took a manila envelope out of her purse. 'Oh Serena, I have something for you.'

'Reeee-ally, what?' Serena trilled.

'It's a sub-lease,' Amanda said, slapping it on the dining-room table in front of Serena.

'A what?' Serena said.

'I rented my apartment to a rock band,' Amanda said, her face bearing a triumphant smile. 'They're using it as a rehearsal space, but only during the day.'

Serena's mouth dropped open and she glared at Amanda. 'They're using it as a rehearsal space?'

Laura gasped. 'Why would you do that?'

Amanda turned to Laura. 'It's been six months

since we read Mom's will. We agreed on a new distribution. Serena, you promised to make the change. I called Sam Hermann last week. You haven't done a thing about it.'

'I've been applying Sebastian to private school,' Serena said. 'I'll get to it.'

'And when you do, I'll arrange another space for the band. Meanwhile, they start rehearsing tomorrow.'

'Come *on*, you can't do that,' Laura said, her eyes blazing.

'Cake please,' Sebastian said.

'Here, Sweetie,' Amanda said, handing him a piece. 'Sure I can. I'm gone all day. It's a way for me to earn extra income.'

'Like you need it,' Serena said, rolling her eyes.

'You don't know what I need,' Amanda snapped.

'How could you do that to us?' Serena said. 'The kids' bedrooms are right over your apartment.'

'Are they?' Amanda said. 'Gosh, I hadn't thought of that.'

'You hadn't *thought* of that?' Serena said.

'Amanda,' Laura said, 'Why would you punish Sebastian and Valentina for something Serena did? And I have to write singing telegrams and promote my music. How am I supposed to work with a rock band playing above my head?'

'Isn't it time you got realistic about your singing career and applied for a normal job?' Amanda said. 'You'd be great in sales. Let me get you an interview at Corcoran.'

'No,' Laura said. 'I'll make it on my own. As a matter of fact, I was just recruited to be a hostess on a private jet for some billionaire. The job pays eighteen thousand a month. You only have to be on call ten days out of thirty *and* they give benefits.'

'Eighteen thousand a month for being a glorified waitress?' Serena said. 'I find that hard to believe.'

'Believe it,' Laura said. 'It's not only serving. They want me to entertain in-flight. My interview's next week. I could fly ten days a month and do my music the other twenty, which is why you can't let a band practice in your apartment.'

'Well, I'm sorry but they needed the space and I could use the income,' Amanda said, reaching into her purse and opening her wallet. 'As soon as Serena does what she promised, I'll move them. Meanwhile, here's ten bucks. Go to Duane Reade and buy yourself some earplugs. Cake?'

Laura picked up her cake and threw it at Amanda. It hit her ear and fell on Serena's Persian rug. 'You're ridiculous, both of you,' she shouted, dashing toward the stairs to the roof.

Serena shrieked. 'Laura, don't! We have ants!'

'Ants?' Amanda said. 'Since when?'

'For the last few weeks,' Serena said, shuddering. 'Those tiny black ones. When the exterminator comes Friday, I'll be sure he sprays everywhere but your apartment so they'll relocate there.'

Amanda shrugged. 'I'll get some Raid.'

'Is Aunt Laura moving her bowels?' Sebastian asked.

'Yes, sweetie,' Amanda said, messing up her nephew's mop of blond hair. 'Shall we give her a prize?'

LAURA

'Sweet is the voice of a sister in the season of sorrow.'

—Benjamin Disraeli

Laura sprinted up the spiral staircase from Serena's dining area to the rooftop terrace. Making her way to the sliding glass door, she surveyed the white leather sofa, which was high style but cold and hard. Serena had arranged a row of black satin pillows against the sofa back in descending order of size like a set of Russian nesting dolls. It was pathological. Laura mixed them all up. Damn Amanda for ruining her party. Things were going so well before she dropped her rock band bombshell. And a pox on Serena for not doing what she promised. Jeez, she thought. How can someone as normal as me have two such demented sisters?

Stepping outside, Laura sat in the woven wicker loveseat. She took a deep breath and centered herself, determined to live in the moment. It was one of those perfect summer evenings, the air crisp and cool. The sun was setting over the Hudson River, painting the sky a watercolor of yellows, golds, light blues, and pinks. Laura closed her eyes and remembered her mother devouring her chocolate birthday cake last year. There was no spinach-and-carrot puree hidden inside. She felt a wave of loneliness. I miss you, Mom, she thought. Are you watching over us? She visualized a young, healthy Sunny standing next to her, stroking her hair. She liked to believe her mother's spirit was with her.

In the months before she died, Sunny didn't want to eat or drink, so Laura was always trying to tempt her with the homemade soups or puddings that Amanda had delivered from Dean and Deluca. Turning her to relieve bedsores, bathing her, changing her diapers, rubbing her feet, brushing her hair and teeth . . . caring for her mother was backbreaking.

Serena suggested moving her to a hospice, but Laura insisted she stay at home. Her soul coach had explained that Sunny must have been afraid to die. Her mother's higher self had chosen to send part of herself to the other side before she made the full transition. Eva believed that many souls make the decision to dim their light and fade out slowly. By the time they die, they don't know what is happening. Eva helped Laura understand that it was the highest possible honor to serve her mother as she transitioned from her physical to her spiritual form. Eva came up with mantras and journaling exercises that gave Laura the strength to handle Sunny's decline with patience and grace.

Laura wasn't the only angel walking the last mile with Sunny. By the time Sunny fell ill, she was a fixture in the neighborhood. Everyone knew the cute little lady with the warm smile who always wore the vintage red pillbox hat. After 9/11, she went door to door volunteering to help local merchants with whatever they needed, since no one was shopping in Tribeca and many stores had to let employees go. She arranged flowers, baked cookies, mopped floors, organized merchandise on shelves – no job was too small.

When the shop owners and restaurateurs heard she was sick, they returned the favor. Tribeca Cleaners took care of her laundry. The Bouley Bakery sent over fresh raspberry scones (her favorite) and homemade breads every few days. Duane Park Flowers delivered bright arrangements each week. The yarn shop on Franklin Street organized a blanketing bee where local residents knitted colorful squares that were assembled into a soft, comfy cover for Sunny's bed. New Yorkers have a reputation for being impatient and curt, but they're not. When a beloved neighbor needs help, they're as dependable as panhandlers in the subway.

Laura remembered what a hard time her sisters had showing up for Sunny in her final decline. They couldn't bear that she didn't recognize them and used that as an excuse not to visit. Laura never felt that way. To her, being with Mom was a blessing. At night, she would brush Sunny's hair, tuck her in, and read her to sleep like she was a little girl. 'Mr Sandman is here. Better shut your eyes,' she would say.

In the mornings, Laura would open the blinds to fill the room with light. Often, after she woke up, Sunny would spin the craziest yarns from her scrambled brain.

'Are you my nurse?' Laura remembered her saying one morning.

'No silly, it's me, Laura,' she said. 'Your daughter.'

'Oh, right,' Mom said.

Laura was never sure if Sunny really remembered or had just gotten very good at covering up the holes in her memory. 'Did you sleep well?' Laura would ask.

'Not a wink,' Sunny said. 'You didn't hear the noise?'

'What noise?'

'That young man who came to my bed. We made an awful racket.'

'A man came to your bed?'

'Yes, indeed. George.' Mom said. 'Gosh, he was handsome, like Paul Newman. And he crawled under the covers and wanted to make love. But he didn't know what to do. I had to teach him how to pleasure a woman.'

'He was a virgin?' Laura asked.

'Not when I got through with him.' Sunny giggled.

Laura swatted her mother. 'You're terrible.' The woman is sixty-one years old, bedridden, and still getting it, Laura thought, at least in her dreams. How bad can Alzheimer's be?

Her mother gasped. 'Oh good Lord, what if I'm pregnant?'

Laura chuckled at the memory. By then, the tough loving warrior known as Sunny Moon had dissipated like ocean mist. Thankfully, Laura had had her mother to stand up for her when she was a kid, though. Laura suffered from dyslexia and had been a terrible student. In those days, the unenlightened didn't call what she had dyslexia. They called it dumb.

She remembered the time in ninth grade when the principal, Miss Carp, had strolled into her geometry classroom to popinspect everyone's notebook. When she flipped through Laura's and saw all her F's, she held it up for all to see. 'F, F, C-minus, D, F,' she announced. 'What are you, stupid?'

Laura burned with shame as her classmates' eyes bore into her. 'Is that a rhetorical question?' she asked.

The next day, Sunny was sitting in Miss Carp's office before the first bell rang. She brought Amanda along to make sure she didn't stab the woman in both eyes with a number-two pencil. Laura was humiliated that her mother and sister had come to confront the principal. It was bad enough to be the class dimwit.

'How dare you call my daughter stupid,' Sunny said. 'I'm pulling her out of your *stupid* school.'

Miss Carp's eyes were wide with shock. Few parents dared to stand up to old fish-breath. 'Have you seen your daughter's grades? What would *you* call her?'

Sunny stood and stuck her face right in Miss Carp's. 'I'd call her an exceptionally talented and socially adept young woman who may not be a successful academic, but will be a successful human being, no thanks to idiots like you.'

'That's right,' Amanda said. 'And you call yourself an educator.' Amanda spat on the floor in disgust. Laura couldn't believe she did that. There had to be laws against spitting in the principals' offices.

With that, Sunny yanked Laura out of John F. Kennedy High and marched her over to the High School for the Performing Arts (actually, they took the subway). 'I should have sent you here in the first place,' her mother said. 'I don't know what I was thinking.' Sunny explained to the more enlightened principal of Performing Arts what had just happened to Laura at JFK High. He invited Laura to audition right then and there. She sang her rendition of *Over the Rainbow* and he accepted her on the spot. From then on, Laura wasn't a failure in school. She was a star.

Laura gazed at the red sky over the Hudson River. Mama, what would I have done without you, she thought, reaching into her pocket and pulling out the paper she had found taped to the bottom of her mother's rug the night before. She had been rolling it up to move into her own bedroom and there it was. After Sunny knew she was sick, but before she lost her faculties, she had written God knows how many notes to her daughters and hidden them around their apartments. A few were discovered before she died, most after.

This is so totally Mom, Laura thought after finding the first one. When the girls were little, she was always sneaking love notes into their school lunch boxes and sweater pockets, or under their pillows at night. But after Sunny was dead, getting messages from her felt a bit creepy. It was as if her mother – the strong, fierce Sunny of old – was talking to them from the other side.

Sometimes Sunny's letters were long and heartfelt, other times they were short bits of advice, family recipes, or quick reminders she wanted to be sure to tell her girls. So far, Serena had uncovered the most notes because she was a neat freak. Laura and Amanda, neither of whom was a meticulous housekeeper, had each found a few. Laura had planned to read the new note to Amanda and Serena, but their fight cut the party short. Now she reread her mother's familiar penmanship.

My dear beautiful Laura,

Are you having a good day? How I wish I could be there to give you a hug. Do you know how grateful I am to have you as my daughter? I am grateful for your beautiful smile. I am grateful for your rich singing voice. I am grateful for your curly blond hair, your clear turquoise eyes, your deep adorable dimples, your strong Moon chin, your lovely figure and every one of your perfect little freckles. I am grateful that you hold my hand when we take walks. I am grateful that you talk to me about Heaven. I am grateful that you make me tuna fish salad with green apples. I am grateful that you took me to the Statue of Liberty last week (or was it last month?). In all the years I lived here, I never got to see that proud lady up close. I am grateful for time, for every minute I get to spend with you and your sisters. Now that my battery is running out, I savor every second that I live (at least, the ones I'm aware of, which are getting to be fewer and fewer). Until we meet again in Heaven, make the most of these moments, my lovely, big-hearted Laura. Don't get sucked into Serena and Amanda's silly melodramas. Let those two duke it out (and you know they will no matter what you or I say).

Love you forever and ever,
Mom

How did you know? Laura wondered. It seemed that whenever she uncovered a message from Sunny, it was exactly what she needed to hear. Laura loved when the cosmos gave her little winks like that.

A man snuck up behind her and cupped his hands around her shoulders. The faint smell of his cologne was unmistakable.

At forty, Elliott appeared more like a movie star than the behind-the-scenes television director he was. Sleek and polished, tall and muscular, he had a full head of curly salt-and-pepper hair, burning black eyes that could pull off an endless assortment of lethal gazes, and the smile of a leading man.

'Elliott, don't,' she said, pulling away, folding the letter and sticking it in her back pocket.

'I can't help myself,' he pouted.

Laura blamed herself for Elliott's advances. The day after Sunny's funeral, she had asked her sisters to stay home to honor their mother's memory. But Amanda had planned a trip to the Caribbean months earlier that she didn't want to miss. Serena insisted on taking the children to the Madison Prep Fair, hoping to hobnob with the principal or head of admissions so they would have a leg up when they applied. Amanda suggested she invite some girlfriends over to keep her company, but she had lost touch with most of her friends during their mother's six-year decline.

Alone in the empty apartment, Laura felt lost. Going about her day seemed disrespectful. She couldn't bring herself to look at her mother's room, much less clean out her things. Wearing her short, white satin bathrobe, her hair pulled back in a pony-tail, she stood in her kitchen staring blankly into the refrigerator at Sunny's split pea soup, remembering how she'd fed it to her only three days before. She smelled his cologne before she saw him.

'Are you alright?' he asked kindly. 'Can I keep you company for a while?'

Laura glanced at him and nodded, her eyes filled with tears. She couldn't speak.

Gently, he nudged Laura away from the fridge and closed the door. He pulled her into his arms and held her as she sobbed. 'Shhh, shhh, it's okay,' he said, sweetly rubbing her back, offering her the comfort she craved.

For the first time in ages, Laura felt like she wasn't alone contending with her mother's painful ending. This tall, muscular man was here, protecting her, holding a space for her heart to heal. Then he released her from their embrace, untied the pink polka-dot ribbon with which she'd pulled back her honey-blond hair, and began kissing her neck and then her lips – soft, sweet, delicious kisses that nourished Laura's soul.

As he pressed his body into hers, she could feel his erection against her belly. Softly, he inched his fingers under her robe, cupping a breast, playing with her nipple. Then slowly he slipped his hand away from her chest, down over her belly, until he reached the top of her panties and slid his fingers inside. Laura couldn't stand it. She untied her robe and let it fall to the floor. 'You are so beautiful,' he said, drinking her in. There were tears in his eyes. She wrapped him in her arms, smelling him, feeling his body pressed next to hers, reveling in the power of the human touch.

'*Ooh baby,*' he crooned in her ear, '*When I get that feeling/I want sexual healing.*'

'Elliott?' Laura said. It was as if a clock radio had clicked on with a Marvin Gaye tune, awakening her from a dream. 'What are we doing?' Laura grabbed her robe and tried to cover herself. Oh my God, Elliott! she thought. I almost had sex with my sister's husband. Dashing to the bathroom, she gulped a mouthful of Listerine, swishing it around and spitting it into the sink. Then she took another swig and another until she had emptied the bottle. Sticking her head out the door, Laura shouted, 'Elliott, I'm taking a shower. When I get out, you'd better be gone. This never happened, and nothing like it will ever happen again. Ever!'

Now, as he flirted with her on his own roof while his wife served spinach-laced chocolate cake downstairs, she blew off his advances. 'Remember what we said – never again.' Laura shook her blond locks away from his roving fingers. Why is it, she thought, that the only men who ever want you are the ones you don't want?

In college, Laura had experimented with her sexuality, dating men and women to see which felt more right. At Juilliard, she was president of the Gay and Lesbian Society. She later decided that it had been a phase. Over the last few years, there had been so many guys vying for her attention that she had to give them nicknames to keep them straight. There was Mr Mensch, Mr Muscles, Mr Millionaire, Mr Master of the Universe, and Mr Larry David (a dead ringer, not the real thing). With her wild golden hair, angelic face, beauty queen legs, and slim figure, Laura was a beacon for male attention. So far, she hadn't come across anyone resembling her soul mate, but that was fine with her. Laura had set her singing aspirations aside for six years to take care of Sunny. Now, her career took priority. There would always be time to find a man, but a girl has to be young, beautiful, and talented to make it in the music industry. This was her last chance, and she was determined to succeed.

Laura glanced at Elliott and smiled in spite of herself. That man can charm the scales off a snake, she thought. Every day, women threw themselves at him. But Laura would have none of it. 'Serena has some news for you,' Laura said, trying to redirect his attention the way one would a misbehaving toddler.

'Really, what?' he said, taking a Heineken out of the mini-fridge, and flipping the top off with a bottle opener.

'I don't want to steal her thunder. Let's just say you might want to get a lawyer.'

Elliott's eyes widened. 'She's asking for a divorce? Well, maybe it's for the best.'

'Noooo,' she said. 'Serena would *never* divorce you. Amanda's rented her apartment as practice space to a rock band during the day.'

'Oh, not my problem. I'm gone by eight,' Elliott said, shrugging.

'Don't you ever think about anyone else? Like your children, who sleep right above where the band will be practicing, or your wife? Serena says you guys are going to Phoenix tomorrow.' Laura said. 'Why don't you give her extra attention while you're there? Try to rekindle your passion.'

He sat on the love seat, slithered closer to Laura, and guzzled half his beer. 'I know she's your sister,' he said, 'but we're miserable. She doesn't even pretend to be interested in me anymore. The last time we had sex was before Valentina was born. Maybe you can talk to her, remind her she has a husband with needs.'

Laura stood. She hated to hear that her sister's marriage was in trouble. 'You guys need to talk to a counselor, not to me.'

'When I married her, she was so attentive,' Elliott continued, 'but now all she cares about is children, potty training, private schools, play dates. I may as well not be in this marriage for as much as Serena notices me.'

Laura felt for Elliott. She had watched Serena shut him out after the children were born, and had even offered to babysit them for a weekend so Serena and Elliott could get away alone. 'Why would I give birth to them, only to go off and leave them with a stranger?' Serena had said at the time.

'I'm *hardly* a stranger,' Laura said.

Still, Serena wouldn't budge. She prided herself on never having spent a night away from her children. Laura thought her sister carried much of the blame for the problems in her marriage. But she didn't want Elliott to tell her their private details. It made her feel like a traitor. 'Look, I know you're frustrated, but . . .'

'*There* you are,' Serena said, as she popped up from the stairs. 'I need to speak to Elliott about *your* sister.'

'My sister?' Laura said.

'She's dead to me. El, you off the phone?'

'He's off,' Laura said. 'We're coming down. And don't talk about Amanda like that. You'll attract terrible energy her way. I gave you *The Secret*. Didn't you read it?'

'Thanks for the talk,' Elliott said to Laura as she trotted downstairs. 'Don't be a stranger.'

Don't be a stranger indeed, she thought. Her family was completely dysfunctional. What had made her think things could ever be otherwise?

AMANDA

'Lord help the sister who comes between me and my man.'

—Irving Berlin

After the fight with Serena, Amanda let herself into her now-one-floor apartment. Catching her reflection in the vestibule mirror as she entered, she cringed at what she saw – a used-up forty year old trying to draw attention to herself with long, bright pumpkin-colored hair. From a distance or in muted lighting, she could fool people, but otherwise the wrinkles and bags under her eyes gave away her age. Amanda knew the drill. When a woman hits forty she has one of two choices: let herself become the frump nature intended or devote herself to exercise, dermatology, plastic surgery, hair, nails, waxing, cosmetic dentistry – the never-ending treadmill of middle-aged maintenance. Forty was 'the new thirty' only if you had a buttload of time and money to devote to backwards aging. Amanda often wished she had given up years ago and moved to the suburbs, where she could wear elastic-waist jeans and shop at malls.

Her sisters had it made. Laura was beautiful, sweet, and optimistic. She actually believed that being a good person and working hard would get her everything she wanted in life. Serena was prickly, judgmental, and self-centered, but that didn't keep her from having a loving husband, two beautiful kids, and financial freedom. Amanda felt an intense ache in her heart for the dream of love, happiness, and security that had passed her by.

She plopped onto the comfy sofa. A minor storm of dust and feathers exploded into the air as her body made contact with the fluffy cushion. 'Aaaaaaa!' Amanda shouted as she waved her hands in frustration. Serena was making her crazy. Why wouldn't she take care of the will like she promised? All her life, Amanda had given, given, given to Serena. Now, for once, Serena could really do something for her, but she wouldn't.

Amanda recalled the endless months they had spent at Methodist Hospital when Serena suffered from leukemia. When the doctors told her the massive chemo infusion had not put Serena into remission, it was like a punch in the solar plexus. Her little sister would die without a bone marrow transplant. Amanda couldn't let it happen. Thank God, Laura was a close enough match to be Serena's donor. Still, it was far from a sure thing. The procedure carried a higher risk of graft-versus-host disease because Laura's bone marrow wasn't a perfect match. Serena's first hospital roommate, a fifteen year old named Amy Gordon, had succumbed from that disease after her transplant.

'Is this going to hurt?' Laura asked Sunny as she lay waiting on the gurney next to her sister. Sunny was holding Serena's hand. Everyone in the room except Serena was wearing a surgical mask, a gown, a paper cap, and booties. Amanda had pulled her mask down to confer with the doctor right outside the door.

'I'm sorry,' the doctor said, 'but we just got a call from your insurance company. They reversed their decision to cover the transplant.'

Amanda felt bile rise in her throat. 'Why? I thought it was all approved.'

'Now they say the procedure's experimental.'

'But it isn't,' Amanda implored. 'You do it all the time with success. We've already started. Serena has no immune system. She'll die without the transplant.'

'It's a travesty,' the doctor said. 'Your insurance company pulls this stunt regularly to get out of paying. By the time the family wins the appeal, the patient has expired and the carrier's obligation is over.'

Amanda glanced at Serena. She was frail and pallid, her skin practically translucent. With no hair or eyelashes, her face swollen from prednisone, she was barely recognizable as Amanda's beautiful sister.

'I'll cover it,' Amanda said, her voice trembling. Her real estate practice was steadily building and she had managed to set aside eighty grand in a retirement account. Whatever the cost, she would pay. 'How much?'

'About a hundred thousand. That's quite a burden for one person to shoulder.'

Amanda gulped, but did not hesitate. 'It's no burden. She's my sister.'

'You and your mother need to go to the business office across the street to change the paperwork,' he said. 'As soon as that's done, we'll start the procedure.'

Amanda stuck her head into the room. 'Mom, I need you to come with me across the street. Laura, if they take you before we're back, we'll be waiting when you wake up. Everything's going to be fine.'

If it hadn't been for Amanda reaching into her own pocket, Serena would have died. She wouldn't have had Sebastian and Valentina or married Elliott. Amanda glanced at the family portrait sitting on the coffee table that they had taken at Serena's wedding. There, standing between Serena and Amanda, was Elliott with his killer smile.

Elliott Skank. Oh sure, his last name could send your gag reflex into overtime until you discovered he was part of the Skank Oil family. Amanda *gave* Elliott to Serena, for God's sake. Eight years ago Thanksgiving she'd brought him home to meet her sisters and mother. They'd gone on two successful dates, falling into bed together after the second. He mentioned he was planning to have turkey dinner at Three Guys Coffee Shop, so she invited him to join her family. 'I really like him, Mom,' she had told Sunny. 'He's smart, handsome, successful. He could be the one.' She thought of her mother, so full of life that night. Her real name was Susanne, but everyone called her Sunny. She used to introduce herself as 'Sunny Moon. It's an oxymoron, get it? The moon isn't sunny. That's what makes it so funny! Ha-ha-ha-ha.' She always got a polite laugh over that.

'So, Elliott,' Sunny said, as she passed him the cranberries, 'What brings you to the city?'

'You know the show *Law and Order*? I'm assistant-directing a spinoff they have called "Special Victims Unit." It's about an elite squad of detectives that investigate sex crimes.'

'Elliott works in television,' Amanda said with pride. 'He used to direct *Seinfeld*.' She was excited to be dating a man who was connected in Hollywood. Who knows, maybe he could introduce her to celebrities who would buy apartments from her. When you sold property in New York City, it was imperative to pair up with someone equally successful but in a different field, as this opened up a whole new pipeline of potential buyers.

'Wow,' Sunny said. 'You could be on television yourself. Has anyone ever told you, you're the image of Elliott Gould?'

'Nope, you're the first.' He took a spoonful of gravy and poured it over his mashed potatoes.

'Do you know Jerry Seinfeld?' Sunny asked.

56

'Yes, Jerry and I are friends,' Elliott said, after swallowing a mouthful of potatoes.

'You know Jerry Seinfeld?' Sunny asked. 'How?'

'Elliott used to work on the show, Mom, remember? He just moved here from L.A.,' Amanda explained. Lately, Sunny had been forgetting things and searching for words. Amanda wondered if she should take her to a doctor.

'Do you think you can get me on an episode of *Law and Order*?' Laura said. 'I'm going to be famous someday.'

'Yeah, someday you'll make the cover of *Toenails Today*,' Serena said. 'You know, that free rag they give you at the Korean manicure salons.'

'Shut up,' Laura said. 'Mom, tell her not to tease me.'

'Serena, you know how sensitive Laura is,' Sunny said, helping herself to a generous spoonful of dressing.

'For God's sake, she's going to college soon. It's time she toughened up,' Serena said. 'You should stop buying her those Earth Shoes.'

'What's wrong with them?' Laura said, admiring her feet. 'We get them for half price.'

'They're so 1950's-polio-victim,' Serena said. 'All you need is a brace to complete the look.'

Laura kicked her shoes off. 'Bet you wouldn't say that if there was a polio victim sitting at the table.'

'Please, I am nothing if not sensitive,' Serena said. 'Who gave a toothbrush and toothpaste to that toothless lady who begs at the corner so she can save the two brown teeth she has left? Me, that's who!'

'Oh, excuse me while I call the Vatican to nominate you for sainthood,' Laura said, rolling her eyes.

'So, Serena,' Elliott said, breaking the tension. 'Are you in college?'

'No,' Serena said. 'I'm with Versace. See? Ta-da!' She pushed her chair back and gestured to her short, tight black dress, which was from the designer's current collection.

Amanda noticed that Elliott kept stealing glances at Serena, not that she blamed him. Serena radiated such beauty that sometimes she herself couldn't look at her. It was like staring into the sun. 'I'm really proud of her,' Amanda said. 'She studied at FIT.'

'Amanda paid for me to go,' Serena said. 'I'm thankful to her for that.'

'She just bought us a new roof for this house,' Sunny added. 'I'm thankful for no more leaks.'

'On this Thanksgiving as on every Thanksgiving, we are grateful for Amanda who takes such good care of us,' Serena said. 'Yadda yadda yadda.'

'Serena, you're embarrassing me,' Amanda admonished. But really she was pleased by the attention. Helping her mother and sisters was Amanda's raison d'être. She couldn't imagine what she would do or who she would be if she weren't the family caretaker.

'Elliott, would you like to go for a walk after

dinner?' Sunny said. 'I can take you around, show you the neighborhood.'

'I don't mind taking him,' Serena said. 'We were practically the first residents in Tribeca.' In one motion, she took her long brown hair and twisted it into a bun that stayed on her head without a rubber band.

'Mom, why don't you let Serena go with him?' Amanda said. 'You're always getting lost these days.' Amanda began collecting the plates from the table. 'You guys go. We'll do the dishes.'

Amanda later learned it was the walk that did it. With every cast-iron or brick building Serena pointed out, each cobblestone street, every old factory that was being converted into lofts, Elliott became more and more entranced. A week later, he invited her to help him shop for Amanda's Christmas present and they ended up in bed for an entire weekend.

Amanda blamed herself. She should have let Sunny or Laura take him around the neighborhood, not Serena. When Elliott and Serena confessed their attraction and asked Amanda's permission to date, she was gracious about it. What choice did she have? In a way she was relieved. Amanda had spent most of her adult life taking care of Serena. First, when she was a little girl and their mother went back to work, she'd pick her up from school, make dinner, help her with homework. Then there were the FIT tuition payments and the whopping hospital bills for the leukemia treatments, which went on for two years.

59

When Elliott expressed his desire for Serena, Amanda thought, let someone else take care of her for a change. For a moment she felt guilty for her selfish reaction, but only for a moment.

A year and a half later, Serena became a Skank at a lavish wedding at the Hotel Pierre on Central Park South. Elliott did not offer to pay for the festivities. Like many old-money families, his were as tight-fisted as they were rich. Plus, they had multiplied like hamsters since the first generation, producing scores of Skanks who wanted to get their grubby little paws on the family fortune. So much of it was tied up in trusts that Elliott would be in adult diapers before he saw his first dollar. No worries! Amanda picked up the slack.

By then she was seriously involved with Riley Trumbo, the son of Harley Trumbo, the flamboyant real estate tycoon. How brilliant of me to have given Elliott to Serena, she thought at the time. If I hadn't, I'd never have met Riley. They made a striking couple – he at 6'7", she at 5'7", separated by a foot of height and a lifetime of growing up in different worlds.

Riley was the hardworking, hard-charging son of a bigger-than-life father. Ruggedly handsome with slate-gray eyes, a thick head of black slicked-back hair, and a nose left crooked by years of polo injuries, he spent most of his time working out, working the charity circuit, or working for his father. This worked out perfectly for Amanda, who worked all the time herself.

To Amanda, life with Riley was excruciatingly divine. The couple split their time between his apartment on Fifth Avenue and the family compound in Bridgehampton. There were exotic vacations by private jet, weekly massages, daily trainers – Riley was only too happy to share his good fortune. Amanda knew he adored her. He introduced her to the upper echelons of Manhattan, taking her to all the right charity balls and inviting her to wine and dine with his wealthy socialite friends. To Amanda, Riley was exactly the kind of guy a budding real estate superstar like her should be seeing. In the time they dated, she became the eleventh-highest-grossing realtor in Manhattan just by buying and selling apartments through their social network.

Confident that she would soon be part of the Trumbo clan, Amanda spared no expense on the wedding she threw for Serena – it was pretentious, over-the-top, and extravagant to the point of being obscene – everything Serena dreamed of and more. With Elliott's Hollywood connections, Serena's fashion contacts, and Riley's society friends all attending, papers ranging from the *New York Times* to the *National Enquirer* covered the nuptials. Amanda enjoyed the media attention, which would do nothing but bolster her already sizzling career, and Serena was thrilled beyond life itself to be the main event at such a spectacle.

'Amanda, I don't know how to thank you,' Serena said, hugging her sister. 'This is the most beautiful wedding I've ever been to. I can't believe it's *mine.*'

'Oh, stop,' Amanda said, like it was nothing. But it was everything. Amanda's greatest source of pride was the exquisite care she took of her sisters and mother. 'That's what family does. We support each other, right, Riley?'

'So I've been told,' Riley said.

'Amanda, Serena, come on,' Laura said. 'The makeup artist wants to touch us up before the pictures.'

'Riley, honey, we're about to take family shots,' Amanda said, smoothing the front of her floor-length, strapless turquoise silk gown that set off her red hair to its fullest advantage. She gestured toward the photographer and his assistant, who were adjusting the lights. 'Why don't you stay and be in some?'

Riley fiddled with the collar of his tuxedo shirt. 'I'm not a *real* relative – not yet, anyway,' he said, not looking her in the eye. 'Tell you what, I'll go get a drink. Find me as soon as you're done.' He gave her a peck on the cheek.

'Sure,' Amanda said, smiling to cover her disappointment. She would have gladly posed in his family's pictures if he'd asked.

Amanda's face remained motionless as the stylist added powder to her nose and repainted her lips, but her eyes followed Riley as he made his escape. Then she joined everyone for the endless iterations of family shots that photographers insist upon – the Moon sisters with Sunny, the Moon sisters together, each Moon sister alone, the Moon sisters and Sunny with Elliott, the Moon family with Elliott's family, and on and on.

Forty-five minutes later, Amanda made her way to the reception. She scanned the bar for Riley, checked the appetizer table, searched the dance floor, and even asked Elliott's uncle to look inside the men's room. He was nowhere to be found. 'Have you seen Riley?' Amanda asked his friends. No one had. Amanda worried that something was wrong. She decided to check out the room they had booked for the night. Maybe he went there to freshen up. As she crossed the lobby to the elevator, she spotted him nestled on a plush sofa engaged in lively conversation with Sofia di Carlo, the elegant twenty-year-old Italian countess who had recently arrived in Manhattan to attend NYU film school. There were two empty champagne flutes on the coffee table in front of them. Sofia was a tall, blue-eyed brunette who had the quiet confidence and natural elegance of someone who came from generations of entitlement. Amanda had gotten to know her when she helped her buy a three-bedroom unit with terrace at Zeckendorf Tower on Union Square. Riley had introduced them.

'There you are,' Amanda chirped. 'I've been looking for you.'

'Oh, we wanted to escape the madness in there,' Sofia said. 'Why not take a break? Join us for a drink?'

'No, I can't,' Amanda said. 'I'm the host. But Riley, we're about to start dinner. Do you want to come back with me?'

'Of course,' Riley said, ever the gentleman. 'Shall we?' he said to Sofia, offering an arm to each lady, escorting them back to the reception.

That was the last evening Riley ever spent with Amanda. Three weeks later, pictures of him and Sofia appeared in the Style section of the *Times*. He had taken her to the Hamptons Classic Horse Show. He never officially broke it off with Amanda; he just stopped calling. Amanda was crushed. She couldn't understand why he'd left her, but fierce pride prevented her from confronting him. She could only surmise it was because she wasn't Sofia. Ten months later, Riley married Sofia in a sumptuous ceremony at the Pierre, where sparks had first flown. Amanda was not invited. Five years after they married, Sofia left him and moved back to Italy with their only daughter. Amanda secretly hoped she would hear from Riley after that, but he never called.

Following Amanda's split from Riley, her pipeline to wealthy socialites buying and selling real estate dried up. She had to fight and scrape to get clients the old-fashioned way. In the months afterward, she made a decent living, but nothing close to what she'd done as Riley's girl. Then, a year after Serena's wedding, she heard that Donatella Versace was interviewing realtors to sell her late brother's thirty million dollar townhouse at 5 East Sixty-fourth Street. It's all about who you know, she thought. This could be my chance to land on top again.

'Introduce us, that's all I ask,' Amanda said, sitting across the desk from Serena at Versace's Manhattan office.

'I'm not sure,' Serena said, stacking her notepads from largest on the bottom to smallest on top. 'She's so unpredictable. You never know what's going to set her off.'

'Serena, I'm a great broker,' Amanda said, practically begging. 'Everyone who works with me loves me. As long as I can get in front of her, I can sell her.'

Serena shook her head nervously. 'I don't like to use my contacts for personal favors,' she said. 'What if she hires you and it doesn't work out? She'd blame me. It's risky. Let me sleep on it.'

Of course, she never made the introduction, Amanda thought, bitterly. Serena is a taker. That's what she does. She let me support her all her life. She let Laura save her life and give her children life. Now, the one thing I ask of Serena – to fix the will – she won't do. Even if she knew the trouble I was in, she wouldn't care. Serena cares about one thing: Serena. Amanda shivered. How can someone as normal as me have such a psycho as a sister?

Sitting up, Amanda glanced once more at the family portrait they had taken at Serena's wedding. Everyone looked radiant except for Amanda herself, whose eyes betrayed her profound longing that night. She reached for the slim drawer beneath the coffee table. Inside, she kept the notes she had found hidden by her mother in the apartment, along with a petit-point evening bag Sunny had given her when she went to her first dance in middle school. A month after her mom's funeral, she found this folded inside:

> To my giving, brave, guardian angel Amanda,
>
> Thank you for all the beautiful assistance you have given your sisters and me through the years. My biggest regret is that you had to grow up so fast and take on too much. At the same time, I don't know what we would have done without you. Darling Amanda, your sisters are all grown up now. They can take care of themselves.
>
> You're strong; it's true. But I know there are times when you are tired, lonely, afraid, and sad, times when you need someone to lean on. Be kind to yourself, dear Amanda. I filled this evening bag with kisses before I tucked this note inside. Open it anytime you need me and all my love will come spilling out to embrace and hold you and let you know that everything is going to be all right.
>
> Love forever,
> Mom

Amanda held the open bag up to her cheek, closed her eyes, and felt her mother's presence. Sunny always knew what to say to make her feel better, even when she wasn't there.

SERENA

'Before marriage, a man declares that he would lay down his life to serve you; after marriage, he won't even lay down his newspaper to talk to you.'

—Helen Rowland

'Sweetie, you have to turn off your BlackBerry,' Serena said, having just arranged the items in her seat pocket from largest in the back – United's *Hemisphere* magazine – to smallest in the front – the vomit bag. Since they were flying to Phoenix for a vacation, she had dressed casually in her thousand-dollar black APO jeans, which she had gotten for free through industry connections, and a coal-black cashmere sweater. She wore flat Dolce & Gabbana boots from last season.

In deference to the recession, Serena had decided to stop acquiring new designer clothes, except for samples that fashion houses gave her for free. She was committed to following Michelle Obama's lead and shopping with the masses. It was her way of contributing to the recovery.

Elliott raised his hand. 'One second,' he said as he continued typing onto his handheld.

'El, will you *please* keep Valentina busy while I deal with Sebastian?' she said. Serena tried to contain her son, who was squirming to get out of his seatbelt. Valentina was across the aisle next to Elliott, making high-pitched squeaks about wanting to get fed. Elliott did his best, playing peek-a-boo from behind the BlackBerry, but Valentina didn't respond to him and began whimpering. 'Oh, forget it,' Serena said scornfully. 'Do I have to do everything?' She took her pudgy daughter from Elliott and latched her onto her breast, praying she could get her fed before take-off. The baby needed to be strapped in. If she wasn't and, God forbid, the plane crashed, she would shoot out of her mother's arms like an errant missile. Serena had seen a report about that on *20/20*.

Thankfully, Sebastian settled down, peering intently out the window. As Valentina suckled, Serena showed her flash cards of simple words with corresponding pictures and read them to her. Serena estimated that Valentina could already read sixty words herself. It was too bad she couldn't talk and show off her advanced skill, maybe even appear on the *Today Show*. At four, Sebastian was already devouring chapter books, but she could have had him reading by one if she had known to use the flash cards on him.

Serena glanced at Elliott, who was smiling as he

tapped away. She hated competing with that stupid device. When she and Elliott first got married, there would have been no contest. He pursued her like a hot film deal. He loved the fact that she worked in the executive offices of Versace, and not just because of the discounts. Back then, she was a siren. At work, he was the all-powerful director. At home, he was helpless in Serena's orbit. Back then, it pleased him to please her – jewelry, clothes, exotic trips. Back then, they couldn't keep their hands off each other.

Before Sebastian, sex for Serena and Elliott was fun and playful. They would share their fantasies with each other and act them out. Sometimes she would pretend to pick him up in a bar and take him home for a one-night stand. Other times, Elliott would grab Serena, blindfold her, and 'force' himself upon her. The more she resisted, the hotter the sex. To celebrate the one-year anniversary of their meeting, Serena made Elliott lick Thanksgiving dinner off her naked body. At the first Golden Globe Awards dinner they attended together, Serena gave Elliott a hand-job under the table. Finding creative ways to turn each other on became a game to them, one they were both eager to play.

After Sebastian, sex was straightforward 'wham, bam, thank you ma'am' intercourse – that is, the few times they'd done it in the last four years. Serena wondered if she'd made a mistake by having a baby so soon, but after Laura had offered to be their egg donor, she'd decided to say yes in case, God forbid, her sister changed her mind. When Serena imagined having a baby, she saw herself bathed in golden light like Mother Mary holding an angelic sleeping child with Elliott gazing lovingly over her shoulder. In reality, she had become enslaved to this screaming, squirming, pooping, puking, and eating machine who never let her sleep through the night. She was terrified of him.

The spell Serena had over Elliott shifted as soon as they brought Sebastian home. He began working until midnight a lot, and when he'd come home earlier, he'd get on the phone with his editors or producers. Eventually, he'd climb into bed and put his BlackBerry under the pillow. She felt it vibrating and sensed him checking it through the night.

Serena suspected that Elliott fooled around. A week after her mother died, on her way to the dry cleaner, she found a pink ribbon and a long blond hair in his pants pocket. It wasn't proof positive, but it was a wake-up call. If, God forbid, they divorced, she would need a substantial nest egg to survive.

When she and Elliott married, they signed a prenup. That's to be expected when you marry a Skank. The family fortune had to be protected. In the event of divorce, each party would keep what they brought into and earned during the marriage. Serena was well paid in her career, so

70

she didn't care. Knowing she was infertile, she planned to work her way to the top of the fashion industry. Their unexpected decision to have children brought that plan to an abrupt end. The truth was, Serena hardly had any savings. Recently, she'd started taking five hundred dollars a week from the ATM and hiding it in a safety deposit box for the kids' financial security.

With her husband off in his own world, Serena vowed to put all her intelligence, love, and ambition into parenting. If she didn't do it, Elliott wouldn't. Truth be told, he hardly knew his children. She felt an overwhelming responsibility to give her son, and later her daughter, a perfect upbringing. After her father died, her mother had had to work two jobs to pay the bills. Serena would never leave her children all day the way Sunny had. As long as she was healthy, she would always be available to them, no matter what. With the added specter of recurring cancer lurking in the back of her mind, Serena strived to make every single second with her children count.

Serena shuddered as she recalled the bleak eternity spent at Methodist Hospital when she had leukemia. It was the day of the transplant. Amanda snuck out of the room to speak to the doctor. Serena's mouth was filled with sores, an angry red rash covered her skin, and her organs felt bruised from so much vomiting.

Laura and Serena were lying next to each other in gurneys, waiting for Laura to be taken to the operating room. Even though Serena was in a morphine induced haze, she remembered praying, 'Please, Lord, let this work. I'm afraid to die. Give me another chance, please!'

'I don't want to do this,' Laura cried, interrupting Serena's prayer. 'Don't make me. It's gonna hurt.'

Sunny took Laura's hand and gave it a squeeze. 'Honey, it'll hurt a lot more if we lose Serena. Now come on, show some courage.'

'Please, Laura,' Serena croaked, her voice hoarse with mucositis. 'I want to live.' This can't be happening, she thought as a fat tear slipped down her cheek.

'Shhh,' Sunny said. She glimpsed up and signaled to the nurse with her eyes. Discreetly, she injected a sedative into Laura's IV until her eyes grew heavy and closed.

Serena let out a sob. 'Thanks, Mom,' was all she could say.

Sunny winked at Serena. 'Hush now. What's a sore hip next to a lifetime without her sister? Someday she'll thank me.'

Amanda stuck her head back into the room. 'Mom, why don't you come with me? Let's go across the street to that spa. By the time we get massages and facials, Laura will be out of surgery and Serena will have had her rescue dose of bone marrow.'

Sunny gave Serena a quick kiss on the cheek, then dropped her hand and took off with Amanda.

'Wait! Don't leave me alone,' she cried. But her voice was so weak, Sunny and Amanda never looked back.

What a nightmare, Serena remembered. Laura tried to take back her bone marrow and Amanda and Mom didn't care enough to hold a vigil during the procedure. That's when Serena realized there was no one in life she could count on but herself.

That, she told herself, was why she had to take her time before changing the will. Amanda made plenty in real estate and Laura lived simply. What did they need with the inheritance? Amanda estimated that the house was worth more than twelve million dollars, although who knows if she could unload it in this ailing real estate market. Frankly, she wouldn't mind selling it. Serena had always considered herself an upper-east-sider trapped in a downtowner's body. She felt far more *simpatico* with the restrained, status-conscious uptowners than the loosey-goosey, label-may-care downtowners.

If she managed to sell the house and paid the taxes, she would be left with about eight million. Let's see, she thought. The way the stock market's been acting lately, I'd have to put that in a conservative investment; say treasury bills that return three percent. What's that? Two hundred and fifty thousand? After taxes, I'd get to keep a hundred and twenty-five thousand. You can't raise a family in Manhattan on that.

God forbid we have to move to the suburbs, she

thought. Nothing good ever came from nature. She shuddered at the thought of those goddam birds and their incessant singing. No, for now the inheritance stays in my name. Amanda and Laura won't do anything rash. They'll hang around waiting for their share of the booty, although that comes at a price. Right now, Amanda's furious with me, she thought. Heck, Amanda hasn't forgiven me since she asked for that introduction to Donatella Versace. I wish I could tell her that I asked, *I did*. But Donatella refused to work with her because Sofia di Carlo was an important client she couldn't afford to offend. How could I tell Amanda the truth when she was so brokenhearted about Riley? *I couldn't*. At least I did one thing right. I named the children Sebastian and Valentina. Laura always wanted those names for her first children and let's face it, Sebastian and Valentina are hers biologically. She deserved to be honored in that way.

Yesterday, before Amanda ruined Laura's party, Serena started to confide in her sisters about the problems she and Elliott were having. But she stopped herself. Her sisters thought she was living a fairy tale with her perfect marriage and two adorable children. Serena's life gave them hope that they, too, could have a happily-ever-after ending. It was better that she hadn't opened up. Why shatter their illusions by telling them the ugly truth about her marriage?

Valentina finished suckling at Serena's right

breast, so Serena moved her over to the left. Her little eyelids were heavy and she was starting to doze. Sebastian was craning to see the luggage being loaded into the plane. She glanced Elliott's way and noticed his fiery eyes and thick lashes. He's so handsome with that curly hair, she thought, I can't remember the last time I ran my hands through it. We couldn't keep our hands off each other while we dated, but our marriage has been practically celibate. How is that possible? We *must* have sex on this trip, she thought. If not, what chance do we have? But deep down, Serena was petrified. They were so out of the habit of being intimate with each other. How would she even initiate lovemaking?

The steward floated down the aisle picking up everyone's drink as the plane backed away from the gate. An announcement was made that they would soon be taking off so passengers should turn off their electronic devices.

'You'll have to shut that BlackBerry off,' the steward said. Elliott held up his finger to indicate he needed a moment.

Sebastian began squirming while his impish freckled face turned various shades of red. 'Mommy, I have to move my bowels,' he cried out, pulling his tan corduroy elastic-waist pants down.

'Baby, not now,' Serena said. 'You have to hold it. Squeeze your buttocks together like this.' She tried to demonstrate but it was as difficult as trying

75

to teach a toddler to blow his nose. Sebastian hadn't learned to do that yet either. It was odd that such a gifted child could not master nose-blowing. She made a mental note to call an occupational therapist.

'I can't wait,' he cried. His pants were off and he had wiggled out of the belt.

The steward strode past. 'Mrs Skank, you need to keep your son in his seat.' This was first class, so he knew her name.

'I'm trying, but he has an emergency,' Serena said. The plane was taxiing toward the runway. Serena figured she'd have just enough time to get Sebastion to the toilet before takeoff. She disconnected Valentina from her breast and plunked her into Elliott's arms. Black and white flash cards scattered all over the seats and into the aisle. The child howled at the abrupt interruption of her meal. Everyone in first class was giving her dirty looks.

'Calm her down,' Serena said to Elliott as she swept Sebastian toward the bathroom. She plopped him on the toilet and told him to make it snappy. There was no way she was going to let him backtrack on his training at this point. He'd been one hundred percent diaper-independent before Valentina was born, routinely discharging his load every morning after his egg-white-and-soy-cheese omelet and before nursery school. But with the addition of a sibling, he backslid, demanding the use of Pull-Ups and pacifiers. This child development nightmare had to stop and it had to stop now. Their appointment with Madison Prep was coming right up.

There was urgent knocking at the door. 'Mrs Skank, you need to go back to your seat. We can't take off with you in there.'

'One second,' she said. 'Sebastian, *hurry.*'

'*Nobody knows the trouble I've seen,*' the boy crooned. He'd been singing old spiritual songs ever since Serena took him to see the Harlem Gospel Choir perform at the Ebenezer Gospel Tabernacle.

Serena started to pull him off the toilet. He screamed. 'Mommy! Not yet!'

'Mrs Skank, take your seat NOW,' the steward yelled.

'Serena, get out of there,' Elliott demanded through the door.

Serena knew he had Valentina in his arms because she recognized her distinctive howl for food. He's made no progress in calming her down as I asked him to, she thought. Why do I have to do everything in this family? 'He's almost done,' Serena cried. Her chest tightened. Anxiety rose inside her, constricting the air from her lungs so that she could barely breathe.

'Jeez, Serena,' Elliott screamed. 'You're causing a scene!' Valentina cried louder.

Frazzled, Serena scooped Sebastian off the can and stuck a toilet-paper plug in his butt. She unlatched the door with her elbow and hustled him back to their seats. With the boy in one arm, she used her other arm to open the overhead compartment and pull out his porta-potty, which was a feat since she was 5'2" and not wearing heels. She slammed the compartment door shut, dropped the potty in the aisle, and stuck Sebastian on top of it. His contorted face turned red as he moved his bowels. First class immediately reeked. There were groans from all sides.

'I'm sorry, I'm so sorry,' Serena said to the other passengers. God, she thought, twisting her hair into a tight knot, the pressure is killing me. I never felt this stressed in business, not once. Sebastian's face was returning to normal. Serena lifted him up, wiped him quickly, and put the *Hemisphere* magazine over the porta-potty to contain the smell. As fast as she could, she strapped Sebastian and his naked bottom in before securing her own belt.

'Forgive us,' she said to Elliott and then to everyone around her. 'It was an emergency.' Elliott's eyes danced over her with contempt. Why can't he be more supportive? she wondered. Serena felt so alone as a parent that she wanted to weep.

'Christ, we're returning to the gate,' Elliott hissed. 'What have you done?'

Serena peered out the window and realized that the airport was getting closer and closer. She unhooked her belt and rushed forward to the steward.

'Do you not know the meaning of the words "take your seat?"' he said, rather rudely, Serena thought. This wasn't the kind of treatment one expected to receive in first class. When they got back from Phoenix, she would write a letter to the president of United Airlines.

'Please,' Serena said, 'tell them it's okay to take off. I won't get up again. My son needed to go and I had to . . .'

The door to the cockpit opened and a silver-haired captain stepped out. 'Ma'am, will you please sit down?' he said crabbily. 'You have inconvenienced a planeload of passengers already.' He was so tall and stern that Serena obeyed. Elliott handed a wailing Valentina over to her as soon as she buckled up.

When the plane stopped at the gate, the steward opened the door. Captain Crabby made his way back and ordered the family off the plane.

An angry shadow passed across Elliott's face. 'What?' he said. 'Captain, please. I'm sorry for my wife's behavior, but she won't do it again. She didn't understand . . .'

The captain pointed to the door. 'We can do this the easy way or the hard way,' he said.

'Excuse me,' Serena said. 'But is this any way to treat four passengers who paid full price for their first-class tickets? We didn't even use miles, although we could have. Elliot's Premier, you know. He's a director on *Law and Order*, Special Victims Unit . . .'

The captain was unmoved. 'Off,' he said, pointing to the door. 'Now.'

Elliott acquiesced and scooped up his things. He unstrapped Valentina's car seat and stormed off the plane with it under his arm, leaving Serena to struggle with the baby and Sebastian all by herself. As she carried the kids out, she kicked the magazine off the porta-potty in silent protest.

At the end of the jetway, Serena found Elliott arguing with two uniformed officials from United. He's being awfully pushy, she thought, which is no way to get what you want in these times of heightened security and no-nonsense airport employees. 'It's okay,' she said, with Valentina resting on her outstretched hip and Sebastian holding her hand. 'Let's just calm down.'

'Serena,' Elliott said, giving her a searing glare. 'They're putting us on United's no-fly list.'

'Forget it,' Serena said. 'I would never fly United again anyway. We'll go away another time on another carrier.'

'There may not be another time, Serena, because airlines share their no-fly lists,' Elliott said, or rather shouted, at her. He turned back to the airport officials and begged them to reconsider, or at least to only put Serena on the no-fly list since she was the guilty one.

Serena's face grew hot and her eyes watered. She couldn't believe Elliott would throw her to the wolves like that in front of her own children.

'Mommy,' Sebastian said, tugging at her sleeve, 'do I get a toy for moving my bowels on the plane?'

LAURA

'Family faces are magic mirrors. Looking at people who belong to us, we see the past, present, and future.

—Gail Lumet Buckley

Every Saturday, when Laura entered Golden Manor Nursing Home, her first thought was of Sunny, who had loved their daycare program. The place was located on Manhattan's Upper East Side in an inconspicuous white brick building on Seventy-sixth Street, right off Second. A great many of the residents suffered from Alzheimer's or other forms of dementia. Some had intact minds but had outlived their bodies' ability to transport them. In all but the most miserable weather, the staff would park a gaggle of blanket-wrapped octogenarians in their wheelchairs smack in front of the building like human lawn ornaments. Strolling by, you couldn't miss the sea of spotted scalps through wisps of thinning hair. Those residents who managed to stay awake took great joy in kibitzing with the cute puppies and little children who ambled past with their mommies and care-givers.

Years earlier, Sunny used to enjoy their arts and crafts, singing, old movies, and seated-workout classes. It was here that Laura met the Off Our Rockers Trio, the house band for Golden Manor consisting of John Hazeltine on drums, Stan Garrett on bass, and David Hargrove on piano. These self-proclaimed 'cats' had been world-class musicians in their day. Despite the fact that John weighed three hundred pounds and was confined to an electric Rascal, Stan had inoperable cataracts and couldn't see past his nose even with thick glasses, and David fell asleep between songs, they made sweet music together.

All her life, Laura aspired to become a torch singer like Billie Holiday. After attending the High School for the Performing Arts, she earned a coveted spot at Juilliard. Music was Laura's lifeblood.

One rainy afternoon, when Sunny was attending a weekly concert at Golden Manor, Laura asked the Off Our Rockers Trio if she could sing with them. They were delighted. She performed *April in Paris* with their backup. The crowd went nuts – as nuts as a rec room full of incapacitated senior citizens can get. Soon, she and her mom were minor celebrities at Golden Manor. Laura eventually joined the group as lead singer. In the years that followed, they became like a little family, with David acting as the father she never had, and Stan and John the nutty uncles.

In the last two years of Sunny's illness, it was David who kept Laura's spirits high. Not Amanda, not Serena – David! A tall, long-limbed African American, David had a face of deep, crooked lines with skin like an old polished boot. He had spindly fingers on huge hands that could stretch across two octaves each. Every morning, he would call to see how Sunny and Laura were doing. At least twice a week and sometimes more, he rode the bus a hundred blocks south to Tribeca and read or sang to Sunny while Laura took a much-needed break. When she came home, Laura would fix David a heart-healthy dinner and they'd spend the evening chatting or watching movies. He usually dozed off and spent the night on the sofa bed.

David became Laura's mentor, teaching her the ins and outs of the music business; training her voice; showing her different phrasings, intonations, and interpretations for the classics that he first heard accompanying Sarah Vaughan. David would demonstrate the sound on the keyboard, and then Laura would sing it. It was a master class in jazz vocals, worth more than all her years at Juilliard. Sometimes, after a lesson, she would take him to dinner at his favorite neighborhood restaurant, MaryAnn's, and listen as he recounted stories about the good old days when jazz was the mainstay of American music.

Laura and David got on so brilliantly that she brought him to Eva for a past-life regression. There, she discovered that the two of them had been husband and wife in at least three earlier life-times. It made perfect sense to Laura, who knew in her solar-plexus chakra that David had traveled with her through multiple incarnations. 'It's okay,' she joked. 'I'm giving you permission to date other women.'

Today, as Laura watched her elderly audience shuffle into the rec room at the nursing home, David approached her with a new 'girl' on his arm. He was known as quite the lady-killer at the home despite his reputation for falling asleep during lovemaking. 'Laura, meet Emma Schneiderstern. She just moved in.' He winked at her. Emma blushed. She was a white, shrunken, stooped old bird with random hair patches and a gravelly voice that made her sound like a cartoon. Beside her was a portable oxygen tank on wheels with tubes leading to her nose.

'Pleased to meet you,' Emma said, a lit cigarette hanging from her lips, white smoke wafting to the ceiling.

'Emma, you can't smoke,' Laura said. 'You're on oxygen. You'll blow us up.'

Emma dropped her cigarette on the floor and stamped it out. 'And you can't call me Emma. It's *Mrs Schneiderstern* to you. She looks like a hussy,' she said to David under her breath. 'I don't see how you could have married her, not in *any* lifetime.'

'Mrs Schneiderstern, you shouldn't call me a hussy to my face, even if you think that,' Laura said, wondering if Emma might be suffering from some sort of mental decline that impaired her self-censoring abilities. That was what happened to Bea

Arthur's mother on *The Golden Girls*. She knew because they had that series running on a continuous loop in the card room at Golden Manor.

'C'mon, Emma, I'll get you a front-row seat,' David said.

As if in slow motion, nurses, patients, and visitors filed into the large game room, where concerts were held. It wasn't the ideal venue for performing, with its unmistakable smell of senior citizens outliving their expiration dates. Still, after the custodian set up rows of folding metal chairs and a small wooden stage on the scuffed linoleum floor, it felt like a mini-theater. Residents who still had their memories intact looked forward to the weekly concert. Those lacking the neural synapses to anticipate the band, apparently enjoyed listening all the same.

Laura took the stage. Her curly golden hair cascaded loosely down her back. Today she wore a vintage midnight-blue crepe strapless top with a feathered skirt that she had picked up for a song at the City Opera thrift shop, the best second-hand store in Manhattan. The wealthiest socialites sent their finest designer castoffs there to benefit a most worthy cause. 'Ladies and gentlemen,' Laura said, 'it's Saturday at Golden Manor Nursing Home and what are we . . . ?'

'Off Our Rockers!' The visitors and staff yelled. The residents of the center were quiet. A few had dozed off. That was okay. The band was used to playing against a backdrop of snores and phlegmy snorts.

Laura led the band through their playlist, songs from an era when the patients were raising families and building careers. A few remembered the lyrics; Alzheimer's wiped away short-term memory before long-term. *Summertime, Cheek to Cheek, A Fine Romance, I Won't Dance* – the audience swayed to the beat, many closing their eyes and going back in their minds to a time when they were happy and whole. Oh, how Laura loved to perform! As John launched into his drum solo, she thought about the billionaire's private-jet gig that paid so well. Please God, let me get that job so I can spend my time promoting this band.

As Laura picked up the song again, she noticed Joey Martin, the actor and director, sitting next to blue-haired Miriam Goldofsky. His bald head, chipmunk cheeks, and barbed-wire eyebrows were unmistakable. Holding the old lady's hand, he danced with her as best he could while she sat rigid in her wheelchair. This was a first. No one famous had ever come to any of her retirement-home concerts, unless you counted Dr Blood who performed at their Halloween party. He had been the subject of an obscure but critically acclaimed documentary in the nineties. 'Does anybody have a request?' Laura asked.

'"The Best Is Yet to Come",' a nurse shouted.

'Maybe for you, sister,' Emma cried. 'We've got one foot in the ground.'

Laura wasn't sure she approved of Emma dating David. The older you get, the more you need upbeat people in your life, she thought. Who needs cranky, embittered friends like Emma, who see the grave as half-full, not half-empty? The band launched into the song despite the heckling.

'Before we close, let me introduce my mates here,' Laura said. 'On electric wheelchair, we have John Hazeltine, behind those thick glasses is Stan Garrett, and of course, that's the incomparable David Hargrove sleeping at the piano.' David insisted Laura make fun of them when she introduced the band. He wanted everyone to know that they were in on the joke.

The audience applauded with great enthusiasm and appreciation.

The band ended with *They Can't Take That Away from Me*. Afterward, Laura mingled with the crowd. For some reason, the residents always wanted to touch her skin and stroke her hair following a performance. When she passed Joey Martin, he shook her hand, then didn't let go.

'That was great,' he enthused. 'And you, I can't get over your voice. It's so sweet and high, like Joni Mitchell in her heyday, but you swing like a jazz vocalist. Peggy Lee comes to mind. And I love the band. Never seen a group quite like it. It's life-affirming to watch.'

'Thanks,' Laura said. 'That means a lot coming from you.'

Joey sidled a little closer. 'Can I ask you a favor? Will you introduce me to David Hargrove? He used to play with Miles Davis, didn't he?'

'Yes, and Dizzy Gillespie,' she said. 'David,' she called, 'Can you come over?'

David strolled over sans Mrs Schneiderstern, for which Laura was relieved.

'Whoa,' Joey Martin said, 'I can't believe I'm meeting the great David Hargrove. I'm a huge fan, *huge*! You played piano with everyone, didn't you?'

'Why thank you, son,' David said. 'It's true. I am one of the greats.'

'David,' Laura said, swatting him playfully. 'Don't be so modest.'

'When you're as old as Moses,' David said, 'you may as well tell it like it is.'

Joey Martin laughed. 'You, I like,' he said. 'And that gives me an idea. My next film'll be shooting in Manhattan with Julia Roberts and George Clooney. I'd love to use the band for a scene,' he said. 'You interested?'

David grinned broadly. 'You damn right we are. Hey Stan, John, want to be in a movie?' he called to them. Neither responded – they were hard of hearing after so many years of playing.

'We'd been thinking of Norah Jones, but your band would be more interesting visually. There's real color here,' he said.

Laura practically tinkled in her pants. 'We're nothing if not colorful,' she squealed.

Joey shook his head with disbelief. 'Pinch me! The great Dave Hargrove is going to play in one of my movies. I want you on camera.' Joey appeared lost in thought for a moment. 'It's possible we could use you for the whole sound-track. Do you have a CD?'

Never in her wildest dreams would Laura have imagined getting the gig of a lifetime through Golden Manor. She knew that Rob Reiner had made Harry Connick, Jr.'s career when he hired him to do the soundtrack for *When Harry Met Sally*. Finally, she and the band would get their big break. It's karma, she thought. You give to the elderly and the elderly give back to you.

Act calm, she told herself. Ohmmm, ohmmm. 'Ohm, we don't have a CD but we do have a DVD of the show. Mrs Steuben's grandson shot it last summer. The sound quality's not the greatest, but you can take a copy and show it around.'

'That'll work,' Joey said. 'I know how good you sound. It's the visual gestalt of the group that's so compelling.'

Mrs Schneiderstern approached David, a lit cigarette hanging from her mouth once more. 'Mrs Schneiderstern, no smoking when you're on oxygen, remember? You'll blow us all to kingdom come.'

'I never smoke with this thing on,' she declared, the cigarette dangling dangerously. 'That would be suicidal.'

David gingerly plucked it from her lips and stamped it out with his brown loafer.

'If you want to use us, I suggest you do it soon, before Mrs Schneiderstern does us all in. I'll get you a DVD,' Laura said to Joey Martin.

'You'll hear from me,' he said. 'And Mr Hargrove, it has been an honor to meet you.'

Laura was thrilled beyond belief. She couldn't wait to call Mom and tell her. Then she remembered she couldn't. Instead, she closed her eyes and told Sunny the exciting news in a prayer, wondering all along how much of a hand her mother had in her good fortune.

AMANDA

*'Big sisters are the crab grass in the lawn of
life.'*

　　　　　　　　　　　　—Charles M Schulz

Amanda took a sip of coffee from a cereal
bowl-sized ceramic mug. She was sitting
at the far back table at Kitchenette, a
shabby-chic comfort-food restaurant in her neighborhood. Across from her was Richie, her
'personal banker.' Ten years her junior, he had
black hair slicked back in a pompadour, a dark
complexion and glistening brown eyes fringed
with lashes so long they cast shadows on his
cheeks. He wore fresh Levis and a white muscle
shirt that showed off his baseball-sized biceps, two
on each arm. Anyone catching a glimpse of them
would have thought they were on a date. Nothing
could be further from the truth.

Amanda slid a thick envelope across the table.
'Here. Ten thousand dollars, a show of good faith.'

'That's not enough, Red.' Richie said. He had
anointed her 'Red' the first time they met, in

91

deference to her hair. Amanda had anointed him 'Richard' in deference to the threat he posed.

'I know, Richard, I'm sorry, but listen. I'm about to close a huge deal. As soon as I do, I'll be able to pay the whole loan back *with* interest.' Amanda's underarms felt clammy beneath her navy St John Knit dress.

Richie stuck a fork into his omelet. Yellow cheese oozed out and white smoke wafted into the air. 'I'll try to hold my employer off, a week, maybe two. If you don't pay up by then, there *will* be blood. Nothing personal. I like you, Red, but this is the last cordial meeting we'll have, if you know what I mean.'

Amanda's heart raced and her breath became shallow. Last cordial meeting? *Blood?* What had she been thinking getting involved with a loan shark? She'd seen something like this on *Law and Order* once. A nice, respectable professional woman stupidly borrowed from the mob. The cops found her sliced into human confetti and stuffed down a trash chute.

Damn her big-shot client and his 'can't lose' investment strategy. A few weeks before Sunny died, her nest egg had dwindled to practically nothing and the medical bills were piling up. Amanda used the power of attorney Sunny had given her to take out a four million dollar mortgage against the Duane Street house. One of her Wall Street clients advised her it was fool-hardy to have all the family's assets tied up in real estate.

At least a third should be liquid. As a personal favor, he hooked Amanda up with an investment advisor who usually only worked with the super-rich and well-connected. After spending a hundred grand on doctor bills, she placed the remaining millions with the money manager, confident that diversifying was the smart thing to do in such an uncertain economy. She never mentioned this to her sisters. For years, she'd handled the family's legal and financial affairs and they'd never shown the slightest interest.

Unfortunately, the advisor Amanda invested with was Bernie Madoff. A mere four days after handing over the check, Madoff confessed to running a fifty-billion-dollar Ponzi scheme, the largest fraud in the history of the world. When Amanda heard the news, she rushed over to his office, hoping against hope that he hadn't cashed the check. The crush of reporters outside the building made it impossible to get through, but a call to her bank confirmed that the check had been deposited into Madoff's account, which had been frozen by the Securities and Exchange Commission. The money had disappeared.

Amanda wanted to shake this shark in sheik's clothing and ask him, 'Why? How could you steal from widows and charities and hardworking people?' But she'd have to get in line behind thousands of other victims. She was wracked with despair that the money was gone, but even more devastated by the shame she felt over violating her sisters' trust. All their lives they had depended on her to take care of them. If only she'd done more research, asked the right questions, she might have figured out that this was a scam. When her client told her the fund returned one percent a month in good times and bad, she should have known that was too good to be true. Amanda had invested foolishly and now her sisters would suffer. She wished she was brave enough to tell them the truth, but she couldn't get the words out of her mouth.

Making everything worse, the credit market imploded, sending real estate plummeting. Amanda's sales dipped seventy percent. She fell behind on the mortgage payments. At least I'll inherit a third of the Duane Street property, she thought. We'll sell the house and I'll repay the loan with my share. Laura and Serena never have to know.

When the inheritance didn't pan out and Bank of America threatened to foreclose, Amanda borrowed a hundred grand from a 'private lender' to bring her mortgage payments current. A colleague at work made the introduction. She never dreamed that the 'banker' was a loan shark. Who knew there really *were* loan sharks in this world? She had always thought of them as an urban myth.

Amanda's mouth was dry with fear. 'Richard, when you say there will be *blood*, what *exactly* do you mean?'

'What do you think? I have to hurt you, break a bone, maybe two, spill some blood,' he said, eying her with an expression that was both nonchalant and forbidding. 'Pass the ketchup, please?'

Amanda's heart thumped so hard that her ribs ached. Richie's biceps were covered in tattoos that screamed 'hoodlum' (in her opinion). Prison tats no doubt, she thought, as she slid the bottle of red liquid over. I'm so fucked. 'Richard, I swear I'll have the money soon. I'm getting a big commission on a Park Avenue co-op sale. All we need is board approval and that'll be no problem with this family. And I have other deals in the hopper as well.'

'Then I suggest you get moving,' he said, flicking back his black, shiny hair. 'You're too pretty to rough up. That's the one part of my job I get no joy out of.' He let out a sigh of regret. 'But wuddaya gonna do, Red?'

Amanda swallowed hard. 'I'll bet you hate that,' she said, taking a sip of water to wet her parched throat. She had no appetite for the thick stack of blueberry pancakes sitting in front of her. 'You seem like a good person. Do you have a girlfriend?'

Richie's eyes bored into hers. 'Let's not talk personal. It'll make it harder for me to do my job if it comes to that. Think of me as the cancer doctor who doesn't get close to his patients, if you know what I mean.'

'I do know,' Amanda said, wanting more than

anything to get personal with Richie. That was the whole reason she'd suggested to him that they have breakfast together. Amanda was convinced that if he could experience what a good human being she was, he'd cut her a break. 'My little sister had cancer. I met lots of doctors who were strictly business. It was their self-preservation strategy. I was only asking if you had a girlfriend. A handsome guy like you must.'

'I said no personal talk,' he snapped, his voice as icy as a January freeze.

Amanda shrank back, dropped her eyes, and began picking blueberries out of her cold pancakes with her fork.

Richie grabbed the honey in the plastic bear and squeezed a glob onto his buttermilk biscuit. 'Keep it business – that's the first thing they teach you at CIA training.' He bit into his biscuit and honey dripped down his chin.

'Were you in the CIA?' Amanda said.

'Still am, Red,' Richie said, dipping his napkin into her water and wiping his chin. 'I do this on the side to pick up extra cash. If you knew what the government pays its assassins, you'd be scandalized. Lucky for me, in this economy, collectors are in high demand.'

Amanda's stomach dropped. 'But your *real* job is to assassinate people?'

Richie leaned forward. 'Government enemies. Terrorists that infiltrate our shores. Assholes who offend the wrong people.'

Great. Of all the loan sharks in New York City, mine is certifiably insane, she thought.

He rubbed his leg against Amanda's. 'You feel my piece?'

Amanda nodded slowly, her eyes growing rounder and rounder. 'My gosh. It's so big and hard. I mean, oh God, I didn't mean it like *that*,' she said. 'I wouldn't talk dirty to you. Now *that*'s personal. And certainly not at this family restaurant. Not anywhere really. You're my assassin. I mean . . . collector.' Shut up, Amanda, she told herself. 'Oh, fuck, I'm scared of you,' she said, her voice small and frightened.

'Good, Red,' Richie said, 'you should be.' He pushed his chair back, stood, dropped his napkin on Amanda's cold pancakes, and disappeared without even offering to cover his half of the tab.

SEBASTIAN

'When I grow up I want to be a little boy.'
— Joseph Heller

Sebastian hated when his parents didn't talk to each other. On the way home from the airport that day, no one spoke and they weren't even playing the quiet game. This was happening more and more. The only thing that brought them together as a family was when he moved his bowels. Everyone would smile and applaud. If he could make ten times a day, his mommy and daddy would be happy. But there was only so much he could do in that department.

What Sebastian wanted more than anything right now was his pacifier. When his parents' silence hung in the air like a stinky diaper, nothing helped more than sucking and chewing on a rubber dummy. His mother had forbidden him to use them anymore, so he had to suck in secret, the way she smoked in secret. She wasn't paying attention, so he reached down behind the back seat and pulled one out. It was covered in hair and dirt, but Sebastian had an itch that needed to be scratched. He stuck it in his mouth and chewed furiously. Ahhhh, he thought.

Mommy continued to face forward. He hoped his luck would hold out. Lately, she was calling him her 'little man.' All she did these days was care for him, feed his useless sister, and sneak smokes. Daddy was never home anymore. Sebastian didn't like the way home felt. Every day after school, Mommy would take him to one of his extra-curakulas – French on Monday, Chinese on Tuesday, violin on Wednesday, yoga on Thursday, Mini-Mensa on Friday, fun math on Saturday. Grownups think that singing about numbers makes them fun. Sebastian disagreed. Mommy was helping Sebastian find his passion so that he could get into a good school next year. A kid had to have passion to make it in kinder-garten these days.

'Since we're not going to Phoenix,' Serena said, 'I'll call the Metropolitan Opera. They're having tryouts for the children's chorus soon. Maybe I can get him a spot.'

'What are you talking about?' Elliott said, 'Sebastian can't sing.'

Serena shook her head sadly. 'That's how little you know. Our boy has a fine voice. Sebastian, how would you like to be onstage during the opera?'

Sebastian would not like that at all. He would rather play with cars and trucks. And *not* with his play tutor supervising.

'That would be a plume in his cap for his résumé,' Serena said. 'But I wonder if the opera would accept him before his interviews. They're coming right up.'

'Then you'd better get on it,' Elliott teased.

Sebastian noticed that his father was smiling at his mother when he said that. If it would make them happy, then fine. He would do it. He hoped he might be in an opera that had animals in it, like some of the ones his mother had taken him to. Live animals make everything better. He took a few more sucks on his pacifier and then stuck it back behind the seat.

When they got home, Daddy unloaded the car and carried everything upstairs. Sebastian was sorry the trip got cancelled. He had been counting on seeing his first real snake. They lived in the desert. Sebastian loved nature and wished he could live where there were trees and birds. Mommy put good-for-nothing Valentina down for a nap while Sebastian colored in his room. Sebastian didn't know how she could sleep through the loud music playing on the floor below. He was chewing his dummy when he heard his mother's footsteps coming down the stairs. Quickly, he stuffed it down his Pull-Up.

Serena stuck her head in. 'Sweetie, Daddy has gone back to work. What would you like to do this afternoon?'

'Play cars?' Sebastian said.

'Why would you want to play when you could

be learning? I know,' Mommy said, her eyes wide and her voice all excited, 'instead of *playing* with the cars, why don't we *count* them? And then, we can sort them by colors and make a graph showing the number and colors of your collection. Graphing is fun, don't you think?'

'No,' Sebastian said.

'C'mon,' Mommy said. 'We can sing the graphing song together. That'll make it like a party, right? It would make me so happy to see how smart you are in math. You want to make Mommy happy, don't you?'

'Yes,' Sebastian said. He hated when Mommy played the happy card. Of course he wanted to make her happy, unlike Daddy, who made her sad. Sebastian knew Mommy's happiness was all up to him. It was a big responsibility.

AMANDA

Amanda arrived at the Bullocks' eight million dollar apartment on the corner of Seventy-eighth and Fifth Avenue. Although their current apartment offered location and light, the new one boasted location, light, *and* space, the killer combo reserved for Manhattan's most privileged residents. Today Amanda wore her red zebra print St John Knit with a matching black feather-trimmed cape. She had sold a seven million dollar duplex at Trump Tower wearing this outfit, so it was lucky. Amanda needed all the luck she could get. The only thing standing between this family and the fifteen million dollar apartment on Park Avenue and Seventieth that they coveted was the co-op board interview scheduled for four that afternoon. The only thing standing between Amanda and two broken kneecaps was this deal closing.

At one p.m., thirty-six-year-old Tabby Bullock and her five-year-old daughter, Diva, were having their matching chestnut hair blown straight by George, the same hairdresser who did Meredith Viera, from the *Today Show*. His partner, Scott, had finished touching up Tabby's roots and was packing up to go to his next client.

Tabby's four-year-old son, Winston the Third, a freckled brunette, was running around the apartment with a wet Pull-Up on his head. Noodle, the family's white Maltese, was still at the groomers'. Tabby's husband, Winston the Second, had picked an inopportune time to take a quick jog around the Reservoir. At fifty-five, he was heir to a major pharmaceutical fortune, but he reminded Amanda of one of those idiot savants who lived on a different existential plane from everyone around him. When one was as rich as Winston the Second, weird behavior was considered cute instead of annoying. Amanda was miffed. She needed to counsel the family on what to expect at the board interview and how to conduct themselves, but no one was close to being ready.

When Amanda was dating Riley Trumbo, she was one of the top-grossing agents at Corcoran. That was a lifetime ago. Lately, it felt like she couldn't sell a carrot stick to an anorexic. Still, she had faith that today was the day things would turn around.

Amanda had been in real estate long enough to

know that when it was bad, it was very bad, but when it was good, there was nothing more thrilling. She'd fallen into the business through a twist of fate, the year her father drowned himself. She had barely returned from her second semester of Yale Drama School when Sunny got the call that her husband was missing. The family drove to East Hampton with high hopes for a happy ending, only to have them dashed. On their return, Sunny locked herself in the master bedroom, wailing so loud and so plaintively that Amanda was convinced she would harm herself. Serena sat outside her mother's door whimpering, curled in a fetal position. Laura was in the kitchen making peanut-butter-and-jelly sandwiches, trying to help in the only way she knew how.

Using a bobby pin, Amanda picked the lock and let herself into her mother's bedroom. Sunny lay under the covers sobbing, her eyes red and swollen, her shoulders and chest heaving as she hugged a pillow. 'I'm so sorry, Mama,' Amanda said, embracing Sunny's tiny form.

'It's all m-m-my f-f-fault,' Mom wept. 'I did this to h-h-him.'

'No, you didn't,' Amanda said. 'It was his choice and it was selfish.'

Sunny sat up and sniffed, trying to compose herself. 'No, I pushed him. I may as well have held him under the water myself,' she said, choking back a sob until it escaped of its own accord. Fat tears spilled down her face and soaked into the white cotton sheets. 'I can't do this alone, I *can't*,' she wept, surrendering to the tsunami of grief that wracked her body.

'You don't have to,' Amanda said, frightened by her mother's surprising fragility. 'I'll take a year off, find a job. We'll get through this together.' It was the last thing she wanted to do, but what choice did she have? Sunny would never be able to make a living and take care of two little girls by herself, not in her state of mind. I'll go back to school next year, she promised herself.

Luckily, the Moons' neighbor was a successful condominium developer. As a gesture of kindness to the battered family, he hired Amanda to show apartments in a building he had recently completed near First and Eighty-fourth. In Amanda's second month on the job, she happened to be observed by Barbara Corcoran, who told her she'd make a great salesperson. Barbara stole her away, offering an entry-level position in her company's busiest office on Madison Avenue.

One evening, about a week after starting, she was asked to show a Beekman Place apartment to a couple who were in from Chicago for just one night. On arrival, they discovered that the owner had turned off the electricity when he moved out. 'No problem,' Amanda said. 'I'll be right back.' She ran to Duane Reade, bought flash-lights, and showed the apartment in the dark. The couple made an offer on the spot. Amanda figured if she could sell apartments by flashlight, she must be cut out for the profession. A year later, she let her one-year deferment from Yale lapse. Her income was too important to the family to give up. One thing led to another, and twenty years later Amanda was still flogging real estate.

Most of the time, she loved it. There was something deliciously voyeuristic about going into strangers' homes, getting to know them through their art, possessions, books, and photos. To Amanda, real estate was like dating. You're introduced to different places until you find one especially attractive. You decide you want to see it again and go back to get to know it better. Or maybe it's love at first sight. You wonder if you could live happily ever after there. Finally, you decide it's 'the one' and make a proposal to buy it. It was a ritual Amanda never tired of, possibly because she'd gone out on so few dates since Riley dumped her.

Amanda glanced around the sun-filled room, admiring the Bullocks' display of Picassos, Cézannes, Monets, de Koonings, and Lassiters – and this was just the bedroom suite. What a life Tabby Bullock had, to never have to worry about money, to be surrounded by beautiful things, with pleasant servants to do her bidding. But was she happy? Hell yes, Amanda thought. She glimpsed a small Pissarro set on an end table in Tabby's sitting area. If I slipped that into my purse, my troubles would be over. Stop! I'm not *that* desperate. 'I love your paintings,' Amanda said over the sound of the blow-dryer. 'Which of you is the collector?'

'It's Winston's family. But I'll tell you a secret. They're all fake,' she shouted. 'It's too risky to hang them with so many people coming and going all the time. There's an artist named Ham who lives in Harlem. He copies all our acquisitions. We hang the reproductions and store the originals in the vault.'

George finished Tabby's blowout and stood back to admire his work. Her shoulder-length brown hair was straight and silky.

'I never would have known,' Amanda said, studying the Pissarro, er, Ham on the table. She was no art expert, but it looked authentic to her. No point in stealing it, though. Not that she ever would.

'He's amazing,' Tabby said. 'Every clump of paint on his reproductions is identical to the original. And his drawings, forget about it. Between you and me,' she whispered, 'I had all my important jewelry copied as well. A second wife can never be too careful.'

Amanda knew that lots of women married to rich men did this. She couldn't believe all the secrets her clients had entrusted her with through the years. Didn't they know there was no such thing as client-real estate agent privilege?

Tabby's assistant opened the dressing-room door and delivered Noodle, who resembled a four-legged mop with her long, luscious, freshly styled fur. As soon as the Maltese saw Amanda, he went off on an incessant yappy-dog barking spree.

'Shhhh,' Amanda said, 'calm down now. Should I give her a treat?'

'No,' Tabby said, 'sometimes she gets this way with strangers. Maybe we should medicate her before the interview.'

Amanda was loath to drug a dog without vet supervision. Last year, a client gave Valium to his golden retriever and the poor pooch went into such a stupor during the interview that he had to be carried out. Ever since, Amanda agreed to Valium for her human clients but not their dogs. It was unfortunate that this particular board was so picky that they insisted on meeting both children and pets. This was technically against the law, but if you complained, you'd never get in.

When Amanda tried to pet Noodle, the dog howled.

'Noodle, what's gotten into you today?' Tabby said.

'Since when is she so vocal?' Amanda said, a worry line growing between her brows. 'That's not good. Can she sit on command? They'll expect her to do that for the doorman.'

'I'd say . . . mmm . . . yeah, sure,' Tabby said. 'Noodle, sit. Sit!'

Noodle chased her tail.

'Oh dear,' Tabby said. 'This won't hurt our chances, will it? I suppose we could give her to my parents.'

'NO!' Diva shouted, curling her lower lip down to her chin. 'She's *my* puppy.'

'No one's getting rid of Noodle,' Amanda said as she dialed her assistant. 'Nikki, call Starpetz and see if you can get your hands on a white long-haired Maltese, stat! We need a stand-in for the Bullock interview today by three o'clock. I'll take a cell phone shot of their dog and send it to you. Find as close a match as you can.' Starpetz was a talent agency that represented animal actors across the city. Their dogs were the utmost professionals and were often available last-minute. Because of union rules, the pooch would have to be paid the full-day rate, but it would be worth it.

By two-thirty, the entire family was gathered in the living room for their final instructions. Winston the Third was dressed in a hand-embroidered olive-green outfit from Bon Point. Tabby and Diva wore matching navy Dior suits with Barbara Bush pearls. Winston the Second was crisp and businesslike in his charcoal pinstriped Armani and shiny black Gucci shoes. His thinning salt-and-pepper hair was still wet from his post-run shower.

'You all look like you're going to a funeral,' Amanda said on inspection. 'Perfect! Except Winston, wear your glasses. They make you seem even more conservative. And Tabby, don't take that Kelly bag. Carry something tasteful but not recognizable. There's a woman on this board. You don't want to outshine her.'

'I could give this to her,' Tabby said.

'No,' Amanda said, 'anyone who lives in that building can afford one herself.'

'I have Noodle's pedigree papers and résumé,' Winston the Second said, 'along with a certified copy of his height and weight from the vet.'

'Great,' Amanda said. 'And bring his diploma from Berkeley Kline.' Berkeley Kline was the crème de la crème of dog-training academies in the City. Amanda was surprised they'd let Noodle graduate. Today she was behaving like a complete animal.

The doorbell rang and Amanda's assistant, Nikki, swept in carrying a white Maltese that was a dead ringer for Noodle. 'Here's Puddle, your substitute dog,' Nikki said, handing the pup to Diva. 'You may have seen her on *Gossip Girl.*'

'Coo-ol, she's famous!' Diva said.

'You're not allowed to watch *Gossip Girl*,' Tabby said.

'Daddy lets me,' Diva said. 'I've never held an actor dog before.'

'Yes, and *you* have to *act* like she's Noodle,' Amanda said. 'Do you think you can do that?'

'You want me to lie? Mommy, the mean lady is a liar,' Diva said.

'Darling, don't call Amanda mean,' Tabby said.

'Can I call her a liar?' Diva said.

'I'm not asking you to lie,' Amanda said, 'I'm asking you to *act*, like Puddle does on television.'

'I've got the board package here,' Winston the

Second said, waving a phonebook-thick binder. 'Any last-minute words of wisdom?'

Amanda kneeled in front of Diva and Winston the Third. 'Kids, you're going to go with Mommy and Daddy to a boring grownup meeting but we're going to make a game out of it. Does that sound fun?'

Diva stared at Amanda, her eyes like almond slivers. Winston the Third pulled a bloody booger out of his nose and wiped it on his sister's cheek.

'Stop it,' Diva shouted, swatting him hard on the leg.

Winston the Third sniffled and his eyes filled.

'Ah-ah-ah!' Amanda said, picking the booger off Diva's face.

'We'll have no tears at the meeting. When you're there, you two are going to play the quiet game. Who knows how to play that?'

Diva's hand shot up like a missile. 'I do, I do. We zip our lips, right?'

'Right,' Amanda said.

Diva raised her hand again.

'Yes, Diva,' Amanda said.

'How do we win?'

'You win if you're quiet the whole time and you don't hit each other.'

'What about putting a booger on Winston? That's not hitting, right?' Diva asked.

'No, you automatically lose if you do anything booger-related. What should the prize be?' Amanda asked.

'Dylan's Candy Bar after!' Diva shouted.

'You got it,' Amanda said, 'but when you're at the meeting, don't say a word; pretend you don't speak English.'

Diva grinned widely, revealing a large gap where her two front teeth used to be.

Amanda turned to the parents. 'Now, remember, these people are not your friends. Be cordial but not chatty. This board usually asks about the last time you saw a lawyer. Say it was when you wrote your wills. We don't want them to think you're litigious. Tabby, don't tell them you work with the Homeless Coalition. They'll think you're planning to invite homeless people to your apartment. Winston, try not to show your personality. Be as bland as possible. If they ask you if you have any questions, you don't. If they ask if you intend to renovate, you don't . . .'

'But you know we plan to build a D-U-N-G-E-O-N off the bedroom,' Winston the Second said, whispering when he spelled it. 'Shouldn't we mention that?'

What planet is this guy from? Amanda thought. Do I really need to say that a co-op board from a top building would not take kindly to applicants who included dungeon blueprints in their package? Obviously I do. 'Once you close, wait a few months, then submit a renovation package. You can have a change of heart *after* you're in.' Let the architect deal with it, she thought. 'Winston, you answer the financial questions.

Tabby, you answer the questions about family and anything else. I don't want you tripping over each other's words. And whatever you do, don't disagree in front of them. Oh, and you never have parties, no one plays an instrument, and you don't want to run for the board, ever. Are we clear?'

Winston the Second saluted. 'Ma'am, yes ma'am,' he said.

Amanda smiled. 'You guys are going to be fantastic!'

'Would you come with us?' Tabby asked. 'For moral support?'

Amanda knew she was gifted at getting families approved by co-ops. Her record was so outstanding that in certain circles she was known as 'the board whisperer.' However, she worked her magic *behind* the scenes. It was rare for a broker to attend a board interview. On the other hand, closing this deal would get Richie off her back and save her from bodily harm. Winston the Second was odd even as eccentric billionaires went. You never knew what he would say. Luckily, she had socialized with Lionell Creed and his wife, and Creed was on the board. Maybe he would let her sit in. 'If they'll allow it,' Amanda said. 'But you do the talking.'

'Unless we get in trouble. We can have a safe word like we do when we have rough S-E-X,' Winston the Second said, whispering when he spelled it. 'You know, if we're not comfortable, we'll say our code word and you can jump in to help.'

'Sounds like a plan.' Amanda checked her watch. It was a quarter till four. They had to get moving. She had a car waiting downstairs. Amanda always arranged to have her clients driven to closings in her firm's chauffeured Rolls-Royce. For the ride home, she would serve Cristal champagne, Beluga caviar and black-and-white cookies from William Greenberg Desserts. It was one more thing that set her apart from the competition.

'Daddy,' Diva said. 'What's rough S-E-X?'

'It's . . . it's something Mommy and Daddy do for fun, like you ride on merry-go-rounds or roller-coasters,' Tabby said.

I really don't need to hear this, Amanda thought.

'Remember how loud I screamed on Space Mountain?' Diva said. 'Do you scream when you do rough S-E-X?'

'Mommy does,' Winston the Second said.

'Winston, *please*,' Tabby said. 'Keep talking like that in front of our children and I'll divorce you.'

'Mommy, no. No divorce!' Diva shouted.

'Mommy doesn't mean it,' Winston the Second added sheepishly.

'If we find ourselves in trouble, our safe word will be "divorce,"' Tabby said. 'And I do mean it.'

'There's not going to be any trouble,' Amanda said. 'You guys will be awesome. Come, your chariot awaits.'

LAURA

Laura stood in front of the imposing black wrought-iron gate that kept the riffraff away from the crème de la crème who attended Madison Prep. Beneath her winter coat, she wore her daytime Catholic-schoolgirl uniform – a short red plaid skirt and matching tie, tight white top that showed a hint of cleavage, knee socks and black patent-leather Maryjanes. Her blond hair had been pulled into two pigtails, one above each ear. For daytime gigs, her costumes were G-rated. From nine to five, her clients tended toward corporate executives celebrating birthdays, ladies being recognized for their charity work, hospital patients who needed cheering, that sort of thing. Often she found herself wearing giant yellow chicken suits or gorilla outfits, but the boys who had hired her asked for something sexy, but not too sexy, for

115

their favorite biology teacher who was leaving mid-term for personal reasons.

After Laura joined the Off Our Rockers Trio (now a quartet), she managed to get them a weekly gig at Vines on West Fourteenth. The group played for love and not money, as the club paid one hundred dollars a night for the four musicians. Still, it gave John, Stan, and David a reason to live, or so they said, and it gave Laura a chance to practice and improve her technique. To make ends meet, Laura offered singing telegrams on Craigslist. That worked out brilliantly while her mother was sick because she only had to leave her for an hour or so at a time and the pay was good. Plus, she was talented and quick at making up songs to fit any occasion.

During the day, the work was all fun and innocent. At night, she mostly performed at bachelor parties or gave sexy dances for big birthday boys. If she were willing to strip, she could have charged at least fifty dollars more per telegram, but she wasn't comfortable with that.

With Sunny gone, Laura had hoped to focus all her energy on her music career – creating a website for the group, getting record producers to come to their gigs at Vines, scouring the city for more lucrative performance venues. Lately, she had been distracted from her goal by having to promote her singing telegrams because business was so slow. If the hostess job on that billionaire's jet came through, she planned to give up the singing telegram business and work exclusively for the band when she wasn't flying. Meanwhile, she stood waiting in her Catholic-schoolgirl uniform.

The male custodian in navy overalls manning the reception desk released her without hesitation to a black-haired twelve year old boy wearing gray slacks, a blue blazer, and a red tie who introduced himself as Martin.

Martin escorted Laura to his classroom. The hallway walls were decorated with class art projects – self-portraits, still-life drawings, papier-mâché masks. They ambled past a huge glass-and-walnut case filled with trophies and awards won for athletic achievement. A large sign listed and congratulated this semester's honor-roll students. Laura shivered. School buildings gave her the willies. 'Does your teacher suspect anything?' she asked, as they made their way down the deserted hallway.

'No,' Martin said. 'I pretended to have a stomach-ache to get out of class. He's going to be so surprised.'

'And Mr Shine is your biology teacher?' Laura said.

'Yes, he's mad-old, but he's sick,' Martin said.

'By "sick," do you mean "cool?"' Laura asked.

'Oh yeah,' Martin said. 'He's sick like cool.'

'By "old" do you mean he's over thirty?' Laura asked.

Martin's eyes widened. 'No, he's like *forty!*'

'Wow! Ancient. Why's he leaving?' Laura asked.

'His wife died. He's staying home with his

daughter,' Martin explained. 'That's the rumor. Do we pay now or after?'

'Now is good,' she said. Laura had cut her fee for this one. Normally, she didn't get out of bed for less than two hundred bucks, but these boys were paying for it themselves, so she'd agreed to sing for fifty.

Martin handed her a huge, messy wad of one-dollar bills and a sandwich bag filled with quarters. Laura's heart melted. She was used to singing for corporate bigwigs and upwardly mobiles. This was the first time a bunch of kids had gotten together and paid for her services out of their allowance.

Laura squeezed the boy's hand. 'Let's have some fun with this, okay?' She laid her coat in front of the thick wooden classroom door in preparation. Martin's eyes were full of mischief. What a cutie, Laura thought. She wanted to put him in her pocket and take him home with her.

Wasn't this the school Serena wanted so much for Sebastian? She was pretty sure it was. This is a sign, she thought. My being here means this is the school Sebastian is meant to attend. If all the boys are as sweet as young Martin here, this would be the perfect place for him. Sebastian's a sensitive child who's been saddled with a crazy mother and an absentee father. He'll need all the nice friends he can get.

As they entered the classroom, Laura spied a tall, lean, light-skinned African American man with reading glasses parked on top of his neatly cropped brown hair. He wore khaki pants and a

118

tweed jacket. Standing at the blackboard, he was diagramming a crude drawing of the human heart.

There were about twenty boys in the class, all dressed exactly like Martin. They turned at once and gaped at Laura in her costume. You could have heard a stick of chalk drop.

Mr Shine turned around and dropped his chalk. Everyone heard it. The boys burst into laughter. He stared at Laura, speechless.

'Gentlemen! May I have your attention, PUH-LEASE!' Laura shouted.

A short, towheaded boy pulled out a video camera and started recording. Laura cleared her throat and began to sing the original song containing tidbits the boys had given her about their teacher. She had written it to the tune of 'Auld Lang Syne.'

Should old acquaintance be forgot
And never brought to mind,
You're leaving us, we like it not
We'll miss you, Mr Shine!

You're outta here for greener grass
We're stuck with Miss Dekwaengler,
Without you in biology class
We'll probably have to strangle her.

The cops got mad on April Fools'
When we told an awesome tale,
And now we know despite the rules
You'll bail us out of jail.

We used to hate this stuffy place
Until you came along,
The uniform still sucks, but now
We feel like we belong.

We never would have had you if
We'd gone to public school,
And best of all, we learned from you
That teachers can be cool!

At this point in the song, Laura launched into a kazoo solo while she simultaneously tap-danced on a two-by-two fold-up parquet floor that she'd brought for the occasion.

As Laura performed, Mr Shine's eyes welled as he gazed into the classroom of adoring boys who beamed with pleasure at the gift they had given him. Laura felt transported; how he must love those boys, and how they loved him! This was why she did singing telegrams. Being part of her customers' most special moments was such a high. Well, not so much when working the bar mitzvah circuit, but certainly when surprising a couple with a fiftieth anniversary song or cheering up a cancer patient.

That was what gave Laura the idea to do singing telegrams in the first place – Serena's classmates from FIT had sent her one after the umpteenth time she had been rushed to the hospital for complications from leukemia. On this particular visit, Serena had awakened in the night with blood leaking from every orifice of her body. After a week of

transfusions, intravenous fluids, and heavy medications, her vital organs were in danger of failing. There
was talk of Laura donating a kidney, which she was
more than willing to do. Then, on the tenth day,
Serena woke up feeling better, her organs began to
function, and color rose to her cheeks – crisis averted
along with the need for a kidney transplant. That
afternoon, as Laura sat by her sister's side, painting
her nails with clear varnish, a scantily dressed, hunky
doctor burst into the room and delivered a singing
telegram to the tune of *Moon River*:

> *Se-re-na, we miss your lovely smile*
> *You've been through quite a trial, okay*
> *Oh style-setter; please get better*
> *Without you beside us it's no fun to play . . .*

It was the first time Laura had seen her sister
laugh in ten days. Now, as Laura belted out the
finishing line of Mr Shine's classroom tribute, she
realized this was her favorite singing telegram ever.

The boys jumped up and applauded when she
took a bow, screaming, 'That was so fire!' 'Wasn't
that dope?' They clapped as if Laura was their
favorite rap artist, then rushed up and gathered
around their teacher, giving each other high-fives
for pulling it off.

Suddenly, the door swung open and in strode a
fiftysomething woman with a prune-pursed
mouth, a glaring facial mole, and auburn hair
wound into a tight bun at the base of her crepey

neck. She wore a classic brown suit with a cream-colored silk blouse, sensible black shoes, and no jewelry except for a gold chain around her neck to hold her reading glasses. 'What is going on? Cease and desist immediately!' She spoke with a heavy German accent and clapped twice like she was reprimanding a dog.

Laura was glad she hadn't run into Frau Blucher earlier. She extended her hand gingerly. 'I'm Laura Moon. The boys hired me to sing a good-bye song for Mr Shine.'

'I'm Ms Dekwaengler, admissions and diversity director,' the woman said, bowing her head down and up like she was, queen. 'I heard a disturbance coming from this room.'

Laura wondered if she might say something that would help her nephew's chances of getting accepted here. Except for Ms Dekwaengler, this seemed like a wonderful school. She pulled the admissions director aside so she could speak to her privately.

'My sister, Serena Skank, talks about Madison Prep all the time,' Laura said. 'I know they're inter-viewing here soon. She's sure Sebastian would fit right in. I can't wait to call her and tell her I met you, but I'll have to wait because she's . . . she's . . . she's getting an award today. Yes, she and Elliott, her husband, from the Skank Oil family, gave a multi-thousand . . . million dollar donation to Elliott's elementary-school alma mater. They're very philanthropic. But don't tell them I told you.

They prefer to give anonymously. And they never admit to their generosity.'

'Skank Oil?' Ms Dekwaengler said, her eyes wide as bratwurst slices. 'Then I look forward to meeting your sister and her family.' She retreated to the door, grabbed Laura's coat, and thrust it at her. 'For heaven's sake, cover yourself.'

Laura glanced at her skimpy costume and felt diminished. She hoped Ms Dekwaengler wouldn't deduct points from Sebastian's application because of his shameless aunt.

The boys had already returned to their seats. Mr Shine stepped in. 'It's all right, Ms Dekwaengler, she delivered a singing telegram. It was good, clean, fun; a gift from my boys.'

'That costume is completely inappropriate for a roomful of prepubescent young men,' Ms Dekwaengler said, hoity-toitily. 'This is an institution of learning.'

Mr Shine took Laura's hand before she could leave. 'Ignore her,' he whispered, his tender eyes gleaming with tears. 'And thank you. You have no idea how much this meant to me. I'll never forget it.'

Laura flashed her dazzling smile at him. 'Aww, shucks,' she said, giving him a light kiss on the cheek. 'I'm only sorry that my nephew didn't attend this school while you were here teaching. The boys obviously love you, and I can see why.'

Mr Shine was beaming with the compliment. Laura was so naturally adorable and sweet that no man could resist her charm, not even mad-old Mr Shine.

AMANDA

'There are no good girls gone wrong – just bad girls found out.'

—Mae West

A manda's nerves were buzzing as she escorted the Bullocks into Lionell Creed's Park Avenue apartment. His twenty-five-year-old wife greeted them at the door, holding their new baby boy in her arms. Lionell, the president of the board, had agreed to allow Amanda to join him and the other members in his home conference room. It was unusual, he said, but they had once permitted another family to bring their broker. That was because they didn't speak English, but still Lionell allowed it.

The four Bullocks and their actor pet filed into the sun-filled room and took seats across from Mr Creed, a white-haired gent who was in remarkably good shape for a new father pushing eighty; Mrs Brewster, an elegant, Chanel-clad matron with lacquered auburn hair that smelled of fresh spray, and Mr Peter Rodgers, a man so bald and rotund that he resembled a hard-boiled egg in a suit.

Each had a copy of the Bullocks' thick board package at his or her place. Winston the Third's curly brown hair barely cleared the table and Diva's face was visible from the nose up. Amanda thought that was good. The less seen and heard of the children, the better.

'We see you're paying cash for the co-op,' Mr Creed began.

'Right,' Winston the Second said, 'and as you can see from our package, money's not an issue.'

'We like to see one hundred and fifty million in liquid assets before we consider an applicant,' Mr Rodgers sniffed.

'As well you should,' Winston the Second said. 'If you want, we'll pay our maintenance fees a year in advance. Twenty years even.'

Amanda almost rolled her eyes. She couldn't believe how the other one-tenth-of-one percent lived, always trying to one-up one another. It was so unfair. Winston the Second hadn't done a thing to earn a penny of his fortune. She wanted to slap him.

'That won't be necessary,' Mrs Brewster said. 'Our building is solid financially.'

'Your finances don't worry us, but we have a few questions about the children,' Lionell Creed said. 'There is only one other family with a child living here, and that's my wife and myself, not that we discriminate, but young families don't usually desire such a white-glove building. Are you aware of that?'

'No, we weren't,' Tabby said. 'But our kids don't need to make friends in the building. They have plenty in the neighborhood.'

Amanda instinctively jumped in. 'Not that those friends will be coming over. Little Winston and Diva will visit them in *their* buildings.'

'Diva,' Mrs Brewster asked kindly, 'do you ever play in the lobby of your building, or in the hallways?'

'Oh yes, Daddy and me play catch in the hall,' she said.

'That was once,' Winston the Second said. 'When it was snowing outside.'

'Daddy, you're funny,' Diva said. 'We do it all the time.'

Amanda's heart sank. It was one thing to inspect an applicant's kids during an interview, but to ask them questions was playing dirty. Damn children for always telling the truth.

Mrs Brewster turned to the little boy. 'Winston, what about you? Do you ever play in the hall?'

Winston shook his head and pretended to zip his lips.

'Darling, it's okay, you can answer the question,' Tabby said.

Once again, Winston played deaf and dumb.

'He likes to pretend that he can't talk,' Amanda said. 'It's a game, one that won't disturb the neighbors.'

Diva's hand shot up. 'I play that game too. If we're quiet today we get to go to Dylan's Candy Bar. Amanda bribed us.'

Amanda felt the blood rushing to her face. Calm down, she told herself, bribing children is a time-honored tradition in New York City.

'So, what I'm trying to understand is, are you a quiet family or a noisy family?' Mrs Brewster said.

'Oh no, we're quiet as mices,' Diva confirmed. 'Except when Mommy and Daddy have rough S-E-X and then Mommy screams like she's on a roller-coaster.' Diva let out a piercing, high-pitched screech to demonstrate her point.

Mr Rodgers' mouth dropped open so wide you could see his tonsillectomy scar.

'Diva, please,' Winston the Second said.

'It's true, Daddy. You said so yourself.' Diva turned to Mrs Brewster. 'We're not allowed to lie.'

'That's good. It's wrong to lie,' Mrs Brewster said. She glared at Amanda. 'You know, brokers who tell their clients to lie go straight to H-E-L-L.'

'I would never do that,' Amanda said, mortified.

Diva raised her hand urgently. 'Oh oh oh,' she said. 'You did *so* tell us to lie. You know how I know?'

'How do you know,' Mrs Brewster asked. 'Tell us.'

'You see that dog? He's not really ours. No, he's an actor from *Gossip Girl*. He acts better than Noodle so that's why we borrowed him just for today. Isn't that right, Winston?'

Little Winston remained stone-faced and zipped his lips.

'Divorce,' Tabby said. '*Divorce.*'

'Mommy, no! No!' Diva screamed. 'Don't say

that. No divorce.' Tears started down her face, though she blinked hard to stop them.

'Thanks for coming,' Mr Rodgers said, pushing his chair back. 'This interview is over.'

'Wait, wait,' Amanda said, her apricot-colored hair damp with sweat, her green eyes darting urgently about, her kneecaps aching with dread. 'May I speak on behalf of this family?'

The board members glanced at each other. Then Lionell Creed gave Amanda the nod.

'First of all, the Bullocks couldn't be more solid financially,' she started. 'Second, the children heard some things they shouldn't have . . . on TV . . . and that's what they were referring to. They have no idea what rough S-E-X is. I have been in their apartment any number of times. It's no noisier than your apartment or mine. And anyway, they're buying a whole floor and laying down thick Persian rugs, so their neighbors wouldn't be disturbed even if they got a bit rowdy . . . which they won't. Mr Bullock will gladly put in writing that he will never play ball with the children in the halls. *Never!* And the only reason we borrowed this dog today was because the real Noodle had diarrhea and we didn't want to postpone this interview yet again.' This was a lie but Amanda was desperate. She prayed Little Big Mouth would keep her toothless trap tightly shut.

'You can see from Noodle's résumé that he has a stellar pedigree,' she said. 'His grandfather placed first at Westminster in his breed and Noodle himself graduated top of his class at Berkeley Kline. Plus, what you may not have noticed in the package is that Mrs Bullock is chairwoman of the Committee for a Better Park Avenue, so she has tremendous influence over anything that happens in and around the building. Wouldn't someone like that be an asset to you?'

'Could you do anything about that noisy Puerto Rican Day Parade and all those drunkards who wander onto our street?' Mr Rodgers asked.

'Absolutely,' Tabby said. 'I could get the police to block the side streets leading to our building between Park and Madison. I also happen to know that the city is planning to tear up sections of Park to replace corroded pipes. I could make sure they don't jackhammer the street near us, but access our section from as far away as possible.'

Amanda didn't think Tabby could really do that, but it sounded good.

Mrs Brewster sighed resignedly. 'You seem like a lovely family,' she said. 'But we have a firm rule here that if we discover that someone lied in their package or presentation, it's an automatic no. All you had to do was tell us Noodle had diarrhea. We would have excused him. I'm sorry.'

Amanda's breath became short and her body began to tremble. The Bullock deal was dead. She feared she might be next.

SERENA

'If you bungle raising your children, I don't think whatever else you do well matters very much.'
—Jacqueline Kennedy Onassis

Serena sat at the kitchen table with Roseanne Schmidt, the latest three hundred dollar an hour consultant (this one an admissions advisor) to join Team Skank. Today, Serena had on the black pantsuit she had purchased from J. Crew for her new recession-chic wardrobe. It was the first thing she'd worn from a mass retailer in years and though the material was rather coarse, it made her feel good to join other Americans who were 'keeping it real' by cutting back and spending responsibly.

'Cookie?' Serena offered. 'They're made with legumes and Brussels sprouts but you can't taste them.'

'What is that pounding noise I hear?' Roseanne asked, helping herself to two.

'It's the rock band that rents our second floor,'

130

Serena moaned. 'Can you believe the sound travels all the way up here?'

'Pardon my asking, but why would you lease an apartment to a rock band?' Roseanne said.

Serena threw up her hands in exasperation. 'I know. I know. I'm one of three sisters, the only *normal* one. My younger sister floats aimlessly through life. My older sister, well, she's impossible. She rented her apartment to the band to annoy me.'

'Oh, come on,' Roseanne said, 'No one is that obnoxious.'

'You don't know Amanda,' Serena said. 'In college, I had leukemia. She alienated all the doctors and nurses at the hospital; she was *such* a bitch to them. They took it out on *me*, the sick patient, withholding towels and sheets and pillow-cases because of her attitude. It upsets me to think about it.' She checked her watch. 'Elliott should be here any moment.'

Roseanne smiled, revealing a set of coffee-stained teeth that matched her ill-fitting suit. With her cropped silver hair, school-marm glasses, and clipped tone of voice, she projected the image of no-nonsense professional that she was. 'Well, you and Elliott'll be happy to know that Sebastian is ready for his Madison Prep interview,' Roseanne said. 'I've tutored him on anything they might ask. Here, I recorded these CDs for him to listen to over the next few nights.'

Serena took them in hand. Roseanne Schmidt

was the only admissions consultant in the city who provided her families with customized CDs so children could prep subliminally for their kindergarten admissions tests. Supposedly, she had worked with both Spike Lee's and Diana Ross's children. Choosing an advisor so committed to diversity in private schools made Serena feel like she was giving back somehow.

Sebastian was sitting at his pint-sized table coloring away on a picture he had been working on since Roseanne arrived.

'Would you like to see how smart he is?' Roseanne said, wandering over to him.

Serena nodded enthusiastically.

'What's that a picture of, Sebastian?' Roseanne said.

Sebastian glanced up for a moment, his golden hair shimmering. 'God,' he said, going back to his paper and adding a purple flourish.

Roseanne regarded his drawing. 'But Sebastian, nobody knows what God looks like.'

'They will when I'm finished!' Sebastian said, with a proud grin on his freckled face.

'Sebastian, if the teacher asks you to draw a picture in one of your interviews, make something that everyone agrees on, like a house or a person. That's very important. Now tell me, what color is the sky?' Roseanne asked.

'Yellow!' he shouted.

'No,' Roseanne said, 'It's blue.'

'Nuh-uh, not my favorite sky,' he said.

'Oh, right,' Serena said, slapping her forehead. 'I took him to the Met to see paintings by Monet.'

'It's red, too!' Sebastian said.

'Sebastian, for the purposes of your interview, the sky is blue, the grass is green, and the sun is yellow, got it?' Roseanne said.

'Pee-pee is yellow,' he said.

'Yes, and aren't you smart to notice that,' Serena said. 'But when you're interviewing, always call things by their proper names. How many times have we discussed that pee pee is *urine*?'

'Like Martin Van Buren!' Sebastian cried.

'And who was he?' Roseanne said.

'Mmmm, I don't remember,' he said.

Roseanne turned to Serena and frowned. 'I thought you worked with a prenatal tutor. Didn't she give you a civics CD to play for him *in utero*? The names of our presidents should be imprinted in his brain.' She shook her head and went back to her young charge. 'Now, Sebastian, if you had four cookies and you ate three, what would you have?'

'Diabetes!' he shouted.

'Sorry, I'm always telling him he'll get diabetes if he eats sweets,' Serena said. 'Should I stop saying that?'

'Sebastian,' Roseanne admonished, 'we went over this, remember? Four cookies minus three cookies is a SUB-TRAC-TION question. Now, listen carefully for another SUB-TRAC-TION question.'

Sebastian glared at Roseanne. It was obvious he didn't appreciate being treated like a three-year-old.

'If you had five tomatoes and you ate two, how many would be left?'

Sebastian stood up and stuck his face in Roseanne's. 'Five,' he said. 'I hate tomatoes. I won't eat them. You can't make me.'

'Just rip Mommy's heart out,' Serena moaned, crumpling in her chair. Sebastian was a disaster. It was as if none of the work he'd done with Roseanne or the hours of subliminal CDs had stuck. 'Sebastian, you need to cooperate. This is *very, very* important. Mommy only loves smart boys, not dumb boys.'

Sebastian lowered his eyes and curled his lips down.

'If you don't get into Madison Prep, you'll have to go to public school,' Roseanne said.

'God forbid,' Serena said. 'Half those kids will end up in jail before high school.' She shivered. 'They'll make you pass through a metal detector and pat you down for weapons before letting you in.'

'So, focus, Sebastian,' Roseanne said. 'Your entire future depends on it. Now, take this pencil and draw a triangle.'

'I can't,' Sebastian said.

'Yes, you can,' Roseanne said.

'No, I can't,' he said.

'Why can't you?'

'Because I don't want to,' Sebastian said, folding his arms across his chest.

'Sebastian, c'mon, you draw terrific triangles. Show us how well you draw them.'

'Stop torturing me,' he cried, his eyes welling. 'Can't you see I'm only four?'

'Torturing – now *there's* an advanced vocabulary word!' Serena said with pride.

'Sebastian,' Roseanne said, 'in certain African tribes, four is old enough to get married. So come on, act your age.'

'She's right,' Serena said. 'Do you want to stay in nursery school forever?'

'Yesssss,' Sebastian whined. 'I love Miss Carol. She smells like cherries.'

Black ants marched boldly in a line across the kitchen floor, snagging every healthy cookie crumb in their path. *Smush.* Serena stamped out their insignificant insect lives. 'You do *not* want to stay at your school,' she said. 'You want to go to Madison Prep.' Grabbing a tissue, she wiped up the smear of black ant carcasses and tossed it into a wastebasket. 'Please don't tell your clients we have ants,' she said to Roseanne. 'These old houses. It's impossible to get rid of them.'

'Have your maid scrub everything down with bleach and put cloves along your baseboards,' Roseanne suggested.

'We don't have a maid,' Serena said with pride. 'God forbid my children grow up feeling entitled. Besides, I'm a bit of a germophobe. I enjoy doing it myself.'

Sebastian reached down his pants and pulled out a pacifier. He stuck it into his mouth and sucked it defiantly. Try and stop me, his eyes said.

'Sebastian, no,' Serena cried. 'That's filthy. You're too old.' She didn't know which objection to make first.

He turned and bolted downstairs.

'Ignore him. He just wants attention. I'll run down to Starbucks while he acts out,' Roseanne said. 'Want anything?'

Serena shook her head, then rubbed her temples. What was Sebastian thinking? He knew the rules about pacifiers. Clearly the boy needed a child psychiatrist. So many city kids do these days. She would get on that this afternoon. Being a mother was the hardest thing she had ever done. And applying to private school was second only to having leukemia.

She took a cigarette out of her bra, padded over to the window, and lit up. Valentina sat on the other side of the room in her bouncy chair next to the TV, quietly chewing one of the Berlitz Spanish DVDs that Serena had given her after she uttered her first word – 'filthy.' Serena had never smoked with one of her children so close by, but today she felt out of control. She didn't know how much longer she could keep up the standards she had set for herself.

What if Sebastian blew his interview? Madison Prep was the only first-tier school in the City that she wanted. If he got into a second- or, God forbid, a third-tier school, they'd have to slink away to Scarsdale and tell their friends that they wanted to raise their children with trees and a back-yard . . . as if any rational parent would actually choose trees and a backyard for their children when they could have Manhattan. Serena puffed furiously at the very idea, blowing the smoke outside.

Her cell phone rang – it played the *Law and Order* signature sound – THONK-THONK! 'I'm sorry, honey, but I can't make the meeting today,' Elliott said. 'There's a problem with the opening of this week's show. It's too similar to that teacher in the Bronx who got whacked last week by one of her students during detention. We're re-shooting it in a gym.'

'You're re-shooting it in a gym? But you *have* to come,' Serena said. 'It's our last practice interview before the real one.'

'Haven't we practiced enough already? We're both good on our feet,' Elliott said. 'It'd look better if we didn't sound rehearsed.'

'We won't sound rehearsed. Roseanne is coaching us on how to make our answers sound extemporaneous and off-the-cuff,' Serena said. 'I paid extra for that.'

'Let this session be just for you, then,' Elliott said, 'I have to stay and direct this scene. And anyway, don't we get extra points because I work on a famous show?'

'Noooo,' Serena said, 'Directors don't count.

You have to be front-of-camera famous to get celebrity consideration.' It was common knowledge that well-known people had a huge advantage. Every private school competed to attract the children of movie stars and athletes. It gave them tremendous prestige to rattle off a list of luminaries whose spawn graced their halls. According to Roseanne, Sidwell Friends didn't even ask the Obamas the question other prospective parents had to answer: 'If your child was a fruit, what fruit would she be, and why?' No, they let Sasha and Malia waltz right in just because their father was President. Damn those celebrity kids, Serena thought. Like they don't have enough advantages already!

'Well, I still can't make it,' he said. 'Sorry.'

'Okay, fine, Mr Emmy-Winning-Director. Don't practice for the most important meeting of your son's life, Mr *Law-and-Order*-von-Gravy-Train, but you'd better be at the *real* meeting on Friday,' Serena hissed.

Elliott sighed. 'I will. I promise. Serena, it'll be okay. We're smart, witty people. Remember us? We were the couple everyone wanted to be. Let's be that couple for the school, okay?'

'Fine, good-bye. I love you,' Serena said. Even though she was mad at him, she always said 'I love you' when she said good-bye in case either of them died before they saw each other again. Serena slumped in her seat. What was with Elliott? she wondered. He was too busy for his own family. If he wasn't directing, he was editing. If he wasn't editing, he was casting. How could he be so present for his work and so absent for the people who loved him? If I had a cancer recurrence, would he be 'too busy' to come to the hospital?

She recalled the day they met. Elliott had recently moved to the city and her sister Amanda was trying to sell him an apartment. Amanda invited him to their Thanksgiving dinner on the pretext of not wanting him to be alone for the holiday. Serena knew that Amanda's real motive was to get in good with Elliott by setting him up with her. It was obvious by the way she pushed them to go off by themselves and take a walk.

Back then, Elliott would do anything for her. If she'd asked him to join her in line at the Motor Vehicle Department, he would have jumped at the chance. But here she was asking him to do something for the good of Sebastian's future and he refused. Does he not care about his son? Oh Jesus, if I keep this up, I'm going to drive him away. I've got to back off. Somehow we have to get in sync again, like we used to be. Even he said it: 'We *were* the couple everyone *wanted* to be,' not 'We *are* the couple everyone *wants* to be.'

Serena opened a drawer and took out a crème-colored card she had recently found tucked inside her wedding album. It was one of her mother's infamous notes, hidden where Serena could find it, after Sunny learned she would soon fade away from Alzheimer's.

Darling Serena,
How are you doing today? Don't you worry; things will get better. I have to wonder if, by the time you read this, you have children. Give them a big smooch from their Grandma Sunny if you do. I love them even though we've never met. Whether you have children or not, you are blessed. I see how Elliott worships you. Be sure he always knows that you are his biggest fan, that you think he is a great man, and that you appreciate everything he does and is. Even when you don't feel this way, find something right about him. In fact, tonight, cook him his favorite meal, rub his feet, initiate lovemaking. A smart wife makes her husband feel needed and appreciated. My mother said that this was the secret to her marriage, and Grandma and Grampa were married for fifty-seven years. I didn't listen to my mother and, well, you know how that story ended.
Love and kisses,
Mom

Serena gulped. Jeez, I'm doing a terrible job of appreciating Elliott, she thought. Please don't let our marriage end like Mom's. I'll try harder. I *have* to try harder.

Sebastian came running in carrying his porta-potty. 'Look, Mommy, look at my poop!'

'What? Oh, no, honey. Call it by its proper name – *stool*, remember?' Serena said. She peeked inside. A few years ago, Donatella Versace used to ask her opinion on silk chiffon versus silk crepe for her latest couture creation. Now she was opining on poop. For the love of God, what had her life come to? Truth be told, she was sick and tired of having to be the perfect mother. If only Elliott was one of those super-involved fathers like some of the kids at Sebastian's nursery school had, fathers who walked their children in the morning or volunteered to decorate for parties. At Sebastian's last parent-teacher conference, Miss Carol had been shocked to learn the boy actually had a father.

Serena snapped out of it and focused on the job she had signed up for – motherhood. 'I'm proud of you for moving your bowels and making that stool, honey,' she said. 'But I'm mad at you for using a pacifier. Smart kids who go to big-boy school don't need dummies, okay? Do you know why they call them dummies?'

Sebastian shook his head.

'Because every time you suck on one, you lose IQ points. You don't want to lose IQ points, do you?'

Sebastian's eyes grew wide. 'No,' he said. 'What are IQ points?'

'They're a measure of how smart you are,' Serena said. 'The more you have, the smarter you are. The more you lose, the dumber you get.'

141

'Do you think I'm dumb, Mommy?' Sebastian asked.

'No, you're brilliant. And I'm not just saying that because I'm your mother. Stanford-Binet says you're a genius, too.'

'Can I have a kiss, Mommy?'

Serena gave her son a big smack on the cheek.

Sebastian's mouth broke into a goofy smile. 'Mommy, your kisses make me smarter.'

At that moment, Serena loved her boy more than anything in the world. She thought of her father and wondered how he could have walked into the sea while his little girl waited for him alone on the beach. What kind of monster parent would do that? 'Give me a hug,' Serena said.

Sebastian jumped into his mother's arms and gave her a big squeeze. Serena felt something hard in his Pull-Up. Wasn't he too young for that? She would have to call a pediatric urologist immediately. But then she realized that the shape of the protuberance was square. Reaching inside, she extracted Roseanne's iPhone. 'Sebastian, no,' she groaned.

'It's for you, Mommy! A present. So you and Daddy can talk more. I love you.'

AMANDA

'She's the kind of girl who climbed the ladder of success wrong by wrong.'

—Mae West

To the Bullocks' credit, they didn't immediately fire Amanda over the board debacle. 'We'll find something else,' Tabby said. 'Let's only look at condos or townhouses. I never want to go through a co-op interview again.'

'I'll pull up listings that fit your criteria and we'll talk tomorrow,' Amanda said. 'Thank you for being so cool about this.'

'It wasn't your fault,' Tabby said.

But Amanda knew it was. She should never have brought in that substitute dog. They could have claimed Noodle was sick and that would have been the end of it. Lesson learned. Meanwhile, she wondered if she could push through any other deals to raise cash quickly. Unfortunately, the pipeline had slowed to a trickle. Maybe a friend could lend me money, she thought. But who? She ticked off all her friends in her mind and realized

143

none was close enough to ask for a six-figure loan. Maybe I could hire Ham, the artist, to copy the Lassiter sketch, sell the real thing, and hang the forgery. No one would ever know, since Serena refused to sell it. Oh God, this is what desperation feels like, she thought miserably.

Shuffling down Third Avenue, Amanda noticed that the pristine glass-and-steel towers that usually seemed so electric and inviting to her today looked bleak and depressing. She wished she could afford to see Dr Schnur, her old psychologist. But at two hundred dollars per fifty-minute session, that was out of the question.

Amanda gazed up and realized she was two blocks from the Trumbo Building, an elaborate, fifty-story neo-gothic stone tribute to Harley Trumbo, his contribution to the New York City skyline. She wondered if Riley was in today. The last time she'd seen him was the weekend of Serena's wedding, although she regularly cut out his picture from the Style section, always with a different woman since he'd broken up with Sofia. Such a pompous ass, she thought. *I wonder how he's doing? Is he dating anyone? I should pay him a visit.* What am I saying, he's a good-for-nothing jerk. He threw me away like a piece of chewed gum. Riley *owes* me. Hmmm, maybe *he* would lend me the money I need. *That's nuts. I could never ask him.* Why not? He probably doesn't remember my name, the dirty rat-bastard. As Amanda considered her crazy idea, she found herself heading straight toward the Trumbo Building and through its automatic revolving doors. *What the heck,* she thought. *All he can do is not see me, or tell me to take a hike. I'd be no worse off.*

If nothing else, Amanda's real estate agent experience had given her brass ovaries. 'I'm here to see Riley Trumbo,' Amanda announced to the uniformed guard behind the security desk. 'Name's Amanda Moon.'

He tapped into his computer, then shook his head. 'You're not on the list. I'll have to call up.'

Amanda's stomach clenched as the guard punched in the number. *What am I doing?* she thought. *Have I no shame?* No, apparently not.

'He'll see you,' the guard said, handing her a sticky white security badge to slap onto her red St John Knit zebra-print cape. She peeled it off as soon as she reached the elevator.

Amanda couldn't believe she was going to Riley's office. As the private elevator made its way up to the executive suite, she wished she had thought this through better. How would she explain why she was here? Should she get right down to business or accuse him of being a goddam fucking son-of-a-bitch cowardly cockroach for dumping her without explanation? Calling him a goddam fucking son-of-a-bitch cowardly cockroach wouldn't help her cause, she realized. Take the high road. Act like I'm over it, over him, and life for me is good. Checking her reflection in the mirrored back wall of the elevator, she rather liked how her flaming orange hair cascaded in soft waves over her shoulders and down her back. She adjusted her feather-trimmed cape, then applied her red lipstick just before the '*ding*' announced she had reached the fiftieth floor.

As the doors opened, there stood Riley Trumbo, all 6'7' of him, in his custom-tailored navy pinstriped suit and freshly shined black Italian shoes. His formerly thick head of slicked-back hair had turned gray and thinned considerably, his broken nose had been straightened, and between his eyes were deep furrows born of sleepless nights over all those big-money responsibilities, she supposed. He looked old and she wondered if he was thinking the same thing about her.

Then he grinned and his whole face lit up, his gray-speckled eyes matching the sparkle of his smile. That was the Riley she knew, the Riley she had loved. Amanda couldn't believe it. He's happy to see me, she realized. And I'm happy to see him. I want to hug him. No wait, I want to kick him in the balls.

'Amanda Moon. How long has it been?'

Act like you don't care, she told herself. Play it cool. 'Seven years, eleven months, and four days,' she said. 'I only know because Serena celebrated her anniversary eleven months and four days ago and the last time I . . .'

'Come here, you,' he said, sweeping her into his massive arms, picking her up off the floor, and giving her a big, wet kiss on her freshly painted lips. When he put her down, he was wearing her red lipstick. She giggled.

Amanda noticed that Riley's secretary was typing away at her computer, artfully ignoring the former lovers.

'Let's go to my office and catch up,' he said, escorting her through his double walnut doors, which led to a long white-and-peach marble hallway and an office the size Amanda's apartment had been before she gave half of it back to Serena. It had a fully equipped Miele kitchen, a dining area that doubled as a conference room complete with silk Persian carpets and priceless antiques, a lusciously furnished living-area-slash-office, a bedroom with an oversized sleigh bed to accommodate his big-and-tall-man body when he pulled all-nighters, and finally a marble bathroom with a Jacuzzi and steam shower.

The office was luxury at its finest, the architectural equivalent of a Louis Vuitton bag. Amanda recognized the decor as coming from the same firm that had designed the interior of his private jet. Oh for the days of Riley's Gulfstream, she mused, such a civilized way to travel. In some ways, she hated being inside his world again. It felt like a schoolyard taunt. This could have been Amanda's, but for . . . but for what?

Riley gestured for Amanda to make herself comfortable on his thick down sofa and offered her a glass of Dom Perignon, which she readily accepted. Sitting beside him, smelling his spicy after-shave, she desperately wanted to touch him. Instead she ran her fingers through her own fiery hair.

'This is a surprise. What brings you here after all these years?' Riley asked, tilting his head curiously.

Amanda paused, held out five fingers, and pretended to admire her new French manicure as a delay tactic while she considered what to say. 'I was on your block and I saw your building and, I don't know, I got to wondering if you were inside and what you were up to. I suppose I'm finally over what happened between us.'

'Me too,' Riley said, nodding his head slowly. 'Seeing you now, all the anger I felt back then just vanished. I think I can finally forgive you.'

Amanda took a quick breath of utter shock. '*You forgive me?* I should be forgiving *you*. *You're* the one who disappeared without a word.'

'No I didn't,' Riley said. 'You walked out on *me*. I called you after Serena's wedding and you never called back. I must have left five messages, maybe more. Finally, I figured you dumped me. I turned to Sofia to lick my wounds.'

'You left *five* messages?' Amanda said, incredulous that she didn't get any of them. 'How is that possible?'

'You tell me,' Riley said. 'I left messages at your house with the people staying there for the wedding. Plus I called your cell several times.'

'Nobody told me,' Amanda said. 'It was all those

148

Hollywood people Elliott invited. I swear they have ADD. And that was a terrible cell phone. It never got reception, remember? Why didn't you come find me? Please don't tell me it was all a misunderstanding.' She let out an involuntary groan that sounded animalistic.

Riley's jaw dropped. 'Jesus, no,' he said. The expression on his face was of disbelief.

'You could have e-mailed or texted me,' she said weakly.

'I didn't do that back then.' He shut his eyes in disgust. 'What a fucking waste.'

Amanda sighed, wishing she could go back in time. I never should have assumed he didn't want me, she thought. I should have confronted him. 'My father just up and left me one day,' she whispered. 'It seemed logical that you had done the same thing.'

Riley refilled her glass with champagne. There were tears in his eyes. 'I loved you so much back then. How could you have *thought* that?'

'I'm so sorry,' Amanda said, moving onto his lap. She held him tightly as she took in his comforting scent. Finally, she released him from her embrace and brought her head back until she felt his warm breath on her cheek. Her eyes searched his face, probing his thoughts. Suddenly, she felt a rush of desire and had to kiss him. Slowly, she brought her lips to his, dry and barely a whisper at first, but then firmly and urgently.

Riley scooped her up Rhett Butler-style and

carried her to his bed, then gently eased her down. Amanda's heart thumped hard against her chest. Discarding her cape, she pulled the matching dress over her head, blushing when she realized she was wearing undies and a bra that had long ago lost their elegance. These were exactly the kind of undergarments Sunny told her never to go out in lest she get into an accident and the paramedics had to cut her out of her clothes. Fortunately, Riley was too busy stripping off his business suit and dropping it into a pile to notice.

Making love with Riley seemed like the absolute right thing to do. It felt as if no time had passed since their last night together. Though their bodies were softer and Riley's hair was thinner, Amanda couldn't get enough of him. She hungered for the feel of his fingers and lips caressing every curve of her body. She craved the weight of him on top of her, the salty taste of his body and the feel of him inside her. All the years of anger toward him vanished and she just wanted to love him and make up for lost time. For a brief moment, Amanda forgot how angry she was with Serena, how dire things had gotten at work, how much of her family's money she'd lost, or how Richie had threatened to spill her blood. Amanda felt safe in his arms. Now that Riley was back, she could face her troubles with him by her side.

After, Riley held her and they cuddled the way they used to. His arms enveloped her as she buried her face against his throat and felt the rhythm of his heart beating. Riley would protect her. She had come home. As he ran his hands lightly up and down her back, she shivered.

'You have a daughter?' Amanda said. She wanted to know everything about Riley, catch up on the years they had been apart.

'Yes, Angelica,' he said. 'She's beautiful.'

'Don't you miss her?' Amanda said.

'I do, but it won't be for long.'

'What do you mean?' Amanda said. 'Is she coming here?'

Riley sighed. He brushed back Amanda's fiery bangs and gazed into her eyes. 'Oh Amanda, you and I are star-crossed. Next week, I'm moving to Italy.'

Amanda sat up straight. 'You're moving to Italy? But why?'

'My wife and I are giving it another shot,' he said, as though resigned to a course of action not of his choosing. 'There's too much rich history between us to throw it away.'

'What? But you can't do that. What about your business? Fuck your business. You just fucked *me*. Why would you do that if you were going back to your wife?' Amanda's face burned with anger.

Riley's face held a hurt expression. 'Because I couldn't resist you,' he said. 'Because we never got to say a proper good-bye.'

Amanda fell back in the bed and covered her face with her hands. 'You shit. Why didn't you tell me before we . . .'

'Well excu-use me,' he said. 'You wanted this as much as I did. You kissed me first.'

Amanda shook her head. 'I would have restrained myself if I'd known you were going back to your wife.' She hung her head and tried to stifle her tears. 'Why didn't I go see you when I thought you'd left me?'

'You were always so damn proud,' he said. 'My friends couldn't believe a girl like you would dump me like that.'

'A girl like *me*? I guess that's why they've all given me the cold shoulder since we broke up,' Amanda said. 'The ones who used to be clients never used me again.'

'Anytime someone in my circle breaks up with someone, they do that,' he said. 'Loyalty, you know.'

'So you didn't tell them to blackball me?' Amanda said, brushing back a shock of hair from her face.

Riley shook his head. 'How could you think that?' he said, not looking her in the eye. It was a non-look that Amanda recalled from their time together, the same non-look he gave her right before he went off with Sofia de Carlo at Serena's wedding. He was lying. He had been lying to her this whole time. I'm such an idiot, she thought, screwed by Riley Trumbo not once, but twice.

'You should be grateful I introduced you to them in the first place. As I recall, you made a lot of money selling them property.'

'Yeah, thanks a lot, Riley,' Amanda said, rolling her eyes.

'What? You're doing alright now though, right?' he said as if he cared. 'In real estate, I mean.'

'Now that you mention it, *no*,' she said. 'I'm *really* struggling.' It was humiliating to admit the truth to Riley, but she gave it a shot. If nothing else, maybe she could guilt-trip him into helping her. Amanda went on to explain how she'd lost millions of her family's money and then borrowed from a loan shark to save the house from being foreclosed. 'If I don't pay him back in the next week or two with interest, he's going to hurt me. As in break my kneecaps. This is no joke. I'm scared.'

'Jesus, you should get out of town,' Riley advised.

'What I really need is for you to lend me the money,' she said. 'It would be short-term. I have several deals on the verge of closing. You'd get it back.'

'Is that why you came to see me today?' Riley asked. 'I'm disappointed.'

Amanda crossed her arms beneath her breasts and thrust out her chin defiantly. 'Well, I'm disappointed in *you* for giving me that bullshit story about thinking I broke up with *you* and then screwing me without telling me you were going back to Sofia. And anyway, you're rich. I'm desperate. What do you expect?'

Riley got out of bed and stepped into his boxers. 'I'd like to help you but I've got problems of my own,' he said. 'My father is furious that I'm leaving the business for Italy. He says if I go, he's cutting me out of his will and making Angelica his sole beneficiary. After everything I've done for him and his goddam company. But who cares? Sofia's family is loaded.'

'Come on,' Amanda said, gesturing toward the room, the luxurious office-apartment. 'What about all this?'

'None of it's mine,' he said dismissively. 'You don't need me, Amanda. You're resourceful. You'll figure something out.' He retreated to the bathroom and shut the door.

Amanda heard the shower running. She shook her hands at God in frustration. I'm such a schmuck, she thought. No, wait! I didn't do anything wrong. He did! I believed him. He took advantage. Well, fuck you, Riley Trumbo, she thought, whipping the covers off the bed in a rage. Amanda marched over to his pants, which he'd left in a pile on the floor with the rest of his clothes, and dug into his pockets until she found his cell phone.

Acting quickly, she dashed over to the office area, to Riley's desk. On top of it, in a sterling-silver frame, sat a black-and-white portrait of him, Sofia and Angelica on a beach, like one of those Ralph Lauren fantasy families. Engulfed with hot anger at him and the world at large, Amanda plunked her naked body in his leather chair, held the portrait next to her breasts, and snapped a cell phone photo of herself from the neck down. She noticed the *New York Times* strewn on the floor beside his chair. Picking up the front page, she photographed herself holding it so the date could be seen in a close-up. It was a trick she had learned watching *Law and Order* kidnapping stories. Then she went back to the bedroom and took another picture of her naked self, holding Riley's family portrait in his unmade bed. Finally, she took a nude shot of herself and the photo next to his pile of clothes strewn about the ground. She checked the digital photos to make sure she had cut off her head each time, and she had. *Whom* Riley was screwing didn't matter. What mattered was that on the eve of reconciling with his wife, he was screwing another woman.

Amanda quickly scrolled through his address book, found Sofia's number, and sent the incriminating photos to her phone. Let him explain *that* to his beloved loaded wife with whom he shares such a fucking rich history, she thought. After stuffing his cell phone back in his pants, Amanda threw on her clothes and hightailed it out the door, down the elevator, and onto the bustling Midtown street. There was no need for a proper goodbye.

LAURA

'Resolve to take fate by the throat and shake a living out of her.'
—Louisa May Alcott

It was Thursday night at the Vine and the place was jumping.

Laura wore her favorite body-hugging red dress with fishnet stockings and patent leather stilettos she had borrowed from Serena. Dr Marc Tannenbaum, a Park Avenue plastic surgeon renowned for his luscious lips (not his personally, but the ones he gave his patients), sat in the front row moving to the beat.

When Laura met him, she dubbed him Dr Marvelous because he danced like Fred Astaire. It was the day her client, Brooke, got married at the Peninsula Hotel. Brooke had hired Laura to deliver a singing telegram to her new husband, Aidan, a cardiologist at Lennox Hill. Laura wore her sexy cupid costume, a sheer red boa trimmed teddy complete with wings and a bow and arrow, and started with a kazoo solo to

the tune of Sonny and Cher's, 'I Got You, Babe.'
Then she launched into her song:

They say you'd never commit to me
Why buy the cow when the milk was free
Well I don't know if all that's true
'Cause here we are, and Babe, I've married
  you . . .

The groom was delighted and the crowd
laughed and clapped. Just as she was sneaking
out, the best man asked her to dance. At first
she declined because she didn't know how to do
those old-fashioned steps, plus she was dressed
as a cupid. But he told her to lock eyes with him
and her body would know exactly what to do.
She did what he said and it worked. With
Dr Marvelous leading, Laura felt like Ginger
Rogers. It was pure magic. Marc was six feet tall
and had olive skin, wavy brown hair, powerful
shoulders, a slim waist and a head that was a tad
small for his body.

Later, after several glasses of champagne, Marc
slipped into the conversation that he was gay. This
wasn't a total surprise given his remarkable skills
on the dance floor combined with his counter-
clockwise hair whorl (which Laura had read in
New York magazine was a leading indicator of
gayness). *Que sera, sera*, she thought. Laura invited
him to come hear her sing and soon he was one
of her most loyal followers, bringing groups of

friends to see her every week, really helping her build her fan base.

Laura always enjoyed the crowd at the Vine. It was unexpected and eclectic. There were young and beautiful socialites, tourists, hot actors, ageless jazz fans, and rockin' seniors. Everyone partied and appreciated the remarkable sound that the Off Our Rockers Quartet brought to the club, which was located in the basement of an Italian restaurant that had been a speakeasy during Prohibition.

'Ladies and gentlemen, we're going to end this set with our favorite number, "The Best Is Yet to Come," but before we do, let me introduce the band,' Laura said. 'On electric wheelchair, we have John Hazeltine; behind those thick glasses is Stan Garrett, and of course, the unstoppable David Hargrove is napping at the piano.' The audience applauded and hooted with appreciation. David startled himself awake and made a gentle salute.

Sunny had always come along when Laura started playing at the Vine. She loved the old stand-ards and remembered most lyrics written before 1960. By then, she had shrunk to under five feet, her brown hair had gone gray, and she never went out without her red pillbox hat. Laura was proud to introduce her. 'Ladies and gentlemen, sitting to our right is Sunny Moon, my mother, who loves to dance if anyone wants to ask her.' Usually someone asked and twirled her around the floor a few times. Too bad she's not here now, Laura thought. Dr Marvelous would make her feel like a princess.

Sunny's last visit to the Vine had been four years earlier. Laura was singing 'Que Sera, Sera,' the jazz arrangement where there were three *Seras* instead of two. While Laura wasn't paying attention, Mom went to the bathroom. Usually someone accompanied her in case she got lost. This time, she found it herself, but she came out wearing her top but no bottom, sat at her table, and resumed drinking her chocolate milk as if nothing was amiss. Laura didn't notice it, but John did. He buzzed over to her in the middle of the set and laid his jacket on her lap. After, he caught Laura's eye and shrugged. '*Que sera sera sera,*' he said.

When Laura worked nights after that, she would put Sunny to bed with an Ambien and turn on the baby monitor so Serena would hear her if she woke up. She never did.

After the set, John and Stan bellied up to the bar while David closed his eyes and snoozed. Laura sat with Dr Marvelous. 'Watching you perform makes me feel like we're in the old New York of the nineteen-forties,' he said. 'I could listen to you all night long.'

'Really, Marc,' Laura said, 'Because I could dance with you all night long.' She squeezed his hand. 'Too bad they don't have a *Dancing with the Stars* for regular people. You could win that.'

'You think?' Dr Marvelous said, smiling proudly.

'Thank you. You know why I became a good dancer?'

'Why?'

'As a teenager, I was a geek. I took dance lessons to help me build confidence. I've always been sensitive about my small head.'

'Your head's not small,' Laura lied. 'Why would you say that?'

'Okay, my body's too big for my head,' he said. 'Is that better?'

Laura laughed. 'Okay, your head may be small but, well, you know what they say about men with small heads.'

'What?' he said.

'You know, small head, big . . .' she said, making Groucho Marx eyebrows at him.

'Wallet?' he teased.

'Stop,' she giggled. 'Would I pull your head, I mean leg? We say "small head, big heart," silly.' Poor Marc, she thought. He spends his whole life making Park Avenue socialites more beautiful, but no operation in the world could make his head bigger. For his sake, she hoped afros would come back into style.

Laura noticed John approaching the drums. 'Oops, I got to go. Time for the last set.'

She settled herself onstage as John and Stan put down their drinks. 'Shall we do "Ill Wind"?' she asked.

'Yes, but nudge David. He's sleeping,' Stan said. 'Again.'

Laura shook him softly. Then she shook him harder. He didn't wake up. She felt his wrist for a pulse, but there was none. Her heart lurched and she screamed in a voice she didn't recognize. Collecting her wits, she yelled, 'Is there a doctor in the house? Someone please call nine-one-one!'

There were cries and gasps. 'I'm a pharmaceutical-supply sales-woman,' someone shouted. She rushed to the stage and felt David's neck, checking for signs of life.

Suddenly, Marc pushed the saleswoman aside. 'Make room,' he said. 'I'm a doctor. Lay him down.'

'Give this man space,' Laura shouted.

Two customers sitting up front jumped in and helped David to the ground, then stepped back. Marc compressed David's chest, pinched his nose, and breathed into his mouth. He kept at it. Nothing happened for what seemed like eternity. Marc finally glanced up, his eyes misting with tears. 'At least he died doing what he loved.'

'Don't stop,' Laura pleaded. 'He's not dead yet.' *Live, David, live,* she begged silently. Laura thought of the night last spring when he brought her back to his small room at Golden Manor and showed her his most prized possession – a framed poster-sized photo taken in the summer of 1958 in front of a brownstone on East 126th Street in Harlem. There he stood, cool as ice, his brash young self, between Dizzy Gillespie and Thelonious Monk, in the class portrait of America's greatest jazz musicians. 'See, the cats all signed their names over their pictures,' David had said. 'This photo is worth a lot of bread.' So many of those musicians had passed on. *Don't join them, David*, Laura prayed.

Reaching over, she positioned David's hands facing palms-upward. Then she stood above him and imagined a healing stream of light coming from Heaven, moving through her body, enveloping David, infusing him with life. She had studied this Bruno Groning healing method at the Omega Institute the summer before. This was her first time performing it in an emergency situation. As she meditated on beaming the light, tears poured down her face and her heart felt like it was bursting open. She sensed a direct connection to God as she conducted the powerful life-infusing energy to her beloved mentor.

David's head twitched and color returned to his lips.

As Marc continued with his chest compressions and mouth-to-mouth resuscitation, Laura kept sending David the healing stream, bathing him in its purifying light. Suddenly, he gasped.

Marc cried, 'He's breathing!'

Oh my God, Laura thought. It works.

Two paramedics rushed inside and took over. Soon, David was lying on a gurney and being rolled out the door.

An hour later, at the St Vincent's Hospital emergency room, Marc brought two cups of steaming black coffee to John Hazeltine and Stan Garrett.

'How much longer do you think it'll be?' John asked, his foot jiggling nervously.

'They're working on him in the back,' Laura said. 'Pray.'

'If he dies, do you think Joey Martin will still want us in his movie?' John asked, driving his electric wheelchair a few feet to get his coffee from Marc.

'John, how can you even think of that right now?' Laura said, appalled.

'I'm just *saying*. David was the one he knew,' John said. 'He was why Martin wanted us.'

'Please don't talk about him in the past tense,' Laura said nervously. 'You'll attract the wrong energy his way.'

'Damn Blue Cross and Blue Shield,' Stan said. 'If he dies, they'll have blood on their hands.'

'What do you mean?' Laura said.

'Last month, Dave's doctor wanted to put in a pacemaker after those irregular heartbeat episodes he had,' Stan explained. 'Said it was a matter of time before his old pump stopped altogether. But the insurance company wouldn't cover it. 'Some stupid excuse about Dave being too old. Bastards.'

'I hate insurance companies. What does a pacemaker even cost?' Laura asked.

'About twenty grand all in,' Marc said. 'But I could arrange to get it done for him for ten. My best friend is a cardiologist and my brother is an anesthesiologist.'

'Would you do that?' Laura said.

'Of course I would. My favorite band wouldn't be the same without David at piano.'

Laura threw her arms around Marc. 'Thank you! You are a saint.'

Marc blushed. 'Yeah, yeah,' he said modestly. 'I'm like Jesus without the beard.'

Laura laughed. 'You are; it's true.'

'Anyway,' Marc said, 'I can get the doctors to donate their services. The hospital expenses should only be about ten grand.'

'Only? May as well be ten million,' John said, shaking his head. 'David's behind on his rent at Golden Manor. He got an eviction notice last week.'

'They would evict a man his age?' Laura said, practically choking on her words.

Stan shrugged. 'They evicted Emma Schneiderstern, and she was eighty-six.'

'That was because she set her room on fire, not because of rent.' John said.

A portly, young doctor dressed in head-to-toe green scrubs appeared at the waiting-room door. He resembled a lima bean. 'David Hargrove's family?'

Laura's stomach turned a flip. She tried to read the doctor's expression, whether he was bringing good or bad news, but she couldn't. She wondered if they taught that in medical school – Straight Face 101.

Stan stood. 'We're all the family he has.'

'The orderly is taking him to his room,' Doctor

Lima Bean said. 'We want to keep him overnight for observation.' He wrote a name on a prescription pad. 'Here's a cardiac specialist he *must* go see when he's released. He needs a pacemaker as soon as possible.'

Laura let out an enormous sigh of relief. 'He made it. Yes!' She hugged Marc. 'Thank you. Thank you for being there tonight.' Losing David would be unthinkable. She knew she could offer him a place to live if Golden Manor kicked him out. It was paying for the pacemaker that had her stumped. She was barely making ends meet herself. *Amanda,* she thought. Thank goodness I have a successful sister.

Marc, John, and Stan took off as Laura made herself comfortable in the mint-green plastic chair by David's bed. She didn't want him to be alone when he woke up. There was a line attached to a vein on top of his hand, one up his nose, and a chorus of monitors bleeping. The antiseptic smell of hospital was overwhelming.

Laura kissed David's forehead. 'Don't worry. We'll do whatever it takes to save you,' she said. She watched his chest rise up and down slowly. He was sleeping. Laura was doing her best to stay awake in case there was a Code Blue. That happened all the time on *ER*.

She pulled out her cell phone and dialed Amanda's number. This couldn't wait until morning. If Amanda would lend her the money,

David could stay put and have the pacemaker implanted tomorrow.

'Hello,' Amanda mumbled.

'Amanda, it's me,' Laura said softly. 'I'm calling to ask for your help. David had a heart attack tonight. He needs a pace-maker. Without it, he could *die*.'

'Huh? Who's David?'

'You know, my pianist,' Laura said. 'You've met him a thousand times.'

'Oh *that* David, sorry. I'm half asleep. Wait, are you saying you want *me* to pay for that?' Amanda said. 'No, no. If it were you, that would be one thing. But your friend should go to *his* family.' She sounded less groggy.

'He has no living relatives. He's *more* than a friend, you *know* that,' Laura begged. 'Please, I promise to pay you back as soon as I can. The operation should cost twenty thousand but I have a doctor friend who can get it done for half that.' Laura noticed that David's eyes were fluttering. Was he waking up? That would be a good sign.

'What doctor friend?' Amanda said.

'A guy I met at Brooke's wedding,' Laura said.

'You're dating a doctor? Since when?' Amanda said. 'And, no. I'm really sorry, but I'm not in a position to help. They declared a cease-sell on Manhattan apartments, in case you hadn't noticed.'

'Can't you take it from savings?' Laura said. 'Please?'

'I wish I could, but I can't,' Amanda said.

'There's . . . there's something you need to know that I haven't wanted to tell you.'

'What?' Laura said. 'That your investments have lost half their value? I know what's happening with the economy. But I'm talking about a measly ten grand. I'd pay you back, with interest.'

'No, that's not it. Oh, never mind. Ask Serena. She's the heiress.'

'Yes, but she has property, no cash,' Laura said.

'You're resourceful,' Amanda said. 'You'll think of something. Try out for *American Idol*. Sell Mom's furniture. Hold a benefit concert.'

Damn, Laura thought as she hung up. Why would Amanda be so selfish? Quickly, before she chickened out, she dialed Serena's number.

'Who died?' Serena said, picking up on the first ring.

'No one,' Laura said. 'It's me. Why are you up?'

'I'm nursing Valentina,' Serena said. 'What's wrong? It's three a.m.'

Laura decided to pull out all stops for this. If Serena refused her, she had nowhere else to turn. 'Serena, I've always been there for you anytime you needed help, would you agree?'

'Well, yeah, I suppose . . .'

'Now I need something from you.'

Serena groaned. 'Let's hear it.'

'I need a kidney,' Laura whispered. 'I'm at St Vincent's. If you can come down in the morning, they can do the compatibility tests and the operation the next day.'

167

'*What?*' Serena said. 'You don't need my kidney. And even if you did, I'm a mother now. I can't go having elective surgery. Tell Amanda to donate *her* kidney.'

'You won't give me your kidney? I was once prepared to give you one of *my* kidneys. But, no hard feelings. Tell you what,' Laura said. 'Instead of donating your kidney, how about loaning me ten thousand bucks?' Laura figured ten grand would seem like subway fare after being asked for a kidney.

'Laura, what are you babbling on about?' Serena said. 'Wait, I'm switching breasts.'

Laura could hear Valentina making little kittenish noises in the background. Her eyes filled as she caught a glimpse of David's small figure in the bed. Since they'd arrived, he seemed to have shrunken. His cheeks and eye sockets were caving in by the hour, casting a skeletal pall over his face. 'You know my piano player, David? His heart stopped tonight. If he doesn't get a pacemaker soon, he'll die. He doesn't have the money. Please, you *have* to lend it to me,' she said. 'Anytime you've needed me, I've been there.'

'I wish I could help,' Serena said. 'But the economy is terrible. You can't expect me to pay to save some stranger's life at a time when I'm coloring my own hair and shopping at the Gap. Besides, David's not related to us.'

'He is to *me*,' Laura said. 'Can't you take out a

mortgage on the house? Or ask Elliott. Or borrow from savings. I swear I'll pay you back.'

'Laura, I want to help you, I do. But you're being unreasonable. David's not your responsibility. Besides, he's old. Maybe you should let nature take its course.'

'Forget it, Serena. You're lucky I didn't let nature take its course when you had leukemia or wanted children,' Laura said, snapping her cell phone shut. I don't get it, she thought. How can someone as giving as me end up with two such selfish sisters? She'd always considered Amanda and Serena her safety net, the two people she could go to if there was no one else. Obviously she couldn't count on them. I'll have to be my own safety net from now on, she thought.

Tiny beads of sweat had formed on David's forehead. His eyes fluttered and remained open for a second, just long enough to show a flicker of recognition that Laura was by his side. 'I'm here, David,' she said. 'You're going to get well. We'll play together again soon. Everything's going to be fine.' Laura believed that with all her heart. She wished she knew how she would make it happen.

SEBASTIAN

'Of all the animals, the boy is the most unman-ageable.'

—Plato

At precisely eight a.m., Elliott, Serena, and Sebastian were sitting in the waiting room outside the office of Admissions Head Vera Dekwaengler. Sebastian wore gray slacks, a blue blazer, and a red tie, the uniform for Madison Prep. Roseanne, the admissions consultant, had selected his outfit. She said that if Sebastian dressed like a Madison Prep boy, Ms Dekwaengler would *subliminally* see him as one and would be more likely to offer him a place. Sebastian didn't know exactly what that meant, but he thought it had something to do with subway trains.

Elliott, who never dressed up for work, wore a dark-blue suit and a burgundy tie. He checked his gold watch. 'How much longer are they going to keep us waiting?'

'Act like you're happy to be here,' Serena said.

Elliott broke into a jack-o'-lantern grin. 'If I were a dog, my tail would be wagging.'

Sebastian giggled. 'Daddy, you're silly.'

'Turn off your cell phone. Stop checking your Rolex. You weren't supposed to wear such an expensive watch, remember?' Serena said under her breath.

'For God's sake, relax, we're not in the interview yet,' Elliott whispered, a smile frozen on his face. 'And I have to keep track of the time. I have a plane to catch. You didn't tell me I wasn't supposed to wear this.'

'You'd have heard if you'd come to the accessories briefing. Keep smiling. The secretary's watching,' Serena said. 'Roseanne says she takes notes and reports everything that happens out here. The wait is a key part of the interview. That's why they're holding us here. Don't screw it up.' Serena squeezed her husband's hand and gave him a peck on the cheek. 'Pretend we're a happy family, okay?'

Serena pulled a copy of *Charlotte's Web* out of her bag. 'Sebastian, how about I read this to you? Let's put Ruthie away for now.' Ruthie was his baby doll. It was one of the many girl toys Mommy had given him in an effort to counter social stereotypes. With the exception of Ruthie, his mini ironing board, and Pepe-from-next-door's dress-up clothes, Sebastian preferred boy toys.

Sebastian grinned. He loved *Charlotte's Web*. Snuggling close, he listened as she read the words and acted out the different parts. Mommy was going the extra mile today by giving special voices to the characters. Before Valentina was born, she always acted out the parts when she read to him. But he couldn't remember the last time she'd done that for him. Oh for the good old days when it was all about me, he thought.

Suddenly, a school official wearing a Madison Prep uniform who looked like a man and a woman at the same time approached. He/she reminded Sebastian of Tinky Winky the Teletubby. Sebastian had never seen the actual show on TV, but he and Mommy often worked out to their exercise video.

Sebastian remembered Roseanne talking about this person in hushed tones. No one knew if he/she was a man or a woman. His/her name was Chappy Comstock and Roseanne said he/she was famous amongst private school parents and nursery school directors. Chappy had short brown hair, bushy brows, beady eyes, and a chin out of which odd hairs sprung. A boy, definitely a boy, Sebastian thought.

'Are you ready to show me how smart you are?' Mr/Miss Chappy said.

'No, thank you,' Sebastian said, hiding behind Mommy as best he could. A girl, definitely a girl, Sebastian thought after hearing her voice. But she didn't have breasts or smell like cherries. Sebastian did not know whether this person had a penis or a vagina, but he knew he did not want him/her for a teacher. He wanted Miss Carol.

'Don't be silly,' Serena told her son. 'You go on with mis . . . Professor Comstock. We'll be waiting for you out here.'

'No, Mommy,' Sebastian said, curling into a ball. 'He scares me.'

'Sebastian,' Elliott said, 'Go on. Mr Comstock is your friend.'

'If it would make him more comfortable,' Mr/Miss Chappy said, 'I can play with Sebastian *after* you meet with Ms Dekwaengler. There's another boy waiting to be tested.'

'That won't be . . .' Serena started.

'Yes, Mommy, *please*,' Sebastian begged.

'Okay, okay,' she said. As Mr /Miss Chappy left, Serena turned to Elliott and said, 'If you had attended the briefings with Roseanne, you would have known *not* to call Comstock a *mister*. Damn your super-important I'm-such-a-big-shot director job.'

'*That's* not a man?' Elliott whispered.

'No, Daddy, it's a Teletubby, half human, half tubby,' Sebastian said, loud enough to catch the secretary's ear.

'Shhh, Sebastian, use your spa voice,' Serena said, with her finger to her mouth.

The headmistress opened her door and invited the threesome inside her office. It smelled like hamster. She was a wrinkled old lady with a brown bun. Her eyes popped out of her head like a goldfish's. There was a chocolate chip on her cheek. After a bit of handshaking and chit-chatting,

Ms Dekwaengler pulled out Sebastian's file and turned to his application. Sebastian remembered Roseanne typing these out for Mommy. Several lines were now colored in yellow. 'It says here that you have a wide variety of interests, young man. What do you want to be when you grow up?'

Sebastian paused as though he needed to ponder the infinite possibilities, but in truth, he knew exactly what he hoped to someday become. 'A flower girl,' he said. That was what Pepe-from-next-door wanted to be, and it sounded swell to him.

'A flower girl?' Elliott repeated, in a disapproving voice.

'A flower boy?' Sebastian said.

'What kind of father-son things do you two do together?' Ms Dekwaengler asked.

Elliott cocked his head into a thoughtful pose. 'Hmmm,' he said. 'Well. Gosh. Uhm, sometimes we . . . It's sort of . . .'

'Elliott takes Sebastian to the set all the time,' Serena said quickly. 'He's teaching him how to be a director. And they love to cook together. Love, love, love it.'

'We do?' Sebastian asked brightly. 'What do we cook?'

Ms Dekwaengler made one of those teacher tongue-clucking sounds. 'Sebastian, your mommy says that you're a math whiz. Can you tell me how many pencils are in my cup?'

Sebastian could see there were five. 'Seven,' he said.

'Sebastian,' Serena said, 'Come on. You know the answer to that.' Her eyes were pleading with him.

'Four,' Sebastian said. It didn't take a certified genius to know that his only chance to stay with Miss Carol was to mess up this interview. And Sebastian was a certified genius, so he really *did* know.

'C'mon, Sport,' Daddy said. 'Stop fooling around. You know how to count.'

'Sebastian's being humble, Ms Dekwaengler,' Serena said. 'When he was two and a half, his nursery school insisted we give him the Stanford-Binet because he was so advanced. His IQ is second only to Einstein's.'

'He can add three-digit numbers in his head already,' Elliott said.

Ms Dekwaengler cleared her throat and turned to Elliott and Serena. 'Yes, I'm sure he can. It says here that *you* are a television director and *you* are a housewife.'

'Yes,' Serena said. 'Before having kids, I handled all the publicity for Versace. Donatella Versace was my immediate boss. I'm sure I can get donations from her for your auctions, or maybe she'll offer an internship. Oh, and Elliott's a director for *Law and Order*. He can get you parts on the show, you know, to auction off for the annual benefit.'

'Is there anything else you want to tell me?' Ms Dekwaengler asked expectantly.

'Now that you mention it,' Serena said. 'You really ought to get that mole on your face examined.

Sebastian's psycho-pharmacologist had one like it and it turned out to be malignant. They had to dig out half his cheek. Then they tried to fix it with regular plastic surgery and . . . well, one thing led to another and,' she lowered her voice, 'do you remember last year when they transplanted that face from a cadaver at New York Hospital?'

Elliott made monster eyeballs at Serena, the exact same kind he made when Sebastian boxed Valentina's ears when he thought no one was looking.

'Ms Dick-Wiggler, I think your mole is *radiant*,' Sebastian said, using a vocabulary word from *Charlotte's Web*.

Ms Dekwaengler's mouth flapped open but no sound came out.

'I think what Ms Dekwaengler meant to ask us was, is there anything you want to tell her about us or our son,' Elliott said.

'Oh. Well, as you may have noticed from our application,' Serena said, 'we live downtown. I know most of your families are from the Upper East Side, so we would bring a fresh breath of geographic diversity to your community . . .'

'That's not what I mean,' Ms Dekwaengler said, with a no-nonsense expression on her puckered face. 'I'll be blunt here if you don't mind.'

'By all means,' Elliott said.

'Blunt is good,' Serena added.

'I have blunt scissors at home,' Sebastian said.

Ms Dekwaengler cleared her throat. 'If you were

to join the school, we've been led to believe that you would want to be leaders in annual fund-giving, perhaps even members of our Golden Circle.'

'When you say "leaders,"' Elliott started, 'what exactly do you mean? Would we make phone calls to other parents soliciting donations?'

'Oh no,' Ms Dekwaengler laughed. 'We don't ask our Golden Circle families to do *that* sort of work.'

'How sizable a donation would you expect from us?' Elliott asked.

Ms Dekwaengler cleared her throat. 'To be part of our elite Golden Circle, you would donate at least a million.'

'Dollars?' Serena said.

'No, rubles,' Elliott joked. 'Seriously, I think we could do it in rubles.'

'What are you talking about?' Serena said.

'A million rubles is about forty thousand dollars,' Elliott said. 'We could donate that over four years.'

'Oh,' Ms Dekwaengler said. 'I was given to understand that you were a very generous family.'

'Really?' Serena said. 'Who told you that?'

'They couldn't be more wrong,' Elliott said.

'Your sister,' Ms Dekwaengler said. 'She performed here. Didn't she mention it?'

'No,' Serena said. 'She delivered a singing telegram?'

'That's right,' Ms Dekwaengler said. 'Wearing practically nothing. But she did mention your connection to the Skank Oil family.'

'Maybe we should talk about Sebastian,' Serena said. 'Isn't that who we're here to discuss?'

'That and my cancerous mole, it seems,' Ms Dekwaengler sniffed.

'Sorry. I should have waited to mention it in my thank-you letter.' Serena conceded. 'If it's an admissions crime for me to care that you never suffer the ravages of cancer as I once did, then I plead guilty.'

Elliott leaned in to the admissions director's desk. 'Ms Dekwaengler, if Sebastian gets in, we would *definitely* give as generously as we could not only of our money but of our time, and certainly I could arrange for parts or internships on *Law and Order*, and Serena has great connections with Versace and all of the fashion community, you know, for auction contributions. But we're not in a position to donate a million dollars. Laura may have exaggerated a bit.'

'So you *would* aim to be leaders in annual fund-giving,' Ms Dekwaengler said.

'Yes, if you'll include donations besides cash,' Serena said. Both she and Elliott nodded.

Ms Dekwaengler nodded along with them.

From all the head-bobbing amongst the grownups, Sebastian could see that things were going well, *too well*, he thought. Something had to be done . . . now! He wiggled out of his chair, stood, and dropped his pants. 'Look at my Pull-Ups, everyone! They have airplanes on them. Whee-eee!' Then he reached into them, pulled out two dummies, and popped them both in his mouth at the same time – the double dummy suck, one of his earliest inventions. Putting his hand under his other arm, he made loud armpit farts like Pepe-from-next-door had taught him. Then he stopped and gazed at the grownups with an expression that said, 'Ta-da!'

'Sebastian, what are you *doing?* Put your pants on this instant!' Serena cried, trying to yank the dummies from his lips. But Sebastian was ahead of her. Quick as lightning, he whisked them down into his Pull-Ups.

Ms Dekwaengler perused Sebastian's application. 'It says here that he's toilet-trained. And it doesn't say anything about an oral fixation.'

'Obviously he's a little unnerved by this process,' Elliott said. 'We were taking extra precautions with the training pants, that's all.'

'I don't know where he got those pacifiers,' Serena said. 'He hasn't used one in years.'

'As long as this is an aberration,' Ms Dekwaengler said. She turned to Sebastian. 'We can only accept *big* boys at Madison Prep. You *are* a big boy, aren't you?'

Sebastian's shoulder's drooped. He glimpsed his mother and father. They gazed back at him with the same pride he saw in their eyes when he did something clever, like sing *London Bridge is Falling Down* in Chinese or name all the bones in the human body. Then he regarded Ms Dekwaengler. She was smiling at him. He cast a glance out her door and saw Mr/Miss Chappy, the Teletubby teacher, tottering toward them. The adults had backed him into a corner from which there was no escape. He needed a plan and he needed one fast.

Sebastian clutched his chest, collapsed to the ground, and began gasping for air. 'I can't breathe! I can't breathe!' He coughed loudly. 'I'm dying!' He made his eyes bug out and crumpled to the ground, acting as dead as he could. It was his rendition of the death scene he had witnessed when his mother took him to see that boring play, *Romeo and Harriet*, at the Public Theater.

'For God's sake, Elliott, do something,' Serena shouted.

Elliott dropped to his knees and tickled his son's underarms. Sebastian burst into laughter. 'No, no Daddy, stop it,' he giggled.

'Sebastian, get up,' Elliott said. 'You're not dying.'

'I am so,' he squeaked.

'What is *wrong* with that child?' Ms Dekwaengler said.

'Nothing a little fresh air won't cure. We're sorry, Ms Dekwaengler, really sorry,' Elliott said, sweeping the boy into his arms and toting him out. The last thing Sebastian heard his mother say was, 'Thanks. It was a pleasure to meet you. Did I mention that your school is our first choice?'

LAURA

'A ministering angel shall my sister be.'
—William Shakespeare

After spending a sleepless night at the hospital, Laura was a mess. Her blond curls were tangled and her red cocktail dress was wrinkled and pungent. Exhausted and starving, she took a quick detour for a bite at Bubby's, feeding every expired parking meter she passed on the way for good karma.

In Laura's opinion, Bubby's was the best comfort food restaurant in Tribeca. Oh sure, Amanda favored Kitchenette for home-cooking fare, but she begged to differ. Small and homey, Bubby's made everything from scratch. Their pancakes were the fluffiest, their pies the flakiest, and their macaroni the cheesiest. For dairy products, they relied on their own cows that fed on nothing but grass on a small family farm upstate. Laura knew that once you've tasted dairy products from private cows, there was no going back.

Inside, the air was sweet, thick, and warm. For

a weekday morning, the place was hopping. The hostess estimated a fifteen-minute wait. As Laura contemplated whether to stay or go, she saw a familiar face. Who is that? she wondered. He was eating with a little girl who looked about six or seven. Friends of Serena's? An actor on TV? A neighbor? It hit her: Mr Shine, the biology teacher she'd serenaded at Madison Prep.

She was too tired to make conversation. Then again, he had an empty seat at his table. Surely he'd invite her to join them. Hunger trumped fatigue.

'Excuse me, Mr Shine,' Laura said, 'but do you remember me?'

He stood and smiled. 'You're the singing telegram lady. This is my daughter, Violet. And please, call me Charles. Join us, will you?'

'Thanks. I'm Laura Moon,' she said, noticing just how good-looking Charles Shine was for a man so mad-old. His skin was toffee-colored, his almond-shaped eyes were golden-brown, and his smile could light up Yankee Stadium if they hadn't just closed it forever. Today, he wore jeans and a soft black sweater. He seemed far more relaxed than he had at school.

'You're dressed awfully fancy,' Violet said. 'Are you a hooker?'

'Violet!' Charles admonished.

Wow! What a pip, Laura thought. Violet was small and dainty with curly, untamed shoulder-length hair – dark like her father's. She had honey-brown

182

skin, and her green eyes were enormous, like one of those Japanese *anime* children. Violet was dressed in jeans and a Miley Cyrus T-shirt. A pink Hello Kitty backpack hung on the back of her chair.

'I'm a singer, not a hooker,' Laura said. 'And how do you know about hookers? Never mind, don't tell me. The reason I'm dressed like this is because I didn't go home last night. My bandmate had a heart attack. I stayed with him in the hospital.'

Violet made a sour face. 'I hate hospitals. People die in hospitals.'

'Will your bandmate be okay?' Charles asked, his eyes filled with concern.

'He needs a pacemaker,' Laura said. 'I've got to raise ten thousand dollars to help him pay for it.'

'That would take a lot of singing telegrams,' Charles said.

Laura nodded. 'You got that right. But the good news is, when I left him this morning, he was doing much better.'

A waiter appeared with French toast and oatmeal for Charles and Violet. 'Can I bring you some coffee or juice?' he asked.

'Coffee, please,' Laura said. 'And I'll have the farmer's breakfast. I'm famished.'

'What are you doing so far downtown?' Charles said. 'Do you live around here?'

'On Duane Street. You?'

'We're on Greenwich,' Violet said, as she doused

her French toast with maple syrup. 'Next to the Food Emporium. I'm in third grade at P.S. two thirty-four. My teacher's Mrs Porzio. She's the best!'

'No private school for her, even though you taught at Madison Prep?' Laura asked Charles.

'P.S. two thirty-four has a fine program,' Charles said. 'It's around the corner and it's free.'

'Free is good,' Laura said. 'Is today a holiday?'

'Parent-teacher conferences,' Charles said. 'It's why I left Madison Prep. My wife, Rachel, died a year and a half ago and I wanted to be present for Violet.' His throat caught when he mentioned his wife.

'I'm sorry,' Laura said. 'You must miss her very much.'

Charles and Violet nodded in unison as the waiter delivered Laura's coffee and farmer's breakfast of scrambled eggs, bacon, hash browns, and a country biscuit.

'That was fast,' Laura said.

'Would you excuse me?' Charles said. He headed toward the restroom.

The moment he was out of sight, Violet grabbed Laura's wrist as if for dear life. 'You're nice. Do you like my father?'

'Well, yes,' Laura said. 'He seems . . .'

'Good! Because he needs a wife,' Violet said urgently. 'Real bad. Ever since Mommy died, he's been a mess. He cries after he puts me to bed. He's up half the night. We *have* to help him.'

Laura's heart ached for this little girl who was

trying to solve such a grown-up problem. 'Violet, I can see you're really worried about your father. The thing is, after someone dies, it's okay to feel sad and to cry. That's how we heal. You know, my mom died earlier this year. I still cry.'

'You do?' Violet said, her eyes like saucers. 'Me too!'

'Everyone needs to grieve,' Laura said. 'You, me, your daddy.

Here's a secret: When I feel alone or afraid, I imagine that my mother, who's now an angel, is sitting next to me stroking my hair. You should try that. And the truth is, your mother probably really *is* there stroking your hair, because our loved ones never really leave us.' Laura bit into her eggs, which were hot and buttery.

'I'll try it. I will. But back to my dad. Do you think you might want to marry him? He showers every day even though no one makes him,' Violet said earnestly.

Laura smiled despite Violet's urgency. 'I can see he's a very special man.'

'Plus, I could use a mother. Don't worry, I'm in therapy. I know that no one can take Mommy's place, blah, blah, blah. But I'm poised on the brink of womanhood. Soon, I'll have questions that Daddy can't answer, like how do I know if a boy likes me? Am I ready for a training bra? Do I need extra protection for my heavy days?'

'How old *are* you?' Laura asked, trying to keep a straight face.

'Eight,' Violet said, with steely determination in her eyes. 'Will you be my mother? Teach me the womanly ways?'

Laura's eyes brimmed with tenderness. She would gladly help Violet, but it wasn't her place. Charles would have to find his own true love and future mother for her. 'Maybe your dad's not ready to date,' she said. 'But I'll tell you what, if he asks me, I'll say yes.' She wasn't sure about Charles, who was now making his way back to the table, but she definitely wanted to get to know Violet better.

'Daddy,' Violet said. 'Would you like to have dinner with Laura tonight?'

Charles cocked his head curiously. 'Are you playing matchmaker again?'

Laura spread some strawberry jam on her biscuit. 'Your daughter is concerned about you. She thinks you need to get married again.'

Charles gazed at Violet with a mixture of sadness and love so tender that Laura averted her eyes. 'I thought the two of us were doing pretty well. Aren't I here for you?'

'Daddy, this is unhealthy. You're smothering me. It's time you find a girl your own age. How can I be expected to master long division and take care of you at the same time?' Violet reached behind her hair and unclasped a silver necklace she was wearing. A strand of her brown hair was caught in the clasp. Attached to the chain was a charm shaped like half a heart. 'Here,' she said, handing it to Charles. 'Till you're ready to love someone besides me with your *whole* heart, you wear both halves.'

Charles' eyes dropped in disappointment. 'Really? You don't want it anymore?' He turned to Laura. 'I gave this to Violet after Rachel died. See, the halves are magnetized so they'll stick together, like the two of us.' Taking the charm off her necklace, he transferred it to his chain. 'There, are you happy? I'll wear this till I'm ready to love again with my whole heart, if that day ever comes.'

Laura swallowed the lump in her throat. She wished she could help Charles and Violet. Then she was overcome by a giant yawn which reminded her how tired she was. Slipping a twenty-dollar bill and her singing telegram business card on the table, she stood up. 'I need to get some sleep,' she said. 'Let me know if you'd like to get together, Charles. And Violet, call me anytime you want to talk.'

'Sorry I called you a hooker,' Violet whispered. 'I don't even know what that is.'

AMANDA

'Those who do not complain are never pitied.'
—Jane Austen

Amanda checked her black-and-white houndstooth St John Knit dress and freshened her red lipstick in the mirrored private elevator on the way to Penthouse Four. When the door opened with a soft *ding*, she poked her head inside. 'Yoo-hoo, anyone home?' She was seeing Cookie and Pansy Kellogh at Pansy's seventeen-room duplex overlooking Central Park and the Metropolitan Museum of Art. Considered one of the grandest prewar penthouses in Manhattan, the sprawling apartment boasted eighteen-foot ceilings, a dramatic gold stairway that swept up and to two sides, floors of Italian marble from Michelangelo's quarry, antique Persian rugs, a cavernous ballroom brought over piece by piece from a seventeenth-century Venetian doge's palace, four massive wood-burning fireplaces, and a glass-enclosed solarium opening onto an enormous wrap terrace.

As Amanda made her way through the marble entrance gallery and two-story living room toward the master suite of Pansy's legendary home, she felt depressed. And it wasn't just because Pansy's unbridled wealth reminded Amanda of her financial predicament, although that would have been enough. No, she was depressed because Pansy Kellogh was in the last stage of cancer, drugged within an inch of unconsciousness, and could pass at any moment. That reminded her of losing her own mother, and it made her sad.

Happily, Amanda had found a Russian billionnaire who offered thirty-eight million for the place, having only seen photos of it online. Sadly, if Pansy died before both parties signed the contract and the down payment was deposited, the apartment would fall into Pansy's estate, where it would linger in probate for months, and the buyer would pull out. Happily, Amanda had the listing for the apartment, so she wouldn't have to split her commission with another broker, only with her own firm. This sale would put $1.6 million in her pocket and release her from loanshark hell. Screw Riley Trumbo, she thought. I'll get the money myself. And when I do, I'll lend Laura whatever she needs. Hell, when this sale closes, I'll *give* her the money.

Sixty-two-year-old Cookie Kellogh was Pansy's never-married socialite daughter. She was slim as a cigarette holder with an Annette Funicello hairdo that hadn't evolved since 1960. Her spiked eyelashes made her appear perpetually surprised. She and

Pansy were inseparable. Amanda had met them ten years earlier, when mother and daughter were being pushed in matching wheelchairs down the United terminal at La Guardia to catch the noon flight to Palm-Beach. Cookie had confided to Amanda that neither of them was disabled, but they always ordered wheel-chairs when they flew so the airlines would give them personal valets on both ends. 'It takes the sting out of flying when you can't take the private jet,' she said. 'You should try it.'

Today, the shades were down and Cookie was weeping at her mother's side. Pansy lay motionless in a king-sized canopied bed.

Seeing the two of them, Amanda thought back to her own 24/7 vigil over her sister when she had leukemia. Serena had suffered devastating reactions to some of the chemotherapy side-effect medicines, drugs that doctors regularly prescribed for patients going through similar treatment. For their own convenience, they would order the same medications for all the patients on the leukemia floor. When the nurses would come in to administer a particular drug to Serena, Amanda would tell them that she couldn't tolerate it. This threw everyone into a tailspin. The doctor would have to be recalled, and that threw off his schedule. He would yell at the nurse for not pointing out Serena's special requirements. The nurses would scream at the doctor for not reading the chart, often taking their anger and frustration out on Serena for having such a bitch for a sister. But it couldn't be helped. The overworked doctors and nurses at the understaffed hospital screwed up on Serena's medication so often that it required Amanda's constant vigilance and aggressive defense to make sure her sister was safe. It would have been better if Sunny could have taken on the role of protector, but she was too shell-shocked by her daughter's life-threatening illness to reliably check and recheck every dose of medication.

Amanda's stomach dropped when she saw Pansy's inert form. 'Is she . . .'

Pansy turned her head slightly toward Amanda. 'No,' she croaked. 'I'm not dead yet.' Someone, Cookie most likely, had made up Pansy's face as if she were going out for a night at the opera. She had on blue eyeshadow, fake lashes, pink lipstick, and rouge. All this was set off by a pair of shiny pear-shaped diamond drop earrings and a delicately embroidered pink satin bed jacket. Wouldn't it be uncomfortable to die so heavily made up? Amanda thought.

Cookie bit her lower lip. 'Soon.' She raised her arms toward the Swarovski crystal chandelier and wailed. 'I don't . . . huh . . . huh . . . know how I can go on without Mother.'

'I can hear you,' Pansy moaned, a line of drool spilling from her lips.

'Sorry, M-Mother,' Cookie said, wiping Pansy's mouth and then stroking her thin pinkish hair. It was moist from sweat around her forehead.

Amanda sat at the foot of the bed. 'I know how you feel. I miss my mother so much.'

Cookie blew her nose. 'She was my best friend. We did everything together.'

'Do, we *do* everything together,' Pansy moaned, an ominous gurgling sound coming from her throat. 'I'm still breathing.'

Amanda knew she had to tread a delicate line. She felt terrible imposing on this family at a time like this. Cookie had piles of money. She could sell the apartment now or later, it made no difference to her. But this commission was Amanda's lifeline. 'Cookie, Pansy, I don't want to be a bother to you, but I have the contract for the sale of the apartment. If you'll sign the places I've tabbed, the deal will be done and I can get out of your way.'

Cookie took the contract and flipped through it. 'I don't know,' she said, 'there's always hope she could turn around.'

Amanda felt like shaking Cookie. Look at her! she wanted to shout. She weighs seventy pounds. Her face is concave, her eye-sockets are blue, and her skin is yellow. Sign the contract now, woman!

Pansy's chest began to heave painfully and she made a strange rasping noise. Amanda prayed it wasn't the death rattle.

'Mother, are you alright?' Cookie said, leaping to her side and kissing her sunken cheek.

Pansy whispered something to Cookie that Amanda couldn't hear. Cookie beckoned Amanda over. 'Mother would like a healthy green-vegetable drink. There's a Jamba Juice on Lexington.'

Is she kidding me? Amanda wondered. Don't

rich people have servants for this sort of thing? Where's the cook, for God's sake? And doesn't she know a healthy drink can't help her now? Amanda tried to stay cool. 'Okay, I'll be back in a flash. Will you sign the papers while I'm gone? Your mother can stay in the apartment as long as she likes,' Amanda lied, knowing Pansy had very little time. 'After she's gone, which I'm sure will be ages from now, we could close *then* and this would be one less thing for you to worry about.'

Cookie took the documents and set them on the nightstand. 'I'll read this while you're getting the juice. Make sure the drink is all vegetable. Fruit gives Mama gas.' She turned back and laid her head on her mother's chest.

Gas is the least of her worries now, Amanda thought. She made her way back through Pansy's massive apartment and took the private elevator down to the street. It was midday, and the sidewalk in front of Pansy's apartment was packed with locals and tourists who had come to visit the museum or stroll through Central Park. Amanda rounded the corner and spied a Jamba Juice a few blocks east. She tried to dash over, but she kept getting stuck behind lollygagging visitors who were gazing around and taking pictures. Two jeans-clad women strolling ahead of her who were snapping photos every three steps proved impossible to pass. 'Excuse me, but do you think you could take up even *more* of the sidewalk and walk even *slower* than you already are?' Amanda exploded. She was a bird's nest of raw nerves.

One of them turned. '*Sor-ree*! I guess it's true what they say about New Yorkers,' she muttered to her friend.

Amanda left them in the dust and hastened to Jamba Juice, but on arrival she discovered that they didn't serve green-vegetable juice.

'You've got to be joking,' she said. 'You're a juice store, for God's sake.'

'Yes,' said the gangly teenager behind the counter, 'but *fruit* is at the core of everything we make. And we never add processed foods like high-fructose corn syrups or trans fats to our drinks. That would be very un-Jamba-like. You might try Eli's on Third. They carry green juice.'

That's right, Amanda thought, slapping her forehead. Eli's has everything.

Amanda hoofed toward Third as quickly as she could. What I won't do for a commission, she thought. Just as she approached the store, a black Buick with a dented right fender pulled up. The passenger-side window came down. Richie was driving, and a hulking figure sat in the back. Amanda's heart leapt into her throat. She considered running but she was wearing her six-inch Manolo deal-closers.

'I need a word with you, Red,' he said, leaning over the empty passenger seat and opening the door. 'Get in.'

SEBASTIAN

*'There was a boy called Eustace Clarence
Scrubb, and he almost deserved it.'*

—C.S. Lewis

I t was pouring sheets when the Skanks left
Madison Prep.

Sebastian thought his interview had gone
terrific. He had managed to miss all the questions
Ms Dekwaengler asked him, prove he was potty
challenged, suck two dummies at once, and fake
a heart attack. That should be good for another
year with Miss Carol. I *am* a really smart boy, he
thought, patting the iPhone he'd stolen from
Mr/Miss Chappy and hidden inside his Pull-Up.

'You can write that school off,' Elliott said as
they stood under the canopy in front of the
building. Cold rain poured over the edges like a
waterfall.

'Do you think it went *that* badly?' Serena asked.

Elliott dropped his jaw. 'Are we talking about
the same interview? We're just lucky there's a good
public school in our neighborhood.'

'Public school?' Serena said. 'God forbid! In New York City? Are you nuts?'

'A bunch of guys at *Law and Order* send their kids to P.S. two thirty-four. It can't be that bad.'

'I'm going to kill that little bastard, Pepe, from next door,' Serena muttered. 'You *know* he's the one who convinced Sebastian to want to be a flower girl. And can you believe what Laura said to Ms Dekwaengler? How could she say we were generous? How? If Sebastian doesn't get in, it'll be *her* fault. And Pepe's.'

'Serena, we can't blame anyone but ourselves. We were doomed the minute Sebastian showed off his Pull-Ups and stuck those plugs in his mouth,' Elliott said. 'And not only one – *two*! I thought you had that under control.'

Serena glared at her husband. 'Oh, like it's so easy to control a child!' she screamed. 'You have no idea how hard I work, how much I do, for so little appreciation.'

'Alright, alright,' Elliott said. 'Let's not fight in front of the school.' Elliott's black Town Car pulled up. 'I wish I could give you two a ride, but I'm flying out from JFK and not Newark. I'll call you from L.A.'

'Are you leaving us again, Daddy?' Sebastian said. 'Awww.' His lips curled down in disappointment.

'You can't abandon us. I'll never get a cab with this weather,' Serena said. A torrent of rapids was swooshing down the street and flooding the

196

gutters. A bus sailed by and threw up a wave that broke over Elliott's car.

'Take the subway,' Elliott said. 'Didn't you just take a vow of poverty.'

'Frugality. And El, you know that didn't include giving up taxis,' Serena said.

'Make an exception,' Elliott said, ducking into his car. 'Sebastian'll love it.'

'Oh dear,' Serena said. 'It's been years since I've taken the trains. Do you have any tokens?'

'They take MetroCards now,' Elliott said. 'You can buy one at the token booth.'

'Why do they call it a token booth if they don't take tokens?' Serena snapped. 'Didn't a lunatic just throw some tourist onto the tracks?'

'That was years ago,' Elliott said. 'You'll be fine.' He patted Serena on the head and gave Sebastian a hug and a kiss. 'Take care of Mommy while I'm gone, Sport.'

'Bye, I love you,' Serena said. 'Hope your plane doesn't crash,' she muttered under her breath as she remained under the canopy to secure Sebastian's harness and leash. 'God forbid you jump in front of the train, or worse, some homeless drugged-out maniac pushes you in front of it.' She held him by his leash and popped open her umbrella. They ran toward the station and made their way down the slippery subway stairs. 'Oh Lord, I can't believe I'm doing this,' she said, approaching the token booth and buying a MetroCard for the two of them.

Sebastian was beside himself with excitement. He loved anything with wheels. 'Is this like Thomas the Tank Engine only not a toy?' he asked, clapping his hands with delight.

'Where did you see Thomas the Tank Engine?' Serena said. 'Certainly not at *our* house.'

'The boys at school talk about him,' Sebastian said.

'Well, alright, yes, it's like Thomas I suppose,' she said, holding his harness close as they waited for the subway to come, 'except it's much more dangerous and full of criminals.'

An announcement came over the public address system. 'Ladies and gentlemen, this is an important message from the New York City Police Department. Keep your belongings with you at all times. If you see a suspicious package or activity on the train or platform, do not keep it to yourself. Tell a police officer or MTA employee. Remain alert and have a safe day.'

'Jesus Christ,' Serena fretted. 'Terrorists. I didn't even think of that.' She peered around. 'See those black iron bars, Sebastian? They're to keep lowlifes from jumping the turnstyle. If, God forbid, there's an explosion, how are we supposed to escape this death trap? I pray it doesn't happen until we get off.'

A train pulled up. Serena and Sebastian boarded and found two seats. 'Now sit quietly and don't talk to anyone and whatever you do, don't make eye contact.'

Sebastian surveyed the subway, wondering what dangers lurked around them. The chairs were blue and there were shiny silver poles throughout the car that would be perfect for climbing. At one end, a bunch of teenage students were making lots of racket. Near them sat an old Chinese couple, a family of tourists studying a map, two guys with orange vests and construction hats. A jeans-clad mother with a boy about Sebastian's age sat across from them. He had thick golden hair that looked like sunshine.

The mother was trying to feed a bagel to the boy, but he kept hitting her hand and screaming, 'NO!' She offered him a sippy cup, which he knocked to the other side of the car. He squirmed to the floor and lay down on the filth. As his mother tried to pull him up, he went completely limp and she couldn't manage it. Sebastian noted his slick move for future emergency use.

Serena gazed at Sebastian, who was sitting quietly clutching Ruthie, his baby doll. She gave her son a squeeze. 'So you still take a pacifier, so what.'

Sebastian smiled to himself. Sometimes Mommy was almost like a normal person.

'At least you can control yourself in public,' Serena whispered. 'I can take you out and you never make a scene, not like that horrid little monster over there. I should really get out more amongst the people. It would help me appreciate the blessings I have.'

'Hell! Hell! Hell!' the child shouted as he banged his head on the floor while his mom attempted to lift him.

The woman sitting next to Serena, who was reading a thick book with tiny letters and no pictures, lifted her eyes, leaned over, and said to Serena, 'Thank God for birth control.' Then she saw Sebastian. 'Is he yours? Sorry.'

Sebastian felt terrible for the little boy. Was something wrong in his head to make him act that way? Or had he just come from a kindergarten interview?

'Shhh,' the boy's mother warned, although it did no good. Somehow she managed to get the child off the floor and hold him tight in her arms while he continued to scream and squirm. Eventually he quieted down as his sad mother rocked him back and forth in her arms.

Sebastian stood, pulled a dummy out of his pants, marched over to the kid, and offered it to him. The little boy grabbed it and stuck it into his mouth as if for dear life. Sebastian returned to his seat and glanced back at the boy's mommy, who mouthed the words, 'Thank you.'

'Obviously she didn't see you pull that dummy out of your pants, or she wouldn't have been so grateful,' Serena murmured. 'Why on earth did you do that?'

'He needed it more than I did, Mommy.'

ELLIOTT

'I love being married. It's so great to find one special person you want to annoy for the rest of your life.'

—Rita Rudner

As his black Town Car snailed toward JFK, Elliott thought about Sebastian blowing his interview. That whole system of getting kids into private school pissed him off. They had done an episode of *Law and Order* about that a few years back. An admissions director was murdered and one of the first suspects was a parent whose child hadn't been accepted. Elliott was shocked that didn't happen more often. In the end, the murderer turned out to be the headmaster. It was an affair turned ugly. We're so good at last-minute twists, he thought. It was too bad that his being a director on an Emmy-winning show wasn't enough to get them the celebrity exemption when it came to admissions.

Poor Sebastian. I'd fake a heart attack, too, if I had to go off with that hermaphrodite. That school should make him or her declare a sex and dress appropriately. It's too stressful to ask a small child to go off with someone so ambiguous. Parents should refuse to put their kids through this admissions nonsense. I wish Serena could see that and relax.

Serena. My beautiful Serena, he thought. What happened to you? To us? Serena's transformation from sexy executive to momzilla had been swift and ugly. The more involved she became with the children, the more she squeezed him out of their lives. In the beginning, he would do diapers and get up with Sebastian in the middle of the night, but then Serena would redo the diapers because they weren't on tight enough and send him back to bed because he couldn't help with breastfeeding. Elliott had retreated into his work. What choice did he have? Serena was so busy raising their little resumés that he didn't know her anymore.

I loved her once. He closed his eyes, remembering the woman he had married. She was so much fun back then, so lighthearted and happy. They both loved to laugh and play practical jokes. She knew all the Alfred Hitchcock movies, as did he. She could recite every line from Monty Python and the Holy Grail just like he could. They used to play scenes in bed for giggles. For the first two years, they never spent the night together without making love. He took such pleasure in buying her silky lingerie, blindfolds, and silk bondage cuffs from Kiki Montparnasse, a luxurious store in

SoHo for all things sensuous. Serena would perform hot stripteases for him. Sometimes their sex was kinky; sometimes it was daring like at the Golden Globes, sometimes it was simply sweet and loving. He used to feel compelled to touch her whenever she was near. She adored travel and he was happy to take her wherever she wanted. There were plenty of fights, but it was always worth it for the make-up sex. In the early years, their relationship fizzed like freshly uncorked champagne.

After Sebastian was born, the bubbly went flat. When Valentina came along, it was even more apparent that Serena no longer needed her husband to provide satisfaction. Serena hardly wanted Elliott to touch her. When they had sex, it had to be with the lights off and in the missionary position. She went from vixen to Victorian overnight.

Elliott became a shameless flirt, which worked out well because there were always women vying for his attention. Being a director on *Law and Order* may not get you ahead in the private-school game, but it worked wonders in the dating game. So far, he had managed to keep it innocent, although he'd once almost lost it with Laura. Good thing she stopped them before they went through with it. That would have been unforgivable. But now, he was on his way to meet someone, a beautiful Asian-American actress on his show. She was fifteen years younger, and she got to him in a way that Serena used to. So far, nothing had happened between them except for a bit of BlackBerry sex. Now, he was about to cross a line in his marriage that he never imagined he'd cross.

Elliott gazed out the window at the cars whizzing by and thought of Sebastian and Valentina. They were so innocent and sweet. What he was about to do was as much an affront against them as Serena. He winced at the thought.

He'd grown up in Beverly Hills, and he couldn't remember a time when his father wasn't screwing around. An executive at Skank Oil, his dad traveled three weeks out of every month. The family lived lavishly and was always attended to by servants. The children studied at the best private schools, summered at the finest camps, and never wanted for anything but the attention of their parents. Elliott remembered his mother flitting around the three kids all day and drinking alone at night. Eventually, his father divorced her to marry someone twenty years younger, the second of his four marriages. Elliott and his father didn't speak anymore. The last thing he wanted was to let Sebastian and Valentina down the way his father had let him down. But that was the path he was on.

'Sir, which airline do you need?' the driver asked.

'Hmmm?' Elliott had been lost in his head. 'Delta.'

'Where you off to?' the driver asked.

'The Caribbean,' Elliott said.

'Work or pleasure?'

'I have no idea,' Elliott said.

AMANDA

'A woman is like a teabag, you can't tell how strong she is until you put her in hot water.'
—Nancy Reagan

Amanda had no choice but to get into the front seat of Richie's car. The door locked automatically. 'Richard,' she said, 'I'm literally *about* to make the deal that will allow me to pay back the loan. But I need to pick up some green-vegetable juice for the client. Give me a few hours. Please, *I beg you.*'

Richie wagged his finger back and forth at her. On it he wore a heavy gold ring with a marble-sized blue stone. 'Not so fast, Red. My associates weren't happy with your niggling deposit. In fact, I'd like you to meet Anthony "Kneecap" Santorielli.'

Amanda turned to shake his hand only to hear an animal-like snarl and face the barrel of a big, fat, shiny handgun. The snarly man brandishing the piece was a young, shaven-headed guy wearing an orange muscle shirt. His chest, shoulders, and upper arms were covered with so much black hair that he could have been part Chia Pet. That was as much as Amanda could make out before doing an immediate about-face.

'Anthony's father is your lender, the one you're late paying back. He's here to make sure I deal with deadbeats accordingly, if you know what I mean,' Richie said. 'I've been dispatched to . . .'

'. . . to what? To whack me? Please don't,' Amanda begged, her heart racing. 'I'm so close to having the money to pay you back.'

'Not to whack you,' Richie said. 'If I was going to do that, you wouldn't have seen it coming. But I'm gonna have to hurt you, break a leg or arm, if you know what I mean.' He picked up a large rusty hammer he had stuck in his cup holder to show her his weapon of choice, then set it back down.

What if that isn't rust? she thought. What if it's *dried blood!* Amanda's heart pounded harder. She considered grabbing the hammer and bashing Richie's head in, but with Kneecap sitting in the back seat carrying a piece, that didn't seem wise.

Richie pulled the car over and Kneecap got out in front of Brick Church. 'You'll excuse me,' he said. 'I'd love to stay and watch, but you're Richie's fourth victim, er . . . client today,' he said, 'and I'm due at my kid's nursery school. It's my turn to do patrol.'

After Kneecap slammed the car door, a torrent of tears exploded from Amanda's eyes, cascading down her cheeks. 'Please, I beseech you. Don't . . . huh, huh, huh. I'll do anything. Just don't hurt me.'

Richie scratched his chin thoughtfully. 'Would you sleep with me?'

Amanda gulped. 'Yes, of course.' She hated to think she would stoop that low to save her bones, but under the circumstances it seemed like a no-brainer.

Richie laughed, 'Just toying with you, Red. If I slept with you, I'd have to sleep with every other deadbeat whose balls I'm always breaking.'

'It can be our secret,' Amanda said, wiping her cheeks. She folded her hands in front of her face in begging position. Every molecule of her body was vibrating. All her life she'd wondered how courageous she'd be if faced with a life-and-death situation. Now she knew. Not very.

Richie shook his head sadly. 'Damn, this is the part of my job that I hate.' He genuinely seemed disturbed about his assignment. 'But wuddaya you gonna do, Red?'

The imminent threat of pain gave Amanda an idea. 'I know. Won't you . . . won't you *pretend* to hurt me?'

A gasp escaped Richie's lips. 'That would be lying, Red. I can't do *that.*'

'But Richard, I swear, I've got this sale pending. If it closes, I mean, when it closes, the commission'll be over a million and a half bucks. I'll give you twenty grand right off the top.'

Richie gave her a look that would stop a toddler mid temper tantrum. 'Are you insulting my integrity by offering me a bribe?'

Amanda was confused. You'll beat people up and assassinate them, but you won't lie or take a bribe? 'No, of course not,' she stammered. 'It's just that . . . is your mother still alive?'

Richie glared at Amanda with reproachful eyes. 'I told you I don't mix my personal and business life.'

'Okay, fine, don't tell me,' Amanda said. 'But you *do* have a mother, whether she's here or has passed. What would she say if she saw you right now? She'd tell you to be a gentleman and give the nice young lady a hand, wouldn't she?'

A guilty cloud passed over Richie's face. 'Okay, fine. Tell you what,' he said. 'I'll take you to my brother-in-law on Staten Island. He's a paramedic. We gotta make it look like I roughed you up real bad.'

'Sure, anything,' Amanda said, feeling more relieved than she had in her entire life. Pansy's green juice would have to wait.

Two hours later, Richie dropped her off in front of Pansy's building. 'Remember not to get that wet.' He handed her a Duane Reade bag. 'Here, I got you some medicated powder. Drying plaster causes a nasty rash, if you know what I mean. Don't forget the crutches.'

Amanda hauled her fake broken leg out of the car, hopping about until she balanced on the crutches. At least he topped off the cast below her knee so she had some mobility. 'Thanks, Richard,' she muttered. 'I got to run. Or limp.'

'Forgetting something, Red?' Richie said, handing her the green-vegetable juice he had been considerate enough to pick up while Amanda was getting her cast put on. He smiled at her, his dark eyes gleaming with mischief. He was so attractive at that moment, it was easy for Amanda to forget he killed people for a living.

But there was no time for silly fantasies. She had to get back to Cookie and Pansy and save the sale, if it wasn't too late already. It was cumbersome to maneuver while on crutches and holding a large cup of juice. A doorman wearing a red-and-gold quasi-military uniform offered to carry it upstairs in exchange for a generous tip.

When Amanda finally made her way into Pansy's bedroom, Cookie dropped her jaw. 'Where have you been? Oh my goodness gracious, what happened?'

'I fell, broke my foot,' she said, as the doorman handed Cookie the juice. Richie made her swear not to tell anyone the injury was faked. 'Did you sign the papers?' Amanda was drained from the mental strain of coming within a hair of getting her kneecaps whacked with a hammer. Let's get those papers signed and get me the hell out of here, she thought.

'No, not yet,' Cookie said. 'Mama and I were talking about old times. Now that you're here, I'll read everything. But first, Mama wants one of those soy chocolate puddings they make at Eli's. Would you mind running down to get that for her?'

Amanda was incredulous. Can't Cookie see that

I just broke my foot? she thought. Not that I really did, but if I *really* did, that would be a remarkably selfish request. It makes me sick the way rich people think only of themselves. What if Pansy dies while I'm down buying the pudding? I'll be completely screwed. 'My foot is in a lot of pain,' Amanda started. 'Is there any staff here that might . . . ?'

'I sent everyone home,' Cookie said. 'I didn't want to risk relying on another person watching her even for a minute. What if I was on a break when she passed? Make sure the pudding is soy.'

Yeah, yeah, let me guess, Amanda thought. Dairy gives her gas. She crutched her way out of the building, around the corner, across Madison, Park, and Lexington to Third, hobbling as quickly as she could back to Eli's, walking on the cast itself when no one was looking. At the dessert counter, she discovered that the store was out of soy chocolate pudding. They only had the kind made from milk. It'll have to do, Amanda thought. With great strain, she made her way back, her underarms aching from the hard wooden crutches. In Pansy's kitchen, Amanda put the pudding into a china bowl and found a small silver spoon. To be safe, she stuck the empty container in her purse so Cookie wouldn't see that it wasn't soy.

'Would you mind feeding it to her?' Cookie said, sitting at her mother's desk. 'I want to read through the contract, and then I'll sign it. You're right. Things will be easier later if I take care of this now.'

Thank you, Lord, Amanda thought. *Finally*!

While Cookie perused the contract, Amanda spooned the pudding into Pansy's mouth. Amanda was surprised at how much she was able to eat, considering this was her deathbed and all.

Suddenly, Pansy grabbed Amanda's wrist as though she was about to fall off the edge of a building. Her breathing became labored. It seemed as if she couldn't get air into her windpipe. 'Cookie, something's happening!'

Cookie rushed to her mother's side, dropping the contract on the carpet along the way. 'Mama, Mama, are you alright?'

Pansy's formerly yellow skin tone was turning blue. 'Do you have oxygen?' Amanda cried. 'I don't think she can breathe.'

Cookie shook her head wildly. 'It's like she's having a reaction to something. That pudding didn't have milk in it, did it? She's deathly allergic.'

'No, of course not,' Amanda lied, her face contorted in an expression bordering on hysteria. Oh, fuck! Fuckity fuck fuck fuck! I killed her. Lucky for me she was dying anyway. 'Let's call nine-one-one.'

Pansy wheezed in what little air she could. Her eyes rolled back in her head.

'We have to let her go,' Cookie said, clutching Amanda's arm so hard that her fingernails drew blood, choking back a sob. 'She . . . huh . . . huh . . . made her desires clear on that.'

Pansy deflated like a punctured pool float. Her eyes softly closed until she was perfectly still.

Cookie let out an animal-like wail and took her mother's frail remains into her arms. 'No, Mama, no.' Her body shook with violent cries and gasps.

Amanda picked up the unsigned contract that was strewn about the floor. It would be obscene to try to get Cookie to sign it now. Should she try anyway, she wondered? 'I'll get out of your hair,' Amanda said. 'But before I do, why don't you, uhm, here. Here's a pen.' She set a blue felt-tip marker and the signature page on top of Cookie's dead mother and watched her like a hopeful puppy dog.

Cookie glared at Amanda with such venom that you'd think this whole thing was her fault. Amanda knew that it was, but Cookie didn't, so the evil stare was uncalled for. Her stomach sank when she realized that there was not a vegetable-drink chance in Jamba Juice that Cookie would sign that contract.

The reality of her predicament hit Amanda so hard, she could barely catch her breath. She owed the $100,000 plus 3-percent interest a week, bringing her debt to over $150,000. With the tax rates in New York, she'd have to earn at least $300,000 to net that. She might as well jump into the East River with her heavy cast, because that's where she was going to end up anyway if she couldn't raise the money. Thirty days. Now that her leg was 'broken,' Richie felt he could hold her creditors off that long. 'But not a minute more,' he'd warned.

LAURA

'Help one another is part of the religion of sisterhood.'

—Louisa May Alcott

Later that afternoon, Laura took David home to his cramped studio apartment at Golden Manor. He passed out as soon as his head hit the pillow, as was his usual M.O. Watching him on his sickbed, she thought about all those days and nights at Methodist Hospital when Serena had leukemia. It was supposed to be such a fine cancer institute, but the truth was, there were not enough doctors, nurses, or supplies to go around. They were constantly running out of gowns, sheets, pillowcases, and towels on Serena's floor. Laura, who was a kid at the time, turned herself into the Artful Dodger, slipping into supply closets on other floors and stealing those items for Serena.

During Serena's first round of chemo treatments, the doctor had explained to Sunny and Amanda that because of the nurse strike, there was a shortage of caregivers available who were trained in oncology. Only the sickest patients, those with status five as evidenced by a red sticker and a doctor's initials on their charts, would be tended to by the few experienced nurses who had crossed the picket line. Student nurses and candy stripers, who were pitching in during the crisis, cared for the rest. When no one was paying attention, Laura crawled into the nurse's station, stole a red sticker for her sister's chemo chart, and forged the head doctor's initials. After that, Serena had the best care available.

Sunny encouraged her younger daughter's quasi-criminal behavior. Laura learned an important lesson back then: When someone's survival was at stake, you break the rules.

When David finally opened his eyes, he was in no mood for company.

'Laura, *go* home, don't waste your time with me,' he muttered, his voice hoarse. 'I'm an old dying man. It's fine. I accept it's my time. I only hope I pass before the end of the month when this heartless nursing home evicts me.'

'They're kicking you out at the end of the month?' Laura asked, popping open a 7-Up for him, pouring it into a glass, and sticking a straw in it. 'Here. This'll make you feel better.'

David took a sip of soda and then picked up the eviction notice, dropping it before he could hand it to Laura. 'They gave me thirty days, and that was a week ago. Is that how long the doctor gave me to live if I don't get a pacemaker?'

214

'Now you listen to me. You're not going to die. I won't let you. Your operation is half-covered already. I'm working on raising the rest. And if they kick you out, you can live with me. Mom's room is empty and I'm lonely for a roommate.'

'I couldn't impose,' David said, his eyes downcast.

'Shut your face,' Laura said. 'It's *me* you're talking to, your former wife during the Crusades. Of course you could.'

David's tight expression relaxed into a smile. Laura squeezed his hand, then gave him a kiss. His eyelids fluttered and soon he was snoring. On the wall above his bed hung the autographed class portrait of America's greatest jazz musicians. David had said it was worth a lot of bread. Could it be worth ten grand? Probably not. But still, maybe they could piece the money together by selling several items on eBay, the picture included. Laura didn't like the way David's breathing sounded, but there was nothing she could do, so she left.

Once home, Laura retreated to her mother's storage area. It used to give Sunny so much comfort to sit among the remnants of her life. Laura never knew if she remembered each picture or stick of furniture or piece of clothing, but it grounded her to be near them. Maybe it was the faint smell of Norell that still to this day hung in the air. That was the perfume Sunny had worn every day of her adult life until she didn't remember to put it on anymore.

Laura glanced at the rack filled with the clothes Mom wore before she got sick. It had to be dresses, never pants. Sunny reveled in feeling frilly and girly. Even at the end, she loved it when Laura brushed her hair and tied it back with one of her pink ribbons. Laura took a deeply satisfying breath. To be among her mother's things was the closest thing to being in her arms.

Perching on her mom's old vanity bench, she picked up her bottle of Norell, opened the top, and took in the familiar scent. The vanity itself was white-painted wood with a mirror that could rotate up or down. The matching bench was covered with a faded red velvet cushion. Laura closed her eyes and recalled sitting at the vanity six years earlier, putting on makeup while Sunny, Serena, and Amanda sat on the bed watching her get ready for the big date. Laura's sisters never really believed her singing career would take off. 'What you need to do,' Serena would say, 'is to marry rich. You're beautiful, sweet, smart – well, not book smart, but you have good sense.'

'You're savvy,' Amanda said. 'Street-smart.'

'You'd make the perfect trophy wife,' Serena declared. 'I know that seems crass and tacky, and it kind of is, but I mean it in the best possible way.' Elliott had arranged for Laura to go out with Simon Booker, the producing partner of Dick Wolf, the man who created and owned the *Law and Order* franchise. Simon was twice divorced and shit hundred dollar bills, according to Serena. This was before Sebastian was born and Serena used words like 'shit' instead of 'moved his bowels.'

'Let's hope he's Mr Right,' Laura said.

'Or Mr More-or-Less Right with a deep pocket,' Serena said.

Laura checked herself out in the full-length mirror. She had taken the time to blow out her naturally unruly blond mane. Today it was a silken waterfall, like hair in a shampoo commercial. Serena had borrowed a strapless gold dress from Versace for her to wear. It was tight and short, showing off her figure to its fullest advantage. With her Wolford tights and six-inch Hollywould heels, she was impressed by how sexy she looked. She turned her head upsidedown, and then flipped all her hair back so it appeared thicker, more mussed. 'What do you think?' she asked.

'You are a vision,' Serena said. 'He won't be able to resist you.'

'When I was twenty-one, I didn't look like that,' Amanda said. 'Actually I never looked like that, ever.'

'I'll take that as a compliment,' Laura said, grinning. She turned and checked herself out, pleased with what she saw.

'I'm not too young for him, am I?' Laura said.

Sunny pursed her lips with disapproval. 'You're darn right you're too young.'

'Mom, he's forty-one,' Serena said. 'Twenty

217

years is the perfect age gap for a second wife, or in this case a third wife.'

'If you say,' Laura murmured. Maybe her sisters were right. Maybe her highest and best purpose in life was to decorate the arm of a rich mogul. The odds of finding success as a singer were a million to one, she thought. If her dream didn't pan out, what was she trained to do? Nothing. Today, her greatest asset was her pretty face and hot body. Ten years from now, she'd have fine lines, thinning lips and a drawer full of Spanx. The practical thing was to use her natural assets to attract a husband who could take care of her, but also a man she could fall head over heels for. She hoped Simon Booker was that man.

The doorbell chimed. 'I'll get it,' Amanda said, jumping up. 'Take your time before coming down. And remember, first impressions count. Try to make a memorable entrance. Serena and I will keep him waiting in the vestibule.'

Laura spritzed some of her mother's Norell into the air and then stepped into its vapors. She glanced out the window onto Duane Street. A big, shiny black limo was idling in front. Next to it stood a man wearing a chauffeur's uniform. She squealed with anticipation. 'Mama, look at that,' she said. 'Wouldn't you like me to have that all the time?'

'Marrying a man for his wallet,' Sunny said, shaking her head, 'there's too high a price to be paid.' Her mind was relatively sharp that day. 'But who am I to stop you? Let me go down and meet this . . . this . . . uhm . . . what's the word? Meal ticket.'

Laura wondered if her mother was right. She usually was. But with Simon Booker and his shiny limo waiting for her downstairs, she might as well enjoy herself. Did he bring me flowers? she wondered. Daisies would be lovely.

Languorously, she made her way to the stairs. This was before the house had been divided into separate apartments. There was a single wooden carpeted staircase leading to the entry hall. Laura took her sweet time descending each step, trying not to sound too clunky in her heels. Finally, she turned the last corner and stood on the landing, spotting Simon Booker standing next to Mom, Amanda, and Serena.

Simon gazed up at her expectantly. He was attractive – a foot taller than Amanda, slim, a thick head of dark hair, wearing a handsome blue suit. When he caught sight of the willowy blond poised at the top of the landing, his mouth crinkled into a lopsided smile and his eyes caressed her face, piercing the distance between them. It was a moment so electric and full of promise that Laura grabbed the wall to steady herself.

Mindfully, feeling the sensation of the carpet beneath her heels, holding her chin high, she descended the stairs, silently repeating the mantra Serena had taught her. I am the most desirable woman Simon Booker has ever seen. I am the most desirable woman Simon Booker has ever seen. I am the most . . . 'Arrrrrrrgh!' she screamed as her high heel caught on a small tear in the carpeted staircase. As if in slow motion, she lost her footing and tried to grab the railing, but missed. She felt herself tumbling down the stairs, head over Hollywould heel, her gold dress hiking up to her waist, her legs askew, her head bumping into hard wood edges all the way down to the floor.

When she landed, Laura's face was hot with humiliation. She closed her eyes and groaned. Is my underwear showing? I can't get up, she thought. Oh God, my leg, my leg! Luckily, the big black limousine was waiting right outside to take her to the hospital. Simon Booker asked his uniformed chauffeur to carry her to the car – something about suffering from back spasms. At St Vincent's, Sunny, Amanda, and Serena told Simon to go home; they would wait. Twenty hours later, Laura was released with a broken leg and a concussion. Sunny and Amanda sat by her side the entire night feeding her pain pills, holding ice packs on the hematoma that had erupted from her forehead, waking her every two hours to be sure her condition hadn't worsened.

Early the next afternoon, Serena rapped on the door. 'I have wonderful news,' she said, lunging inside like a bull charging a red cape. 'Simon still wants to take you out, even after what happened. He's giving you another chance. Isn't that great?'

Laura pulled herself up in bed. Her eyes were framed by black, blue, and purple bruises. The knot on her forehead had morphed into a goose egg. 'No, it's not great,' she said. 'That fall was a sign. The universe was telling me I'm not meant to be anyone's trophy wife. From now on, my life is about making music. It's my purpose and it's how I'll support myself.'

As she spoke, Sunny popped open a 7-Up, poured it into a glass, and plopped in a straw. 'That's nice, dear. Here, this'll make you feel better.' Then she went to the closet and brought out the tan-and-white cashmere blanket she had knitted herself and laid it over Laura's covers. 'This'll keep you cozy. Whatever you want to do is fine with us.' Her mother meant that, but Laura could see the disappointment in both of her sisters' eyes. They thought she couldn't make it on her own, that she needed to be taken care of. She would show them. Laura knew she had as much talent as Amanda had drive and Serena had style. The universe had spoken. Her destiny was to enrich people's lives through music, not to be some rich man's plaything.

Now, six years later, Laura glanced around at the furniture, clothes, and boxes. What do you know! There on Sunny's dresser sat the tan-and-white cashmere blanket all folded into a thick square. Beneath it was the colorful knit bedspread the neighbors had made for Sunny toward the end. Her red pillbox hat sat stuffed with tissue paper on top of her bookshelf. Okay, time to get serious. What can we sell? she wondered, scanning the room. On top of the vanity, Laura spotted the envelope containing the inventory Sam Hermann had given her. She tore it open.

Then she caught a glimpse of her mother's enormous armoire, stuck behind the dresser in the back corner. That was the nicest piece she owned, although she never wanted it in her bedroom. It was made of rosewood and had ornately carved angels and flowers across the top. I'll bet *that's* antique, Laura thought. It could be worth something. And what's inside? She put down the envelope and went for the armoire doors. Old-fashioned locks secured them, the kind that could easily be broken into. Laura grabbed a hairpin from her mother's vanity and stuck it in the keyhole. Growing up, she and her sisters used to pick each other's bedroom and diary locks constantly.

The telephone rang. Laura left the pin in the lock and ran to the kitchen to catch the phone. David's doctor had promised to call today. It was probably him.

'Laura Moon? Hold for Joey Martin, please,' a woman said.

Laura's stomach flipped. Oh my God, it's Mr Movie Man! What do I say to him? 'Relax, relax, relax,' she chanted.

'Laura, you were right,' Joey said as soon as he got on. 'The sound on that DVD doesn't do the band justice. When are you playing next?'

'We have a regular gig at Vines, but we're on hiatus right now.'

'What about Golden Manor? I'll be in New York in two weeks. How 'bout I come there. I can visit Aunt Miriam and bring my co-producer and musical director,' he said. 'They're intent on Norah Jones. I told them they had to see you and the band first. It's really the musical director's choice. He's a jazz fan, though. When he sees Dave Hargrove perform, that should sway him.'

Two weeks, Laura thought. *Sheesh*, David's not going to be ready by then. 'Didn't your Aunt Miriam come into Golden Manor with Uncle Isadore?'

'Yes, but he died last year,' Joey said. 'They were married fifty-nine years.'

'I remember him,' Laura said. 'He played harmonica. Sometimes he'd jam with the band.'

'Uncle Isadore jamming?' Joey said. 'I wish I could have seen that.'

'He was great,' Laura said. 'Your Aunt Miriam loved to watch him. And he got such a kick out of it.'

'Thanks for giving him the chance,' Joey said. 'He used to play for me when I was a kid. That and pull nickels out of my ear.'

Laura laughed. 'So you see, you have to fight for our band no matter how we perform because your uncle played with us. We're practically family.'

'You'll perform great,' he said. 'And I'll do my best.'

223

'You know, two weeks from now is a busy time for us,' she started.

'It's the *only* time,' Joey said. 'We start shooting in thirty days. Got to wrap this up.'

Laura hung up and sighed. An astrologist once told her that something huge would happen to her before she turned thirty. Could this be it, the big thing her chart had predicted? Please God, I hope so, she prayed. I don't want to be doing singing telegrams when I'm Aunt Miriam's age. There was very little time before Joey Martin was coming to hear them play. Somehow, she had to conjure the money for David's operation, like, tomorrow.

Laura stuck her head back into her mother's storage room. What could she sell? Most of Sunny's stuff was junk, but the armoire and vanity could be worth something. Between that and David's autographed jazz picture, maybe they could raise ten grand. She made a mental note to call an estate appraiser to come over as soon as possible.

AMANDA

'How do people make it through life without a sister?'

—Sara Corpening

When Amanda got home that evening, she donned an old soft cotton bathrobe. It's so exhausting being me, she thought. I need to lie down right now and think about that. She tried to settle onto her sleek couch, but the plaster cast on her foot was hot, bulky, and heavy. As she reflected on her day, a thick cloud of melancholy descended on her.

First, she accidentally killed Pansy Kellogh, then she faked a broken foot, and finally lost another apartment sale.

When she got back to the office, there was the e-mail from the manager of the rock band that was rehearsing in her apartment. It seems that Serena was calling the police every day to complain that the noise they were making exceeded the weighted decibel level of forty-five that the city statute allowed. They had been issued four $250 tickets so far and after five, the fine goes up to $1,000. He threatened to break the lease if Amanda didn't call off Serena.

Later, she heard from the heiress Julia Crown. Over the last three months, Amanda had squired her about town in her firm's chauffeured Rolls Royce to see ninety-six apartments. Now Julia had left a message saying that she'd found something through a rival broker. Instead of the half million dollar commission Amanda expected, Julia sent her a box of chocolates. They weren't even Godiva. Cheapskate.

Then Thomas Bennett called. He and his third wife were scheduled to meet with the board at 740 Park tomorrow, but he'd just discovered she had been cheating on him with his son from his first marriage, so they would be getting a divorce. Amanda explained to him that if he pulled out, he'd lose his two-million-dollar deposit. Couldn't they pretend to be a happy couple for one more day, get board approval, close, and THEN get a divorce, she had asked him? Thomas was willing but his wife wasn't, not unless he agreed to tear up their pre-nup, which he refused to do. Amanda saw yet another commission slipping through her fingertips.

The capper was when she read this morning's Page Six. Apparently, Riley Trumbo had defied his father and flown to Milan last night to reunite with his beautiful wife Sofia. An inside source said Harley had kicked him out of the family business and disinherited him, but Riley and Sofia were determined to settle into a simpler life in Italy. The way the press romanticized the story you'd think Riley had given up the throne for the woman he loved.

Amanda was so disgusted that she left work early, intending to lay on the couch, eat her stash of black and white cookies, drink expensive wine, and contemplate the pathetic state of her so-called life. Damn you Bernie Madoff for putting me in this miserable position, she thought. Damn me for being so stupid and greedy that I'd give my money to such a charlatan. Stop it! I wasn't alone. Lots of smart people trusted him. Things could be worse. I could have lost everything like that eighty-eight year old Holcaust survivor, that widow whose husband invested their fortune with Madoff in the early nineties. Now she's working as a greeter at Walmart. Amanda shuddered at the thought of this poor woman's fate and took a swig of Merlot.

Amanda must have dozed because when she awoke, her foot was tingling like crazy. She started to jerk but was stopped by the weight of the knee-high plaster cast. 'Shit,' she cried. Her foot *really* itched. It was as if ants were crawling around inside. But that would be impossible because her cast was on tight. Well, it wasn't that tight, she noticed. There was about a quarter inch of breathing space all around. Maybe she had rest-less-leg syndrome. She'd seen a commercial about that. Thank God there is treatment for that now, she thought.

Examining her cast, Amanda saw a buzzing black spot that seemed to be moving. On closer inspection, she realized it was a gaggle of ants crowded around a mess of black and white cookie crumbs near her ankle. She slapped at them several times until they morphed into shriveled black dead-ant dots. But still, the inside of her cast tickled like a thousand mosquito bites. 'Ow, ow, ow, ow, ow,' she shouted, banging the cast with her fist. She lay on the floor and lifted her leg into the air, shaking it so the tiny creatures would spill out, but she still felt them crawling upward toward her foot. How many could there be? she wondered. It was as if an entire ant farm had taken up residence. What if they laid eggs? Eeeww!

Amanda pulled herself up. Hobbling, she made her way to the kitchen and took out a can of Raid. Sticking the top into the tiny space between her leg and cast, she sprayed bug poison down the gap. It pooled into liquid near her knee. Little if any got to the buggy part.

'Stop, stop, breathe, ohmmm,' she told herself. 'Stay calm.' She hobbled to the desk and pulled out a sharp letter opener she could use as a scratcher, and stuck it down the cast, but it wasn't quite long enough to reach the itch. As she wiggled it back and forth, she lost her grip and felt it slide down to her foot.

Amanda sat on her stuffed chair and lifted her

'broken' leg onto the ottoman. A lump formed in her throat. I'm a disaster, she thought. She looked around the room, her eyes stopping at the Lassiter sketch. No, no, she thought, averting her gaze. I can't do it. That would be wrong. But what am I supposed to do? I know. I'll tell Serena the truth. The truth will set me free. No, it won't. Serena would kill me. The itching inside her cast was maddening. She banged at it with her fist until she temporarily stopped the sensation, but then it reappeared somewhere else.

Amanda hobbled over to her computer and googled 'how to kill black ants.' A WikiHow article came up that suggested pouring boiling water on them. Forget it, Amanda thought. It also recommended baby powder. *That* I have, she thought, making her way to the bathroom. Carefully, she filled her palm with Johnson and Johnson's Baby Powder and stuffed it into the crack between her leg and cast. After she emptied the entire bottle into the cast, she lay on the floor and shook her leg every which way. I'm either annihilating them or giving them really soft ant bottoms, she thought. Eventually, there was an eerie calm inside the cast. The baby powder had done its work.

Suddenly, Amanda felt an intense pins and needles sensation in her leg. Damn, she thought. Those buggers bite. This time she googled 'how to treat black ant stings.' Another WikiHow article recommended putting bleach on the affected area. However, it said you must apply it within five minutes of being stung or the ant venom will cause severe itching and swelling. Amanda hustled to the kitchen sink and grabbed some Ajax powder with bleach. Hurrying, she lay on the floor, lifted her leg in the air, and shook it until the baby powder, letter opener and dead ants fell out. Gross! Then, she emptied the entire can of Ajax down her cast. Mercifully, the itching stopped.

Ech! she thought, crumpling to the floor. My life sucks! It's so unfair. Serena has a loving relationship, two perfect children, plenty of money, and Mom's entire estate. Laura is beautiful, talented, and dating a doctor. She's positive about everything, even being disinherited. Her future is wide open. Then there's me. A lifetime of striving has added up to nothing. I lost the family's money, a loan shark is threatening my life, my business is drying up, and my ovaries have shriveled up – not that it matters, because no man will ever love me again.

I should stick my head into the oven and get it over with. Wait. I can't. The oven's electric. Would a microwave work? But no, it would explode my head, and expecting Laura and Serena to clean up my fried brain matter would be selfish. Amanda pulled the feather cushion out from her easy chair and stuck it over her face, but no matter how hard she tried to smother herself, she kept releasing the pressure and breathing. As God is my witness, she thought, I want to *live*!

She reached over and picked up her cell phone.

'Hello, Tabby, it's Amanda. You know that artist you told me about who copies your original pieces? Ham, right? How can I get in touch with him?'

Tabby gave her Ham's number. 'Why are you asking?'

'I have an original Daniel Lassiter sketch that I'd like to sell privately, very discreetly. You don't happen to know anyone in the art world who might be interested?'

'As a matter of fact, I do,' she said. 'I'm married to him.'

LAURA

'To love is to suffer.'

—Woody Allen

With David recuperating, the Off Our Rockers Quartet was officially out of commission. The doctor insisted he limit his exertion until he could get a pacemaker. Stan broached the subject of replacing him, but Laura wouldn't hear of it. Being in the band gave David his dignity. She remembered how she tried to maintain her mother's dignity, even at the end, when she was in diapers. No, she had to raise the money for his procedure and get him back onstage.

Marc had arranged for his personal anesthesiologist to do the operation for free. His former roommate, Aidan, a cardiologist and jazz fan, also offered his services gratis. Marc even volunteered to give David an eyelift while he was under, but David declined. He took pride in the petrified-wood appearance of his skin. He felt it gave him character.

A week after meeting Laura at Bubby's, Charles invited her out for sushi. It had been ages since she had felt so excited for a date. He picked her up at the house and the two of them strolled over to Megu, a Japanese restaurant on Thomas Street. Laura wore a green sweater, black pants, and high-heeled boots. Her curly blond hair was pulled back in a ponytail. 'I didn't realize it was cool out,' she said.

'Take my jacket,' Charles said with concern in his eyes. 'At least put it over your shoulders.'

'Thanks, I will,' Laura said. 'You're such a gentleman.'

Charles held out his hand. He smiled shyly. 'I don't know why, but I have this irresistible urge to hold your hand.'

Laura took his hand and gave him a light kiss on the cheek. She leaned into him, resting her head against his shoulder. There was something sweet and old-fashioned about Charles that appealed to her.

'Have you been able to raise the rest of the money for your friend's operation?' he asked.

They still needed ten thousand dollars to pay for the operating room, the pacemaker, and other costs that Marc couldn't get donated. Laura reached into her purse, opened her wallet, and pulled out a check written to cash for ten thousand dollars. 'Ta da!' She sang triumphantly.

'You got it. Fantastic.'

'Well, no, not yet,' Laura said. 'I wrote the check. Now I'm waiting for the money to show up.'

'Excuse me?' he said. A jackhammer started banging away in the street where a group of men wearing orange vests and yellow hardhats were repairing a sewer line in front of a popular Italian restaurant.

'I'm so confident the money is coming that I went ahead and wrote the check. It's called the law of attraction,' she shouted over the noise. 'This check'll help me suck in the money. I don't know how, but it will.'

Charles squeezed Laura's hand. 'I love your optimism,' he said, his dark eyes warm with amusement.

A garbage truck roared by, almost running over a bike messenger. 'Jeezus! Watch where you're going, you fucking asshole!' the guy yelled. A high-pitched car alarm sounded as music blasted from a passing Cadillac: *Oh, that's the way, uh-huh, uh-huh, I like it, uh-huh, uh-huh.*

'Ahh! Don't you love the sights and sounds of New York!' Charles said, laughing.

Laura noticed the crow's feet that appeared by his eyes when he smiled. As wrinkles went, they were adorable. 'Tell me about Violet,' she said. 'How's she managing?'

Charles appeared thoughtful. 'As well as you'd expect. She and her mother were very close. Rachel took her to school, cooked for her, bathed her, kissed her boo-boos. I was your typical absent working dad. When Rachel died, Violet was devastated. Not only because she missed her mom, but because she was sure I couldn't do her mother's job.'

'It must have been so difficult,' Laura said.

'Oh, sure. There were lots of burned meals and missed appointments, which is why I quit working.'

'Do you like being Mr Mom?' Laura asked.

'More than anything I've ever done,' Charles said, flashing an eager smile. 'Violet's hilarious without meaning to be; she's sweet and loving and tries her hardest to take care of me. I had no idea how delightful she was until Rachel died. Teaching is my second career. Until I was thirty-six, I was a Wall Street trader. It was all-consuming and I didn't quit till I hit my number.'

'Your number?'

'The number of dollars I thought I needed in the bank to never have to work again,' he explained. 'Of course, in this economy, I've lost half my net worth, but I don't care. Now I know there are more important things in life than your bank account. Once I hit my number, I stopped trading and became a biology teacher. Loved every minute of it. But then Rachel died and Violet needed me. Raising her has been an unexpected gift. What about you?'

Laura told him how she'd studied music but set aside her ambitions when her mother got sick. As she spoke, his eyes fixed on hers and his face showed interest, sympathy, and amusement. Laura loved that he listened so attentively. She invited him and Violet to come hear her sing as soon as David got better.

'We'd like that,' Charles said, as they stopped at a red light. A truck from Fresh Direct barreled through the intersection, making it hard to hear. 'Violet really admires you, by the way,' he shouted over the noise. 'Thank you for offering to coach her for the talent show. It's important for a young girl to have a woman in her life.'

Laura blushed. 'Yes, well, I take my job as role model very seriously.' After Laura had told Violet to call her anytime, Violet had taken her up on it. On Monday she'd phoned to discuss a girl named Bijou Hammond who had invited everyone in her class to her Chelsea Piers birthday party except Muffin Whitehead. After consulting with Laura, Violet decided to boycott Bijou's party and make a play-date with Muffin instead. Someone had to take a stand against birthday-party exclusionary practices. On Tuesday and Wednesday she'd called to discuss what song to sing in her school's talent show. Laura convinced her to go with '*Que Sera Sera*' with only two *seras*, since it was a beloved song from days of yore and the mad-old teachers were judging. Violet asked her for help getting ready for the performance.

Charles's cell phone rang. He checked to see who it was and then answered. His face fell. 'That was our babysitter. I'm sorry,' he said to Laura, 'but we're going to have to cut this short. Violet fell while jumping in bed. She hit the side of her desk and sliced her chin open. They're on their way to the NYU emergency room. Forgive me. Rain check?'

'Oh please,' Laura said, raising her arm to hail a cab. 'I'm easy. C'mon, we'll eat at the hospital cafeteria after Violet gets stitched up.' She was enjoying Charles's company, but mainly she wanted to be there for her new, pint-sized BFF.

VIOLET

'I remember my mother's prayers and they have always followed me.'

—Abraham Lincoln

Violet's naturally wide eyes grew even wider as she took in the emergency room at New York Hospital. While Kirsten, her babysitter, filled out forms at the nurse's station, Violet sat perfectly still in her blood-stained Hello Kitty pajamas. Checking her Hello Kitty watch, she wondered what was taking Daddy so long. Hello Kitty was Violet's favorite designer. Tonight, wearing her Hello Kitty clothes and accessories made her feel like she had a friend amidst a sea of battered and bruised humanity.

On Violet's left sat a sweating man who was shaking as if his whole body were in a blender. He held a plastic tray of puke on his lap, into which he would hurl every few minutes. The stench was overpowering. On Violet's right was a guy with a beach-ball belly wearing a thin hospital gown. Folds of flab bulged from every square inch of his body. His shoeless feet were swollen, black, and covered with oozing sores. Violet thought they might fall off.

Holding a towel against her trembling, bleeding chin, Violet tried to be brave. She closed her eyes and imagined her mother sitting next to her instead of the ugly foot man. In her mind's eye, Mommy was gently stroking her hair, telling her everything would be alright, that she would stay with her the whole time. Violet relaxed. It would be okay. Mommy was there.

Suddenly, from behind a closed curtain, a crazy lady started yelling, 'Somebody help me! Help me! They're trying to kill me!' Two nurses ran to her, and soon she stopped screaming. Violet was glad she had shut up but hoped the nurses hadn't killed her.

She took a deep breath to calm herself, but gagged at the vomit odor. If there had been an empty chair, she would have moved.

Violet hated hospitals. She had hoped never to visit one again. After the car hit Mommy, she and Daddy flew to London to be with her. It was hard to believe that the person wrapped in bandages, her face swollen and purple, was really Mommy. Even though she was sleeping, Violet and Daddy sat by her side talking to her. One afternoon, Violet sang her a song she'd learned at school called *Tikki Tikki Tembo*, which means 'The most wonderful thing in the whole wide world.' Before she finished the last verse, alarms started beeping and ringing from the machines Mommy was attached to. Doctors and nurses rushed into the room and worked on her, but Mommy died while Violet stood in the corner hiding her eyes. Violet wondered if you could die from a split open chin.

Then, miraculously, her father and Laura appeared. As soon as she saw them, she burst into tears. She couldn't hold it in anymore. Her impossibly tall daddy kneeled in front of her and took her in his magic arms. She was getting blood all over his blue shirt, but he didn't care. Laura, as welcome a sight as the good witch from *The Wizard of Oz*, ordered the shaky vomit man sitting next to her to move to the quarantine area. 'You're spreading germs to everyone around you!' she yelled. As soon as he left, Laura took his seat. Violet was glad she was there.

When Daddy went to find a doctor, Laura pulled out a Kleenex and wiped Violet's eyes and nose. 'Th-thank you,' she said.

'Shhhh. You're going to be fine,' Laura told her. She lifted her head and pointed to a scar. 'I split my chin open jumping into a swimming pool,' she said. 'Now we can have matching scars. Hey, this'll sound weird, but I sense that your mother is here with you. Did you ask her to come?'

'I did! I did!' Violet said. 'You sense her? You really sense her?' Violet wondered if Laura actually knew she was there or if she was just trying to make her feel better. It didn't matter. She felt better. Violet's chin hardly hurt anymore knowing that Laura was there with her dad. Maybe afterward, they could go to a movie.

The nurse called out, 'Shine, Violet Shine!'

'Here!' Violet said, her hand shooting up like a rocket.

Daddy and Laura came in with her while the doctor gave her three dissolving stitches and a big white chin bandage. Kirsten went home after apologizing for letting this happen to Violet. 'Don't worry,' Violet said, 'we won't sue you, even though we could.'

'C'mon,' Laura said. 'Let's go to the cafeteria. I'll bet they have chocolate ice cream.'

Daddy took the girls' hands and smiled bigger than Violet had seen him smile since Mommy died. 'I think that can be arranged,' he said.

Nya-ah-ah, Violet thought. I couldn't have planned this better if I tried. If she had a mustache, she would have twirled it.

LAURA

'I wrote the story myself. It's about a girl who lost her reputation and never missed it.'
—Mae West

The next day, Laura was in the back seat of a chauffeur-driven black Town Car speeding through the Lincoln Tunnel on her way to Teterboro Airport, where the rich, famous, and powerful flew in and out in their private jets when visiting New York City.

A few weeks earlier, a tall, striking black woman named Tamara overheard Laura asking the manager about openings at Balthazar, a hip restaurant in SoHo that she herself couldn't afford. Laura was told that weekend waitresses there could easily make four or five hundred dollars in a night. She had dressed to impress that day – wearing a short, tight emerald-colored skirt, strappy heels, and a butter-cream silk blouse. Her smooth legs went on forever, and her long blond hair bounced with life. Unfortunately, Balthazar wasn't hiring at the moment. As Laura left the restaurant, Tamara tapped her on the shoulder and asked if she had ever considered hostessing on a private jet.

'No, never,' Laura said. 'Does it pay well?'

'The man I work for pays eighteen thousand a month. You only have to be on call ten days out of thirty and you get benefits.'

'Shut up!' Laura said. 'I don't have to sleep with him, do I?'

'No,' Tamara said, laughing. 'It's typical flight-attendant responsibilities plus some entertaining, but he'd never touch you. He's a well-respected businessman. You'd know his name if I told you.'

'That's perfect. I'm a professional entertainer, a singer,' Laura said.

'Some months you work all ten days,' Tamara said. 'Some months you don't work at all. But you have to be available 24/7 when you're on call. One of our hostesses left last month to get married. I heard you say you were looking for work. That's why I'm asking.'

'How do I sign up?' Laura said. If Tamara had handed her a contract, she would have committed right there and then.

Tamara arranged for Laura to interview with the pilot, who made the hiring decisions. He was waiting for her at the billionaire's jet, which was parked at Teterboro. Today she had dressed with special care, in a tight navy vintage Chloe dress with adorable white patent-leather boots circa 1960. It was all very Anne Marie in *That Girl*. The pilot wouldn't be able to resist her.

Soon she was floating through the revolving door of the terminal, being hit by a *whoof* of cold air. Nathan, the chauffeur who'd driven her to the airport, was escorting her to the jet. This is perfect, she thought. No more singing telegrams. Although she had never been a flight attendant, she had waitressed in college. Plus, six years of waiting on her slowly declining mother had given her a Ph.D. in serving others with a smile. She wondered if she should bring up that experience. Maybe not; it was too depressing.

Just think, in the first month, I'll make enough to cover David's pacemaker and get him back onstage. Then Joey Martin will use us for his movie and the band will *finally* take off. I'm totally getting this gig. How lucky was I to meet Tamara? So lucky!

'There she is,' Nathan said proudly, pointing to an enormous double-decker jumbo jet with four engines, a triumphant testimonial to one man's achievements in business. 'It's a brand-new Airbus A380. That baby cost three-fifty million dollars and another one-hundred-and-fifty million to outfit. They had to extend the runway to accommodate it. Six-thousand square feet inside. See those engines? They're made by Rolls-Royce.'

Laura couldn't believe that regular people were allowed to own planes that big. The thing was colossal. Why someone would want the responsibility for such a behemoth she had no idea. She couldn't imagine having to clean it.

Nathan led her to a set of stairs that went directly

244

into the first deck of the plane. 'The captain is waiting for you,' he said, gesturing toward the door.

A man wearing a blue uniform with a name-plate but no pilot's hat greeted her. He was older, well built, probably fifty, but good-looking in a Bruce-Willis-but-with-hair sort of way.

'Captain Bing, I presume,' Laura said, trying to dazzle him with her smile.

'You must be Laura Moon,' he said. 'Come, let me give you the fifty-cent tour.'

Laura gazed around with astonishment. She was standing in a gorgeous living room that belonged in an apartment on Fifth Avenue, not inside a jet. It was magnificently appointed, with marble floors, light-oak walls, Persian rugs, crystal chandeliers, and an assortment of seating areas with plush sofas and inviting chairs. Paintings by Picasso, Monet, and Chagall hung on the walls. A dazzling spiral staircase led to the upstairs deck.

The captain motioned to Laura to follow him into an airy dining room with a round antique table that seated twelve. Another elegant crystal chandelier hung above it. Laura wondered how safe that was during turbulence. And shouldn't those dining-room chairs have seatbelts?

They wandered through the marble-and-steel kitchen, then over to the gym, which was as well equipped as the New York Sports Club on Reade Street, by Laura's house. There were two locker rooms, each with its own whirlpool bath, sauna, and massage table.

'On the other side of the living room is a private office, library, lounge, and billiard room,' Captain Bing said.

'Where's the lap pool?' Laura joked.

'Upstairs,' he said. 'Between the climbing wall and the private zoo.'

'Really?' Laura said.

'No,' Captain Bing said. 'I'm teasing you.'

Laura noticed he had a funny lisp that made him whistle when he made the 's' sound.

'Would you like to see the bedrooms?'

Hello! Do mansions fly in the air? Of course I want to see the bedrooms, Laura thought. This is the most incredible private plane I've ever seen. Actually, it's the only one I've seen. But still, who lives like this? She was dying to know the identity of the mystery billionaire. It had to be the Sultan of Brunei or an Arabian sheik.

Upstairs, there were four guest bedrooms, one of which Laura would use if she took the job. The owner's quarters were enormous and included a king-sized bed, a mirrored ceiling, his-and-her bathrooms with Jacuzzis that had built-in TVs, his and her dressing areas and a cozy sitting room. Like the rest of the interior, the palette was dark-chocolate and off-white. Except for the mirrored ceiling over the bed, the decor was Zen and tasteful.

'Make yourself comfortable,' the captain said, gesturing toward the plush sofa in the sitting room. 'Can I get you a glass of Cristal?'

Laura said no, since it wasn't even lunchtime and that was her earliest cutoff for alcohol. Still, this billionaire obviously treated his staff right – beautifully designed bedrooms for their use, Cristal champagne, generous salaries. As she sank into the down-filled cushions, she took in the master suite, which was breathtaking.

How cool would it be to work in a setting like this? she thought. Amanda and Serena were going to die when she told them about it. The door to the hallway was open slightly. Suddenly, Tamara came in wearing a long, brightly printed halter dress. Her ebony skin was flawless, her brown eyes bright, and she had a body that seemed to go on forever like a giant exclamation point. She hugged Laura as if she were a long-lost sister and sat down right next to her.

'So, let me tell you more about the position,' Captain Bing said. 'I know Tamara gave you the basics.'

'She did,' Laura said eagerly. 'I just want to know, when can I start?'

Captain Bing laughed. 'Let's see if you're right for the job, shall we? First of all, the man you'll be working for is . . .' he nodded toward a copy of *Forbes*, which was sitting on the coffee table.

'Oh my God,' Laura said, clapping her hand to her mouth. 'You're kidding? He's an icon! Would I get to meet him?' Argh! Calm down, she told herself. Don't act starstruck.

'You'll get to know him *very* well,' Tamara said.

'But you can't talk about him with anyone. Don't even mention his name. You have to sign a confidentiality agreement.'

Laura nodded. 'I can be discreet.'

Captain Bing set a two-page confidentiality agreement and a pen on the table in front of Laura. 'Before we go any further . . .'

'You want me to sign this now? Even though I haven't taken the job?' Laura said. Then she shrugged. 'Why not?' she said, writing her name on the bottom line and sliding the document back across the table.

'So, tell me about yourself. Are you an open-minded person?' Captain Bing said.

Laura cocked her head. 'Open-minded? I think so. I believe in alternative healing methods, reincarnation, ESP. I go to psychics and do energy work. Yes, I'd say I'm open-minded.'

'Good. As you know, this job pays well,' Captain Bing said. 'You'll be expected to perform your typical flight-attendant duties along with a few other special entertainment assignments.'

Laura nodded enthusiastically. 'Yes, yes! Did Tamara mention I'm a singer? It would be my honor to perform for . . . er . . . the boss.' She was careful not to mention his name.

Captain Bing knitted his brow. 'What? No, I don't think you understand,' he said. 'When I say "special entertainment assignments," I mean "*special*" entertainment assignments,' he said making air quotes.

Laura's stomach dropped. She could only imagine what he meant by special with air quotes. Her dream job and David's last hope were fading in memory before they even began. She turned to Tamara. 'I thought you said I wouldn't have to sleep with the boss.'

Tamara shook her head. 'You don't.'

'Oh, whew!' Laura said. 'Sorry! So sorry. I *really* jumped to conclusions there. Forgive me.' She hoped this wouldn't ruin her chances.

'The thing is,' Tamara said, 'he likes to watch.'

'Who likes to watch? And what does he like to watch?' Laura asked, confused.

'Our employer,' Captain Bing said. 'And he would be watching the two of us perform.'

'We'd sing together?' Laura said.

'No, we'd "perform,"' the captain said. He made the air quotes again when he said 'perform.'

Oh, I get it, Laura thought. He's telling me what's expected of me without actually *telling* me. She was so disappointed she wanted to cry. 'Wait, let me get this straight,' she said, closing her eyes and trying to imagine the scene. '*You* and *I* would have sex and Mr Don't-Even-Mention-His-Name would watch?'

'Yes, that's right. He likes to be called "Big Poppa,"' Tamara said. 'It doesn't happen every single time you fly, mind you. Usually he's not alone. Often his wife or kids or business associates are on board. Sometimes he stays in his office and works. Other times, he goes to the gym.'

'At least once a week, he gets everyone together for karaoke,' the captain said. 'You could sing then.'

'But sometimes,' Tamara said, 'if he's by himself and in the mood, he'll send a signal to the cockpit and the captain comes back and either you or I or sometimes both of us would get into the master-suite bed with Captain Bing and have at it. While we're doing our thing, he'll wander in, holding a book or the newspaper, and then he'll sit down on that white chair over there and read and every once in a while peek over the top.'

Laura couldn't believe what she was hearing. It was one thing to have sex in front of the rich kink-job who owned the jet, but with the *pilot*? 'Who would be flying the plane?'

'We put it on autopilot,' Captain Bing said.

Laura's mouth dropped. 'Isn't that dangerous?'

Captain Bing laughed. 'I'm kidding. There's a co-pilot.'

Great, Laura thought, kinky pilot humor. Damn, damn, damn, damn, damn, she thought. This had seemed like the perfect opportunity. Ten days' work in this opulent setting for a bloody fortune, the rest of the month to focus on my music. Laura gave Captain Bing the once-over. Could I do it with him? I've had sex with plenty of less attractive men in my life for free. He's old, though. What if he takes Viagra and gets one of those five-hour erections? Tamara, on the other hand, is striking, not that I'm attracted to her. Still, in my college lesbian days, I made it with a girl or two. But could

250

I debase myself like this? What about Charles? I really like him. What would he think of me if he knew about this? And Violet? What kind of role model would I be if I took the job?

Lately, Laura's singing telegram bookings had been in the crapper. Last month she'd made less than a thousand dollars. When the economy tanked, luxuries like singing telegrams were the first thing people cut from their budgets. She knew she could book more gigs if she stripped, but she couldn't bring herself to do that.

If I can't strip in front of strangers, what makes me think I can fornicate in front of them? Eighteen thousand dollars, that's what, she thought! Even if I do it for a month to cover David's pacemaker and back-rent and then quit, it'd be worth it. I could do that. Maybe Eva could hypnotize me into blocking it from my memory.

Laura thought about her school friend Julie, with whom she'd had lunch last week. Julie married an overweight sixty-year-old industrialist from Long Island who smoked cigars and had an overactive salivary gland. She freely admitted that she'd married him for the apartment on Fifth Avenue, the Gulfstream G550, and the three-hundred-foot yacht. Her pre-nup stipulated once-a-week sex and she faithfully fulfilled her contractual obligation. That wasn't so different from the deal Laura was being offered. *If I do it, she thought, think how interesting my episode of Behind the Music would be.*

Wait. No. Stop. *I need time, she thought. I won't*

decide now. I'll sleep on it. This isn't the kind of decision you make overnight. Her cell phone vibrated in her bag. Laura reached inside and peeked at the caller ID. It was John Hazeltine, who was babysitting David. 'Excuse me, I have to take this. It's about a sick relative.'

'Laura, you'd best come back now,' John said. 'I think we need to take him to the emergency room. His breathing is labored.'

Laura's heart raced. The reality of David's situation bore down upon her like a giant press. His time was running out. He needed the pacemaker now or the end was near. She sensed this in her solar-plexus chakra, which was never wrong. 'Call downstairs for a nurse,' she said. 'Ask her to come up and check on him. I'll be there within an hour.'

Laura snapped her phone shut. It has to be a sign that this call came just when I got the offer to prostitute . . . uhm . . . hostess for this billionaire. It's my destiny to take the job, at least for a month, she decided. 'I'll tell you what,' she said. 'I'll do it. But my price is twenty thousand for ten days a month, cash. And you have to pay me up front, not after.'

Captain Bing cast a glance at Tamara. She nodded slightly. 'I'll go get the contract and the money,' he said. 'Your shift starts a week from tomorrow.'

AMANDA

'There can be no situation in life, in which the conversation of my dear sister will not administer some comfort to me.'
—Mary Montagu

The next morning, wearing her money-green St John Knit dress, Amanda prepared to meet Penny Winkleman, a client who lived in a gorgeous six-story limestone townhouse on Seventy-fourth between Madison and Fifth. Penny was interested in a one-bedroom apartment at the Plaza, the large, ornate hotel (now a condominium) at the southeast corner of Central Park. With its white-gloved doormen, airtight security and glamorous guests like Zelda and F. Scott Fitzgerald, Marilyn Monroe, Liz Taylor, and the Beatles, the enchanting landmark was perhaps most famous for it's six-year-old fictional resident, the mischievous Eloise, whose 'bawth' once flooded the entire hotel. Penny wanted it because her husband traveled six to ten days a year without her and she was afraid to

253

stay alone in the house when he was away. They were asking six million for the unit she was considering. Amanda was determined to drive this sale through as quickly as possible. The Winklemans were all-cash buyers, so they could close and Amanda could collect almost immediately.

Amanda wrapped the Lassiter sketch in brown paper so no one could tell what it was. Her assistant, Nikki, stopped by to pick it up and take it to the Bullocks' where Tabby had arranged to have it appraised before Ham copied it. Winston was considering the piece for his personal collection. Between the Lassiter sketch and Mrs Winkleman, Amanda was sure she could raise the cash to pay Richie back within the month. I'm nothing if not resourceful, she thought.

'What's all that stuff doing on the sidewalk?' Nikki asked when Amanda opened the front door.

'What do you mean?' Amanda said. 'Oh my Lord!' Indeed, there was a forty-eight-inch plasma TV on the sidewalk. Next to it was a pile of Elliott's designer suits, shirts, and shoes, his golf clubs, a Bose stereo, his rare books, and his prized wine collection, some bottles from as long ago as 1955. 'Serena, what are you doing?'

Serena, her hair loose, wearing black leggings, a ratty T-shirt, and flip-flops, answered by taping a big sign on the TV: 'Free Stuff. If you can haul it, you can have it.' Then she went back upstairs for more.

'I call the stereo,' Nikki shouted. She picked it

up and brought it inside. 'Can I leave this here till later?'

'Sure,' Amanda said. 'Take some wine while you're at it.' Then she pointed to the wrapped package leaning against the wall. 'But now, I need you to drop that at Tabby's and then pick up Mrs Winkleman and take her to the Plaza. If I'm not there by ten, have them show her eight-H. I'll catch you as soon as I can.' Why is Serena losing it today? Amanda thought. I don't have time for another Serena crisis. She grabbed her crutches and hobbled outside.

Laura, wearing jeans, a cornflower-blue T-shirt, and running shoes came jogging down the block carrying a white bag from Bubby's. 'Jeez Louise, what's going on out here?' she gasped.

Amanda shook her head in confusion. 'I can only surmise that Elliott pissed her off.'

'Maybe he dumped her,' Laura said.

'If so, Serena is one unhappy dumpee,' Amanda said.

'What happened to your leg?' Laura said.

'I slipped on some steps while showing a brownstone,' Amanda said. 'It's nothing.'

The girls made their way upstairs. Serena stood by her dresser, taking her panties out of the top drawer. Her face was red and wet from crying.

'What's going on?' Laura asked.

Serena sniffed and then pointed to copies of the *News* and *Post* that sat on her bed. One headline read, 'Real Law and Order Drama.' The other

255

read, 'Nightmare on Sandy Lane.' Laura and Amanda each scanned a paper to see what had set Serena off. It seemed that Elliott had been on a tryst with an actress from his show (who played the obligatory young, beautiful DA) at Sandy Lane, a posh resort in the Caribbean. Two nights ago, after dinner, three men followed them back to their hotel room, tied them up, gagged them, pistol-whipped Elliott, and stole their money and valuables. As he tried to reach the phone, the chair Elliott was tied to fell over and he hit his head. He was flown by ambulance jet to Miami where he was being treated for a concussion. The actress was back in Manhattan, bruised and sore but otherwise unharmed. According to the story, her publicist had gone to *People*, *Us*, *InStyle*, and the tabloids with her juicy tale. Both dailies carried a picture of her with a stitched cut near her eye and a swollen cheek. Each printed an inset of a banged-up Elliott in the corner.

'My God,' Amanda said, 'did you *just* find this out?'

'Yes,' Serena said. 'I was taking Sebastian to nursery school when I saw the paper. Elliott hasn't even called me. God – damned fucking bastard. He'd better be on the brink of death or I'll kill him myself. What happened to your leg?'

'I broke it,' Amanda said. 'It's no big deal, not compared to what you're going through.'

Serena sniffled. 'You've got that right.' She began arranging her panties into piles.

Amanda was flabbergasted. She'd always envied

Serena for the life she had created. She seemed to have it all and constantly lorded it over her sisters.

'What are you doing?' Laura asked.

'I'm organizing my panties into g-strings, thongs, bikinis, hip huggers, and granny pants,' she said.

'You're doing that why?' Laura said.

'I have to do something.'

'I thought you and Elliott were happy,' Amanda said.

'So did I. But maybe there've been a few signs of trouble I didn't want to see.'

'Like what?' Laura said, her face flushing.

'I found a pink ribbon and a blond hair in some pants of his I took to the dry-cleaner,' Serena said. She turned toward her sisters and erupted into violent sobs with tears streaming down her face.

'When?' Amanda asked.

'Right after Mom died,' Serena said. 'Do you know what *the worst* thing is?' she cried.

'That the actress he was with is named Bambi?' Amanda said.

'No. Every school we applied to . . . huh huh . . . will see the papers. They hate scandals.'

'Come on, Serena,' Amanda said, putting her arm around her. '*That's* not the worst thing. Your husband's a cheater. You'll have to divorce him. Then you'll be forced to go back to work and be a single mother supporting two children under five. That's *much* worse.'

'You don't know for sure that he cheated,' Laura

said. 'Maybe he didn't go through with it. People change their minds, you know.'

Serena's face bore an incredulous expression. 'Not in my world,' she said. 'And anyway, everyone *thinks* he cheated so he may as well have. Plus, he was stupid enough to get robbed and pistol-whipped and taken advantage of by a publicity-seeking actress. No private school wants a family with that kind of baggage.'

'At least you have your health,' Laura said. 'Anyway, aren't we zoned for a good public school? Who told me that?'

'I did.' Amanda said. 'P.S. two thirty-four. It's a great school and you'll save thirty grand a year per kid.' She was in the bathroom preparing a cold washcloth.

'And don't worry,' Laura said, 'they *have* to take Sebastian, no matter what you and Elliott are like.' She sat on the edge of the bed and picked up the *Post*.

'Public school! My children can't survive in public school. Divorce! How am I going to manage?' Serena wailed. She stacked her panties into one pile, from the granny pants on the bottom to the g-strings on top.

'Would you stop with the underwear already?' Amanda said. 'Lie down.' She gave Serena a cold compress for her face. 'Shhh, relax. It'll be okay. Elliott isn't the first husband who strayed and he won't be the last.'

'Whoa!' Laura said, stopping as she flipped

through the *Post*. 'Serena, did you see this other story?'

'What other story?' Serena said. 'What could possibly interest me beyond the headlines about my husband and his beautiful young fucktress?'

'You're right,' Laura said. 'Nothing could. Forget it.'

Suddenly, they heard Valentina babbling to herself through the baby monitor. 'Should I get her?' Laura said.

Serena shook her head. 'No, wait 'til she cries. Now tell me, what story?'

'You don't want to know,' Laura said.

'I do,' Serena said. 'Anything to get my mind off that God-damned motherfucking husband of mine. Shitheel. Buttwipe. Poopy log.'

'Poopy log?' Amanda said.

'Give her a break,' Laura said. 'Okay, it says here that last night, Christie's auctioned four studies Daniel Lassiter did for paintings in his Sagaponac Light series. Each one will bring between three and four *hundred thousand* dollars. Can you imagine what Mom's drawing is worth? It's from an earlier and more valuable series. I'll bet it'd sell for half a million.'

'You think?' Amanda said, perking up. Would it sell for that much privately? she wondered.

'You better not sell it without making the variation to Mom's will that you promised.' Laura said. 'But after you do, I'm all for cashing out. You'll need the money to pay your divorce lawyer.'

'No,' Amanda said. 'We're not selling it. *Not ever!* We're passing it around between us each year like we said.'

'But before, you wanted to sell it so badly,' Laura said.

'I changed my mind.' Amanda knew that if she replaced the original with a copy by Ham and then Serena or Laura went to sell it, an auction-house expert would immediately know it was a fake. They were smart that way. 'It stays in the family forever. That's final.'

SERENA

'Is solace any more comforting than in the arms of a sister?'

—Alice Walker

'Here,' Laura said, handing her sisters glasses of orange juice and vodka. The three girls sat next to each other in bed, leaning against pillows propped in front of Serena's headboard.

'Do you know what my biggest regret is?' Serena said, adjusting the cold rag on her forehead.

Amanda swallowed her drink. 'Stealing Elliott from me?'

Serena threw the wet rag on the floor. 'I did no such thing!'

'Naming your children Sebastian and Valentina when you knew those were the only two names I ever wanted for my own kids?' Laura said.

'That was to honor you!'

'Committing to give your sisters their rightful inheritance, shortchanging them, then not following through on the meager handout you promised?' Amanda said, taking a swig of her drink.

Serena gasped. 'Shortchanging you?'

'Stealing my Barbie dolls and shaving off their hair?' Laura said.

'Stealing your Barbie dolls?' Serena said, astonished.

'Not getting your breasts enlarged when Elliott would have paid for it?' Amanda said.

Serena's mouth was agape. 'Not getting my breasts enlarged? Jeez, you two must really hate me to kick me this hard while I'm down.'

'We don't hate you, do we?' Laura said.

Amanda hesitated. 'Truthfully? Lately, I only tolerate you because you're my sister. If you were my friend, I wouldn't put up with your behavior.'

'If I was your friend you wouldn't put up with my behavior?' Serena said. 'What do you mean? I behave just fine.'

'You think?' Amanda said. 'Tell me, how does it feel to have some predator take off with your husband? Well, that's how *we* feel about you taking what should have been ours in the first place. You promised to make the variation. What are you waiting for? Seriously, tell us.'

'Sam Hermann said I had two years to do it,' Serena said, her voice hardly more than a whisper.

Amanda shook her head. 'You deserve everything that's happening to you right now.'

'She's got a point,' said Laura. 'This is karmic payback pure and simple.'

'No, it's not,' Serena said. 'I'm entitled to the entire estate, and I'm only sharing it out of the goodness of my heart. Daniel Lassiter was my real father. The only reason we have the house is because Mom sold a painting *my* father gave her. The study for the Goddess series is all I have left of him. These things mean something to me. I'm having a hard time signing them over to you, okay? But I'll do it. Eventually. Can you hand me those cigarettes?' Serena lit up and took a deep puff, flicking ashes on Elliott's *Law and Order* commemorative alarm clock.

'If you're so sure Lassiter was your father, why didn't you make a claim when he died?' Laura said. 'You could have had a share of the estate.'

'I thought about it,' Serena said. 'But it was before Mom got sick. I didn't want to resurrect any old pain.'

'Oh, right, I forgot,' Amanda said, rolling her eyes. 'You're such a humanitarian.'

'Leave her alone,' Laura said. 'Her husband just dumped her.'

Valentina's wails echoed through the baby monitor. 'I'll get her,' Serena said, stubbing her cigarette out on Elliott's Emmy. Soon she returned with the baby and settled into the glider chair to feed her with the bottle.

'What happened to breast milk?' Laura asked, moving to the edge of the bed.

'I decided to wean her. It's enough already,' Serena said. 'Elliott doesn't lift a fucking finger. I do everything for these kids and I'm tired of it.

Schlepping them to all their classes. Feeding them. Bathing them. Taking them to the park. Shopping for them. Being the perfect role model. It's me, me, me, mothering all the time.'

'I thought you loved doing everything?' Amanda said. 'You live for that.'

Serena gave Amanda one of those 'What watermelon truck did you just fall off of?' looks. 'Sometimes I wonder if Elliott even loves his children.'

'Of course he does,' Laura said. 'Every father loves his children.'

'Hello!' Serena said. 'Ours didn't love me. He tried to pawn me off on Daniel Lassiter, as you'll recall.' Serena hung her head. Her stomach muscles clenched up. She hated thinking about her father. That night alone at the beach was the most afraid she'd ever felt.

'Are you sure that was Daniel Lassiter he took you to see?' Laura asked softly.

'Of course. We were in an artist's studio. I've seen pictures of him since.'

'You know,' Laura said to Amanda, 'If Lassiter was her real father, then maybe she should have the house and the painting.'

'Thank you,' Serena said.

'Laura!' Amanda admonished. 'Whose side are you on?'

'I'm serious,' Laura said. 'Have you considered that maybe this was Mom's last wish and you should stop giving Serena a hard time about it?'

'We have no proof he was her father. If he wasn't, she sure as hell should share everything with us,' Amanda said. 'Equally.'

'*Equally?* But don't you see,' Serena said. 'I *need* more than you. If Elliott leaves me, I'll be alone. I have two kids to raise.'

'You aren't the only one with needs,' Amanda said.

'Amanda, you're plenty successful at work,' Serena said. 'Laura, you're going to be in a movie, make a soundtrack. You're both set. When Elliott leaves me, I won't have a clue. I don't know how to do taxes or insurance or . . .'

'C'mon, you'll be fine,' Laura said. 'You've got a place to live, a good public school in your neighborhood, two sisters to help you. Plus, wouldn't you get alimony and child support?'

'Child support, but no alimony. There's a prenup,' Serena said.

'Still, that would help. So maybe you'd have to sell the house. Even if you gave us an equal share of the proceeds,' Amanda said, 'that would be enough to live on if you invested wisely.'

Serena begged to differ. Amanda and Laura had no idea what it cost to raise children in the city these days. Even with her new commitment to austerity, it would be a stretch. They would still need a place to live, clothing, food, utilities, educational toys. Doctor and therapy and tutor bills could not be ignored. She might consider public school if their children weren't so gifted, but in light of their superior intelligence, that would be a terrible mistake. No, she would have to reduce costs elsewhere. Even if she stopped buying organic food, took the subway from time to time, and cut her own hair (God forbid!), it would take a lot more than one-third the value of the house to raise her family in Manhattan. Maybe I should rethink this whole bringing-up-kids-in-New-York-City idea, she thought. Women in Africa manage on so much less.

Serena brought Valentina up to her shoulder, kissed her forehead, and started rubbing her back until she let out a loud, long, sailor burp. All three girls burst out laughing. As Serena contemplated her two sisters, she thought about how she missed the three of them getting along. She didn't want to fight with them. Maybe they wouldn't begrudge her the house and painting if she proved that Lassiter *was* her father, which she knew he was. 'Laura, open the bottom drawer of my bureau and pull out the green box that's there.'

Laura found the cardboard box. 'DNA Solutions? What's this?'

'It's a DNA collection kit,' Serena said. 'I ordered it last year. Lassiter has a daughter named Kate.'

'I remember her,' Amanda said. 'That summer Mom and I spent in the Hamptons, she was at the house a lot. I don't think she lived there, though.'

'Two years ago, I had Sam Hermann send her a letter asking for a DNA test to see if we were related,' Serena said. 'Her lawyer refused. He said the point was moot since the estate had already been settled. I wouldn't be entitled to anything. But I needed the truth. So I ordered that kit.'

'What do you plan to do with it?' Laura said, opening it up.

'I hear Kate has a place in the Hamptons,' Serena said. 'A sample of her DNA would prove once and for all if we shared a parent.'

'Is it a blood test?' Amanda asked, grabbing the box from Laura, scanning the directions on the back.

'Blood, cheek cells, saliva, a used toothbrush, fingernail clippings, hair – any of the above,' Serena said.

'So what would you do? Tackle her on the street and swab her mouth?' Laura said. 'She's not gonna hand you her cells willynilly. She'd be afraid you wanted something.'

'But there's no risk,' Serena said. 'The estate's settled. Even if we *were* related, I'd have no claim. Don't you think she'd want to know if she had a half-sister? Especially if it's me?'

'No,' Amanda said.

'She's kidding,' Laura said.

'No, I'm not.'

'I think you owe it to yourself to find out the truth,' Laura said.

'You owe it to *us*,' Amanda said. 'If he's *not* your biological father, then you have to do the right thing; you have to share the estate.'

'And what if he *is* my father?' Serena said. 'Do I get to keep it all?'

'I suppose,' Amanda said, hesitating.

'Fine,' Serena said. 'I'll tell you what. We'll go to the Hamptons and somehow, I don't know how, but somehow we'll get our hands on Kate's DNA. If Lassiter's *not* my father, we'll share everything equally. And if he is . . .'

'You keep it all,' Laura said.

Amanda considered the proposition. 'Okay, fine, but only if you let *me* go to Sam Hermann to get the variation drafted. If he's your father, I'll tear it up. If he's not, you sign it *immediately*, no screwing around like before.'

Serena nodded. In truth, she had already agreed to give her sisters each a floor in the house and to share the Lassiter sketch. If she lost, she wouldn't have to give them much more. If she won, she would get it all and that would be a huge help if she and Elliott split. 'It's a deal,' she said, extending her hand. The sisters shook on it. 'You're gonna lose,' she said. 'Lassiter's my father.'

'I disagree,' Amanda said. 'Laura was a five-out-of-six-point match for your HLA markers when you needed the bone-marrow transplant. Do you know how low the odds of that are for a half-sibling? Plus, you have the same dimple on your chin that Dad did.'

'Lassiter had a dimple on his chin, too,' Serena said. 'He was my father, and he knew it and that's why he gave Mom the paintings, to take care of *me*.

If he isn't, that would mean the father I *did* have never loved me. I couldn't bear that.'

'We'll know soon enough, won't we?' Laura said, checking her watch. 'Serena, shouldn't you pick up Sebastian?'

'Would you do it? I can't show my face at his nursery school after what Elliott did, filthy pig, may he rot in hell, stinking turd.'

'Uhm, sure. When does he get out?' Laura said.

Serena glanced at the clock. 'Half an hour. You can leave in ten minutes.'

Amanda jumped out of the bed. 'Oh, shoot, Mrs Winkleman! The Plaza!' She pulled out her BlackBerry and made a call. 'No, don't tell me! Yes, it's four thousand a foot. Tell him that's a steal. Three months ago, it was five thousand a foot. Goddammit!' she said, stuffing the phone into her pocket.

'Problem with a sale?' Serena said.

'Her husband's making her choose between a six million dollar villa and vineyard in Tuscany and a one-bedroom apartment at the Plaza. I need to get to him, convince him they can afford both. Laura, will you hand me my crutches? I'll see you later.' She hobbled out the front door.

Laura went to wash her hands while Serena put Valentina on her shoulder for another burp. She must have patted too vigorously because half the contents of the bottle spewed out. It smelled like curdled cheese. 'Shit,' she said, wiping the spittle off the baby's face and the wall. She stuck

269

Valentina into an electric baby-swing, put on her junior headphones, and turned on the 'Encyclopedic Knowledge for Babies' CD. Serena gazed at her beautiful daughter, who began to doze as she swung back and forth. What a blessing she is, Serena thought. And I haven't updated her website in months. It's amazing how many hours she spends in this contraption. When Sebastian was her age, I played and read and sang to him all the time. With Valentina, all I do is park her in the mechanical babysitter and put on an educational CD. I'm pathetic. And poor Sebastian. He's my little genius. He deserves to go to Madison Prep. What kind of mother am I if I can't give him the best education possible? They'd be better off without me.

'You okay?' Laura asked, emerging from the bathroom.

Serena shook her head and shrugged. Her eyes filled.

'Give me a hug,' Laura said. 'C'mon.' Laura took her sister into her arms. As she held her, Serena rubbed circles on her back and began patting her hard. 'Serena, are you burping me?'

'Oh, God, sorry,' she said. 'It's a reflex.'

'So what are you going to do?' Laura asked.

'Hmm? You mean about Elliott?' Serena said.

'About your whole life,' Laura said.

270

SERENA

'There are so many girls, and so few princes.'
—Liza Minnelli

With Elliott due home that afternoon, Serena asked Laura to take the children to Barnes & Noble. She didn't want them to be in the house in case things got ugly. In fact, she was so furious with Elliott that she hid all the kitchen knives so she wouldn't be tempted.

As she soaked in the tub, covered by orange-scented bubbles, Serena wondered where it had all gone wrong. When they first married, Elliott's adoration knew no bounds. He sent her flowers, gave her jewelry, even wrote her bad poetry that gave them both a laugh. Their sex life sizzled. When was the last time they had even spooned in bed? She couldn't remember. Obviously he was getting his cuddles elsewhere.

It's my fault, she decided. I used to be interesting – smart, sexy, successful. What happened? I became Sebastian and Valentina's mommy, that's what happened. Still, that's no excuse. Lots of women with children manage to fill their lives with work, friends, love, travel, passion, and motherhood, don't they? Actually, she didn't know any women like that personally, but she had read about them in Oprah's magazine.

Why did I have children? She couldn't believe she even allowed herself to think such a horrible thought, but it was a good question. Work was a party compared to motherhood. I'm so tired of taking care of them. I hate who I am around them, she realized. How early do boarding schools take kids? Oh God, how could I think that?

Serena understood that she was burned out. She knew something had to give. Reaching over, she dried her hands on a towel and lifted the lid of a seashell-covered box next to the tub. Inside, she kept a little note she had found from her mother a week before she died. It hadn't made sense to her before, but today it resonated:

Serena,
    This has always been one of my favorite quotes. It's by Kahlil Gibran. 'If you love somebody, let them go, for if they return, they were always yours. And if they don't, they never were.' I think of you when I read it because you have always held on to things and people so tightly. Honey, sometimes the best thing you can do is let go. You will be surprised what comes back to you.
    Always,
    Mom

Serena's thoughts were interrupted as Elliott opened the front door. Serena knew it was him because the sound of his entrance was as distinctive as each of her children's cries. A cold knot formed in her stomach. Be strong, she told herself. You can do this.

After drying off, Serena put on a black Chloe skirt with her charcoal cashmere sweater. She stuck her hair in a ponytail, twisted it into a knot, and then put on a pair of one-karat diamond studs. After stepping into her Christian Dior black patent-leather six-inch stiletto boots, she checked out the overall effect in the mirror and decided to add a touch of gloss to her pillowy lips. To face off with Elliott, she wanted to look her best, even if her clothes were last season.

Serena came down the stairs holding copies of the *News* and *Post* as Elliott sifted through the mail like he did every night. He turned and saw her, smiling sheepishly. There was a huge black-and-blue knot on his forehead. She sat on the top step. 'I take it you saw the papers?' she said as she threw them at him. They scattered on the landing.

'Yes, I did,' he said. 'I'm sorry. We were attacked the night I got there. Nothing happened between us, in case you were wondering.'

'I wasn't wondering,' Serena said. 'I don't believe you, in case *you* were wondering.'

He closed his eyes and rubbed his bruise. 'Don't you want to know if I'm okay? I was tied up, pistol-whipped. Look at the rope marks on my hands.' He held out his scarred wrists for inspection. 'I have a concussion.'

'It was in the paper,' she said. 'I'm assuming you're okay since they sent you home.'

'I am. The doctor said I could go back to work on Monday.'

'You *humiliated* us,' Serena said. 'It's a good thing you're not a politician because if you were, I wouldn't be standing next to you at the press conference.'

Elliott's face fell. 'You wouldn't? There was a day when you would have stood by me no matter what.' He sat next to Serena on the step and took her hand. 'I'm sorry. I love the kids and I don't want to lose them. You and I, well, I know things haven't been good lately, but they were once, remember? Maybe we should go to counseling . . . if not for us, for the children. What do you say?'

Serena gestured with her head to a packed suitcase that was set next to the door. 'No, I don't think so. I'm out of here.'

His eyebrows arched in surprise. 'You mean . . . you're just leaving, taking the kids? That's it, no discussion?'

Serena shook her head. 'No, *I'm* leaving. The kids are staying.'

'With who?' Elliott said.

'With you. Their father.'

Elliott looked as if he had come face to face with a hungry black bear growling in the woods. 'But . . . but I don't know how to take care of them,' he said. 'And I have to work.'

Serena could hardly believe she was leaving the children with Elliott. She had never spent one night away from them. But this was something she had to do. Luckily she had long ago compiled a telephone book-sized manual of how she ran the house and raised the children in the event of her untimely demise. 'There's an instruction manual in the kitchen,' she said. 'What they eat, their preferred learning styles, the classes they take, doctors', therapists' and consultants' numbers, babysitters, their calendar, everything you need to know. Valentina has to see her pediatrician on Tuesday. Be sure to put Sebastian on his leash when you go outside. He has his audition with the children's chorus for the Metropolitan Opera on Monday at two. Check his Pull-Ups for hidden pacifiers. There's also an appointment with a child psychologist, Dr Borowitz. She's in the nineties on the Upper East Side. For some reason he's been stealing BlackBerries, Palms, Treos, iPhones. I've caught him several times.'

Elliott shook his head in confusion. 'Where will you be? What if I have questions? You're abandoning them the way your father abandoned you?'

Serena's chest tightened. 'No, it's not like that. I told them I was taking a time-out from Daddy. I'll call them every day. The thing is, I don't like who I am anymore. Not as your wife. Not as their mother. I've failed you and them and most of all, myself. I need some distance and you need to get to know your children. They're your responsibility now.'

Elliott shook his head in disbelief. 'If you leave, I

could sue you for custody. You could lose them forever.'

Serena shrugged. Elliott was about to shit in his pants. The last thing he wanted was sole custody of his children. 'I'm going away with my sisters for a few days,' she said. 'When I get back, I'll stay with Amanda. While I'm gone, I'm going to think about whether or not our marriage is worth saving. You should do the same. Right now, I . . . I need time off.'

'But why?' Elliot said. 'You don't work. You're off every day.'

Serena rolled her eyes in derision. 'I don't work? Try being me for a few days. Maybe you'll understand why I'm leaving.'

Elliott stood and blocked Serena from moving. 'Wait. Who *are* you? My wife wouldn't leave her children. My wife lives for her children.'

Serena kept her voice steady. 'I love the kids. But I don't love being *your wife* anymore.' She pushed Elliott aside and grabbed her suitcase.

Serena slammed the door behind her when she left. If either of them died, her last words to Elliott would be 'I don't love being your wife anymore,' and that was just sad. She collapsed against the vestibule wall, shocked that she'd left her children. What if they hated her for the rest of her life? But she had to go; otherwise she would hate herself for the rest of her life.

SEBASTIAN

'One of the best things in the world to be is a boy; it requires no experience, but needs some practice to be a good one.'
—Charles Dudley Warner

Sebastian and Valentina spent a glorious play-date with Aunt Laura. It was one of those perfect Manhattan days, the sun was shining, not a cloud in the sky; the kind of day that makes a boy happy to be alive. First, Aunt Laura took them to Barnes & Noble, where Clifford the Big Red *Dog* was appearing live and in person. Sebastian explained to Valentina that it was the actual, real Clifford, not just some clown in a dog suit. They bought two of his books and Clifford signed them! Really he paw-printed them because dogs can't write.

Later, Aunt Laura took them to Bed, Bath, and Beyond for a ride in the shopping cart. Mommy never let them do that, on account of how filthy shopping carts are. They're worse than public toilets, she'd say. Aunt Laura let Sebastian sit in the massage chair, but Valentina was too young to have her brain shook like that. On the way home, they ate ice cream from the truck that was idling next to the park and then played in the sand until it got dark. For obvious germ reasons, Mommy didn't let them play in the sand either. The best part of the whole day was that Aunt Laura let Sebastian suck his pacifier anytime he wanted. She didn't even care that he put it back in his mouth after it fell in the sand. He never felt so free in all his life.

While they were digging, he and Aunt Laura had a serious talk about Mommy's time-out. She needed time away from Daddy. That was good because Sebastian needed time away from Mommy. All those classes she took him to were aging him fast. He just wanted to stay home and play with his trucks. He didn't want to count them or graph them or separate them by colors or compare and contrast them or draw them from memory. Can't a boy be a boy instead of a little man?

'Tell me about the night I was born,' Sebastian asked, as he dug in the sand. He loved when Aunt Laura told that story.

'We were sitting at McDonald's having dinner, you know, the one at the end of Chambers Street, when your mommy went into labor.'

'Who was there?'

'Me, Grandma, Aunt Amanda, your mommy and daddy. Anyway, you were coming so fast there wasn't time to go to the hospital. They lined the table with take-out bags and your mommy gave birth right there. The hamburger cook called for an ambulance while your daddy delivered you using French-fry tongs. Valentina, don't eat that square. You'll choke.' Laura grabbed a blue pattern block out of her niece's mouth.

'Aunt Laura, you're silly,' Sebastian said. 'That's a heptagon.'

'Whatever,' she said. 'It's not edible.'

'Tell me the cook's name?'

'What cook?'

'The cook who called the ambulance when I got born.'

'Federico, I think.'

Sebastian clapped his hands. 'Say the bun part.'

'Oh, well, of course they didn't have any blankets to wrap you in, so the baker made a giant hamburger bun with poppy seeds on top and put you inside to keep you warm. You rode to the hospital in that bun. The ambulance driver was hungry and wanted to eat you up but I wouldn't let him.'

Sebastian jumped up and did the wiggle-worm dance that he had invented last year, clapping all the while. Valentina giggled. The more she laughed, the harder Sebastian danced. This was the funnest day he had ever had in his whole life. He was so drunk with joy that he forgot he hated his sister until he remembered. And then it didn't matter.

Sebastian thought of something else. 'Oh, oh, tell me about the poppy seeds.'

'What? You mean how they named poppy seeds after my father, your, Grampa Poppy?' Laura said. 'It's true. Grampa will live forever because people around the world will think of him anytime they eat a poppy seed.'

'Grampa Poppy says I have to be a extra-good boy for Mommy because he was bad to her and he's very sorry.'

Laura's eye's bulged. 'When did he tell you that?'

'In my dream.'

'Ah,' Laura said, nodding. 'Spirits do sometimes visit you in your dreams. It's nothing to be afraid of.'

'I'm not afraid,' Sebastian said. Only one thing scares me, he thought. And that's letting Mommy down, well, that and having vomit come out of my nose.

Later, they returned home. Daddy was sitting on the couch staring at the TV, which was off. The room was pitch black. It smelled like tears.

'Daddy!' Sebastian cried. 'We missed you.' He gave his father a big hug because he seemed like he needed it. 'Guess what? Mommy's taking a time-out. She has a headache in her heart.'

'I know,' Elliott said, switching on a lamp. 'She told me. I'm depending on you to help, Sport.'

Sebastian nodded solemnly. He would not let Daddy down.

'What's with Serena?' Elliott asked Laura.

Laura was changing Valentina on the rug. 'Duh! What do you *think* is with her? She realized she's married to a scumbag.'

Scumbag wasn't one of Sebastian's vocabulary words and he tried to figure out what it meant. He thought it might be one of those favor bags they give you after a birthday party. He wondered if Aunt Laura brought them scumbags as a surprise. He hoped there would be gummy worms.

'I feel terrible,' Elliott said. His head was buried in his hands.

'Yeah, that you got caught,' Laura said. 'I hope you used protection and you haven't exposed Serena to herpes or worse.'

'What's herpes?' Sebastian said, pronouncing the word carefully.

'It's like a cold that turns your skin bright purple,' Laura said, reaching over and tickling her nephew. 'Elliott, can you hand me the cream?'

He gave her the tube of Boudreaux's Butt Paste. 'Serena gave all my stuff away. Everything! Even my wine collection. Did you know that? All I have left are the clothes I packed for my trip.'

Laura glared at her brother-in-law; then went back to diapering Valentina. She blew a loud raspberry on her tummy. Valentina fell into peals of giggles.

'Those robbers could have killed me,' he said. 'No one seems to care about that.'

'If you're shopping for sympathy,' Laura said. 'Go somewhere else.'

'Nothing happened,' Elliott said. 'I swear.'

'Puh-*lease*, you're such a slut,' Laura said. 'Remember who you're talking to.'

Elliott bit his lower lip. 'I was only flirting.'

'What's a slut?' Sebastian asked.

'Nothing,' Laura and Elliott said in unison.

'Here, here's your daughter,' Laura said. She handed a fresh-smelling Valentina to him.

'Would you stay tonight? Show me the ropes?' Elliott said. 'I never paid attention to what Serena was doing.'

'And *that*, as they say, is the problem,' Laura said. 'Well, that and your wandering eye.'

Daddy has a wandering eye? Lexus, a girl in Sebastian's class had one, too. She had to wear a patch. Sebastian wondered if Daddy would have to wear a patch. Then he would look like a pirate. Sebastian was a pirate for Halloween last year. Someday he hoped to be one in real life, that or a flower girl.

Elliott groaned like he had a stomachache. His forehead had broken out in shiny beads of sweat. 'Please stay and show me what to do,' he said. He sounded lost.

'I'll show you, Daddy,' Sebastian said, coming to the rescue. 'I know what to do. You have to make dinner now.'

'Dinner?' he said. 'Jeezus, I don't know how to cook. I don't even know where Serena keeps the baby food. Does Valentina eat, or does she only drink out of those bottles?'

'I guess I'll be going,' Laura said, checking her watch. 'I have plans.'

'Daddy, Tina eats,' Sebastian said.

'Well, as long as you two have everything under control,' Laura said. 'I'll just let myself out.'

Elliott's cell phone rang. 'Tonight?' he said. 'I can't. I'm still getting over this head injury. Tell Michael I need more time.' As he listened, his face became redder and redder. 'Don't even think about it. What happened to me does not belong on *Law and Order*. Don't you dare order a script on it.' He snapped the phone shut, took a deep breath, and grimaced at his son. 'Where's the baby food?'

'Mommy makes it,' Sebastian said. 'We're organic beegens.'

'You mean vegans?'

'That's what I said, Daddy.'

Elliott opened the pantry and scrutinized the contents. 'There's no Gerber's in the house? I didn't know Serena made baby food from scratch. No wonder she's always so cranky.'

'What's Gerbers?'

'I can do this,' Elliott said. 'I can do this. Come on, Sport. We're going to the store to buy baby food for Valentina and then I'm taking you to McDonald's.'

Sebastian's heart leapt into his throat. His mommy had never taken him there, on account of how so many of their burgers suffered from mad cow disease. But he always knew that someday, he would make the pilgrimage to his birthplace. Daddy really understood him. 'Yippee!' he squealed. 'But don't tell Mommy 'cause it's against the rules.'

Elliott sighed. 'Tell you what,' he said. 'I'm new at this fatherhood stuff so while I'm figuring it out, we're going to suspend the rules. When Mommy comes back, whatever she says goes.' He tried to put Valentina into the stroller but she wouldn't stop squirming. Finally, he managed to strap her in and tuck a light blanket around her.

Sebastian reached into his Pull-Up and retrieved a dummy. He was pretty well covered in the rubber-nipple department. The day his mother threw his pacifiers away, he secretly retrieved them from the trash. Now they were tucked away in all the places he might be when the urge struck – chair cushions, behind the carseat, beneath his mattress. That was where he kept the BlackBerries and cell phones he'd been collecting. They used to be for Mommy but now that he and Daddy were closer than ever, they were for Daddy.

As he sucked and chewed his squishy teat, he saw his father in a way he never had. This giant of a man, this man he hardly knew, this man who brought him into the world with a pair of McDonald's French-fry tongs, this man who would break all the rules – let him keep his dummy, run free without a leash, make stool in his Pull-Up, or do whatever else he felt like doing – Sebastian swore in the names of Dipsy, Laa-Laa, Tinky Winky, and Po that he would stand by this man forever. Sebastian hoped Mommy would take a very long time out before coming home.

LAURA

'Can you make a mistake and miss your fate?'
—Carrie Bradshaw, *Sex and the City*

With trepidation, Laura left Elliott alone with his two children. She had promised Charles she would meet him at the Soda Shop on Chambers Street. He had something important to ask her, he had said.

Stepping into the Soda Shop was like taking a trip back in time. It was a picture-perfect soda fountain from 1950's Mayberry, USA, set in bustling downtown Manhattan. With its marble-topped wooden tables, gumball jars, giant counter, and old-fashioned malt and milkshake blenders, the place was the anti-Starbucks.

The bells on the door jangled as Laura floated inside, her blond hair bouncing and loose. She wore the same jeans and vintage Chanel navy blue coat she had on all day with Sebastian and Valentina. Her delicate features brightened upon seeing Charles. He was sitting at a table near the fireplace reading the *New Yorker*.

'Hey you,' he said, setting aside the magazine to give her a kiss. 'I took the liberty of ordering two egg creams.'

'Thanks,' Laura said. 'I've never tried one of those.' She took a big sip through the fat straw. 'Mmmm, yummy,' she said, smiling shyly at Charles. He was dressed casually in jeans, a white cotton shirt, and black Nikes. She noted how lean his body was, like a runner's. 'So, what was so important?'

Charles let out a sigh. 'It's kind of strange, so bear with me,' he said. 'I met with Violet's therapist yesterday. She's been seeing her every week since Rachel died. Dr Borowitz says that you're all Violet talks about in her sessions. She idolizes you. The way you coached her on singing for the talent show, you may as well have saved her life. You're smart, pretty, kind, trustworthy, warm – everything her mother was.'

'I'm crazy about Violet, too,' Laura said, unsure as to where this was going.

Charles dropped his golden-brown eyes. He bit his lower lip. 'Yes, but . . . are you crazy about *me*? I know it's awkward to ask so soon, but the therapist feels strongly that I shouldn't risk letting Violet fall in love with you unless the two of us have a chance for something serious. She feels it would break Violet's heart if you became part of her life and then disappeared.'

Laura wondered if he was asking the question for Violet or for himself.

287

'Not to mention mine,' he added. 'It would break my heart, too.'

Laura was speechless. She adored Violet. Every day she was growing closer to Charles. Was it love? Maybe. She wondered how Charles had become attached to her so quickly. In truth, he hardly knew her. He'd never heard her sing with the band. He hadn't met her sisters. He didn't know about the job she had taken with the kinky billionaire. Would he feel the same if she was completely transparent with him?

She gazed at Charles, who was swallowing nervously. 'What do you want me to say? That I'd like to marry you? I can't say that now. Neither can you. When you get to know me better, you might not want me.'

'I can't think of one reason why I wouldn't want you,' Charles said. 'We need time. I get that. All I'm saying is, for Violet's sake, we shouldn't pursue this unless you think that *with* time, there's a real chance for us.'

Laura wanted to tell Charles yes, of course there's a chance. But right now, her career took priority. She had put it on hold for six years. If she didn't give it everything she had now, when would she? Maintaining a serious relationship would be as consuming as caring for Sunny. What if the movie soundtrack came through? Could she do it justice if she was distracted by love? No, this was the worst possible time to make a commitment to Charles. And it would be cruel

288

to hurt Violet by starting something she couldn't finish.

She took a deep breath; then spoke softly. 'Charles, I think you are an amazing man . . .'

'I knew I shouldn't have brought this up.'

'It's good that you did. If circumstances were different, I would have welcomed the chance to get to know you and love you the way you deserve to be loved. But with the amount of attention I need to give my career right now, I can't say with confidence that things would work out for us.'

'Wait,' Charles said, taking Laura's hand. 'Maybe there's another way. Maybe you could back away from Violet for now and you and I could quietly spend time together and see where this goes . . .'

'You and Violet are a team. No, I'm going to say no. Let's leave it at that. I wouldn't want to break Violet's heart, or yours, or mine.'

Laura leaned over and kissed Charles lightly on the mouth. She left without finishing her egg cream.

Outside, Chambers Street buzzed with pedestrians. Laura turned the corner and dashed down West Broadway toward Duane Park. A hard lump formed in her throat at the thought of never seeing Charles and Violet again. Had she just made the biggest mistake of her life? But no, Charles was right. It would be unfair to lead Violet on if she wasn't prepared to deliver. After six years of being sidetracked from her dream, she couldn't afford another distraction. This was the right thing to do. So many women would adore having a man like Charles. He and Violet would be fine. It hurt now, but with time she would understand the perfection in what she had just done.

AMANDA, SERENA, AND LAURA

'Siblings are the people we practice on, the people who teach us about fairness and co-operation and kindness and caring – quite often the hard way.'

—Pamela Dugdale

'So then what happened?' Amanda asked Serena. They were holding court in a corner booth at Odeon, a neighborhood fixture on West Broadway for over thirty years. In the early days of *Saturday Night Live*, they held weekly cast parties there. For years after, the Art Deco-style restaurant was a celebrity magnet, and it still attracted its share of local luminaries. With Amanda's bright apricot hair, Laura's wild blond curls, and Serena's tight brown ponytail, they looked more like friends than sisters.

'When I told him I was leaving the kids with him, he couldn't believe it. You should have seen his face. He threatened to sue me for custody if I left them, but that's bravado,' Serena said, twisting her wedding band around her ring finger.

'Good for you for speaking your truth,' Laura said, her turquoise eyes fierce with pride. 'That's the Serena I used to know.' As she spoke, she pulled her blond mane back, arranged it into a loose knot, and clipped it up.

'But do you mean it?' Amanda asked, glancing up from her BlackBerry. 'Would you really leave him?'

Serena stroked her chin. 'I think so. He must be miserable or he wouldn't have cheated. He's barely around anyway. And let's face it, this marriage, this life I have, it brings out the worst in me.'

'That's true,' Amanda said, eying her messages. 'It does.'

'You don't have to agree with me,' Serena said, slapping her sister's arm. 'And put away your BlackBerry. That's rude.'

'Sorry,' Amanda said, switching it off. She was expecting to hear from Tabby. They were waiting for the Lassiter appraisal to come in. Hopefully, Winston would extend an offer afterward. If Amanda accepted, Ham would make the replacement copy. Amanda's face flushed at the thought of pulling a fast one on her sisters, but it couldn't be helped. I'm going straight to hell, she thought.

'. . . the thing is, I'm too much of a giver,' Serena continued. 'I always put other people's needs before mine. I never think of myself. Well, no more.'

'Do you ladies know what you want?' Their waitress, a hip black woman with dreadlocks and a nose ring, stood by the table, pad and pencil at the ready.

'My goodness,' Laura said. 'Look at your hands!'

'What?' the waitress said. 'What about my hands?'

'They're gorgeous,' Laura said, holding the waitress's hand and examining it closely. 'Your fingers are so slender and perfect. Have you ever thought about becoming a parts model?'

The waitress smiled shyly. 'You know, I have. But I didn't really have confidence in my parts.'

'Are you kidding?' Laura said. 'Your neck is like Audrey Hepburn's. You could model chokers and necklaces.'

Amanda cleared her throat. 'I'll have the tuna burger with fries, she'll have the free-range roast chicken, and she'll have the blackened salmon.' They always ordered the same thing.

'Wait,' Serena said. 'Tonight I'll have a lobster roll instead of salmon. With a small green salad on the side, no dressing, but don't let the salad touch the lobster roll or I'll send it back.'

'And three glasses of the house chardonnay,' Laura said.

'I can't believe you ordered something different to eat,' Amanda said. 'What's happening to you?'

Serena shrugged. 'I don't know. Elliott's affair woke me up. Things have to change. He's got to participate with the kids. I want a loving husband. If it's not going to be him, it'll be someone else.'

'Well done, Serena,' Laura said. 'I'm proud of you for reclaiming your power.'

'Thanks,' she said. 'My first instinct was to forgive him and stay, but then I reread one of Mom's notes and realized that clinging to a broken marriage wasn't the answer.'

'What about the kids?' Amanda asked. 'Don't they need you?'

'They need their father, too,' Serena said. 'Either Elliott will rise to the occasion or we'll find out once and for all that he's incapable of taking care of them.'

The waitress came over with their drinks. 'Your food will be up in five minutes,' she said.

'Thanks,' Laura said. 'Has anyone told you today what a good waitress you are? Well, you are terrific.' The waitress gave an appreciative giggle.

'Are you trying to date her?' Amanda asked.

'I'm being friendly,' Laura said. 'She's probably an actress or musician like me. And see what great service we're getting?'

'Still, she *is* the help,' Serena said. 'Anyway, what's the game plan?'

Laura's face took on a serious expression. 'Tomorrow, before we leave, I'm bringing you to see my soul coach, Eva. She does early-and past-life regressions using hypnosis. She's taking *you* back to that summer you and Mom spent in the Hamptons when she worked for the Lassiters,' she said, nodding toward Amanda, 'and she's taking *you* back to the time Dad took you to his studio and, well, you know what happened next.'

'Oh no. No, no, no! Count me out,' Serena said, sipping her wine. 'I hate thinking about that day.'

'You have to,' Laura said, 'for two reasons. Clues. Maybe one of you will remember something that will help us know if he's your father . . . or not. And closure. While you're under, you'll be able to say whatever ten-year-old Serena never got to say to Dad before he abandoned you. This'll be transformative,' she said, gently placing her hand over Serena's. 'It's time to put what happened behind you.'

'Seriously, don't ask me to do that,' Serena said, in a small, frightened voice.

'Hey, did I say no when you asked me to cancel my "Children who Remember Past Lives" seminar and babysit your kids today?' Laura said. 'You owe me one. It'll be healing.'

'Why not do it?' Amanda said. 'You ordered something new for dinner. This is just a bigger step outside your comfort zone.'

Serena rolled her eyes. She didn't believe in new-age stuff.

'After we see Eva, we'll pick up a car in Riverdale and go to the Hamptons,' Laura said. 'Who's gonna rent it?'

'I would, but I can't drive,' Serena said.

'Well, neither can I,' Laura said.

'Don't look at me,' Amanda said. 'My foot's in a cast. Okay, fine. I'll arrange for a car through my office *with* a driver.'

'Ask for a hybrid. We should all be trying to reduce our carbon footprint,' Serena said primly.

'I'll see what I can do,' Amanda said.

'Can't you get in trouble for that?' Laura said.

'We're not clients. Maybe we should pay for the car and driver ourselves.'

'Better yet, Serena can pay for it, because she's the heiress among us,' Amanda said.

'I'm on the verge of losing everything,' Serena said. 'Amanda, you cover it. You've got the successful career.'

'Do the words "mortgage crisis" ring a bell to you? How about you, Laura?' Amanda said. 'Didn't you interview for the private-jet flight attendant job?'

'Yep, and I got it,' Laura said, stiffening. 'My first shift starts next week, for ten days. They paid me in advance and I gave all the money to David. He's getting his pacemaker tomorrow and he has to cover three months of back rent at Golden Manor. So don't ask *me* to pay for it.'

'Why would they advance you the money?' Amanda asked. 'They don't even know if you're any good at the job.'

Laura shrugged. 'I asked and they agreed.'

'Don't you find that odd?' Serena said. 'Are you sure these people are on the up and up?'

'Of course I am . . .' Laura started. The waitress delivered the food. 'Thanks, I'm starved.'

'I had sex with Riley Trumbo last week,' Amanda announced out of the blue.

Laura squealed with delight.

Serena's mouth dropped in astonishment. 'How *could* you? He's head over heels for his wife. Don't you read Page Six?'

'They were separated at the time, and he failed to mention her,' Amanda said.

'Didn't you guys see today's *Post*?' Laura said. 'Apparently, he showed up in Italy and his wife refused to take him back. His father says he can't return to the family business either. He's screwed.'

Serena's face fell. 'Why wouldn't she take him back? They were so much in love.'

'Well,' Laura giggled, 'some floozy he was screwing sent naked pictures of herself to Sofia. They published them in the *Post*, with her head cut off and black bars over her private parts.'

Amanda perked up. 'Oh really? How was her body?'

'Nothing special, a bit lumpy,' Laura said. 'Why? It wasn't you, was it?'

'Puh-*lease*! Anyway, the point is, I needed a good ravishing and I went to see him and, well, it happened. I don't regret it. Does anyone want my French fries?'

'I do,' said Serena, grabbing a handful. 'So what excuse did the bastard give for dumping you?'

'We didn't talk about that,' Amanda said, holding a Diana-in-front-of-the-Taj-Mahal pose.

'Well, I for one think you deserve a good piece of ass,' Laura said. 'It's been way too long.'

That was true. After she and Riley had split up, Amanda went on a few dates but never connected with anyone special. Eventually, she announced her retirement from dating after a blind date excused himself to go to the bathroom and never came back. At first, she convinced herself that he'd had a heart attack, died mid-pee, and had already been rushed to the hospital (out the back door so as not to disturb the patrons) by the time she checked the John. But the next week, she'd seen him shopping at Pottery Barn with another woman.

'Now that you're back in the saddle again, Serena and I will help you meet someone else, right, Serena?'

'What about *me*?' Serena whined. 'If Elliott and I split, you'll need to help *me* meet someone.'

'Does it always have to be about you, Serena? Think of me,' Laura said, her eyes welling. 'You know that guy I was going out with, the one whose wife died? We broke up.'

'Oh spare me, you're better off,' Serena said. 'Never date a man with a dead wife. You can never compete.'

AMANDA

'To have a loving relationship with a sister is not simply to have a buddy or a confidant – it is to have a soul mate for life.'
　　　　　　　　　　　—Victoria Secunda

The next morning, Amanda sat with her sisters on the Metro North train to Riverdale, where Laura's soul coach, Eva, lived. Wearing black stretch pants and a turquoise St John Knit sweater, she tried to cover her disappointment as she read a text message. Winston had decided not to buy the Lassiter sketch. In this difficult economy, even billionaires were cutting back. She had been counting on the money from the sale to repay Richie, but without a buyer, she was stuck. Quickly, she typed a message to Nikki, her assistant, asking her to retrieve the drawing and return it to her apartment. She would have to come up with a different plan.

Laura was dressed casually in skinny gray jeans, a fitted white cotton shirt, and a ten-dollar pair of vintage Keds. 'Bad news?' she asked. 'Tell us.'

Amanda's face went red. 'Nothing important. Silly work stuff.'

'Well, you should share it,' Laura said. 'Don't you see how great it is that the three of us are finally talking and supporting one another?' Laura reached over and took Amanda's and Serena's hands, giving them both a squeeze. 'I'm so grateful to have you as my sisters.'

Serena, wearing her usual head-to-toe black, smiled shyly. 'Yeah, me too. Thanks for being there for me after Elliott screwed up, and for helping me figure out the truth about my father. I don't deserve you two.'

'What about you, Amanda?' Laura said. 'Aren't you glad we're mending fences?' Laura and Serena eyed Amanda expectantly.

Amanda managed a smile. 'Yes, of course.' She wondered if this might be a good time to admit that she had lost the four million dollars with Bernie Madoff, a loan shark was threatening her, and she desperately needed her sisters' help. She knew Laura would be sympathetic, but Serena would be furious, especially since the money technically belonged to her. No, there has to be another way, she thought.

'You know where our next trip together should be?' Serena declared. 'A colonics farm! Wouldn't that be fabulous? Juice fasts. Clean colons. Detox! I'm happy to check into it for us.'

Before anyone had a chance to say yes to Serena's enticing offer, Amanda's cell phone rang.

It was Nikki with an update on a client. '*What?*
No, we can't list the apartment until they're gone.
We have to get the hospital bed and all those
supplies out of there, repaint it, and air it out. Of
course it's tragic, but that's what it's going to take.
Tell her we'll help with the move if they need us.'

'What was that about?' Laura asked.

Amanda shook her head sadly. 'I have this family,
Bruce and Debbie Fox. They have a one year old.
Bruce is thirty-six and has pancreatic cancer.
They've spent all their money on medical bills and
now they're desperate to sell the apartment, but
the place looks and smells like death. We have to
clear it out and freshen it up or it'll never sell.'

'Thirty-six with a one year old? That breaks my
heart. Don't you feel like a vulture, selling their
home out from under them?' Laura asked.

'Unloading the apartment and relieving their
financial worries is the kindest and most helpful
thing I could do for them,' Amanda said. 'I hate
it, but it's true.'

'You should get a rabbi or shaman in to bless
the place,' Laura said. 'Or, if you want, I have an
energy healer you can use to change the vibration. Until you do that, it probably won't sell.'

'Give me the name,' Amanda said. 'We can use
all the help we can get on this one.'

'Her card's at home, but I'll give it to you when
we go back. She cleared the energy in my apartment after Mom died. I guess nobody wants to buy
a home where there was so much grief,' Laura said.

'They don't,' Amanda said. 'Apartments sell because of the three D's – death, disease, divorce, and debt.'

'That's four D's,' Serena said.

'I just added the last D because of the recession,' Amanda said. 'Behind every home sale is a story the buyer doesn't want to know.'

'And you'll never tell,' Laura said.

'You know what they say. What people don't know can't hurt them,' Serena added.

Maybe this is my chance to come clean, Amanda thought. The truth could bring us closer together. Then again, it could break us apart forever. 'So, Serena, if I knew some important information that would upset you, would you want me to keep it to myself?'

'Right now? I can't take any more bad news,' she said. 'Why? Is there something you want to tell me?'

Amanda hid her disappointment. 'No, of course not.'

'Oops, here's our stop,' Laura said. 'Don't forget your umbrellas.'

Amanda lay in a lime green La-Z-Boy recliner in the downstairs office of Eva Stein's two-family home, her crutches propped in a corner. Laura and Serena watched while sitting cross-legged on the dusty-smelling mustard shag carpet. Eva's diploma from the College of Metaphysical Studies in Clearwater, Florida hung on the fake-wood-paneled wall.

Dozens of small candles flickered in the dim basement light. Eva stood beside Amanda, taking her through a guided meditation that put her into a hypnotic state.

'Dahling, let's go back to the summer you spent in the Hamptons with your mother,' she said in her thick New York accent. 'Can you remember a special day from that time? Look around and when you're ready, describe where you are.' Eva's reptilian skin gave her the look of a woman in her sixties, but her multi-colored orange spiky hair was that of someone much younger (in spirit, perhaps). An oversized gold Indian tunic worn over butterscotch leggings camouflaged her ample derriere by making her blend into the carpet.

Amanda's eyelids fluttered. She took a minute or so to absorb the scenery. Finally she whispered. 'I'm in the studio, hiding under a bench, behind some boxes, watching Mr Lassiter work. He's handsome, like a movie star, tall, white hair, he's wearing heavy glasses with black frames. I'm being real quiet so I don't get in trouble for spying. It smells like oil paint and turpentine. Mr Lassiter is standing in front of a giant canvas, making a woman's body out of beige and pink. Her breasts are hu-uuge like water balloons. Her eyes are scary. He's painting the face really fast and it's all distorted. I could paint as good as that if I wanted to.'

'Can you describe the room, dear?'

'It's big, white, lots of glass,' she said. 'Off to

the side, there are brushes, scrapers, knives, bottles of oil, paints, cans of turpentine. It's organized and clean, like a science lab but for art supplies. There are bowls of every size filled with paint on a big tabletop that's on one of those wide file cabinets like architects use. In the corner are two giant wooden rocking chairs. I want to rock in them, but I'm not supposed to be here. This is the most boring vacation ever. Mom said we could go to the beach after lunch. Can you hear my stomach rumbling?'

'Is there anyone in the studio with you two, dahling?' Eva said. 'A model, maybe?'

You could see Amanda's eyeballs darting around under her lids. She shook her head no. Then a slow smile spread across her face. 'Wait, Mom just came in. She's carrying a tray. There's milk and a sandwich. Now she's closing the door behind her. She put the tray on the table by the window and she's going over to Mr Lassiter. His arm is on her shoulder. He's all excited, talking to her about his picture. He says she inspired the woman he's painting. Oh my God, if you could see it, you'd know what an insult that is. Mom is much prettier than that gross lady he's making. Now he's washing his hands. I guess he's going to take a break and eat. My foot is asleep.' Amanda started moving her foot in circles. Her eyelids fluttered furiously. 'Stop. No. Why is he kissing Mom?' Amanda squeezed her eyes shut. 'I don't want to watch this.'

'Ask if he gave her the tongue,' Serena said. She was pulling fuzz out of the carpet and rolling it into tight little balls.

'Shhhh,' Eva cautioned.

'What kind of kiss is it?' Eva said.

Amanda shook her head vigorously. She was getting more upset. Her hands were covering her eyes.

'You can walk out if you like, honey,' Eva said. 'They won't notice.'

Amanda nodded. 'Yes, I'm in front of the house now. Nobody saw me leave.'

'Good,' Eva said. 'Relax, dahling. Have a look around. Tell us what you see?'

'There's a pool behind the house. It's dark blue, not very big. Mrs Lassiter is in the kitchen. I can see her through the window looking through a pile of envelopes. Kate is on the side of the house with the hose. She's wearing cutoffs and a red bikini top. They're giving the dogs a bath,' she said.

'Who's Kate?' Eva said.

A fat, white Persian cat glided into the room and leapt onto the La-Z-Boy, then curled up next to Amanda's feet. 'Mr Lassiter's daughter. She's older than me.'

'Is anyone with her, love?'

'Kimberly. Kimberly Fitch. No, Flick,' she said. 'We call her Kimba. She has a car. Sometimes she drives Kate where she needs to go. She runs errands, too.'

'How many dogs are there?' Eva said.

'Two. Golden retrievers. Ginger and Fred. They're all sandy from the beach. That's why they need a bath.'

'What are you going to do now, dahling?' Eva said. 'Are you going to help wash the dogs?'

'No,' Amanda said. 'I'm knocking on the studio door. Mom is too slow.'

'What do you want from her?' Eva said.

'She promised to take me swimming,' Amanda said. 'Okay, she's coming. I'm going to wait on the porch.'

'Good,' Eva said. 'Dahling, when you get to the porch, I want you to find the most comfortable chair to sit in and then I'm going to bring you back.'

Amanda nodded. In her mind, she snuggled into a chaise longue.

'I'm going to slowly count backwards from ten. Ten, nine, eight, start moving your legs slowly. Seven, six, five, now squeeze your hands together. Four, three, two, you can open your eyes anytime you're ready after I say one. You will feel awake and refreshed. Ready. One.'

Amanda began to blink and then opened her eyes. 'That was weird,' she said, taking in her two sisters and Eva, all of whom were staring at her expectantly. 'I felt like I was back at the Lassiter house thirty years ago. I could see every detail. I hadn't thought about that place in years.'

'Do you remember what you saw?' Laura asked, standing up, then helping Serena to her feet.

'Most of it, I think.'

'Did you *really* see Mom kiss Mr Lassiter, or did you imagine it?' Serena said.

'I saw it,' Amanda said. 'I'd completely forgotten about that. But how could I forget something so important?'

'Aha! So they did have an affair,' Serena declared.

'Was it a romantic kiss or a platonic kiss?' Laura asked.

'It was, gosh, an awfully friendly kiss, but not friendly enough to convince me they were lovers.'

'You mentioned someone named Kimberly Flick,' Laura said.

'The assistant,' Amanda said. 'She drove Kate around, ran errands for the family, babysat me a few times. We should try to find her. She might know if there was anything between Mom and Lassiter.'

'Dahling,' Eva said, taking Amanda's hand in hers, 'I'm getting some deeply disturbing vibrations from your aura. Why don't you come in next week and let me do an energy healing?'

Amanda thought she was doing a pretty good job hiding her troubles. She was shocked that her aura would betray her.

'You should do it,' Laura said. 'Eva's the best.'

'I'll let you know after we get back from the Hamptons,' Amanda said. But inside, she knew it would take more than a healing from Eva to cure what was ailing her.

'Come, I'm going to put on some green tea,' Eva said. 'Would you all like a cup? Then, we'll come back and it'll be Serena's turn in the hot seat.'

SERENA

'You keep your past by having sisters. As you get older, they're the only ones who don't get bored if you talk about your memories.'
—Deborah Moggach

'Now we're going to go back to that last trip you took to the Hamptons with your father. Are you ready?' Eva asked.

'Yes,' Serena said with some hesitation. She was reclining in the green La-Z-Boy, her feet propped up, her eyes closed. Eva had put her under and she'd already recounted the story of her fifth birthday party at the Museum of Natural History in excruciating detail right down to the disappointment she felt when her grandmother gave her a wooden coloring box as a gift instead of the Talky Tabitha doll she wanted.

'So, dahling, how are you and your father traveling? By bus?' Eva asked. She was sitting on a metal folding chair beside the recliner. Laura and Amanda were cross-legged on the floor.

Serena shook her head. 'Car.'

'Ah, and are you going straight to Mr Lassiter's studio?'

'No,' Serena said. 'We're stopping for lunch in Southampton, at the Driver's Seat.'

'Is Mr Lassiter with you, dahling?'

Serena shook her head. 'Only me and Dad.'

Amanda's cell phone rang, interrupting Eva's concentration. She fumbled to see who was calling and then turned it off. 'Sorry,' she whispered.

Eva gave her the evil eye before turning back to Serena. 'Can you describe what's around you?'

'We're outside,' Serena said. 'On the patio. Having burgers. There's a bee that keeps buzzing around and I'm afraid of getting stung. If I'm allergic I could die.' Serena swatted her hand in the air.

'What else is happening, dahling?' Eva said.

'The bee flew away. Now I'm reciting all the states in alphabetical order. My daddy likes smart girls, not dumb girls.'

Eva cocked her head. 'How do you know that, dear?'

'He tells me all the time,' Serena said brightly. Suddenly, her face dropped.

'What's the matter?' Eva said.

'I have to hush my face. Daddy's too tired to listen to my yammering. He says it's hard work to take care of a family. I offered to help.'

'What did he say to that?' Eva said.

'He said no,' Serena said, her lower lip curling, her head hanging down. 'If I don't watch my P's and Q's, he's going to sell me to the gypsies.

310

He doesn't mean that. Daddy, can I have a French fry? It's for my doll, not me.' Serena reached over to take an imaginary French fry. She gasped, slapping her mouth with her hand. 'Oh, no, I'm sorry, it was an accident.'

'What happened, dear?' Eva said.

'I spilled my milkshake. Daddy's face is all red and he smacked my back. We're leaving right now.'

'Where are you going?'

'We stopped at the fudge store. Yay! I'm getting Dots and red licorice.' Joy filled Serena's face.

'You're certainly happy, sweetie.'

'Oh yes,' Serena said excitedly. 'Daddy loves me. He bought me candy. We're in the car now.'

'Is he taking you to the beach?'

'No, we're going down a long gravel driveway. There's a big white house ahead and some buildings off to the side. Two old red bicycles are leaning against the wall. We're pulling over to where the bikes are.'

'So, dahling, are you going inside with your dad or staying in the car?' Eva said.

Serena hesitated. 'Going inside. Oh, wow. It's an artist's studio. There are giant canvases everywhere.' Serena held her nose. 'It smells like yuck. A man with white hair and blue eyes is sitting in a rocking chair staring at a painting. He has a butter knife in one hand and a clear brown drink in the other. A cigar is burning in the ashtray on the table next to him. His clothes are rumply like he slept in them. He just saw me and Dad.'

'Is he surprised to see you?' Eva asked.

Serena shook her head. 'Not at all.'

'Did you get his name, dear?'

Serena thought for a moment. 'Mr Lassiter. He asked what I like to do in school. I won't answer because it's none of his beeswax.'

'Are he and your dad talking?'

Serena wrinkled her forehead. After a pause, she said, 'Daddy says *he* should take me. Why would he say that? Mr Lassiter says, no. Daddy says Mr Lassiter can't run out on his responsibilities. Now they're talking about money.'

'Is Mr Lassiter giving your dad money?'

'No, he says he's barely getting by himself. Daddy doesn't believe him. They're fighting.' Serena curled in a fetal position on the La-Z-Boy and covered her ears.

'Dahling, what are they saying?' Eva said.

'They're yelling. I'm scared,' Serena said, squeezing her eyes shut. 'Daddy, Daddy, don't go. What am I supposed to do? Daddy left. Mr Lassiter is running out. Oh, they're coming back. Now Mr Lassiter's rolling up a big painting, lots of colors, very bright. It's on material, you know? He's wrapping it with brown paper and telling Daddy to take it and not to bother him ever again.'

Eva lowered her voice to almost a whisper. 'What are you doing now, honey?'

Serena's eyes danced beneath her lids. 'We're in the car. Daddy won't talk. He's upset. I think at me. He's driving *really* fast. "Daddy, slow down.

You're scaring me." Now he's driving faster. We're not wearing seat belts. I want him to stop.' Serena was quaking all over and tears were coursing down her cheeks. 'We're speeding on a winding road. "Get to the other side! Daddy, please."' Serena covered her eyes. Her body was trembling. Then, she peeked and let out a huge sigh of relief. 'Daddy pulled over. He's quiet. Now he's starting the car. We're driving again, but slow. Whew! It's going to be okay.'

'Shhhh,' Eva said. 'Relax. Take a deep breath. You'll be fine. Where are you stopping?'

'The beach,' Serena said, unfolding from her fetal position, relaxing into the chair. 'It's beautiful. White sand, big mansions, little fences. The sky is hazy. There are sailboats out. We bought a chest of ice and some Cokes from the concession stand.'

'Is anyone else there?' Eva said.

Serena moved her head as though looking around, but her eyes were shut. 'Not many people. It's afternoon. There's a man throwing a stick into the ocean and a big black dog that goes in after it. He keeps coming out and shaking off the water.'

'Does your dad take you into the ocean?'

Serena shook her head. 'He put down the ice-chest filled with Cokes and tied a long rope from my ankle to the handle. I'm not allowed to go any farther than the end of the rope while he takes his walk. He says Mom would kill him if, God forbid, I got swallowed up by the ocean.'

'Now what's happening, sweetie?'

'Daddy gave me his watch to hold. It's in my pocket. I'm asking to go with him, but he says no, I should dig a hole to China. So I'm digging and digging and waiting and waiting.'

'Are you scared?' Eva said.

Serena nodded solemnly. 'It's getting dark. I don't know what to do. There are houses on the beach with lights on, but I can't get to them because I'm not allowed to go farther than the rope. If I spill the melted ice out I could drag the chest with me. But Daddy'll hit me if I disobey. I'm scared. What if a hobo comes? Or a madman? I'll climb in my hole to be safe. It's getting cold. Wow, that was a falling star.'

'Dahling, are you hungry?'

Serena shook her head. 'I'm eating my candy and drinking Coke. There are crawly things in the hole that keep waking me up. Crabs or bugs. Now I'm standing on the beach and watching the waves crashing in the moonlight. I'm looking for Daddy but I don't see him. I think I'll go back in my hole because it's warmer there. No wind. Something cold is waking me up. Oh my goodness, the water came all the way to my hole. I'm getting out. I don't know what happened to Daddy.' Serena screwed up her face like she was about to cry, but she blinked hard to stave off the tears.

'There's a man in blue shorts jogging by with his cocker spaniel. I'm calling him over.' Serena's eyelids fluttered as she saw the scene in her mind. 'I'm telling him what happened and he's untying my rope and taking me to the parking lot. There's a pay phone. He's calling the police.'

Tears spilled down Serena's cheeks. 'Something terrible happened to Daddy or he would of come back for me. Now all these people are at the beach searching. They're walking up and down and there are boats in the water and helicopters flying around. Oh my gosh! Mommy's here and so are my sisters.' Serena hugged her arms around her body and sobbed. 'A-Amanda is h-holding me and we're both c-crying.'

'What do you think happened to your father, honey?'

'I think he drowned himself. Someone said they found his clothes by the beach a mile or so down.'

'Serena, dahling, I want you to go back to that moment when your daddy told you he was going to take a walk and you should stay put. Is there anything you want to say to him before he goes, knowing what you know now?'

Serena burst into tears. Her face became red and splotchy and soon she was gulping back sobs. 'I . . . I'm sorry, Daddy. I should have been a better girl. Did I ruin everything? I didn't mean to. Please don't leave me. I promise to be good. Don't go. Stay with me. I love you so much.'

Eva handed Serena a tissue. She wiped her eyes and blew her nose.

'Now, Serena, imagine that your adult self is

standing on the beach a few yards from where your daddy left you. This is you, a grown woman with two children of your own. Is there anything you want to tell your father before he takes off?'

Serena straightened herself out in the recliner and immediately gave off a more mature demeanor. 'Wait, I need a cigarette.'

'No,' Eva said, 'no smoking when you're in an altered state. Come on, you can do this.'

Serena nodded, then took a deep breath. 'I want to say . . . I want to say that I'm sorry for your pain. I realize now that you never let yourself love me because you didn't think I was yours. You loved Amanda and Laura, but never me. You weren't even nice to me, which was unfair. I was an innocent little girl and you deprived me of a father. I had leukemia and I needed you and you weren't there. I got married and you weren't there to walk me down the aisle. You never got to play with your grandchildren. Now that I have kids, I can't fathom how you left me alone on the beach all night. What were you thinking? I could have been washed out to sea, or kidnapped, or, God forbid, murdered! And you let me dig a hole and sleep in it. Do you know how many children die each year from sandhole collapses? I'm furious at you for killing yourself knowing you had three beautiful girls at home. But you know what? I'm letting you go. All my life, I've been a victim of your suicide. That stops now. I'm forgiving you. Please dear God, release me from that terrible night.'

316

'Good,' Eva said. '*Good!* Now, dahling, I want you to sit or lie down in the sand and relax while I bring you back.'

'Wait,' Amanda whispered. 'Ask her what happened to the painting. Did she leave it at the beach?'

Eva asked her. Serena considered the question for a few moments. 'Ahh! Daddy took it with him when he went for his walk.'

'Shit,' Amanda said in a huff. 'Do you know what that would be worth today? Millions!'

'Anything else?' Eva said.

Amanda shook her head.

'Now, Serena, I'm going to count backwards from ten. Ten, nine, eight, start moving your feet and legs slowly. Seven, six, five, now squeeze your hands together, stretch your arms. Four, three, two, you can open your eyes anytime you're ready after I say one. You will feel awake and refreshed. Ready. One.'

Serena slowly opened her eyes. The room came into focus along with her sisters and Eva, who were staring at her. She felt a sense of tranquility that was unfamiliar to her and wondered if now, after speaking her truth to her father, she might be able to let him go. She hoped so. 'Maybe there really is something to this new-age stuff,' she said.

'Whoa! Be careful,' Laura said, standing up, taking her sister's hand. 'Next you'll be getting your chart done.'

Serena smiled. 'Seriously. I feel so much lighter.'

'That was the idea,' Eva said. 'Do you remember what happened?'

'Yes,' Serena said. She closed her eyes and reviewed what she had seen under hypnosis. 'When we left Lassiter's studio and Dad was driving so crazy, he was trying to kill himself with me in the car.'

'No, he wasn't,' Laura said. 'He was just upset and out of control.'

'No, you're wrong,' Serena said. 'He was doing it on purpose. I can see him now. How could I have forgotten that? Why did he stop himself?'

Amanda situated herself on the arm of the La-Z-Boy. 'He came to his senses. I'm sure he realized he didn't want to hurt you or anyone else.'

'This explains a lot,' Laura said.

'Now we understand why you're so . . . sensitive,' Amanda added.

'Not that you should use this as an excuse for your foibles, because you shouldn't,' Laura said earnestly. 'You said what you had to say to Dad and now you have to let it go.'

'She's right,' Amanda said, her eyes full of compassion. 'You have your own family now and they love you. We all love you.'

'I got it,' Serena said, sitting up straight. 'No child should go through what I did. It's screwed me up long enough. Maybe I need professional help.'

Laura chucked Serena's shoulder. 'We've been saying that for years.'

'What happened after Dad walked off with the painting? Did you ever see it again?' Amanda asked.

Serena shook her head. 'I can only guess that he destroyed it when he killed himself. He was angry at Lassiter.'

'Maybe he left it on the beach and some people found it and took it home,' Laura said.

'Or the tide came and swept it away,' Amanda added.

'One thing's for sure, dahling. *You'll* never see it again.'

SEBASTIAN

'It was nice growing up with someone like you, someone to lean on, someone to count on, someone to tell on!'

—Anonymous

Sebastian skipped into the kitchen and stopped as if someone had hit the freeze button. What in the name of Dipsy, Laa-Laa, Tinky Winky, and Po was going on? Mommy hadn't been gone a day and things were already changing around the house, starting with the fact that it was filthy. After Daddy cooked breakfast, dishes were everywhere. When they went out, he didn't put Sebastian on his leash. He was letting Sebastian wear Pull-Ups whenever he wanted, not just at night.

On the one hand, life with Daddy brought Sebastian back to a simpler time when he could urinate at will. On the other hand, it wasn't right. One of Valentina's stooly diapers sat on the table where Daddy left it. Even Sebastian knew that stool should never be near food. It was teeming with bacteria. All the oatmeal his sister had spit

320

on the floor had dried and would have to be scraped off. Valentina was in the pantry coloring all over her brand-new junior microscope with a purple marker. Daddy hadn't even wiped off her nose crust. The bathroom was flooded after last night's bath. Mold was just a matter of time.

Daddy was wearing his red plaid pajamas even though he'd been awake for hours. He was reading Mommy's instruction manual about what to do. He pulled out an envelope that contained today's schedule clipped to Sebastian's headshot. 'You have a publicity still?' Daddy said.

Sebastian smiled blankly because he didn't know what that was.

'Sebastian,' he said, 'you've got an audition for the children's chorus at the Metropolitan Opera in an hour and a half. Have you got something to sing?'

Sebastian shook his head. Not that he remembered.

'Your mother didn't teach you something?' Elliott said. He seemed angry. Sebastian hoped not at him.

'I can sing "Happy Birthday,"' he said. 'Happy birthday to you, happy birthday to you, happy birthday dear Tina, happy birthday to you! Yay me!' He jumped up and down and clapped for his great singing.

'No, no, no. That won't get you into an opera company,' Elliott said. 'But what do I know about opera? Not a damn thing.'

321

'Daddy, you said damn,' Sebastian said.

'Do you have a problem with that?'

'No,' Sebastian said.

'Wait, I know. Here's what you can sing.' Elliott belted in his best opera voice, 'Figaro. Figaro. FigaroFigaroFigaaa-roh! Now you try it.'

'Figaro. Figaro. FigaroFigaroFigaaa-roh!' Sebastian sang in his soprano lilt.

'You've got to sing bass, like a man,' Elliott said. 'Try it this way.' He lowered his chin to his neck and sang his figaros.

Sebastian followed his father's lead. This time his figaros were a bit lower, but still pretty high.

'Good,' Elliott said. 'Keep practicing.'

'Figaro. Figaro. FigaroFigaroFigaaa-roh!' Sebastian sang.

Elliott's phone rang and he took it in his office, talking as Sebastian sang his audition song in the background. Soon, Sebastian and Valentina were laughing uncontrollably.

'Okay, guys, let's get dressed,' Elliott said after hanging up. He stopped short after spotting the purple Sharpie scribbles covering Sebastian's face, neck, arms, hands, and clothes. 'Oh my God, Valentina, Sebastian, no!' he shouted. 'Sebastian, what did you do? You're a mess. You need a bath.'

'Valentina did it,' Sebastian shouted.

'Valentina!' Elliott accused.

Valentina screwed up her face and exploded in tears as the two men in her life turned on her. Elliott picked her up and comforted her.

Sebastian stripped off his clothes and made for the tub. 'Daddy, I'm helping,' Sebastian said with pride.

Elliott checked his watch. 'We don't have time,' he said. 'Just get some clean clothes on and you'll have to go purple. Hurry.'

Sebastian shrugged and ran downstairs to change. Usually Mommy laid out his clothes, but he was sure he could do it himself. All he needed was somebody to believe in him, and that somebody was Daddy.

Most of Sebastian's clothes were too high to reach. Luckily there were some drawers on the floor that he could manage. Let's see, socks, underwear, T-shirt, oops, no pants. He tried a different drawer. It contained all his Halloween costumes since he was born. Hmm, he thought, everyone wears costumes at the opera. I'll go as a pirate. He slipped on the pirate pants and jacket and checked himself out in the mirror. Something was wrong. Of course! The wig. Once he had his messy black hair and hat on, he was ready to face the world. 'Arrrg, Matey!' he said into the mirror, trying to sound menacing. The purple marks weren't right, so he went to the bathroom, turned on warm water, and soaped up his purple hands. Closing his eyes, he washed his face and dried it. Unfortunately, the clean lines Valentina had made were now blurry and his skin had taken on a violet hue. The fluffy white towel was lavender. All Sebastian could think was, God forbid Mommy ever finds out about this.

When Daddy saw him, he laughed so hard he barked. Sebastian didn't see what was funny. He thought he looked rather dangerous, except for the purple. Damn to Valentina and her damn damn marker! Daddy took a picture of him with his cell phone. 'Your mother has got to see this,' he said. 'She'll have a conniption.' He sent her the photo along with a text message, 'Off to the opera audition.'

The line of mothers with children waiting to try out at the Metropolitan Opera snaked all the way out to the street. This was going to be like that show Sebastian had watched at Aunt Laura's, *American Idol.* He wondered if Simon the mean judge would be inside. Probably, he thought. When he glanced around, he realized that he was the only one in costume with a scribbled-up face. That was good. He would stand out in the best way possible. While Daddy talked to his office on the BlackBerry, Sebastian reached into the bag behind Valentina's stroller and pulled out his headshot. He took Daddy's blue felt-tip pen and drew all over his face in the photo. This way, they'll remember I'm the kid with the marked-up head. I'm a smart boy to think of that, he decided. Every few minutes, he turned around, pulled his pacifier out of his pants, and took a few sucks.

After an hour, they were inside the opera house, almost to the audition room. Things were moving quickly. 'How old are you?' said a pudgy little boy with curly brown hair and lots of freckles who was standing in front of them.

'Four,' Sebastian said.

'You has to be five to be in the opera,' the boy said.

'Then why are you here?' Sebastian asked. He didn't look a day over four and a half.

'My birthday's next month,' he explained. 'Mommy's going to tell them I'm five.' The boy narrowed his eyes suspiciously. 'Say, are you a real pirate?'

Sebastian shrugged. He didn't want to discuss his personal business with this stranger.

When they got to the front of the line, Sebastian watched the curly-brown-haired boy audition. Inside, there was a man at the piano and an old lady with red puffy hair. 'Can you sing "Happy Birthday?"' she asked him.

'Daddy, you have to sing "Happy Birthday." *What am I going to do*?' Sebastian said urgently.

'You know that song,' Elliott said.

'But I practiced "Figaro,"' he said. 'I want to sing "Figaro." I know the words.'

'Sing whatever the lady tells you to sing,' Elliott said.

The boy in front of them finished his performance and took a bow.

'His voice is quite good,' the redheaded lady said. 'But he's fat.' She ogled the child's mother. 'You're fat, too. Put him on a diet and bring him back when he's lost ten pounds. Next.'

Elliott gently pushed Sebastian forward toward the scary lady.

'What in God's name are you wearing?' she asked.

'It's my Pirates of pins-and-ants costume,' Sebastian said. That's what Mommy called it when she bought it for him last Halloween. She let him wear it when they went to that Giblet and Sullivan festival. Serena believed in turning every occasion into a learning opportunity.

'And your face is purple why?' she said.

'Herpes,' he stated.

'Herpes?' she said. 'Are you being fresh?'

'No, he doesn't have herpes,' Elliott said. He was standing in the back of the room with Valentina, who was in her stroller. 'His sister used him as a canvas this morning.'

The red-haired lady laughed, but not in an amused way. 'Go ahead. Can you sing "Happy Birthday?"'

Sebastian lowered his chin to his neck and belted, 'Figaro. Figaro. FigaroFigaroFigaaa-roh!'

'Excuse me, but what did I ask you to sing?' the lady asked.

'"Happy Birthday,"' Sebastian said.

'So sing "Happy Birthday,"' she barked.

Sebastian sang as ordered. He thought he sounded pretty good.

'How old are you?' she asked.

'Five,' Sebastian said. He cast a glance toward Daddy to be sure he'd go along with his story, but his father didn't seem to realize that he hadn't told the truth.

'I'll take him,' the redhead said, 'but it probably won't work out. I have children in the chorus who can *really* sing. This one, he's merely average. Do you mind if he plays a girl? Can I put him in a dress?'

'I guess so,' Elliott said.

'I mind,' Sebastian said. It was one thing to put on a dress when he and Pepe-from-next-door played wedding, but quite another to wear one onstage. He preferred that his public think of him as a boyie boy, not a girlie boy.

'No back-talk, young sir,' she said. 'Bring him to class tomorrow. Here's the schedule. No pirate costume this time. No purple face. Next.'

Sebastian was pleased at the news. It wasn't that he wanted to do this and he definitely didn't want to wear a dress. He would have preferred to stay home and play. But his parents seemed to agree that he should star in the opera, so star in the opera he would. He liked making his parents happy – especially his mother, who made a point of wanting to be made happy by him. Hopefully if she was happy with the job Daddy was doing with him, she wouldn't come home anytime soon.

'C'mon, Sport,' his father said. 'Let's text your mother the good news. One more accomplishment she can put on her, ah, your résumé.

AMANDA, SERENA, AND LAURA

'The best thing about having a sister was that I always had a friend.'

—Cali Rae Turner

'My God,' Laura said, rubbing her face against the seats and breathing in the rich smell, 'this is like butter. I could live here.'

Amanda held out her cell phone camera and took a picture of Laura and Serena in their first-class ride. Dimitri, the uniformed Czech chauffeur, was driving them to East Hampton in the midnight-blue Rolls-Royce that Amanda's firm kept on retainer to transport their most valuable clients. Business had been so slow that no one had used it in weeks. Amanda's boss told her to go ahead and take it since they had to pay for it anyway.

Each of the Hamptons attracts its own breed of second-, third-and fourth-home-owners – the old money of Southampton, new money of Bridgehampton, the low-key money of Sag

Harbor, the far-from-the-maddening-crowd money of Amagansett, the we-don't-need-the-right-address money of Wainscott, the poor-relations money of the Springs, the bridge-and-tunnel-crowd money of Westhampton, and the media-mogul money of East Hampton. They were on their way to the Bullocks' home in East Hampton, a vast Gatsbyesque mansion set behind perfectly manicured hedges and rolling green lawns. The Bullocks' weren't media moguls themselves, but they liked being surrounded by them.

'This is a beautiful drive,' Laura said, admiring the lush green landscape along the way.

'I abhor nature,' Serena said.

'That's just weird,' Laura said. 'Amanda, tell us about this house you borrowed.'

'It belongs to Tabby and Winston Bullock,' Amanda said. 'I failed to get them into the co-op of their dreams and they were really good about it. Now they're looking at condos and brownstones. They only use the East Hampton house in August.'

'Is it super-fancy?' Laura asked.

'That's what I've heard,' Amanda said. 'Plus, if you happen to meet a guy who's into S&M while we're here, invite him over. There's a dungeon. They install one in all their homes.'

Laura clapped her hands with excitement. 'It belongs to the couple you told us about, the sado-masochists who live on Mayor Bloomberg's block. How cute is that?'

Amanda's cell phone rang. As she spoke, she broke into a huge smile. 'That's fantastic! You made the right decision. I'll have my assistant drop a contract off today.' She hung up and began texting furiously.

'Good news?' Laura asked.

'Fantastic!' Amanda said, clacking away on her BlackBerry. 'Remember Mrs Winkleman, the one whose husband wanted her to choose between a one-bedroom at the Plaza and a villa in Tuscany? I pitched him on investing in both. Great real estate fortunes are made by buying at the bottom, not the top. He agreed. I just made a seven million dollar sale at the Plaza!'

'Whoo-hoo! Go Amanda, it's your birthday,' Laura sang. 'Dimitri, can you turn the music up back here?'

'Hey, check this out,' Serena said. She opened the DNA kit and held up a vial containing a couple of dark-brown hairs pulled from the roots. 'They'll get my DNA from this; I'm subject A.' Then she picked up an empty vial. 'We'll put Kate's in here, subject B. Then we mail it to the company in this pouch and wait for the answer.'

Amanda finished her texting and then pulled a sealed tan envelope out of her purse for her sisters to see. 'Now *you* check *this* out.'

'What is it?' Serena said, moving to the beat of the Donna Summer song that was on the radio.

'It's Mom's will and the variation Sam Hermann wrote,' Amanda said. 'I told him what we agreed to and asked him to draw it up. If Lassiter's *not* your father, you're going to sign it and share the estate equally. If he is, Laura and I will tear it up. You keep everything Mom gave you.'

'That's fair,' Serena said. 'But we won't know anything while we're here. It takes a week to get the DNA back.'

'Aww, they get it so much faster on *Law and Order*,' Amanda said.

'That's because they have the lab at police headquarters,' Serena said. 'We're sending this to a remote facility.'

Laura sat back and grinned. To her, happiness was getting along with her sisters. Watching Serena dance in her seat, she remembered visiting her in the hospital one morning when Serena was feeling particularly blue. Laura found her sitting up in bed, her skin practically translucent, her long brown wig sitting crooked on her head, writing out her last will and testament. 'Are you crazy?' Laura said. Even then, before reading *The Secret*, she understood that Serena was inviting death's powerful energy to come calling. Laura put on an Aretha Franklin CD and talked her sister out of bed, dragging her IV pole with bags of medicine dangling from it behind her. 'Let's dance,' Laura said. Serena gaped at her, but she started to move and soon she was getting down. Later, out of breath, laughing, her wig even more askew, Serena made Laura promise to come dance with her more often. After that, Laura stopped by every afternoon with different music. The two of them boogied even when Serena didn't have the energy to stand on her own. That's what sisters do, Laura thought, when all seems lost we make each other dance.

Now that they were adults, Laura wished with all her heart for the idyllic relationship some of the most famous sisters had, like Jennifer and Lynda Lopez, Paris and Nicky Hilton, or those Dixie Chicks. Wait, are they sisters? She wasn't sure. But they did support each other when everyone banned their music after the blond one said she was ashamed that the president was from Texas. That's the bond she yearned for with Serena and Amanda, the kind where they could always speak their truth, where they would stand by each other no matter what terrible mistake any of them made.

Laura thought about asking her sisters' advice on how she might get out of her commitment to the kinky billionaire. But then she'd have to speak her truth – that she'd agreed to let him watch her have sex with that creepy old pilot. No, she was too ashamed. Maybe someday she could be that open with her sisters, but not now. Amanda might understand, but Serena, who didn't have a kinky bone in her body, would judge her harshly.

'Laura, aren't you listening? How are we going to get our hands on Kate's DNA?' Serena said. 'I mean, what should our game plan be?'

'Oh, sorry,' Laura said. 'Um, I guess first we need to find her.'

'According to *New York* magazine, she has a

home in Sag Harbor,' Serena said. 'I tried calling directory assistance, but the number's unlisted.'

'Sag Harbor's small,' Laura said. 'We'll ask around. The locals must know who she is, right? My goodness, the traffic's a mess.' The Long Island Expressway had come to a complete halt.

Amanda rolled her eyes. 'Remind me not to take you two on my next investigation. You can't drive. You don't have a plan on how to get our subject's DNA. You don't even know her address.'

'Well, isn't that part of what we're investigating?' Laura said. 'Where she lives?'

'Hey, I know other stuff about her,' Serena said. 'Her birthday is next week. Her mother never married Lassiter. She went to boarding school in Switzerland. See, I have a whole file on her,' she said, pulling a folder out of her bag and holding it up for inspection.

'None of which helps us find her,' Amanda said. She pulled out her BlackBerry and clicked away. 'Do I have to take care of everything in this family?'

'What are you doing?' Serena asked.

'I happen to know that she recently bought an apartment in Soho. Why, you ask? Because one of my esteemed colleagues sold it to her. *He'll* have her Hamptons address.'

'Show-off,' Serena muttered.

'Excuse me, but if she has an apartment in Soho, then why are we going to the Hamptons?' Laura asked. 'She probably lives less than a mile from us in the city.'

Serena peered out the window in silence.

'Obviously Serena didn't think this little expedition through,' Amanda said.

'If *you* knew she had an apartment so close to us, why didn't *you* speak up?' Serena asked.

'Shhh,' Amanda said, 'I'm texting. Look, traffic's moving again.'

'Serena,' Laura said, 'assuming we find Kate in Sag Harbor, what do you think we should do? Knock on her door and introduce ourselves? Or retrieve her DNA surreptitiously?'

'Surreptitiously,' Serena said. 'If we introduce ourselves first and she tells us to go to hell, it'll be harder to sneak it off her person.'

'Bingo, here's her address in Sag Harbor,' Amanda said, squinting at her BlackBerry.

'Then how do you propose we get her DNA?' Laura said. 'If she doesn't give it willingly, I mean.'

'Hello! My husband directs for *Law and Order*,' Serena said. 'We do it through old-fashioned police work, which I know a lot about, having watched every episode of that show.'

'That makes sense,' Laura said. 'We'll tail her until she's somewhere we can get our hands on her DNA, like a restaurant or hair salon.'

'Exactly,' Serena said. 'And Laura, you can charm your way into getting the waiter or stylist to give us her hair or a used glass.'

'Good thing we have Laura 'you should be a parts model' Moon with us,' Amanda said.

'Yeah, Laura can talk anyone into anything,' Serena said.

'Oh, you guys,' Laura said modestly, her face bright pink. Her cell phone rang and she flipped it open to answer. 'He is? That's fantastic. Give him my love. Tell him I'll visit in a few days.' She snapped the phone closed. 'Alright! David came through his surgery like a champ. He's already home and asked for a steak dinner, not that he's getting one. I'm so relieved.'

'Does that mean he'll be able to play with the band again?' Amanda asked.

'The doctor says he can start practicing in a few days. Hopefully that means he can audition, because Joey Martin and his crew are coming to hear us play next week.'

'That's so exciting,' Amanda said. 'Haven't I always said your music career would be huge?'

Laura rolled her eyes. 'I'll be sure to thank you in my Grammy speech.'

Serena's cell phone rang, indicating a text message. 'Oh My God.' She said. 'What is he thinking?'

'What?' Amanda said.

'Check out this picture.' She passed around the cell phone. '*That's* how Elliott took Sebastian to audition at the Met. In a pirate costume with . . . *what's* all over his face?'

'Scribble marks?' Laura said.

'Give me the phone,' Serena said. 'I'm going to kill him.'

Amanda put her hand over Serena's and stopped her. 'Don't. You said you wanted to let him sink or swim, so let him go. We have a job to do here. Elliott has a job to do there.'

'Right,' Serena said. 'Let him go.' Her brow was scrunched with worry.

'At least he remembered to *take* Sebastian to the audition,' Amanda said.

'I hope he doesn't forget the child psychologist tomorrow,' Serena said. 'See how Sebastian mutilated his face. It's an obvious cry for help.'

'I wouldn't call it . . . never mind. Can we get back to business?' Laura asked. 'I propose we start by having Serena introduce herself. If she sees how badly you want to know the truth, maybe she'll feel the same way and toss a few hairs your way. Sometimes the best route is the most direct.'

'Good idea,' Amanda said. 'If she resists, then Laura and I will go undercover and get the sample without her cooperation.'

'Holy shit!' Serena said.

'What? What?' Laura asked.

She held up her cell phone. 'I just got another text from Elliott. Sebastian was picked for the children's chorus at the Met,' Serena said. 'Do you know what this means?'

'That he'll learn to sing in Italian, Russian, and French before he learns to read?' Laura guessed.

'No, he already reads at third-grade level. It means I'll be schlepping him to the Met for vocal classes and rehearsals twice a week on top of everything else, and waiting for him 'til midnight while he performs in the opera,' she said. 'I'm not sure this is good at all.'

'But what about your résumé, I mean, his?' Laura asked. 'Isn't that why you wanted him to audition?'

'That was before I remembered what it was like to have a day off,' Serena said. 'This is fun. I need to lessen my load with the kids, not add to it. God forbid this separation from Elliott becomes permanent.'

'God forbid,' Amanda said.

'Yes, God forbid,' Laura added.

ELLIOTT

'I cannot think of any need in childhood as strong as the need for a father's protection.'
—Sigmund Freud

fter the audition, Elliott took the children to the park. As he watched Sebastian drive his truck in the sandbox and Valentina stuff handfuls of sand into her violin, he felt a dozen nanny eyes boring into him. He wondered if it was because Sebastian was in his pirate costume. Lesson learned. Don't let Sebastian choose his own outfits in the future. Elliott was wearing a blue Nike sweatsuit, which he only still had because he'd taken it with him to the Caribbean. Maybe later he'd take the kids shopping with him for new clothes. Glancing back at the nannies, Elliott smiled at them. A tall, muscular, light-skinned African American man in his late thirties or early forties acknowledged him. He was dressed casually, in jeans, New Balance running shoes and a Yankees jersey. Elliott wondered if he was a father or a manny. Everyone here seemed to be a caregiver.

As he retrieved Valentina and shook the sand out of her violin, he took in the scene, a world unto itself, so far from his own. Children played with such purpose, he noticed – chasing each other, climbing the monkey bars, flying high and low on the seesaw, swishing down the slide. It reminded him of the set at work: each person doing a job like bees in a hive, a ballet of gaffers, dolly grips, prop masters, set dressers, all working toward the common goal. On the playground, at least at this age, there was no common goal other than to have fun, he supposed. He tried to remember the last time he'd had fun, but he couldn't.

'Come here, my little grapefruit-head,' Elliott said to Valentina. He sat her up on the bench and put her bottle in her hands. He was amazed that she could feed herself at such a young age. Sebastian couldn't, or maybe he just hadn't been around to see it.

'Excuse me. May I ask what you're doing with Serena Skank's children?'

Elliott glanced up and saw the man who had nodded at him before. Of course, he thought, everyone here must know each other. 'I'm their father. Elliott.' He put out a hand.

'Charles Shine,' the man said, shaking hands with Elliott. 'I had no idea they had a father. May I sit?'

Elliott winced. He was right. He'd never taken the kids to the park. 'Be my guest,' he said, gesturing to the bench. 'But what about your kid? Don't you have to keep an eye on him?'

He laughed. 'We regulars watch out for each other's children. While I'm talking to you, someone will keep track of my daughter, Violet.'

'So they know my children?' Elliott said.

'Not well,' he said, 'your wife doesn't let any of us near your two. I'm sorry to have to tell you that she's not terribly popular here.'

'Why not?'

'She's always watching the nannies and reporting them to their employers for mistreating their kids. That's how we met. Last year, she demanded to know who I worked for so she could turn me in for letting Violet climb the big-kid jungle gym when she wasn't yet as tall as the clown's nose,' Charles said.

Elliott rolled his eyes. 'That's Serena. But to be fair, Violet had no business on the big jungle gym if she didn't meet the Parks and Recreation's height requirements.'

Charles stared at him for a moment to see if he was serious, then he made an 'aha' smile. 'Oh, that was a joke.'

Elliott smiled.

'Where is your wife?' Charles asked.

'She's on a trip with her sisters,' Elliott said. 'I took some time off work to watch the kids.'

'Really,' Charles said. 'What did you take time off from?'

'I'm a director for *Law and Order*,' he said. It always

stroked his ego to say those words. He wondered if Charles had read about him in the *Post* and *News*. If he had, he hoped he didn't realize that he was *that* director from the headlines.

'Daddy, look at me!' Sebastian shouted. He dumped a shovelful of sand on his head.

'That's my boy,' he said, grinning.

A little girl ran up to Charles. She had coffee-colored skin like her father's, dark curly hair, and big green eyes. She was wearing jeans and a mud-stained Barbie sweatshirt. Violet seemed older than Sebastian, about seven or eight. 'Daddy, Apple has a new snake. His name is Slick. Do you want to see him?'

'That's okay,' Charles said. 'I'm not fond of reptiles. Violet, meet Mr Skank. Can you say hello?'

'That's a funny name,' Violet said. 'Did kids tease you growing up? Like, did they say your mommy was a crank, and your daddy drank, and you stank?'

Elliott laughed. 'And I lived in a fish tank. Yes, all the time.'

'Bye,' Violet called, already halfway across the playground.

'Are you a stay-at-home dad?' Elliott asked.

Charles nodded. 'This being New York, you're going to ask me what my wife does, what big job she must have that allows me to be Mr Mom. Rachel was an analyst for Cantor Fitzgerald.'

'Oh, I see,' Elliott said, glancing toward the site of the old World Trade Center.

'No, it's not that. A year and a half ago, she was hit by a taxi while on business in London. Looked the wrong way while crossing a street and stepped right in front of the car.'

'That's awful,' Elliott said. 'Violet must really miss her.'

Charles gave a sad smile. 'We both do. At least she had six and a half years with her daughter. Violet rocked her world.'

'I'm sorry,' Elliott said. Charles seemed to be doing a great job under the circumstances. What if he had to raise Sebastian and Valentina alone? he thought. Could he do it? For a moment, he felt deep gratitude toward Serena for being such a dedicated mother. Some might call her obsessed, but at least she was there. Sebastian waved at him. Then he ate a mouthful of sand. What was happening to that boy? Ever since Serena left, Sebastian was like a drunken sailor on shore leave.

'Don't you think you should burp her?' Charles said.

'Oh, right,' Elliott said. Valentina had sucked down most of the bottle without a burp. He put her to his shoulder and started to gently pat her back. Finally she let out a long, loud belch that sounded like a tuba note.

Elliott glanced up, amused to see a cluster of nannies pretending not to watch them. 'Say,' he said, 'Would you and Violet like to join us for an early dinner? I'd love to pick your brain about nutrition. My daughter is used to freshly prepared foods, but I fed her Gerber's yesterday and she gobbled it up. I'm suspicious they put harmful additives in it to make kids love it so much. What do you think?' Elliott couldn't believe those words had come out of his mouth.

AMANDA, SERENA, AND LAURA

'One of the best things about being an adult is the realization that you can share with your sister, and still have plenty for yourself.'
—Betsy Cohen

Amanda's eyes grew wide as she took in the Bullocks' cottage on Lily Pond Lane in East Hampton. It consisted of a sprawling twenty-thousand-square-foot gray-shingle-style mansion, along with a quaint six-thousand-square-foot guest house. It was as if the big house had given birth to the little one, a wee version of itself. From the front were stunning views of Georgica Pond, and in the back, a sweeping panorama of the Atlantic Ocean. All this, plus manicured gardens, pool, tennis court, trampoline, and gymnasium made the home feel more like a luxury spa than a private residence. The gymnasium housed an indoor pool, sauna, steam room, full gym, racquetball court, climbing wall, and billiards and ping-pong tables. They kept peacocks and bees on the property, albeit not together.

Amanda called her sisters to the grand entry hall, where the house staff – maid, butler, cook, and handyman – had gathered to greet them. Mattie, the maid, was a bulgy-eyed Jamaican woman wearing a white uniform. Dee Dee, the cook, looked like a butch Lesbian with her mohawk mullet. Then there was Albert, the thousand-year-old English butler whose face resembled a Sharpei's, and Jed, the boyish handyman, who resembled God's younger brother in a blue-eyed, floppy, sun-kissed hair sort of way. He wore Levis and a black T-shirt that showed off his ripped upper body to its greatest advantage.

'We want to see the dungeon,' Serena announced, all excited.

'Seree-*na*!' Amanda said. 'I'm sure Jed doesn't want to take us.' Amanda immediately glommed onto Jed, whom she found super-attractive for someone so . . . handy. She was in a fantastic mood. The news that the Winklemans were buying that seven million dollar unit at the Plaza could not have come at a better time. This would give her enough to pay off Richie and much of her mortgage. Now she could relax and enjoy being with her sisters, maybe even have a little fling with the handyman.

'Oh no,' Jed said, eagerly. 'I'll show you. Mr Bullock isn't shy about the dungeon. He always includes it when he gives tours of the house. Says he likes to shock his neighbors. In fact, Alfred, why don't you come along?' He motioned with his head toward the butler. 'Alfred keeps the room stocked and cleaned, the machines working, all that.'

Laura giggled. 'You don't mind being the dungeon-master?'

'A butler *liiiives* to please his master and mistress,' Alfred said without a trace of irony.

They made their way toward the master suite, where the dungeon was located. As they wandered through the house, Amanda noticed that everything was in various shades of eggshell and yellow cream, except for the wooden plank espresso floor. The house was full of large-paned windows dressed in sheer gauzy curtains that billowed in the ocean breeze. On the walls hung oversized impressionistic paintings of beaches throughout the area, some with enormous gray-and-brown shingled homes, some with empty dunes that seemed to stretch for miles.

'If you'll follow me,' Jed said, opening the door to the master suite, which was in its own wing far from the rest of the house.

This is lovely, Amanda thought. The walls were painted a soft shade of champagne. Everything was inviting and warm, from the antique lace coverlet on the king-sized bed to the stuffed sofas and plump chairs in the sitting area around the fireplace. The bedroom palette was mostly beige, with accents of powder blue and sand. Handcuffs were discreetly tucked behind the bars of the brass headboard. The carpet was hand-done needle-point.

'How did you break your foot?' Jed asked Amanda.

'It was a silly fall down some steps,' she said, waving it off as though it was nothing, which indeed it was.

'I've never seen such a pretty shade of red hair,' Jed said. 'I'm surprised we've never met. Are you close friends with the Bullocks?'

'Thanks,' Amanda said, her face blushing. 'I work for the Bullocks like you. I'm their real estate broker.'

Jed's eyes crinkled as he grinned. 'What is it Bob Dylan said? You gotta serve somebody.'

'It may be the devil or it may be the lord, but you gotta serve somebody,' Amanda said.

'You like Dylan?' Jed said eagerly.

'*Love* him,' Amanda said.

'You know, I play guitar,' Jed said. 'Maybe later you'll let me sing some of his songs for you.'

Amanda blushed, then smiled shyly. 'I'd like that very much.' Her organs went all aflutter. She wondered if he was as attracted to her as she was to him. Not that he was husband material, because he wasn't. Power realtors like Amanda never hitched their stars to Hamptons handymen. That would be like dating a doorman or marrying a maître d'. It simply wasn't done. Still, he *was* awfully sexy.

'The dungeon's through there,' Jed said, pointing to a door.

'I'm so excited,' Laura said. 'I've never seen an actual S&M torture chamber.'

'Oh, I have,' Serena said. 'Elliott directed a *Law and Order* episode where the victim was strapped by the bad guy into his own equipment. Right as the murderer struck the fatal blow, the victim managed to handcuff the guy to his own wrist. So the victim died and the murderer was stuck without the key. No one knew he was in there so he starved to death. It was gruesome.'

'You are such a know-it-all,' Laura teased.

'It's a gift,' Serena giggled.

Jed cracked one door enough to reveal a closet the size of Amanda's master bedroom. 'I'll let Alfred show you the rest. This bondage stuff makes me jittery as a long-tailed cat in a room full of rocking chairs. Amanda, if you need anything at all, here's my number,' he said, handing her a card.

As soon as he left, Laura gently teased her. 'The handyman gave you his ca-ard, the handyman gave you his ca-ard,' she sang.

'Shhhh,' Amanda said, swatting her. 'He'll hear us.'

Alfred led the way to a second door that opened into the bathing and dressing areas. Inside Mrs Bullock's section was an enormous French-provincial armoire. He opened its doors and pushed a wood panel beneath the bottom drawer, which sprang open to reveal a hidden space. Inside was a set of keys, some modern, some antique. Alfred used one of the newer keys to unlock the door to an enormous closet wallpapered with black leather and stocked with a collection of whips, paddles, chains, wrist and ankle cuffs, leather hoods and muzzles, ropes, electrical tape, leashes, blindfolds, and dildos.

Amanda couldn't believe how well displayed everything was. It was like Barney's for S&M paraphernalia. At the far end of the closet, an open archway revealed another room, this one lined in stone like the Tower of London. It was filled with racks, swings, stockades, bondage chairs, cages, spanking benches, and suspension bars, a veritable Disneyland for sadomasochists.

'The walls are soundproofed with cork,' Alfred said. 'You can scream all you want in the dungeon suite, but no one can hear. If you want to try any of this out, you'll need these keys to get you in and out of the various locks and cuffs. Shall I demonstrate how to use the equipment?' Alfred said. He was perfectly serious, as if he were offering to teach them how to work the Nautilus machines at Barton's Gym.

Amanda giggled. No, she did not want this ancient English butler to show her how the fucking-swing worked. 'That's okay, Alfred. We can imagine.' As a real estate agent, she had uncovered many client secrets just by poking around their homes. Luckily, she would never reveal what she knew to anyone outside her immediate family and closest colleagues at work. Even though the law didn't recognize it, the real estate broker-client privilege was sacred to Amanda.

'I'll leave you to explore,' Alfred said. 'The keys

are in the armoire should you wish to experiment.' He bowed and made his exit.

Amanda excused herself and went to the bathroom. Her stomach had been bothering her all day. When she returned, her sisters were still browsing in the outer room.

'Serena, Laura, come check this out,' Amanda called, leading them to the dungeon. 'It's too bad they don't have diagrams on each machine showing you how to use it.'

'Whoa!' Serena said, when she saw the setup. She fiddled with a leather whip, then moseyed about, examining each piece of equipment. 'This is kinky stuff. You know, I'm kind of turned on by it all.'

'You?' Laura said. 'I don't believe it.'

Serena giggled, then snapped the whip across Amanda's butt.

'Owww!' Amanda said. 'Don't. Pain holds no appeal for me.'

'I can see we'll have to work on loosening you up,' said Laura, swaying back and forth in the fucking-swing. 'What do you think about Jed? You two seemed into each other.'

'You mean, what do I think of him for *me*?' Amanda said.

'Of course I mean for *you*,' Laura said. 'Wouldn't he be fun to hang out with?'

Amanda blushed. 'Well, sure, but he's kind of young. Anyway, a guy that cute, here in the Hamptons, I'm sure he has his pick of women.'

'You're not so bad,' Serena said. 'I can see how you'd catch his eye. Just try not to be so . . . you.'

'What's that supposed to mean?' Amanda said.

'You know, lighten up,' Serena said. 'Relax.'

'*You're* telling *me* to lighten up?' Amanda laughed.

'Maybe later we'll invite him for a drink,' Laura said. 'Then the two of you can go off alone so he can serenade you.'

'You cougar, you!' Serena teased.

Amanda's face turned as red as her hair.

Serena checked her watch. 'It's after four. Don't you think we should try to track down Kate Lassiter's house and see if she's in town?'

'Yes, yes, definitely,' Amanda said, happy for the diversion.

Laura jumped out of the swing and pointed toward the door. 'Let the games begin.'

SERENA

*'Sisters may share the same mother and father
but appear to come from different families.'*
—Anonymous

Dimitri pulled the Rolls around and the
girls piled in. It would take at least thirty
minutes to drive to Sag Harbor in the
afternoon traffic, and then they would need time
to locate Kate's street and house. Serena hoped
they would find it before dark. At this point, they
just wanted to get the lay of the land.

'Serena, what are you doing with those?'
Amanda asked, pulling a blindfold and handcuffs
out of her gold bag that lay on the floor.

'I brought them in case,' she said.

'In case what? In case you have to restrain her
after you meet her?' Amanda said.

'Serena, this girl could be your sister. Cuffing
her is no way to start a healthy relationship,' Laura
said.

'I know,' Serena said. 'They were in case of emergency.' What kind of emergency, Serena had no

idea. She was such a wreck thinking about meeting Kate that her synapses were misfiring.

Amanda shook her head. 'You're crazy.'

'I'm nervous,' Serena said, pressing the button to lower the privacy window. 'Dimitri, are we very close?'

'It should be the next block, according to the GPS,' he said. Dimitri turned down the next street and drove slowly. 'The addresses are hard to read.' Finally, he pulled over in front of a large Federal-style house, one of those 1700s renovated clapboards so common in this old whaling village. 'Here it is,' he said, turning off the motor.

'I don't believe it,' Serena said, staring motionless at the house. 'Inside is the proof I need to show you who my father was.'

'How about proving it to yourself first?' Amanda asked.

'I *know* the answer,' Serena said.

'Why don't you ring the doorbell and introduce yourself?' Laura said. 'If she shoos you away, then *we'll* get the DNA, won't we, Amanda?'

'Sure we will,' Amanda said. She hoped it wouldn't come to that. In her experience, being on crutches took the fun out of DNA capers.

Serena stared at the house. The sun was setting, the lights were on inside, and you could see someone moving around in the kitchen. She gulped. 'Do you really think I should?'

Both sisters nodded.

'What if she wants nothing to do with me?' Serena said.

'Surely you're used to that by now,' Amanda said.

'When you get to the door, explain the situation,' Laura said.

'Try to act like a normal person. You don't want her to think you've stalked her.'

'Even though you have,' Amanda said.

'Amanda, I could use your support instead of your sarcasm, okay?' Serena said. She picked up her bag and opened the door.

'Serena,' Amanda said, grabbing her purse strap. 'I'm behind you; I am. But leave the cuffs and blindfold in the car.'

'Right,' Serena said, tossing them to her sister. She took a deep breath and started toward the house.

ELLIOTT

'All work and no play makes Jack a dull boy.'
—Proverb

'So, Sebastian, tell me about yourself? Whom do you favor?' Charles asked. 'Are you a Barney man or a Wiggles man? Or maybe you like Diego or Dora?' Charles, Elliott and the kids had stopped off at Food Emporium on the way home and picked up ingredients for burgers and a healthy, colorful salad. They had just finished eating and were starting the dishes.

'Are Diego and Dora TV stars? I'm not allowed to watch TV,' Sebastian said.

'You're not?' Violet said. 'Is your mommy a witch?'

'Violet!' Charles said, popping a slice of avocado into his mouth before tossing what was left of the salad. 'That's not nice.'

'I'm just saying . . . witches don't believe in TV. Fiona Finklestein's mom doesn't let her watch TV and everyone says she's a witch.'

'Mommy doesn't let you watch *any* television, Sport?' Elliott said.

355

'No, sometimes we exercise to my Wiggles workout video and Barney Does Mat Pilates tape.'

'You didn't know this?' Charles said.

'I haven't been an attentive father,' Elliott said, his face red. 'That's one reason Serena left me with the kids this week, to teach me a lesson.'

'Mommy teaches me lessons, too,' Sebastian said. 'Now I'm taking singing lessons so I can be in the opera, right, Daddy?'

'Right,' he said. 'In fact, your first one is tomorrow. Wait, I'd better check your schedule.' Elliott went over to the magnetic calendar that was stuck to the fridge to see if they had anything else on the agenda.

'You're a busy boy,' Charles said. 'Do you like taking classes?'

Sebastian shook his head. 'I hate them.' He reached into his Pull-Up to retrieve his dummy and stuck it in his mouth.

'You don't think you should wash that?' Charles said.

'Uh-uh, penis germs are healthy, like soy and tofu,' Sebastian declared.

'Gross,' Violet said. 'You may as well eat boogers.'

'Boogers are protein,' Sebastian said. 'If you were lost in the jungle, boogers could save your life.'

Violet was intrigued. 'Really? I have a year's supply under my desk.'

'Sebastian, you had a Fun with Math class this afternoon and we missed it,' Elliott called from the kitchen.

'Yippee,' Sebastian said, doing his wiggle-worm dance.

Elliott's cellphone rang. It was one of his producers who had been bothering him about commissioning a script based on the Sandy Lane attack. 'Caimin, I told you before, this is my personal tragedy,' Elliott said. 'It's screwed up my marriage. Don't make it fodder for the show.'

'Daddy,' Sebastian said, sticking his face in front of Elliot's.

'No, she's still gone, but I can't get into it right now,' Elliott said. 'Please, there are two kids involved.'

'Daddy,' Sebastian said, pulling at his father's shirt.

'Not now,' Elliott whispered, before resuming his conversation.

'I know, *ripped from the headlines*. That's what we do. Tell you what, next time someone tries to murder *you*, we'll rip that story right off.'

'But Daddy, this is *really* important,' Sebastian begged.

'One second, Caimin. What *is* it?' Elliott said, his face reddening.

'Where's my inventors from the Nineteenth Century T-shirt? I want to show Violet.'

'Sebastian, don't interrupt for things like that,' Elliott said, shooing him off. He turned back to the phone and sighed. He knew there was nothing he could do to stop them, so he had to try to control the story as best he could. 'Okay, fine.'

He checked tomorrow's itinerary for the kids. Jesus Christ, Serena keeps them busy. 'Tell the writer to call me in the morning before ten. Otherwise I'm tied up. Yes, the intruders actually *did* tie me up during the attack. Are you happy? I'll see you Monday.'

When Elliott hung up, he remembered that he needed to find a babysitter in case Serena wasn't back by Monday. Maybe he could bring the kids to work and leave them in his trailer with an assistant. He was starting to enjoy their company.

He heard Valentina stirring. They had left her asleep in her stroller. 'Sorry about that,' Elliott told Charles. 'It was my office.' He undid the safety straps holding his daughter in and picked her up. Dirty diaper, he realized. 'Excuse me while I clean her up.'

'I'll do it if you want to finish the dishes,' Charles said.

'No, I'm fine,' Elliott said. 'She's so sweet and playful when I'm diapering her.'

Elliott changed Valentina and then put her in the swing, which he recently discovered she loved, and turned it on. She broke into a wide irresistible smile and babbled with delight. Watching her, he thought, life doesn't get any better than this. Sebastian was on the floor with Violet, showing her a T-shirt with some obscure inventors on the front. 'Sebastian, why don't you and Violet go downstairs and play?' Elliott suggested.

'You mean in my *room*?' Sebastian said, as though Elliott had suggested he go play in traffic.

'Yeah, sure,' he said.

'But I'm not allowed.'

Elliott slapped himself on the forehead. Right, he thought. Serena kept the kids' rooms dark and cool, a sanctuary for restoration. She didn't believe in mixing play and sleep. It was something she read in the science section of the *Times*.

'It's okay, Sport,' Elliott said. 'For today, you can play in your room.'

'Let's play school,' Violet said. 'I'll be the teacher and you be the naughty pupil.'

'Yippee!' Sebastian raced downstairs with Violet on his heels.

Charles came back to the kitchen holding a family wedding portrait he'd taken off the wall. 'Excuse me, but is this woman Laura Moon?' he asked, a confused expression on his face.

Elliott glanced over at it. 'Yes, that's Laura. She's Serena's sister. Why?'

'Whoa!' Charles said. 'Laura Moon is Serena Skank's sister? I never would have guessed.'

Elliott chuckled. 'Well, they are pretty different. Do you know Laura?'

Charles set the picture down. 'Yes, I do.' He reached behind his neck and removed a silver chain that had two halves of a single heart hanging on it. He handed the necklace to Elliott. 'Do me a favor, would you? Next time you see her, would you give her this for me?'

'Sure,' Elliott said, puzzled. 'What is it?'

'She'll understand,' Charles said.

Elliott shrugged. 'Beer?' He served two cold Heinekens in bottles.

'So, did your wife leave you because you got caught with that other woman in the Caribbean?' Charles asked.

Elliott winced. 'You knew that was me?'

Charles nodded. 'It was all over the papers and the talk of the playground. I can understand why she bolted. It would be humiliating to face the park-bench gossips – the nannies during the week, the parents on weekends. They're ruthless.'

'I feel terrible about what I did,' Elliott said. 'You have to understand, and I'm not making excuses, but people don't have affairs if their relationship is solid. Ours isn't.'

'That sounds like an excuse to me. But knowing your wife as little as I do, it can't be easy being married to her,' Charles conceded. 'No offense.'

'None taken,' Elliott muttered. 'She changed after we had kids. I hardly know the woman she's become, much less love her. She must find it just as hard to love me. I haven't been around for her or the kids. It's a mess.'

Valentina started to whimper. Her swing was slowing down. Elliott gave her a push.

'Take my advice, do whatever you can to make it work,' Charles said. 'You've got two great kids. They need a father *and* a mother. My wife would have given anything to watch her daughter grow up.

You've been given a gift with those two. Can you see that?'

'I do,' Elliott said. 'But with the children comes a crazy wife.'

'You must have loved her once,' Charles said.

'Oh, sure I did,' Elliott said. He paused. It was good to have someone to talk to. 'Say, thanks for the company. I'm surprised you're being so friendly. You read the newspapers. I'm a schmuck.'

Charles burst into a smile. 'Yeah, you seem like one.'

Elliott laughed. Then his face turned sober. 'How could I have spent so much time away? Sebastian and Valentina are amazing kids and I hardly know them. Now I can see why Serena's a little crazy. It's fucking hard to take care of children all day. I had no idea.'

'When she comes back, tell her that,' Charles said.

Elliott nodded. 'I'm going to be around more for her. I will.' His eyes welled and he blinked rapidly.

Charles met Elliott's eyes. 'You'll work this out,' he said. Then he reached over and embraced Elliott with a bear hug, giving him several pats on the back the way guys do when they embrace but want to make it clear to everyone involved that they're straight.

Elliott was grateful for the gesture. Ever since he'd come home, there hadn't been a kind word from anyone except his colleagues at work, and they only wanted his story. He craved a caring expression or healing touch from somebody – anybody, really.

'Daddy,' Sebastian said. 'Come watch us play school.' He sounded a bit shy, like he wasn't sure if he should interrupt his father or not.

Elliott withdrew from Charles's hug. 'Sure, Sport, in a minute.'

Charles stood and checked his watch. 'Actually, I'm afraid we'd better get going. Violet has home-work to do.'

'Violet!' Sebastian screamed at the top of his lungs. 'Time for you to go ho-ome.'

'Thanks for helping with the burgers,' Elliott said. 'In all the years we've lived in Tribeca, I haven't made one friend in the neighborhood.'

'You've got to get out more, pal!'

Violet came bounding up the stairs and Elliott escorted their guests to the front door. 'It was great spending time with you. We'll see you at the park. You like the Yankees, Charles? Maybe we can go sometime.'

'I'd like that,' Charles said, shaking Elliott's hand.

When he got back to the kitchen, Sebastian was standing in front of the refrigerator pushing the water dispenser button and watching liquid over-flow onto the floor. 'What are you doing?' Elliott said.

'A physics experiment,' Sebastian explained.

Elliott steered Sebastian away from the fridge

and the mess. Then he grabbed a kitchen towel and cleaned up the floor. 'He was a nice guy, don't you think?'

'He has the same color skin as Miss Carol,' Sebastian said.

'Miss who?' Elliott asked.

'Da-ad! Miss Carol,' Sebastian said. 'My teacher.'

There's so much I don't know about your life, Elliott thought. Where have I been?

SERENA

'Sisterhood is probably the most competitive relationship within the family, but once sisters are grown, it becomes the strongest relationship.'

—Margaret Mead

Serena took a last look at her sisters before starting the long walk from the curb to the front door of Kate Lassiter's house. She glanced around Kate's property. For someone with such a distinguished pedigree, her home was awfully unassuming, Serena thought. If I were Daniel Lassiter's daughter, his legitimate recognized daughter, I'd have a mansion filled with his paintings. Peeking through the picture window to the side of the front door, she could see the living room and, past that, the kitchen. A blond woman stood at the sink washing dishes, her back to Serena. The air smelled of freshly mowed grass. This is it, she thought, feeling her stomach flip. It's what I've been waiting for all my life – to find out if Kate Lassiter is my sister.

Then Serena realized that, no, that was not what she had been waiting for all her life. She already had two sisters. It was hard enough to maintain a relationship with them. They fought constantly. There were grudges, jealousies, painful memories, resentments – all the emotions that came with being a sister. As it was, the sisters she had didn't understand or appreciate her most of the time. What did she need with another sister who probably wouldn't get her either, a sister who had oodles of money and still chose to live in a tiny unassuming bungalow? What would they have in common? Obviously nothing. No, she did not want another sister in her life. All she wanted was to know who her father was. If she could find this out without meeting Kate, that would be preferable. This must be what it was like to give up a child for adoption, she thought. You're better off never seeing it so you don't risk bonding. That's it, she decided. I'm going back to the car. Serena felt a tap on her shoulder.

'Can I help you?'

'Hhhhhh!' Serena's heart danced in her chest. Turning, she saw a tall, slim gray-haired man in his mid-fifties or so wearing jeans, cowboy boots, and a blue sweater. 'You scared me half to death!' she said.

'Sorry,' he said. 'What can I do for you? And for your friends in the Rolls-Royce.'

Oh dear, she thought. We've been made. That's never good when it happens on *Law and Order*, not that it happened often because the cops are too smart on that show. Think fast. Think fast. 'Is this Kate Lassiter's house?' Oh, damn, that wasn't what I meant.

'Do you have business with her?' he asked.

'Uhm, yes,' Serena said. 'But it's private.'

'Well, then I suggest you write her a letter since you obviously have her address,' he said. 'Excuse me.' He butted in front of Serena and let himself in the front door.

'Wait,' she cried. 'I need to see her.'

The man opened the door a crack. 'What's this about? Are you a friend? Someone she knows?'

'No,' Serena said. 'Actually, you see, well, there's a chance, a very *good* chance, we share the same father.' Serena kicked herself inside. She shouldn't have revealed her status as possible sister. Too late.

He rolled his eyes. 'Oh, you're one of those,' he said. 'If *that's* your business, I suggest you contact a lawyer.' He closed the door like he meant it. That was followed by the click of several locks engaging and the sound of a steel chain going on.

'What happened?' Amanda asked.

'Dimitri, drive,' Serena urged. 'It didn't go well. I talked to a man who basically told me to go jump in a lake when he heard why I was there. Plus, he saw the Rolls and knows we're together. We can't let Kate see you in this car.'

'Who *was* he?' Laura asked. 'What right did he have to keep you from your maybe-sister?'

Serena shrugged. 'Someone in her life, obviously.

366

It sounds like I'm not the first person claiming to be Lassiter's child. He told me to call a lawyer.'

'Well, at least you tried,' Amanda said, her face pale. 'Laura and I will get her DNA. Dimitri, is there a gas station between here and our house? I need to use the restroom.'

'Are you okay?' Serena asked.

'I don't know. My stomach's been funny all afternoon. I've had diarrhea, but I'll live,' Amanda said.

'Electrolytes,' Serena said. 'You need to replace those with a sports drink and you'll feel better.' Serena's cell phone rang. 'Sorry, it's Sebastian.' She had programmed her cell phone number into the speed dial at home so Sebastian could call her anytime. She flipped her phone open and talked with him quietly. Suddenly, she got louder. 'What? WHAT?!'

'What is it?' Laura asked.

'Sebastian just caught Elliott with his arms around another woman,' Serena said.

ELLIOTT

'Never feel remorse for what you have thought about your wife; she has thought much worse things about you.'
—Jean Rostand

Sebastian brought the phone to Elliott after he finished talking with his mother. 'Mommy wants you.'

Elliott was pleased that Serena had asked for him. One day of watching the kids all by himself had shown him how difficult her job was. He planned to tell Serena this, to acknowledge the hard work she had put in and thank her. That's a step in the right direction, he thought.

'So, Sebastian tells me he saw you kissing another woman,' Serena said. 'I'm gone one day and already you bring one of your girlfriends into the house.'

'What?' Elliott said. 'What are you talking about?'

'What am I talking about? Children don't lie, Elliott,' she said. 'Sebastian told me that when he came to find you, you were having a hug. Who was it, Elliott? That actress you took to the Caribbean?'

'Oh, no,' Elliott laughed. 'It wasn't a woman. It was a man.'

'It was a man?' Serena said.

'Violet's father. He offered me a friendly hug, that's all.'

'A friendly hug, that's all?' Serena said.

'He felt sorry for me because I was attacked in the Caribbean,' he explained.

'He felt sorry for you because you were attacked in the Caribbean?'

'That's right,' Elliott said. 'What Sebastian saw was an *innocent* hug. A *man* hug.'

'A man hug? I don't believe you. If it had been a man, Sebastian would have said.'

'It was, I swear,' Elliott said. 'You can ask Charles when you get back. Taking care of the kids is hard work. I invited him over so I'd have someone to talk to.'

'Whatever,' Serena said. 'I'd better go.'

Elliott leaned against the wall in Sebastian's room. He was sitting on the floor, trying to hold Valentina in his lap while she squirmed and wriggled. Pulling out his cell phone, he saw that he had missed eleven calls, all from his office. While he listened to his messages, Sebastian prepared to jump from the top bunk into the inflatable ball pit he had dragged into his room. 'Wait,' Elliott yelled. 'There aren't enough balls to jump. Here, climb in.' He set Valentina inside so she could play with her big brother.

What a mess this room had become. He had never seen Sebastian's space strewn with toys before. He started to put them away but then realized that cleaning up the room while kids were playing would be like sweeping the porch in the middle of a sandstorm. He was feeling hungry again and wondered what he could fix. Then he remembered the Gray's Papaya down the street. 'Do you like hotdogs?' he asked Sebastian.

Sebastian stopped bopping Valentina on the head with balls long enough to explain that Mommy only lets him eat soy dogs. 'But if it makes you happy, Daddy, we can eat vile pig dogs.'

Elliott smiled lovingly at his son. He wondered why he told Serena he was having a hug, but decided not to ask. Why make a big deal about it?

'Daddy, I have a surprise for you,' Sebstian said. He had climbed out of the pit. Valentina was completely submerged in balls and emitting squeals of delight. 'Come here.'

Elliott followed his son to his bed.

'Close your eyes.'

Elliott hid his eyes with his hands.

'Now open them.'

Elliott did as told. There, on the floor by Sebastian's bed was a pile of cell phones, iPhones, Black-Berries, Palms, Trios, Sidekicks – every electronic

communication device on the market was represented in his collection.

'These are for you, Daddy,' Sebastian said
proudly. 'Now we can talk to each other all the
time when you're gone. And you can talk to
Mommy whenever you want.'

'Where did you get these?' Elliott asked.

'I found them,' Sebastian said, 'in ladies' purses,
on tables, in pockets.'

Elliott sat on the bed and put Sebastian on his
lap. 'Son, that's stealing. You can't take things that
don't belong to you. It's against the law.'

Sebastian's eyes widened. 'Am I going to jail?
Like public-school children?'

'What are you talking about?' Elliott said.

'Mommy said public school children go to jail.
It makes me sad.'

'She was joking,' Elliott said.

'But it's not funny,' Sebastian said with a serious
face.

'I know,' Elliott said. 'The point is you have to
promise never to take anything that doesn't belong
to you again, okay?'

Sebastian's eyes welled and his lower lip trem-
bled. He reached under his bed and pulled out a
plastic Duane Reade bag. 'Here Daddy. I stealed
something else.'

Elliott peeked inside. It was filled with twelve-
packs of condoms, all the same brand. 'Where did
you get *these*?'

'At the drug store. See the mommy and daddy

371

on the picture,' he said. 'They're kissing.' He gazed at his father expectantly.

'So?' Elliott said.

'They're happy,' Sebastian explained. 'You and Mommy can use these and be happy, too.'

Elliott sighed. If only it were that simple.

AMANDA

'Two scorpions living in the same hole will get along better than two sisters living in the same house.'

—Arabian proverb

O n the way to dinner that night, Amanda called and invited Jed to join them. Laura insisted after Amanda reminded her that they had a tentative date for him to play guitar and sing Bob Dylan songs. He said he would be delighted. 'Remember, this is a practice date,' Amanda told her sisters. 'I could never have a serious relationship with a guy like Jed.'

'Why not?' Laura said. 'Too young? Too cute? Too nice?'

'No, too outside my social circle,' Amanda said under her breath. 'No one would use me as a broker if I married a handyman. People in Manhattan are so shallow.'

'Then have fun with him. Nothing serious,' Laura said. 'And make sure to drive home with *him* instead of us.'

'Isn't that too forward?' Amanda said. 'Won't he know I like him then?'

'Aha! So you *do* find him attractive?' Laura said. 'Even though he's a mere handyman?'

Amanda rolled her eyes. 'Of course *I* do. I'm as down-to-earth as they come. It's my clients who are judgmental.'

Laura squeezed Amanda's hand. 'Would you shut up and enjoy?'

'You know what?' Amanda said. 'I will. I'm in a great mood tonight.' It's amazing what selling a seven million dollar apartment does for my confidence, she thought.

Dimitri dropped the girls off at the American Hotel and drove off to find a more casual diner for himself.

Amanda felt a bittersweet affection for the American Hotel. She had enjoyed many a memorable meal there with Riley Trumbo and his privileged posse. The hotel had always been the grande dame of Main Street in Sag Harbor. Built in the 1800s, the Victorian landmark harkened back to the town's whaling heyday. It had a wraparound porch for outdoor eating and drinking, four separate dining rooms, and a massive wooden bar overseen by a dead moose head.

As the waif-thin hostess accompanied them to their table, Amanda navigated the room with her bulky crutches. The atmosphere was clubby, like everyone knew one another. People were laughing, drinking, and toasting as waiters uncorked bottles.

A rugged gray-bearded man sat reading the paper in a cozy stuffed chair in front of a roaring fire. An enormous white-and-silver Alaskan malamute slept at his feet. A large table of casually dressed thirtysomethings was singing 'Happy Birthday' as a chocolate torte was placed in front of the cute guy sitting on the end. Laura could have sworn it was Hugh Grant. The sisters were seated in one of the old-fashioned, romantic rooms in the back. Off to the side, a silver-haired man played piano softly.

'Is that Hugh Grant over there?' Amanda asked the hostess.

The hostess nodded. 'They're making a movie in town,' she said. 'Last week, they shot some scenes right here in the bar.'

'I hope you got to be an extra,' Laura said, taking her seat.

She giggled. 'As a matter of fact, I did. We all did.'

'That's so cool for you!' Amanda enthused. She was in fantastic spirits. Her financial worries were over and Jed would be joining them soon.

'Laura, where did you get that ribbon?' Serena asked when they were seated. 'Did you take it from my house?'

Laura was wearing white pants with a burgundy sweater. Her blond hair was pulled back into a ponytail and tied with a pink polka-dot ribbon. 'It's from that fabric store on Fourteenth Street. I got it ages ago, why?'

Serena's eyes narrowed. 'That's the same ribbon I found in Elliott's pants, along with a long blond hair. I can't believe you'd betray me like that! You're trying to spoil my life, aren't you? You've always wanted whatever I had.'

Laura stared at her sister looking blank, shocked, and shaken.

'Oh, come on,' Amanda said. 'Laura would never do anything like that.' Amanda was incredulous that Serena could think such a thing about their younger sister. Laura was all about honor and karma and doing the right thing. The idea was insane.

'I kept the blond hair,' Serena said. 'Maybe I'll send for DNA analysis against hair from Laura's brush and we'll just see.'

'Hello!' Laura said, her voice an octave higher than usual. 'Nothing's ever happened between me and your husband. I probably left the ribbon at your house and Elliott picked it up.'

'Serena, you're being paranoid,' Amanda said. 'It's unattractive.'

Serena rolled her eyes and turned away, spotting Jed as he came in and looked around the room for them. 'Jed,' she called. 'Here we are.'

Jed flashed a smile of recognition and joined them. He was wearing a boxy blue Brooks Brothers blue suit and smelled of Old Spice.

Thank God, Amanda thought. Next subject! She smoothed her hair nervously. 'Jed, you look handsome tonight.'

He blushed. 'Thanks, so do you . . . look pretty, I mean.' Tonight Amanda had foregone her St John Knits for a pair of slim black pants, a plain white shirt topped off by a silver-and-turquoise beaded necklace, and a pink faux-snake-skin cowboy boot for her good foot. Her curly red hair was worn loose around her face. 'Oh, excuse me, but I have to take this,' she said, checking her BlackBerry which had vibrated, indicating a call.

'Hey there Penny, congratulations on getting the apartment at the Plaza. I'm thrilled for you.' While Amanda spoke to her client, her face fell and body deflated. 'Oh my God, no. I'm so sorry. Of course you have to focus on chemo right now. You'll be in my prayers.' As she closed her cell phone, her eyes filled with tears and she took a deep breath to keep herself together. She felt like she might throw up.

'What happened?' Laura said.

'Penny Winkleman got some bad test results today. Her breast cancer came back,' Amanda said. 'Her husband doesn't want to buy her a new apartment until he's sure she's going to live.'

'He sounds like a real charmer,' Laura said. 'I'm sorry about the sale falling through.'

'It's okay. I'll live,' Amanda said. 'Hopefully Penny will, too. Poor thing, what is she going to do?' Hell, what am *I* going to do? Amanda wondered. She bit her lip and closed her eyes. Fuck, fuck, fuck, fuck, fuck, she thought. What options are left? she thought. Getting a piece of

Mom's estate. That's it. Stop. There's nothing to be done now. I'll figure it out later. This will all work out, she told herself. Focus on dinner and Jed. I feel like screaming, crying, and tearing my fingernails out, but I *have* to act normal. Act normal. Act normal. Ohmmm.

An aging waitress with sun-damaged skin and coffee-stained teeth came over with menus and wine lists. 'What do you recommend?' Laura asked.

'Tonight our special appetizer is rare ostrich served with truffle risotto cake,' she said. 'It's very popular.'

'I'm so hungry I could eat a skunk's bottom,' Jed said. 'But instead I'll have steak made from a cow, well done, with a baked potato,' Jed said. 'My tastes are simple.'

'There's nothing wrong with simple taste,' Amanda said. Her tastes were simple, too. She and Jed had so much in common it was frightening. Maybe the two of them could run away together to a place where Richie could never find them.

'Give us a minute,' Laura said to the waitress. Everyone studied their menus. When the waitress returned, Laura ordered Caesar salad and rack of lamb. Serena ordered parmesan risotto to be followed by lobster, while Amanda opted for plain roast chicken and ginger ale since her stomach was still bothering her.

'Oh, and a bottle of Cristal,' Serena said.

'You must be celebrating,' Jed said.

'No, drowning my sorrows,' Serena explained. 'But I'll do it in style.'

'Sorry to hear that,' Jed said.

'That's okay. What about you? Do you like champagne?' Serena asked. She reached over and put her hand over his.

Amanda kicked Serena hard under the table. Tonight, Serena was wearing a black va-va-voom cocktail dress that fit like a bustier, and black leather stiletto boots. You psychopathic tart, Amanda said telepathically to her. Don't even think about stealing another man from me.

'I prefer Miller Lite,' he said, discreetly pulling his hand away.

'So Jed,' Amanda said, gently touching his shoulder, 'tell us about yourself. Have you been the Bullocks' caretaker for a long time?'

As Jed told the girls how he had moved to Long Island from Texas, where he used to caretake on a working cattle ranch, the waitress poured them each a glass of champagne, then stored the rest on ice.

'That's fascinating,' Serena said, slugging down her flute of Cristal. 'Would you pour me more, please?'

'Sure,' Jed said. 'Anyway, the Bullocks visited the owners of the ranch a few years ago and we got to talking one night and I guess they liked me. Before they left, Mrs Bullock offered me a job managing their Long Island property.'

'I can certainly see what she saw in you,' Serena said, flashing a suggestive smile. 'Could I have another glass of bubbly?'

'My pleasure,' Jed said, filling her glass. The bottle was empty, so he signaled to the waitress for another.

'Serena, slow down,' Amanda hissed.

'Shhh, you're not the boss of me,' she said. 'Say, how's your diarrhea? Better?'

Amanda cringed.

'Jed, I can't help but notice how muscular you are,' Serena said, squeezing his biceps through his coat jacket.

Oh yeah, like hell you notice how muscular he is under that loose-fitting blazer, Amanda thought.

'I guess it takes a lot of strength to take charge of a property like you do,' Serena said, smiling at him.

Serena looked like a lioness about to tear into her prey. Amanda could practically see saliva dripping down her canines. She turned to Laura, stuck her finger down her throat and pretended to gag. Laura giggled.

The waitress showed up with their appetizers and another bottle of champagne. Thank God, Amanda thought. Everyone must have been hungry, because soon all you could hear was the sound of silverware clinking and heavy chewing.

Amanda downed her ginger ale. 'Jed, since you've lived here, have you ever met a woman named Kate Lassiter?'

'As a matter of fact,' Jed said, 'every year, there's an artists-versus-writers charity softball game in East Hampton. I believe she plays for the artists' team.'

'Tell me, when did they start that tradition?' Serena said, slurring her words. 'Like, did all the Hamptons' luminaries used to play? Was it Truman Capote, Herman Melville, and F. Scott Fitzgerald versus Jackson Pollock, Lee Krasner, and Daniel Lassiter? Oh wait; maybe they weren't all alive at the same time. Jed, would you mind pouring me another?' She held out her glass for him. 'It'll be my last, I swear.'

'I'm not counting,' he said.

Amanda scowled at her. 'I am.'

'How's the risotto?' Laura asked.

'Mmm, deeee-licious,' Serena said, licking her lips slowly and sensually. 'Jed, you have to try this.' She put some on her fork and fed it to him like he was a baby.

A busboy cleared away the plates so that the waitress could put down the entrees. 'Careful, hot plates,' she warned.

'With the artists-versus-writers game, they're pretty loose with the qualifications,' Jed said. 'Last year, Rudy Giuliani played for the writers and Alec Baldwin was an artist.'

'Giuliani wrote a book, you know,' Serena said, 'about leadership.' She picked up Jed's steak knife and began cutting his meat into bite-sized pieces. 'And it's fair to say that actors are artists.'

'Serena, what are you doing?' Laura asked.

'I'm cutting Jed's meat,' she said. 'Oh God, I'm sorry. It's just that I'm so used to cutting Sebastian's food.'

'Your thought light ain't lit right now, is it?' Jed said, chuckling.

'No, it ain't,' Serena said. 'In fact, I'm feeling kind of sick. I need air. Would you mind driving me home? We can get doggie bags for the rest of our food.'

Jed glanced at Amanda and then at Serena. 'Oh, well, I guess I could drive you.'

Amanda shot a warning glance toward Serena. For Jed's sake, she tried not to show the murderous thoughts that were raging through her mind.

Jed called the waitress over. She took their plates to box up the leftovers.

Amanda leered at Serena, who seemed oblivious to her sister's feelings. She seethed as Serena wrapped her bare shoulders in a black pashmina shawl and made her way toward the door.

What a night! Amanda thought. Penny Winkleman gets a cancer diagnosis and torpedoes my sale; Serena steals another man from me and ruins my evening. As the devil herself disappeared with Jed in tow, Amanda caught a familiar face nursing a whisky at the bar. Another famous actor? Then she gasped. Fuck! Richie. Is he following me?

'Excuse me for a minute,' Amanda said to Laura.

She handed her American Express card to the waitress and crutched over to him.

'What are *you* doing here?' she whispered.

Richie turned and smiled, his eyes crinkling in amusement. 'What? No, hello, how are you? Can I buy you a drink?'

'Don't change the subject,' Amanda said. 'You told me I had a month. Why are you here?'

'I'm here to tell you I resigned your account,' Richie said. 'The bastards kidnapped and beat the living crap out of the teenage son of one of my clients. I can't work with lenders who undermine my authority like that.'

Amanda's insides twisted with panic at the thought of Kneecap roughing up her family. 'Shit! That's terrible.' She hated being chased by collectors, but at least Richie had shown some compassion. God knows who would be assigned to take his place.

'W-would they d-do something like that to me? Hurt my sisters or niece or nephew?'

'Of course they would,' Richie said. 'They want your money in two weeks and if you're late, or even if you're not, they might decide to teach you a lesson you'll never forget.'

Amanda felt like a five-hundred-pound man was sitting on her chest. 'Two weeks? Oh my God! Help me, Richard.'

'That's why I'm here, to *warn* you,' Richie said. 'Get that loan paid off or the result could be, well, it hurts my brain cells to think about it.' He nodded to the bartender to pour him another whisky.

Amanda gulped. 'I'm working on something now and if things fall the way I hope, I should be able to make the deadline. But please, go back to them; tell them you'll stay on my account as long as they leave my family alone. I can fake new injuries if it comes to that. I *beg* you, Richard. I'd owe you forever if you'd do that.'

'Would you sleep with me?' he said, smiling.

'Don't joke,' Amanda said, slapping his arm, which she immediately regretted.

'Who said I was joking?' he said, making his eyebrows go up and down suggestively. 'Unfortunately for you, Red, these are individuals I do not care to do business with, if you know what I mean. But I'll give your proposition some thought. In the meantime, don't screw around. Find the money, okay?' He slapped a twenty on the bar, downed the whisky the bartender had just set in front of him, kissed Amanda on the cheek, and walked out the front door.

Amanda's heart was pounding so hard she could hear it. Fuck, she thought. Richie was serious. Two weeks? Now my family's at risk! What have I done? Lassiter had better not turn out to be Serena's father. If he is, I get nothing. She took a deep breath to collect herself and went to the bathroom. Her teeth, knees, hands – every moving part of her was trembling. Relax, she told herself. It's going to be okay. It's going to be okay. It's going to be okay. Amanda repeated this mantra about fifty times until her heartbeat slowed and she felt calmer. She turned on the cold water and splashed her face. Composed, she returned to the table.

'You okay? Your face is flushed,' Laura said.

Amanda could see that her sister was concerned. Maybe I should tell the truth. *No!* Laura can't help. Last week, she asked to borrow ten grand. She looks up to me. If I confess, she'll think I'm foolish and irresponsible, which I am, but I can't let her know it. Amanda took a long, steady breath. 'I'm fine. Did the waitress bring our check?'

'Not yet. I can't believe Serena went home with Jed,' Laura said.

'That's right!' Amanda said, recalling what had happened before Richie showed up and spooked her. 'Didn't we invite Jed for *me? She's* married. And *he's* gone home with *her?'*

'She wasn't feeling well,' Laura said. 'Obviously she drank too much.'

'That's bullshit,' Amanda said. 'She just can't stand the fact that a man might be interested in me. What's taking our waitress so long?'

'Remember, she said Sebastian caught Elliott with another woman today,' Laura said. 'That must've thrown her over the edge. Maybe it's hitting her that her marriage can't be saved.'

'Why do you make excuses for her?' Amanda said. 'She's always behaved like a miserable twat.'

'I think that experience of being left on the beach alone when Dad committed suicide screwed her up,'

Laura said. 'And all those years of going through cancer had to take their toll. She's our sister. We *have* to love her. We *have* to give her a free ride.'

'Do we?' Amanda asked. 'You know who I think deserves a free ride? You. You gave Serena your bone marrow and your eggs. You gave her life and children. You put your own life on hold for six years to take care of Mom. You know who else deserves a free ride? Me. I gave up college and supported you, Serena, and Mom after Dad died. Each of us has suffered and sacrificed. That doesn't give *us* a free pass to be miserable twats.'

The waitress approached their table. 'Excuse me, but your card was declined.'

Declined, Amanda thought. Shit. Without AMEX, I don't have credit. I'm screwed.

'Use this,' Laura said, handing over her debit card. 'I deposited a thousand from my flight-attendant advance into my account.'

'That should just about cover the tab after all the Cristal Serena ordered,' Amanda said.

'I think you're being too hard on her. She was willing to give you a third of Mom's painting and a floor of the house without even knowing if Lassiter was her father.'

'Yes, but you'll note that she never got around to signing the papers,' Amanda said. 'I just had Sam Hermann draw up the variation, dividing everything into thirds.'

'But only if Lassiter doesn't turn out to be her father,' Laura said.

'I know, I know.' Amanda reached into her bag, pulled out the envelope containing the legal documents, and ripped it open. She scanned the variation Sam had drawn up. Then she flipped through the will. Her eyes bugged out.

'What is it?' Laura asked.

'Huh. Nothing,' Amanda said. 'A bunch of legalese.' But that wasn't true. Amanda had noticed three witness signatures on Sunny's will. The last one was Serena's. She'd *known* she was getting the whole estate all along. Most likely, she'd engineered it. All that feigning surprise had been a big fat lie.

'She's a pain, I'll admit it,' Laura said. 'But all we have in life is one another. Can't you try to get along with her?'

Amanda started to tell Laura what she had discovered but stopped. Why burst her bubble until she confronted Serena with the evidence? She would do that tonight.

SERENA

'You can kid the world. But not your sister.'
—Charlotte Gray

Jed had to pull the Escalade over so that Serena could throw up. Once she did, she felt better. They stopped at a 7-Eleven so she could get a soda to settle her stomach and wash away the nasty bile taste in her mouth.

'Thanks, Jed,' she said. 'I'm so embarrassed. Believe it or not, I'm a teetotaler.'

'Really?' Jed said. 'Then why'd you drink so much tonight?'

Serena sighed. 'My life is in a shambles. I'm pretty sure my husband's been cheating on me with my little sister. And last week he was caught with an actress in the Caribbean. Today he entertained another woman at home right in front of my children. He claimed it was a man, a friend, but I don't believe him. It's so upsetting.'

'Sounds like you're better off without him,' Jed said as he punched in the gate code and drove down the long gravel driveway.

When they got out of the car, Serena tightened her shawl around her shoulders and gazed at the sky. 'The air feels great,' she said. 'My gosh, will you look at all those stars. We rarely see stars in Manhattan. Too much light from the buildings.'

Jed stood next to her peering up at the night sky. 'Beautiful. Would you like a smoke?' He offered her a Camel.

'Yes, definitely.' It wasn't her eco-friendly brand, but she craved a cigarette. He lit it for her. Such a gentleman, she thought. 'Thanks,' she said, sucking the smoke deep into her lungs. What a nasty habit. God forbid the kids ever do this. She regarded Jed.

'What?' he said.

'Nothing,' Serena said. She knew Amanda was going to kill her for asking Jed to drive her home. They had invited him to dinner for Amanda. She was the single one. But it was better for everyone that she asked him for a ride. What if she had thrown up at the restaurant? That would have been horrible. Serena knew that Amanda would find it more horrible that she stole Jed out from under her nose. Why did she always do the wrong thing when it came to her sisters? She couldn't help herself. When either of them had something good, she wanted it. 'I've been a bad girl.'

'What did you say?' Jed asked.

Did I say that aloud? she wondered. 'I . . . I said that I've been a bad girl. I stole you from my sister. I deserve to be punished.'

'Don't worry about it,' Jed said, blowing a line of blue smoke out of his mouth.

Serena nodded. 'No, it was wrong. Someone needs to turn me over his knee and give me a whupping. Would you come to the dungeon and teach me a lesson?' She couldn't believe she had asked Jed this. She was a cautious person, and what did she know about this man? He could be Mr Jed Goodbar for all she knew. But today, when they had toured the dungeon, something inside her loins had awakened. She was curious to know why people got turned on by pain. Who better to research S&M with than with a guy she'd probably never see again? 'You are such a big, strong man, and if anyone would know how to punish a wicked girl like me, it would be you. Please, I *beg* to be disciplined for my misbehavior.'

Jed's jaw dropped. 'Well, butter my butt and call me a biscuit! You want me to spank you? If you insist,' he said. He took her by the hand, and they made their way inside and upstairs. Serena wandered into the torture chamber where there were all kinds of machines that she didn't know how to use. Why hadn't she let Albert give them an orientation to the equipment when he offered? There were swings, a gynecologist's table, a stockade, a rack, tables with straps and pulleys, all manner of lounge chairs Serena had no idea how to sit or lie on. There was even a large, bouncy Pilates ball with a rubber penis sticking up from the top. You could pleasure yourself and work out at the same time with that, Serena realized with a giggle. How efficient.

She turned and caught Jed standing outside the doorway. His eyes were wide and he was biting his lower lip.

'You afraid?' Serena asked seductively. 'Come on, Big Boy, teach Little Mama a lesson she won't forget.'

'I-I tell you, when it comes to normal sex I'm first in line, but this . . . this kinky stuff,' he said. 'It's not my scene. Albert's into it. Do you want me to get him?'

Blecch. Not that stuffy English fart. *Eew! Feh! Pish!* Let that geezer slap my ass with his bare hand? She needed a shower just thinking about it. 'No, not Albert, *you!*'

Jed shook his head and backed away. Then he was gone.

'What a baby,' Serena muttered. She glanced around the room for something to try. Peeking inside the half-open closet, she saw rubber pants, patent-leather stiletto boots, face masks, and other sex costumes. For a laugh, she decided to try on the black, skintight Spandex bodysuit with tit and ass cutouts. She giggled as she shed her clothes and squeezed into it. After positioning the holes so her butt and breasts were exposed, she slipped on the patent-leather boots, which came to her thighs because she was so short. Serena checked herself out in the full-length mirror. I look ridiculous, she thought at first. No, no, it's kind of hot, really. 'Grrrrr,' she growled at her reflection, emitting a tigress sound she thought S&M practitioners might make.

Serena sighed. It made her sad to see herself like this – all dressed up with no one to whip. Why don't Elliott and I have kinky sex anymore? Probably because we don't have sex at all, she thought. She missed the role-playing they used to do. Her favorite was when she'd be the naughty student and he'd be the horny professor. If we get back together, maybe we could try that again.

Serena wondered if being whipped would turn her on. That was something they'd never tried. A stiff leather switch hung on a hook. She grabbed it, bent over a bench that seemed to have been made for spanking, and snapped the whip across her butt a few times. It was awkward, but felt nice. A high-pitched whizzing sounded in the air as she did it again. *Thwack, thwack*! Oh my God, that hurts but ooh, in such a pleasurable way. Then she used the switch to tickle and tease herself. When she could no longer stand it, *thwack, thwack, thwack*, three hard strikes. Her ass was throbbing. Serena breathed hard and moaned from the delicious pain. She couldn't believe what she'd been missing all these years.

Next, Serena moseyed over to a piece of equipment that resembled a pommel horse. She leaned over the saddle, hiking her ass up. Positioned toward the bottom of the legs were steel cuffs for her wrists and ankles. Serena slipped her hands and feet in and closed them just barely so they wouldn't lock. She wanted to imagine what it was like to be held hostage in a giant sex toy. With her hands restrained she couldn't whip herself, so she fantasized that Jed was behind her smacking her ass with his calloused bare hands. *Thwack, thwack!* Oh lord, what am I doing? she thought, breaking the spell. I'm a registered Republican with two children and eleven applications to Manhattan's top private schools. No, go back. Again she imagined Jed spanking her tight little ass. *Thwack, thwack!* Oh, Jed! Writhing in pleasure, she squeezed the legs of the pommel horse, inadvertently depressing a latch that automatically clicked all four cuffs closed.

Fuck, she thought. Did this thing lock? She squeezed the legs again, over and over, hoping to find the release button. There didn't seem to be one. She needed a key. Oh God, she thought. This isn't happening. I'm imprisoned in . . . what the hell *is* this thing! 'Help! Help!' Serena screamed to no avail. Albert had told them the cork-lined room was soundproof. She collapsed against the pommel horse. There was no escape.

Serena's heart began to pound from the claustrophobia of being trapped. She inhaled deeply to keep from having a full-blown panic attack. It's going to be okay. It's going to be okay. It's going to be okay. Serena repeated this mantra until her heartbeat slowed and she felt calmer. Her nose was stuffed up from the way her head was hanging down.

Why did I put on this ridiculous outfit? My butt is freezing, she thought. Maybe God is punishing me. No, that can't be. Serena's nose itched, but there was no way to scratch it. She rubbed her face against her arm but couldn't reach the spot. To take her mind off her predicament, she sang. 'A hundred bottles of beer on the wall, a hundred bottles of beer, take one down, pass it around, ninety-nine bottles of beer on the wall . . .'

'. . . six bottles of beer on the wall, six bottles of beer . . .'

After what seemed like days in captivity, but could have been hours or minutes, she heard the sound of two crutches clapping. 'There you are,' Amanda said. 'I was wondering what happened to you. That's quite a show you put on before.'

Serena's first thought was, thank God I'll be rescued. Her second thought was, a show? How long has Amanda been watching me? Did she see me whipping myself? Please, anything but that!

'Amanda, I've never been so glad to see you,' Serena said. 'I'm locked in.' This was embarrassing beyond belief. She glimpsed her sister's pink faux-snakeskin boot and plaster-encased foot circling her like a buzzard.

'What in God's name are you wearing?' Amanda said. 'Do you realize how fat that cutout makes your ass look?'

'Amanda, stop.' Serena knew Amanda wasn't going to let her off the hook easily. She would lord this over her for the rest of her life.

'Aren't you a bit, I don't know, *conservative* for dungeon-play, Miss PTA-president-La-Leche-League-perfect-mother?'

'It was sexual experimentation, nothing more,' Serena said. 'Surely you've done that in your life? Well, maybe not.'

'Do you really think you're in a position to get sassy with me?' Amanda said.

Serena's head was filled with blood from being upside down and she worried that an aneurysm could kill her at any moment. God forbid I die in this position. 'I'm sorry. Please,' she pleaded. 'The keys. They're in the armoire.'

'Serena Lou Skank, all jammed up, as they say on *Law and Order*. How're you gonna get out of this one?'

'Amanda, come on,' Serena shouted. 'I'm begging you. This is humiliating.'

'Is it, now?' Amanda said. 'You know what's humiliating? It's humiliating to invite a man to dinner with me and watch him go home with *you*.'

'I'm sorry,' Serena said. 'I shouldn't have done that.'

'And to walk in and find you using our host's S&M equipment after they so generously let us stay in their home, well, that's just gross,' Amanda said. '*Especially* to find you using it on *yourself*.'

'Stop. I didn't *want* to do it alone. I wanted to try it with Jed,' Serena screamed.

'Oh, so you shouldn't have gone home with him, but it was okay to dress like a Frederick's of

Hollywood poster girl and have rough sex with him?' Amanda said.

'No, of course not. If it makes you feel any better, he rejected me,' Serena said.

'Thank you. That does make me feel better,' Amanda said.

'Laura. Laura!' Serena screamed. 'LAURA!!'

'She's on the other side of the house,' Amanda said. 'No one can hear you. Jed told me what happened. He said you begged to be taught a lesson. I'm surprised at you. You're usually such a prude.'

Serena groaned. 'I was depressed about Elliott and said screw it, you know? I'm an idiot.'

'Yes, that's true. Tell you what, we'll keep this little episode between us,' Amanda said. She went over to the armoire and took out five or six sets of keys. After trying several different ones unsuccessfully, she managed to open the cuff on Serena's right hand and to unlock the ankle restraints. Then she returned the keys.

'What about my left hand?' Serena said, still bent over the pommel horse.

Amanda remained quiet as she rifled Serena's purse and pulled out her cell phone. She dropped it next to her foot.

'You're not going to leave me like this?' Serena cried, straining her neck to see Amanda. 'What am I supposed to do?'

'Use the phone,' Amanda said. 'Try nine-one-one. Or Elliott. Or call one of your friends. Oh,

I forgot. You don't have any. Whatever. You're resourceful. But don't call me, because I'm not answering and Laura left her cell phone in the city.'

'You are such a bitch,' Serena said. 'I *thought* it before but now I *know*.'

'Me?' Amanda said, her mouth open in shock. 'After all I've done for you, how can you say I'm a bitch?'

'Oh please,' Serena said, her upside-down head bobbing as she spoke. 'Let me count the ways. Remember how you offended every doctor and nurse at Methodist Hospital? *Bitch*. And then, oh my God, then you didn't even wait for me during the transplant. You took Mom to a spa. *Bitch*. And it's not only you. It's Laura, too. She tried to take back her bone marrow, *Indian-giver bitch*.'

'What are you talking about?' Amanda said, incredulous. 'Mom and I left you to fill out forms after we found out the insurance company wouldn't cover the transplant. We had to change all the paperwork since I was paying for every-thing myself. If I hadn't done that, you would have died. And if I offended the doctors and nurses at Methodist Hospital, it was because they constantly made mistakes with your treatment and I called them on it every time. Do you know how often I caught them giving you someone else's chemotherapy drug, or preparing the wrong medicine, or screwing up the dose? If I hadn't watched them like a hawk, you would have died.

You'd do the same thing if one of your kids was in the hospital.'

'Really?' Serena said, craning her neck awkwardly. 'That's what happened?'

'Yes, that's what happened. And Laura never tried to take back her bone marrow,' Amanda said. 'She would have given you her kidney if you'd needed it to save your sorry life. We all would have. Not only that, she snuck around the hospital stealing towels and sheets for you that they didn't have on your floor.'

'You mean the nurses weren't withholding that stuff because you were such a bitch to them?'

'No,' Amanda said, 'there weren't enough supplies to go around.'

Serena shook her head in disbelief. 'All these years, I thought . . . well, I'm sorry. Maybe you're not a bitch in general, but you're a bitch if you don't unlock me now.'

'After what you did tonight?' Amanda said.

'Please, forgive me,' Serena said, 'I don't know why I acted so badly. It's Elliott's fault. Running off with that actress to the islands. Carrying on with another woman today. And Dad abandoned me in the Hamptons all those years ago when he killed himself. That really screwed me up . . .'

'Serena,' Amanda said. 'When are you going to take responsibility for your behavior? Tell me, whose fault was it when you stole our inheritance? Sebastian's? Valentina's?'

'I didn't steal it. It was Mom's decision.'

'I just saw the will,' Amanda said. '*You* witnessed it. Tell me, how did it happen that Mom changed her mind about dividing everything equally? And you'd better tell me the truth!' *Thwack!* Amanda slapped her butt with the end of her crutch.

'Amanda, stop!' Serena said. 'That hurts.'

'Tell me the truth or I'll do it again and harder.'

'Okay, okay,' Serena said. 'It was right after she was diagnosed. I suggested that she revisit her will since we knew she wouldn't have her faculties much longer. On the way to the lawyer's, I told her that if she left everything to me, I would make sure she was cared for with love and dignity until the end. And – and – and I said that if you and Laura did your part in looking after her, I'd make sure you were both taken care of. And that's exactly what I did, right? I agreed to share the house and the painting with you. You and Laura are the ones who said I could have it all if Lassiter turned out to be my father. That wasn't my idea.'

'That's it? You didn't lie to her or trick her or scare her or push her or . . .'

'No! What kind of person do you think I am?'

'You are a piece of work,' Amanda said. 'Tell you what, you begged to be taught a lesson, so let me teach you one. When I leave, think about *why* what you did was wrong. Ask yourself how you could betray me and Laura, the two people who love you most in the world, the two people who saved your life. The two people who never failed to stand by you no matter how neurotic you acted. When you wanted to find out if Lassiter was your father, we were there. When Elliott screwed up, we were there. I can't speak for Laura, but after this trip, you and I are done.' With that, Amanda flipped off the light and power-crutched out the door.

SERENA

'Between sisters, often, the child's cry never dies down. "Never leave me," it says; "do not abandon me."'

—Louise Bernikow

'Amanda, no!' Serena cried. 'Don't leave me alone. Amanda! *Amanda!*'

Shit, I can't stay here all night, Serena thought. Breathe, breathe, she told herself. Calm down. It's going to be okay. It's going to be okay. It's going to be okay.

Now that she had one arm and her legs free, she wobbled her feet around the pommel horse until her entire body was on one side. Finally she could sit and bend her arms and legs. The stone floor felt like ice through the butt cutout in her Spandex bodysuit. Still, it feels good to be right-side-up, she thought.

The apparatus didn't look that heavy. Maybe I can move it over to the armoire where the keys to the cuffs are. Or if I can reach my clothes, I can cover up and call 911 for help, she thought.

She pushed the horse to see how heavy it was. Damn! Bolted to the floor. There's no way out.

'Laura! LAURA!' she screamed. 'HELP! Somebody, ANYBODY, HELP!' I'll call Elliott, she thought. No, he can't see me like this. I acted so righteous over his indiscretions. Gosh, I'm tired. What time is it? It's got to be past midnight. How long since Amanda left? Surely she's coming back. What if, God forbid, Amanda gets into a car accident and dies and there's no phone reception so I can't call for help and no one knows where I am? I could starve to death like that murderer who was cuffed to his victim on *Law and Order*. Or what if, God forbid, the house catches fire and I can't get out? That would serve Amanda right, she thought. If I were burned to death in a fire, I'd finally get the pity from her I deserve. Ow, is that a steel rash on my wrist?

Serena tried to grab her clothes but they were beyond reach. She lay back down and curled into a tight ball around the base of the pommel horse. Maybe I can sleep. In the morning, if Amanda doesn't come back, I'll call the police. I'll be a laughingstock at the precinct. If this happened on *Law and Order*, Detectives Munch and Fin would have a field day. Jeez, if Elliott finds out about this, I'll be watching it on *Law and Order*. They're always ripping things from the headlines. Oh God, please don't let this make the headlines.

How can Amanda abandon me overnight the way Dad did, in the Hamptons no less? With my history, this could trigger a devastating flashback. But what does she care? I need to pee . . . I mean urinate. Why is this happening to me? Face it; this is my fault. I drove Amanda and Laura away. When you screw with someone's inheritance or steal their boyfriend, they're gonna hate you. I deserve this. Why do I always want what they have? I should be happy when something good happens to them, but instead I want to die inside.

How can Amanda say I don't take responsibility for my behavior? she wondered. I guess I do blame a lot of things on Dad for abandoning me at the beach that night. But it was traumatic! Of course it screwed me up. And whose personality wouldn't be affected by years of illness, of facing death every single day? She sighed. Look where it all got me, she thought, glancing around the cold dungeon, the ridiculous bottomless catsuit she was wearing, her bound wrist, which was mottled with bumpy red spots. I have to become a better person. If I get out of here, God, I promise to stop making excuses.

Serena thought about how vulnerable Sunny had been the day Serena got her to change her will. She had just been diagnosed and was petrified at losing her memory and identity. I took advantage of her. No, I *screwed* her. I screwed my sisters. After all they did for me. Paying for my leukemia treatment. Making sure I got the right medicines. Donating bone marrow. Giving me eggs so I could have children. Standing by me when Elliott betrayed me. Coming with me to find out who my father was. What have I done for them? Nothing.

A lump came to her throat and her eyes filled. Tears spilled down her face as she sobbed in loud gulping waves that no one could hear. What's wrong with me? I'm a monster. I'm sorry, she cried. Forgive me. Serena wasn't sure whose forgiveness she wanted – her sister's? Her husband's? Her mother's? Her father's? Her own? All of the above.

No, she thought, wiping her snotty nose on the arm of her bottomless leotard, I used to be a monster, but that's over. Get me through this ordeal and you'll see what a good person I can be. God, please, everyone deserves a second chance.

AMANDA

'Sister to sister we will always be, a couple of nuts on the family tree.'

—Anonymous

It was before seven a.m. when Amanda stole back into the dungeon to check on Serena. Amanda hadn't been able to sleep. After the Winkleman deal fell through, Richie's unexpected visit, and her sister's treachery, her brain was buzzing. What was with Serena, going off with Jed like that? And what kind of person would steal an inheritance from her own sisters? Sure, she had considered replacing their mother's drawing with a fake, but that would have been a victimless crime born out of desperation and genuine need. Serena had acted out of greed. As if all this wasn't enough, Amanda was petrified that her lenders would come after her family like Richie warned.

In her hand, Amanda carried the contract she had handwritten that morning, plus a copy she made using the Bullocks' scanner. With Serena's signature on this document, she could make the loan shark go away. The family would be safe.

'Serena, wake up,' she said, tapping her softly with the end of her crutch.

Serena shook her head. 'Huh, what? Where am I? Oh, thank God. I'm alive!' She sat up even though her hand was awkwardly cuffed to the pommel horse's leg. Her eyes were puffy, mascara was smeared down her face, and her brown hair was like matted steel wool. One of her breasts was inside the body suit and one was sticking out through a hole.

'Are you letting me go?'

'Not yet,' Amanda said. 'I have a proposition for you.'

'I need to pe . . . urinate first,' Serena said. 'Can you let me out? For a minute. You can put me back.'

'Nooooo,' Amanda said. 'Listen up. I am going to make sure the DNA test shows you're Lassiter's daughter. According to the deal you made with Laura and me, you'll get to keep everything. But instead, you'll sign half the assets over to me.'

'You mean cut Laura out?' Serena said.

'Well, yes, technically speaking, but she'd be cut out anyway if it turned out you *are* Lassiter's daughter, which you're sure you are, so she isn't really losing anything,' Amanda said. 'Plus, if by some slim chance you aren't Lassiter's daughter, we'd split the assets equally and you'd only get to keep a third. This way you're guaranteed half.'

Serena leaned back on the pommel horse. 'How can you cheat Laura like that? Aren't you the one who condemned *me* for trying to screw my sisters?'

'Yes, I am,' Amanda said, cringing inside. The last thing she wanted to do was betray her little sister, but if she didn't go through with her plan, everyone she loved, including Sebastian and Valentina, was in danger. 'For reasons I can't divulge, I have no choice but to do this. Laura will be fine. She'll sing in that movie and make lots of money and become a star . . .'

'Yeah, sure she will,' Serena scoffed. 'And I'm Honk the Wondergoose.'

Amanda ignored her sister's sarcasm. 'Plus she's got that new job as a private-jet stewardess. She won't be hurting. And when the market's better, I'll earn back what I took from her and make it up to her. I'll . . . I'll buy her a house or whatever she needs. Here. Sign.' Amanda hated herself for what she was doing.

'No,' Serena said, shaking her matted hair. 'I turned over a new leaf. This goes against every-thing I stand for . . . *now*. Laura has been nothing but loyal to us. I can't betray her.'

'All your life you're a sneaky, lying, underhanded pain-in-the-butt sister and *today* you decide to go goody-goody on me?' Amanda said, rolling her eyes. 'No.' She pushed the contract against the pommel horse leg and stuck a pen into Serena's uncuffed hand.

'Please, I need to pee,' Serena said. 'And I refuse to compound my offense against Mom by betraying Laura to cover up what I did.'

Amanda was getting impatient. 'If Laura understood why I was doing this, she would tell you to sign. Trust me. If you sign, I'll let you pee.'

'How can I trust you when you're asking me to do something so untrustworthy? Fuck it; give me the pen. My bladder's about to burst . . .'

'Sign both copies and keep one.' Amanda didn't think a contract like this would hold up in court, but she figured Serena would honor it just to keep Laura from finding out that she'd duped Mom into giving her everything.

Serena completed her signature. 'My, my, my, Amanda. How low we have sunk,' she said. 'You're officially as bad as I *used* to be.'

'No, unlike the way you *used* to be, *I'm* going to take care of Laura.' In her head, Amanda asked God to forgive her.

'And I was going to take care of the two of you,' Serena said. 'The road to hell is paved with good intentions. Isn't that what they say?'

Amanda folded Serena's copy of the contract and stuck it into her sister's purse. 'I'll see you later.' She had a lot to do if she was going to pull this off.

'Wait, what about me?' Serena shouted. 'Unlock my cuff. You said you'd let me urinate if I signed your agreement.'

Amanda dumped a ceramic bowl filled with gags

and blind-folds onto the floor and handed it to Serena. 'Use this.'

'You can't be serious,' Serena cried. 'Release me, please!'

'You got yourself into this mess,' Amanda said. 'You get yourself out.'

ELLIOTT

'Most American children suffer too much
mother and too little father.'
—Gloria Steinem

'Jeezus,' Elliott said, 'your dance card is full today.' Now that the kids were dressed and fed, he was checking Sebastian's Week-at-a-Glance. This morning he had an appointment with Dr Borowitz in the nineties on the Upper East Side. Then they had less than an hour to get to Lincoln Center on the West Side for Sebastian's first opera-singing class. At the same time, Valentina was scheduled for French lessons on the East Side. French lessons? She can only say five English words. Later, there was a lecture on 'Children of Privilege: A Parent's Guide to Keeping Them Real' at the Jewish Community Center back on the West Side. There was no way Elliott would be able to navigate all those back-and-forth destinations while managing meals, diapers, dressing, naps, and baths. Okay, I get it. A mother's work is never done, he thought.

'Let's stay home and play,' Sebastian said. 'I won't tell Mommy.'

'Tell you what,' Elliott said, 'we'll take the subway up to Dr Borowitz's office and get you to your opera class and then decide.'

'I love the subway,' Sebastian said. He jumped up from the floor where he had been pretending to be a boa constrictor about to devour Valentina, put on his jacket, reached into his Pull-Up to retrieve a dummy and announced, 'I'm ready.'

Dr Borowitz was in one of those offices shared by a number of unaffiliated psychologists. The waiting room needed a fresh coat of white paint. The seats were black leather and chrome, circa 1970. There were a few cheap tables from IKEA scattered about. Everyone who was waiting avoided making eye contact with everyone else because they were there to see a psychologist and no one wanted to infringe on anyone's privacy even though pretty much everyone in Manhattan saw a shrink. Sebastian found a *Highlights* magazine and brought it to Elliott. 'Want to help me find hidden pictures?' he asked, pulling out his pacifier to speak.

'Can't right now, Sport,' he said. 'Valentina needs to go to sleep.' She was half-crying and half-dozing. Elliott bounced her up and down as he paced back and forth the way he had seen a nanny do it on the playground. 'But you can sit on the floor and find the pictures yourself. You're a smart boy.'

'I am?' Sebastian said. 'Do you think?' His face beamed with pride.

'I know,' Elliott said.

Sebastian put his pacifier back into his mouth, settled on to the carpet and began searching for the hidden ice cream cone, hammer, and fishing hook that were supposedly in the bigger picture somewhere. Soon he got bored of that and began turning the top right corner of each page down into a little triangle. The challenge was to make each triangle on every page the exact same size.

An older woman poked her head out of one of the unmarked offices. She wore a navy-blue pants suit and sensible off-white heels. She was tall and slightly stooped, with a birdlike nose, bright green eyes, milky white skin, and cropped reddish-brown hair. Elliott immediately pegged her for a Freudian.

'Sebastian?' she said.

Sebastian glanced at the woman and then at Elliott. He went back to turning down page corners.

Elliott put Valentina into her stroller and gave her her red puppy, the special stuffed animal that she never left home without. 'C'mon, Sport,' he said.

Sebastian grabbed his father's hand and followed, sticking the *Highlights* magazine down the back of his pants.

'Would you like to lie on the couch?' the woman asked as they entered the office.

Sebastian shook his head.

'Could I ask you to remove your pacifier?' she said.

Sebastian shook his head.

She turned her attention to Elliott. 'What brings you here today? Is it that he doesn't obey authority? His oral fixation? His kleptomania? His obsessive-compulsive disorder?'

'I guess you could say it's the kleptomania,' Elliott said. 'Sebastian has been stealing cell phones and BlackBerries and such. My wife thought he should talk to someone about it.'

Sebastian pulled his pacifier out of his mouth. 'I'm not going to do it anymore. Stealing is against the law.'

'What about that magazine you just put down your pants?' Dr Borowitz asked.

Sebastian gasped in outrage. 'I was just warming it up for the next kid!'

'And what about the condoms?' Elliott asked. 'Will you stop taking those, too?'

'The what?' Sebastian asked.

'You know, the happy-Mommy-and-Daddy packages you took from the drug store,' he said.

'Oh,' Sebastian said, curling his lips down. 'Do I have to?'

Dr Borowitz raised her eyebrows. 'He was stealing condoms with pictures of happy couples on the box?'

Elliott nodded. 'Is that serious?'

'I don't know. What do *you* think?' Dr Borowitz said.

'You're the professional,' Elliott said, but it didn't take a professional to explain why Sebastian was attracted to that condom box.

'Sebastian, there are a bunch of toys in the corner,' Dr Borowitz said. 'Why don't you play over there while I talk to your daddy?'

Sebastian shrugged. He sidled over to an irresistible wooden dollhouse and plopped down in front of it. It had miniature painted furniture and red-and-white-checkered curtains on all the windows. Reaching inside, he pulled out the mommy, daddy, baby, and brother dolls. Sebastian glanced at his father, who was talking softly with the doctor. He started to play house with the dolls.

'What color is blood?' Sebastian asked, speaking for the mommy doll.

'Green,' the brother doll said.

'Blood is not green. It's red,' the mommy doll said. 'You are a dummy. Mommies like smart boys, not dumb boys.'

'Does somebody in your home say things like that to him?' Dr Borowitz whispered.

'No, no,' Elliott said. 'He must have seen it on TV.' Then he remembered that Sebastian didn't watch TV.

'I'm not a dumb boy,' the brother doll said. 'I have hundreds and hundreds of IQ points. Bugs do so have green blood.'

'I'll be right back,' the mommy doll said. 'Valentina's crying.'

'I'll get her,' the brother doll said. He went into

414

the next room, picked up the Valentina doll, and stuffed her into the playhouse toilet.

'Sebastian, what have you done?' the mommy doll said. 'You're acting like a child. For God's sake, you're almost five.'

'Oh look, Daddy's home,' the brother doll said. 'Yay!'

'Hi, family,' the daddy doll said. 'I have to go right back to work. We're shooting tonight.'

'Please stay home, Daddy,' the brother doll said.

'No, I have more important things to do,' the daddy doll said.

Elliott blushed. 'I don't know where he's getting this.'

'I think we should schedule a standing appointment every week,' Dr Borowitz said. 'Twice a week would be better.'

'I'm sure it would,' Elliott said. 'If you really think he needs it . . .' His phone vibrated, so he flipped it open. 'Oh my God, we have to go.'

'What is it?' Dr Borowitz said.

'It's my wife,' Elliott said. 'She's naked and handcuffed in some S&M dungeon in East Hampton. We have to get her out of there.'

'Sir, I strongly recommend that you consider family therapy,' Dr Borowitz said.

'We'll get back to you,' Elliott said, rushing out the door with Valentina in her stroller and Sebastian in tow.

'Sebastian,' the doctor called. 'My dolls, please.'

Sebastian reached inside his Pull-Ups and

retrieved the mommy, daddy, baby, and brother dolls, along with the *Highlights* magazine he'd stolen from the waiting room.

'What a family,' the doctor muttered, shaking her head.

AMANDA

'Sisters function as safety nets in a chaotic world simply by being there for each other.'
—Carol Saline

Sitting at the breakfast table in the Bullocks' kitchen, Amanda typed into her BlackBerry. 'Well, what do you know? We've caught a break. While you were taking a shower, guess who I found?'

'Who?' Laura said, biting into a piece of buttered wheat toast. She'd just gotten out of the shower, and her long blond hair was still wet.

'Kimba Flick,' Amanda said. 'The Lassiters' old assistant. She lives here. Said we could stop by this morning.'

'She never got married?' Laura said.

'No, she did,' Amanda said. 'But luckily she got divorced and went back to her old name. More toast? Coffee?'

'No, I'm good. You learned all that before I finished my shower? *You are* resourceful,' Laura said.

'It's true. Sometimes I scare myself. C'mon, time's a-wastin'.'

'Wait, what about Serena?' Laura said. 'Isn't she coming?'

'I checked on her while you were in the bathroom,' Amanda said. 'She's too hung over. Said we should go ahead without her.'

'Well, I hope she learned her lesson,' Laura said, grabbing a hardboiled egg for the road.

'I'm pretty sure she has,' Amanda said.

Kimba lived in the estate section of Southampton, a block from the beach. As Dimitri drove them, Amanda noticed a black car lurking behind them at every turn. Are we being followed? she wondered, a wave of apprehension sweeping through her. It looked like Richie's car, which made Amanda feel slightly better. Richie had lost all credibility as a vicious gangster when he let Amanda fake her broken leg. Dimitri stopped the Rolls in front of a gate and pressed the intercom button. Soon they were gliding down a long gravel driveway toward an enormous three-story brown shingled home, leaving the black car out of sight.

'I thought her name was Flick,' Laura said.

'It is, why?' Amanda asked.

'It says 'Levy' on the mailbox,' Laura said.

'Maybe that's her married name,' Amanda said. 'It must be.'

'Didn't you say she went back to her maiden name?' Laura asked.

'She did,' Amanda said. 'I guess she hasn't had a chance to change the sign.'

The front door opened and a large woman in a flowery muumuu emerged waving. She had long gray hair, laughing blue eyes, and an infectious toothy smile.

'Oh my God,' Amanda said. 'She looks exactly the same, only older and fatter and grayer.'

'She's probably thinking the same thing about you,' Laura said.

'At least I haven't surrendered to the muumuu,' Amanda said.

The car pulled to a stop and Amanda jumped out. 'Kimba, you haven't changed a bit,' she said, giving her a hug.

Kimba stepped back and gave Amanda the once-over. 'And you. You're all grown up. In my mind, you were still a spunky ten year old.'

'I'm forty now,' Amanda said. 'It's been thirty years. This is my baby sister, Laura.'

'I'm not a baby,' Laura said.

'You'll always be my baby sister,' Amanda said, 'even when you're seventy.'

Kimba motioned for them to come inside. She led the way to her country kitchen and invited them to sit at her long distressed-wood table. There were fresh cupcakes right out of the oven, waiting to be iced. 'I'd offer you those but I'm making them for someone else. How about some tea?' Kimba asked. Amanda and Laura nodded, so she put the kettle on the gas stove.

'Your house,' Amanda said. 'It's beautiful. What kind of work do you do?'

'If you mean what did I do to afford this place, I assisted the Lassiters the summer I met you. Daniel promised to pay me four dollars an hour at the end of the summer, but instead he gave me a painting. Boy, was I pissed at the time.' Kimba took three mugs out of the cupboard and placed a fresh tea bag in each one. 'Green tea, that's all I have,' she said.

'Why would he give you a painting instead of cash?' Laura asked. 'Wasn't he already famous by then? That *had* to be worth more than your salary.'

'Apparently he was having money problems that summer. From what people say, he went through many booms and busts during his life,' Kimba said. 'When things were tight, his work was his currency.'

'What did you do with the painting?' Amanda asked.

'Nothing. I stuck it in my room and went back to college,' Kimba said. 'Later I got married, had two daughters of my own, twins. They're in graduate school now. In the meantime, I got divorced. My mom died three years ago. When I was cleaning out her house, I found the painting in the top of my closet exactly where I'd left it. Sold it for enough money to buy this home, put the girls through college, and fund my retirement. I tell you, that summer was the most lucrative job I ever had.'

'Can I rub your head?' Laura asked. 'I could

420

use some luck just like that.' Kimba bent her head down and Laura rubbed it.

Amanda laughed. 'It was our mom's best-paying job, too. Did you know he gave her *two* paintings?'

'No, but I'm not surprised,' Kimba said. 'Like I said, there are plenty of people who made small fortunes because Daniel couldn't pay his household bills.'

The kettle whistled and Kimba turned off the stove. She poured three mugs of tea and let them steep.

'Do you remember,' Laura started, 'did he ever romance women outside of his marriage?'

Kimba laughed. 'Oh my lord, yes. He was a well-known womanizer. Such a handsome guy, so charismatic.'

'Did he and our mother have some sort of relationship?' Laura asked.

Kimba cocked her head thoughtfully. 'They were quite friendly. I remember that. But an affair? Why do you ask?' She handed each sister a cup of tea as she spoke. Then she placed a bottle of honey and three spoons on the table.

'Amanda remembers them kissing that summer they were here. When Mom left, he gave her a painting and a sketch. We just thought, why would he give someone paintings unless they had something going?' Laura said.

Kimba shrugged. 'I do recall seeing them together quite a bit, so I suppose it's possible. With his reputation, it wouldn't surprise me.'

'Do you still know Kate?' Amanda said.

'Oh, sure,' Kimba said. 'This is a small community. She's a lovely person, raises money for local causes, lives in the area part-time. We see each other. In fact, we're going to the birthday party of a mutual friend tomorrow, a backyard barbecue. But it's Kate's birthday next week, so I was going to take her those cupcakes. Nothing fancy; she's very down-to-earth.'

'Do you think she'd remember me?' Amanda said. 'I remember her. You used to drive us to the beach on the afternoons my mom had to work. Kate loved to swim. She taught me how to bodysurf.'

'Of course she'd remember you,' Kimba said.

'I would love to see her again.'

'Really?' Kimba said. 'I'm sure that could be arranged.'

'Oh, wait, I know,' Amanda said. 'Let's surprise her. Tell her you want to do something special with her before the party tomorrow. You could go for lunch or, oh, this is better, take her for a manicure or pedicure. Then I'll show up and wish her a happy birthday.'

'I'll ask if she wants to do that,' Kimba said. 'You can't think of any reason she wouldn't be happy to see you, can you?'

'No, of course not,' Amanda said. 'It'll be a great surprise.'

ELLIOTT

'A dress that zips up the back will bring a husband and wife together.'
> —James H. Boren

After he'd dropped the kids off with Charles and Violet, it took Elliott less than two hours to drive to East Hampton, a record for him. Serena was in trouble. For the first time in years, she needed him. He was happy to oblige.

Elliott pulled up to the ornate iron gate in front of the Bullock estate and rang to be let in. The gate opened slowly. As soon as he could get the car through, he floored it, sending up gravel and dirt in its wake. He pounded on the door for entry and a distinguished English butler dressed in a tuxedo answered.

'Yes, may I assist?' he said.

'My wife, Serena, she's tied up somewhere in this house,' Elliott said. 'I mean really tied up, with hand-cuffs. Do you have any idea where she could be?'

The butler appeared thoughtful for a few moments. 'Hmmm,' he said, scratching his chin.

Elliott grabbed him by the collar of his jacket. 'Think, man, think!'

'Oh, I believe I know where she might be,' he said. 'Follow me.' He led Elliott upstairs and down a long hallway into a master bedroom suite, through a closet, and into a space that appeared to be a showcase for S&M paraphernalia. 'You might try going through there,' he said, gesturing toward an arched doorway. Then he respectfully retreated from the room.

Elliott barged in. It appeared to be some sort of medieval torture chamber. There on the stone floor lay Serena, half-naked, one arm cuffed to the leg of a piece of gymnastics equipment. She looked like an unmade bed. 'Oh my God,' he said. He ran back out to the master bedroom, grabbed a cashmere throw, and brought it to Serena. 'Here, baby,' he said, covering her up.

'The keys are in the armoire,' she said.

'I'll get them,' Elliott said. He dashed over and was back by Serena's side in a flash with a ring of keys, wiggling each one into the lock, attempting to release her from the steel cuff that held her hostage. 'One more second,' he said. 'There.'

Serena hightailed it to the bathroom.

I'm not going to ask, Elliott thought. If she wants to tell me, fine, but I'm not pressing her. This is my own damn fault. She wouldn't have been here if I hadn't screwed up. He glanced around the room, astonished at the elaborate torture chamber that had been set up in this stately mansion in

424

East Hampton. It's remarkable, he thought, making a mental note to use this as a location for *Law and Order*.

A few minutes later, Serena appeared wearing a soft pink bathrobe. Her face was scrubbed clean and her hair brushed and loose. She looked pretty and feminine and vulnerable, very different from the take-no-prisoners momzilla of late.

'El,' she said, 'thank you for coming.' Elliott sat down on the floor, his back against the wall, and Serena crawled into his lap. She put her arms around him and he held her while she sobbed. 'I'm so sorry. I'm so sorry,' was all she could say.

'Are you okay?' Elliott asked. 'You're not hurt?'

Serena shook her head.

'I'm the one who's sorry,' Elliott said. 'I've been a selfish ass. Forgive me.' He rocked his wife until her tears stopped. It felt right to have her in his arms again. He kissed her lightly on her head, soft comforting kisses that made him feel needed.

Serena relaxed into his arms. 'Where are the kids?' she said.

'Charles has them,' Elliott said. 'See, I really *was* with him. He was the only person I knew to ask.'

'You'll have to introduce me to him so I can say thanks,' Serena said. 'God, I need a cigarette.' She stood and drifted over to her purse, pulled out an American Spirit, and lit up. Taking a drag, she blew a stream of smoke out of her nose and mouth. She hiked herself up onto the gynecologist's table, facing Elliott, who sat on the floor.

'Since when did you . . . never mind,' Elliott said. He hated that Serena, a former cancer patient, would smoke. But this wasn't the time to hassle her. Right now, all he wanted was to make up with his wife and take her home. The last few days with his children had made him realize how much he loved them. He didn't want to become one of those every-other-weekend fathers. Somehow, he and Serena had to find the love that had brought them together in the first place. 'I . . . I really enjoyed being with the kids. Thanks for making me see what I've been missing. I'm sorry I've been such an absent husband. Until now, I had no idea how hard you worked.'

Serena cocked her head in surprise. 'Really? You mean that?'

Elliott nodded. 'When you left me alone with the children, I thought it was the worst thing that could happen. But it's been a gift. I'm just sorry for what I did to drive you away.' Elliott truly regretted how he'd ignored his wife and children for so long. Still, he wondered if Serena would admit to being part of the problem. Then they could really work this out. Both of them had to change.

Serena took a drag of her cigarette and blew a white line of smoke away from Elliott. 'I want to believe that you're really sorry,' Serena started, 'but after the way you've been since Sebastian was born . . .'

The way *I've* been? The way *I've* been? What about *you*? Elliott wanted to shout. But he didn't.

426

Stay cool, he told himself. 'Do you remember how we *both* were before we had kids? We were successful at work, hip, fun, interesting people. Remember how we used to laugh? Look at us now. Do you recognize either of us? I don't. What do you say we try to get back to being those people again?'

'I could try,' Serena murmured. 'But first I have to ask you something and I beg you to tell me the truth. Did you sleep with Laura?'

'What?' Elliott said indignantly. 'How can you think that? She's your sister.' Elliott's mind flashed back to the moment after Sunny died when he almost made love with Laura. Thank God she stopped me, he thought.

Serena took a deep drag from her cigarette and exhaled. 'Good, because I could never forgive that. Although I can't really blame you for cheating. I suppose I haven't been the easiest person to live with.'

'You think?' Elliott joked. 'I'm kidding,' he smiled. 'Neither of us has been easy.' He gave the dungeon the once over. 'This is some setup they have here.'

'I know. Can you believe how professionally it was done?'

'Remember how we used to role-play when we first got together?' Elliott said.

'I was thinking about that last night,' Serena agreed. 'We had great sex in those days. It was exciting and dangerous, you know?'

'Never perfunctory,' Elliott said.

'No, never.' Serena stubbed out her cigarette on one of the stirrups at the end of the gynecologist's table.

'It could be good again, the sex, the marriage,' Elliott said, his eyes brimming with hope.

Serena hopped off the table, went over to Elliott, and crawled back into his open arms. 'I've been awful,' she said. 'Being responsible for two kids by myself made me temporarily insane. If you'll help me more, I think I can relax about mother-hood, not be such a drill sergeant.'

'I'll help you,' Elliott said. 'I would have before, but I didn't think you needed me.'

'How could you think that?' Serena said. 'I need you desperately. The thing I'm most afraid of is that you'll leave me like my father did.'

Elliott pulled her closer. 'Baby, I'm not going anywhere without you. It's you, me, Sebastian, and Valentina. We're Skanks, and Skanks stick together.'

'You know what,' Serena said. 'Let's pull all our applications. Amanda says P.S. two thirty-four is a fine school. Sebastian doesn't need all the pressure I was putting on him. I'm sure that's why he was stealing those cell phones.'

'And condoms,' Elliott added.

'Condoms? Why would he steal those?'

'He was attracted to the picture of the happy couple on the wrapper,' Elliott said. 'That's all he wants from us.'

A slow smile spread across Serena's face. 'You know what might make us a happy couple again?

428

If we had one of these dungeons in our house. Our sex life would be so much more fun, don't you think? If I had a regular outlet for fun in my life, I'd be a more relaxed mother.'

Elliott went into Marvin Gaye mode. He couldn't help himself. 'Ooh baby,' he sang, '*I'm hot just like an oven; I need some lovin' . . . And when I get that feeling, I want sexual healing,*' he crooned into her ear.

Serena swatted him playfully. 'You're such a cornball.'

Elliott lifted her hair out of her face and kissed her slowly, softly, gently caressing her tongue with his. He was overwhelmed by the deep sense of contentment that came with having her back in his arms again. He wanted to make her happy, protect her, be there for her like he'd promised when they first got married. Serena rested her head on Elliott's shoulder.

'So,' he whispered, 'It's gonna take a dungeon to make you a better mother?'

'It beats a minivan.' She giggled.

'And this won't violate your vow of frugality?' Elliott said. 'It could be expensive to build.'

'No,' Serena said. 'You see, I misunderstood. Last week, a professor on TV was saying that if you *have* money, cutting spending is the *worst* thing you can do for the economy.'

'So let me get this straight. If we put one of these dungeons in our house, we'd be helping our country.'

'Yes, it'd be patriotic of us,' Serena said.

'Why not! Hey, that gives me an idea.' Elliott glanced around the room. 'Let's get a desk where you could be the naughty intern and I could be the president.'

Serena smiled, getting more excited. 'And a whole bondage – slave section. This stuff really turns me on. I could ask Mrs Bullock who she used to put the room together.'

'That's a great idea,' Elliott said. 'This would be the perfect home-improvement project to bring us together.'

'But we'll have to keep the kids away from it,' Serena said.

'An S&M dungeon is no place for children,' Elliott agreed.

'I miss them so much,' Serena said.

'Come on,' Elliott said. 'Let me take you home.'

AMANDA AND LAURA

'When sisters stand shoulder to shoulder, who stands a chance against us?'
—Pam Brown

The next morning, Amanda and Laura sat in the back of the Rolls-Royce as Dimitri drove them to the Dashing Diva in Southampton, where Kimba had invited Kate for a birthday manicure. On their return the day before, Alfred had told them that Elliott had come to pick up Serena. She would not be joining them for the rest of the trip. Later, Jed apologized for going off with Serena. Amanda accepted his apology, but not his invitation to dinner.

'Did you call Serena?' Laura asked. 'Is she feeling better?'

'She's fine,' Amanda said. 'Elliott's taking care of her.'

'So it was perfect that she over-drank the other night,' Laura said. 'Maybe they'll reconcile.'

'Maybe,' Amanda said.

'Do you see that black car behind us?' Laura

431

said. 'I think it's following us. I noticed the same car just about everywhere we went yesterday, and now here it is again.'

Amanda peered out the rear window but couldn't identify the driver. 'You're imagining things,' she said.

Laura glanced back nervously. 'Did you bring the video camera?'

'Check,' Amanda said. 'You got the song?'

'Check,' Laura said. 'What time is the appointment?'

'Eleven,' Amanda said. 'You did a nice job with the costume, by the way.'

'Thanks,' Laura said. 'I had to improvise.' In an effort to resemble a Bob Fosse dancer, she was wearing a black bikini, stiletto heels, long black gloves, and a sequined top hat, all items she had found around the house. She wore a floor-length Blackglama mink over the ensemble for cover. She searched for something fake, but Tabby Bullock didn't own anything but the best. In principle, Laura liked to keep her performances cruelty-free – no fur, feathers, silk, wool, or leather. It wasn't that she herself was an animal-rights activist; it was that she liked to be sensitive to her singing-telegram recipients who might be.

'Make sure to get me on tape so we can give it to her as a souvenir,' Laura said. Even though they were on a mission, she wanted to make Kate's birthday special. Laura was customer-service-oriented that way.

Dimitri pulled into the parking lot of Dashing Diva. Opening the door for the girls, he handed Amanda her crutches. 'I'll wait right here,' he said.

As they entered, a young Korean woman asked if they'd like to have manicures. 'Give us a minute,' Laura said. She glanced around the room and saw Kimba, wearing a different muumuu, sitting at the pedicure station with a woman whom she assumed was Kate. Laura couldn't quite fathom that they were finally meeting Serena's possible sister. She didn't look anything like Serena, though. Her long hair was blond and her eyes green. She was tall, slim, and beautiful in a middle-aged, crunchy-granola sort of way. She and Kimba were laughing.

'Let me get closer to them,' Amanda whispered, crutching her way toward the pedicure area.

Laura noticed that Kate had one foot in the soapy water and the other out. Her manicurist had just cut her toenails on one foot and was about to start on the other. They had arrived in the nick of time.

Amanda pulled on her earlobe, a signal to Laura to get started.

Laura situated herself in front of Kate and pushed the PLAY button on her iPod speaker. She whipped off her coat and then let it slowly drop to the floor. All eyes were on her half-naked body as she cried:

'Ladies and gentlemen – mostly ladies! May I have your attention PUH-LEASE?

> *The minute I walked in the joint*
> *I could see you were a girl of distinction*
> *Who's turning one year older*
> *So good-looking, with nails so fine . . .'*

Laura sang, picking up Kate's hands and admiring them, deftly turning her away from Amanda for a few moments.

> *'Now wouldn't you like to know what's goin' on*
>   *in my mind?*
> *Well, let me get right to the point!* (Bump.
>   Bump.)
> *All the fellas must be crazy for your'* – She
>   paused saucily – *'man-i-cure . . .*
> *Hey there, Ka-ate! You could give us lessons for*
>   *sure!'*

As Laura sang, Amanda asked Kate's manicurist if she could use her seat to record the performance up close. By all means, the manicurist said. Well, actually, she was a gum-snapping local from Manorville, so she merely said, 'Oh yeah, sure.' As Amanda taped with one hand, she used the other to sweep Kate's toenail clippings into a baggie that she'd brought for the occasion. No one except Laura noticed how she purloined Kate's body bits; all eyes were glued to the bumping and grinding birthday performance.

At this point, Laura launched into a sexy kazoo solo while she simultaneously danced on the floor, having not brought her two-by-two fold-up parquet floor with her for the occasion. When she finished, everyone in the shop applauded and there were calls for an encore.

Amanda introduced herself to Kate. 'Do you remember me?' she said. 'Thirty years ago my mother worked for your father. You taught me to bodysurf.'

Kate cocked her head thoughtfully. 'I'm sorry,' she said. 'I don't . . . It's been a long time.'

'It's okay,' Amanda said. She cast her eyes down. 'You must meet a lot of people.'

Laura felt sad for Amanda. She thought about what a big part Kate and her father had played in her own family's lives, and yet her family was nothing to them. Poor Serena, who had talked herself into believing Daniel Lassiter was her father. You can't really blame her, she thought. Everyone said Daddy never wanted anything to do with her. Laura was too young to remember it herself. Who in those circumstances wouldn't fantasize about having a rich and famous father? And in her case, there was evidence that it might be true. Soon they would have their answer.

'Thanks for the song,' Kate said. 'I didn't see *that* coming.'

'Neither did I,' Kimba said. 'Do you have a card?'

Laura flashed her infectious smile as she handed each of them one of her singing telegram cards. 'Kate, you have a happy birthday and an abundant life. We'll get this transferred to a DVD and send it to you, okay?'

'That'd be great,' Kate said. 'Can I give you my address?'

'That's okay,' Laura said. 'We have it.'

Amanda ran into Jed as she helped Dimitri pack up the Rolls for their journey home.

'Is your sister doing okay?' he asked. 'She looked "rode hard and put away wet" when she left yesterday.'

'What does that mean?'

'Like she'd been through an ordeal,' Jed explained.

'Oh no, she was fine,' Amanda lied. In hindsight, she deeply regretted leaving her sister tied up all night and then not releasing her in the morning. She'd called to check on her, but Serena wouldn't pick up. After all that had happened, she probably needed time to cool off. Serena and Amanda had spent a lifetime fighting and making up. Amanda prayed they would eventually work this out.

On the more positive side, Richie had called to say he had insinuated himself back onto her case. Someone had to take a stand against unfair collection practices, he told her. It was one thing to break the debtor's bones, but to hurt innocent family members went beyond the boundaries of moral decency, even for him, and *he* was a CIA assassin.

'One more thing, Red,' he said. 'You said you'd owe me forever if I took you back on. Did you mean it?'

'Of course I did,' Amanda said.

'Because I plan to collect,' he said.

'Is that a threat, Richard?'

'No, baby, that's a promise,' he said.

Amanda's stomach flipped. She wasn't sure what he meant by that, but she secretly longed to find out.

LAURA

'How do people make it through life without a sister?'

—Sara Corpening

When she got home, Laura knocked on Serena's door. Sebastian answered.

'Aunt Laura,' he cried with delight. 'You come for dinner?'

'No, I thought I'd stop by and see how everyone's doing,' she said. 'Where's Mommy and Daddy?'

'In the kitchen,' he said. 'Daddy's cooking.'

'I didn't know he cooked,' Laura said.

'My daddy's a fine cook,' Sebastian said.

Laura followed her nephew into the kitchen where, indeed, Elliott was sporting a white chef's apron while scrambling eggs. Valentina was in her high chair wearing only a diaper and gulping Gerber's applesauce, half of which hadn't made it into her mouth. Serena, dressed casually in jeans, a white Hanes T-shirt, and pink flip-flops, was feeding Valentina while studying the label on the bottle. 'You're right, El, there really isn't

438

anything wrong with store-bought baby food. It's apples and ascorbic acid. I know I always like ascorbic acid in my food, what about you?'

'I just added a dash to the eggs,' Elliott said.

'Mommy, Aunt Laura is here,' Sebastian announced.

'You want to join us for dinner?' Serena asked. 'Elliott's making eggs.'

Elliott turned around and waved his spatula. 'With ascorbic acid.'

'No, no, that's okay,' Laura said. 'I have plans.' She was going to visit David, who was feeling so much better now that Emma Schneiderstern was back to sleeping over. Emma no longer lived at Golden Manor. They had kicked her out for torching her room. But she had stood by David throughout his pacemaker ordeal and the two were closer than ever. Since she was banned from the home, his friends were sneaking her in through the back door. Breaking the rules brought an element of danger to the nursing home that the more daring residents enjoyed.

Serena wiped Valentina's mouth with her Chinese alphabet bib and gestured for Laura to follow her into the den.

'I wanted to tell you that Amanda and I got DNA from Kate Lassiter. We'll know soon if you're related.'

'That's great,' Serena said. 'How did you manage it?'

Laura told her how she'd delivered a singing

telegram to Kate while Amanda had stolen her toenail clippings during a birthday pedicure. She glanced at Serena's bookshelf and noticed that all her books had been shelved by spine color. Yellow blended into orange, which blended into red, which blended into purple, and so on. 'Wow, I've never seen books organized that way.'

'Thanks. I got tired of shelving them from smallest to largest,' Serena said.

'The eggs are ready,' Elliott called from the kitchen. 'You want some?'

'No, I have too much going on,' Laura said. 'I'm seeing David and I have to pack for my trip.'

'Where are you going?' Serena asked.

'My job with that billionaire starts Tuesday,' she said. 'I have to be at Teterboro at eight. It's a ten-day shift. They paid me twenty grand, so guess I better show up. And don't forget my Joey Martin audition tomorrow.'

'We'll be there,' Serena said. 'Say, what was the name of that billionaire you're working for?'

'I'm not allowed to say. They made me sign a confidentiality agreement. But if the movie gig comes through, I'm backing out of the job. I'd just as soon repay the twenty grand and wish him *sayonara*.'

Serena eyed Laura suspiciously. 'There's something you're not telling me. No one pays a stewardess twenty grand for ten days, especially in this economy. Are you sure this is legit?'

Laura shrugged and glanced away from her sister.

'It isn't, is it?' Serena said. 'Do you have to sleep with him or smuggle drugs or something?'

'No-ooooh,' Laura said, her voice wavering. 'He's rich and pays accordingly.' Drop it, Laura said with her eyes. This is hard enough without making me lie about it. Then she thought, maybe I should tell her the truth. She could help me think of a way out. Nah, the only way out is to return the twenty grand, and Serena doesn't have that.

Serena's eyes grew narrow. 'He's rich and pays accordingly, huh? So you wouldn't mind if I showed up and assessed the situation for myself. You *are* my little sister, you know.'

Laura's mouth dropped open. 'Don't you dare! It's my first day on the job.'

'Serena,' Elliott called. 'Dinner.'

'Laura, I don't want you getting in over your head,' Serena said, strolling back to the kitchen. 'You're too nice. People take advantage of you.'

'I know what I'm doing,' Laura assured her.

Serena gave her husband a big hug from behind. He turned around and kissed her on the lips. You could have knocked Laura over with a tiddlywink. What had inspired this change of heart? Was Serena no longer afraid Elliott would leave her? Usually the tension was palpable when these two were together. Now nothing seemed tense at all. Something was very wrong.

Elliott brought plates of eggs and buttered toast to the table. 'C'mon Sebastian, let's go wash your hands,' he said, taking his son's hand and gently directing him toward the bathroom. 'I love eating breakfast food for dinner. Don't you?'

'Me too, Daddy,' Sebastian said. 'Let's do it every night.'

'You sure you aren't hungry?' Serena asked.

'No, no, a thousand times no,' Laura said, laughing. 'It's nice to see you and Elliott getting along so well. What happened?'

'I had a very long night to think about the person I've become and I didn't like her,' Serena said. 'And Elliott got to live my life for a few days. We have a new appreciation of each other.'

'Guess what?' Elliott said, as he returned. 'Serena and I are going to build our own . . .'

'Elliott, shhhh,' Serena said. 'Not in front of the children.'

'Sorry,' Elliott said. 'It's a secret.'

'I love secrets,' Sebastian said. 'You want to know my secret?'

'Sure,' Laura said. 'Tell us.'

'If I told you, *it wouldn't be a secret*,' Sebastian said, beaming.

'Has anyone ever told you how smart you are?' Laura said, giving his nose an affectionate wiggle. 'Because you are.'

'Thank you, Aunt Laura. It's true.'

AMANDA

'I felt it shelter to speak to you.'
—Emily Dickinson

Amanda carried two full bags of freshly prepared dishes from Whole Foods. Like many New Yorkers, Amanda reheated; she didn't cook. The only use she had for her oven was to store off-season sweaters.

Holding a bag in each hand while also grasping the handle of her crutches, she felt hot and heavily loaded down. Why did I buy so much? she thought. No, no, it's good for me. Schlepping these groceries is as close to a workout as I've had in months. Still, it was late. Amanda was beat. She just wanted to get home and curl up in her pajamas.

The street was empty as she crutched past P.S. two thirty-four. The children were gone, at home nestled in their beds. That's where I should be, she thought. As she made her way toward Duane Street, she heard a rustling sound behind her. Quickly she turned and saw two rather large figures lurking about half a block behind her. Instinct told her they were up to no good. Her heart racing like a motor, Amanda moved faster and from the sound of their footsteps knew they had picked up speed. Shit, she thought, her eyes darting around for a well-lit street with pedestrians. Unfortunately, this part of Tribeca was a dead zone after six o'clock.

Amanda felt lightheaded. Sweat prickled on her face. Her bags magically became twice as heavy. She thought about ditching them but then decided they could be used as weapons. If these men meant to hurt her, she could swing them hard against their faces, maybe knock them out. Then she realized that bags of pre-cooked food in little cardboard containers wouldn't pack much punch. I'll whack them with my crutches, she decided.

Sensing the men getting closer, Amanda felt a cold knot of fear. She turned left on Church, speed-crutching toward Chambers Street, which was usually busier. A bus roared by leaving a cloud of exhaust in its wake. She passed a pile of stuffed black garbage bags awaiting pickup. The scent of something dead wafted through the air. Amanda felt out of breath and her mouth was bone-dry. Is this it? Am I going to die tonight?

Suddenly, a pair of hands grabbed her and swung her around, knocking both crutches and bags of groceries to the ground. None other than Anthony 'Kneecap' Santorielli shoved her into a darkened doorway. Amanda crumpled to the ground in true cowardly fashion.

'Get up,' Kneecap said. An older man stood behind him leering at Amanda. He was stocky with long hairy arms, a Cro Magnon holdover that hadn't gotten the memo on evolution.

'Okay, okay,' Amanda said, but she felt paralyzed. Come on legs; be brave, she thought. Don't let me down now.

Kneecap grabbed her collar and in one motion lifted her and shoved her against the wall. 'You're overdue on your loan, sister. We're getting impatient.' His breath stank of coffee and cigarettes.

'I – I told Richard . . .'

'You told Richard what?' said a familiar voice.

Amanda's head jerked toward the sound. There stood Richie. He wore Levis, a black sweatshirt, and Nikes, his wavy black pompadour tucked inside a Yankees cap. Richie's jaws were clenched and he glared at Kneecap like a lion ready to pounce. Amanda practically swooned.

'Dude, we were just messin' with her,' Kneecap said. 'Weren't we, Thor?'

'Yeah, givin' her shit, heh, heh, heh, heh,' Thor said.

'I don't mess with *your* clients,' Richie said, his black eyes focused like lasers on Kneecap's. 'So I'd appreciate the same consideration, *dude.*'

The way he said it, you knew he meant it. Without a word, Kneecap skulked away with Thor at his heels.

Amanda's legs buckled, sending her back to the pavement as she burst into tears of relief. *What have I done? Who have I gotten myself involved with?*

Richie was immediately by her side. 'Are you okay, Red? He didn't hurt you, did he?'

Amanda shook her head. She had never felt more grateful to anyone in her life. 'Thank you-ooh,' she said, gulping back tears.

Richie gathered up the scattered food containers and packed them back into their bags. Luckily the cashier at Whole Foods had taped each one shut, so nothing had spilled. Richie helped Amanda to her feet, handed her the crutches, and took the groceries himself. 'Let's get you home,' he said. 'Taxi!'

To Amanda's relief, they didn't run into Serena or Laura at the house. She knew she was a sight. All she wanted was to go upstairs, wash this day away with a hot shower, and climb into bed.

'Can I come inside for few minutes?' Richie said. 'To make sure you're safe.'

'Of course,' Amanda said, unlocking the door. As soon as she shut the door, Amanda threw her crutches on the ground and hobbled over to the couch. She wasn't sure if she would ever be able to get up again.

'Let me put your groceries away,' Richie said, making his way to the kitchen. When he emerged, he was carrying two glasses of Cakebread

Chardonnay from the bottle that had been chilling in the refrigerator.

Amanda had a firm rule not to fraternize with her collector, but since he had just saved her life, or at least her knees, she made an exception. 'Thanks,' she said, taking a glass and gulping down half of it before she realized what she was doing.

'Where's the bathroom?' Richie said.

Amanda pointed the way. Slowly, she sipped her wine, took deep cleansing breaths, and pulled herself back together.

Several minutes passed before Richie returned. 'Come, I made something nice for you,' he said, offering her his hand. 'Don't look,' he said, leading her through the apartment toward the master bath. With her eyes still shut, she smelled a delicate flowery scent and felt warm moist air against her skin. When she opened her eyes, she saw her oversized tub filled with steaming water and frothy bubbles. A symphony of flickering candles placed throughout the room cast a rich orange light against the walls. He had set her iPod and docking station on the dressing table. Frank Sinatra was singing *Strangers in the Night* in the background. It was hokey and adorable and sexy all at the same time, not what she would expect from an outlaw like Richie. Amanda melted.

'Ah . . . ah . . . I don't know what to say,' she whispered. 'This is the sweetest thing . . . but I can't take a bath. My cast.'

'Here,' Richie said, getting on bended knees.

He held open a large, plastic bag from Bed, Bath, and Beyond. 'Step in and I'll tape you up.'

Amanda sat on her dressing table bench as Richie water-proofed her cast. Using thick electrical tape he had found under the sink, he form-fitted the bag to the cast, then created a seal at the knee. 'All done. I think it's safe to bathe now.' Richie excused himself.

Amanda took off her clothes and dropped them in the hamper. Then she stepped into the rich, velvety water and submerged her body, from the tip of her cast to the top of her head. When she came up for air, Richie was standing by the tub, holding two glasses of wine. 'Thank you so much,' she said. 'You don't know how I've longed for a bath.'

'Cheers then,' he said, handing her a glass, making himself comfortable by the side of the tub. 'You are so beautiful, Red.'

He couldn't possibly believe that, she thought. Could he? 'No,' Amanda said, her blush hidden by the candlelight. 'I mean, thank you.' She could hardly fathom that Richie was interested in her romantically. He was a studly, young quasi-criminal. She was a tired, pre-menopausal, staunch follower of the penal code.

'It's true,' Richie said. 'You're beautiful . . . to me. There's something so sweet and vulnerable about you.' He handed her a bath pillow.

Amanda reoriented herself in the tub, with her head on the pillow, her legs crossed so that her castless foot emerged from the bubbles. 'Me? Vulnerable?' Amanda said. 'Oh no, I'm super-competent. I take care of everything for everyone. There's nothing vulnerable about me.'

'That wasn't the case tonight,' Richie said, his hand on her knee. 'Or any other time I've been with you. I see it in your green eyes. I hear it in your sexy voice. I feel it in your hairy leg.'

Amanda dropped her leg back into the tub. 'I'm so embarrassed. I never expected a man to see me in the tub.' She dunked under the bubbles again until she was forced to come up for air.

Richie went over to Amanda's drawer and fished out a razor and shaving cream. 'Here. Give me your leg.'

Amanda did as she was told, draping her good leg over the edge. Richie squeezed out a dollop of cream and spread it up and down. Carefully, he shaved it in gentle, clean lines as Frank Sinatra sang *I've Got You Under My Skin*. 'Perfect,' he said when he was done.

Amanda caressed her butter-smooth leg under the water. Who was this man who was giving her such exquisite attention? He seemed so different from Richie, the collector-thug. Maybe she was seeing him in a different light. She knew she didn't deserve such pampering, but she loved it nonetheless. 'I could get used to this.'

Richie gave her a sly smile. 'Funny. That's what I had in mind.'

Amanda's heart quickened and she felt a flash

of heat surge through her. More than anything, she wanted to touch him, to lose herself in his embrace. She didn't care that he was a hooligan. In fact, his bad-boyness turned her on. Reaching over, she took off Richie's Yankees cap and stroked his wavy black hair. 'Do you want to join me? Because I want you to if you want to.'

Richie unbuttoned his shirt, revealing the ripped torso of a man used to the physical life. That is one fine set of pecs, Amanda thought, gulping. They were so much better than Riley's, whose chest muscles were artificially pumped in the gym. Richie got his the old-fashioned way – wrangling heavy debtors to the ground or pummeling dead-beats. There was something pure and real about Richie; it was a quality she hadn't encountered among the macho power elite.

When Richie's pants and shorts came off, Amanda could barely breathe. Oh my God, she gasped. It was as if Michelangelo's *David* had come to life, stepped into her tub, and begun to caress her skin, whispering sweet words of devotion into her ear. Beneath the warm soapy water, she and Richie gently touched each other's bodies, exploring each other all over, laughing at the pesky air bubble from the bag covering Amanda's cast. Above the water, they reveled in long delicious kisses as rich as melted Godiva chocolate. Amanda felt Richie's erection against her leg and knew that he was ready for her. But when he tried to enter her, they both slipped under the water. It was impossible to find a good position in the soapy tub, which wasn't built for two. Laughing and coughing, Richie helped Amanda out, dried her off, removed the Bed, Bath, and Beyond bag that waterproofed her cast, and led her to the bed, where they made love properly and then fell into a deep, satisfying sleep.

LAURA

For Laura's big moment, she dressed with scrupulous care – her favorite 1950s vintage silk emerald-green form-fitting dress ending above the knee and jeweled six-inch-heeled strappy sandals borrowed from Serena. With her long blond curls bouncing with life, her illegal curves, and her killer talent, Laura owned the room. Granted, it was the rec room in an old folks' home that smelled of Pine-Sol, but she owned it just the same.

Nurse Vanderkwat introduced them. 'Ladies and gentlemen, let's welcome to the Golden Manor stage for the first time in weeks, the Off Our Rockers Quartet, featuring David Hargrove and his new pacemaker on piano, John Hazeltine on drums, Stan Garrett on bass, and of course, the lovely Laura Moon singing lead!'

452

'Fly me to the moon, let me sing among those
  stars
Let me see what spring is like on Jupiter and
  Mars . . .'

The band did all their standards— *April in Paris,
Cheek to Cheek, High Hopes, Nice Work if You Can
Get It* – numbers that most of the elderly audi-
ence had etched into their long-term memories.

Serena, Elliott, and the kids were in the audience
offering moral support. Sebastian was dancing
cheek-to-cheek with Eva, her soul coach, who was
carrying him high in her arms. Amanda sat in the
back row with a hunky guy who appeared to be
much younger than she. Marc Tannenbaum stood
to the side holding hands with his new boyfriend,
a well-built brown-eyed brunette with a movie-star
smile, who he'd just met at a plastic surgeons'
convention. Joey Martin sat front and center, his
Aunt Miriam on one side, Emma Schneiderstern
and her portable oxygen tank on the other.

Behind Joey were two Hollywood-types. Jarrod,
his long-haired, jeans-clad producer, was slight in
stature but generous in snout. Kyle, his silver-haired
musical director, wore a burnt orange silk shirt
unbuttoned to reveal a thick mat of matching red
chest hair. Laura watched them as she sang, noting
their every smile and move to the beat. Were they
enjoying it? They seemed to be. Please, Laura
prayed, let them love us. Let them take us and put
us in their movie and make us stars. This is it, our

big break. Everything depends on Joey, Jarrod, and Kyle. They *will* love us, they *will*, Laura decreed as she sang.

'Ladies and gentlemen, we are so happy to be playing this special concert for you today. On electric wheelchair, we have John Hazeltine, behind those thick glasses is Stan Garrett, the unstoppable David Hargrove is on piano, and I'm Laura Moon. Thank you for coming and we'll see you next Saturday, regular time, for our weekly show here at the Manor.' Everyone burst into applause. Serena and Amanda gave a standing ovation and shouted, 'Brilliant,' 'Encore,' 'We love you.' Laura hoped it wasn't too obvious they were her sisters.

Laura thanked her bandmates and downed a bottle of Evian as Joey Martin conferred with his people. I gave it my all, she thought. Whatever happens is meant to happen. *Que sera, sera*, right?

Joey Martin approached the band. Laura's stomach did a triple flip off the high dive. Her mouth was dry even though she had just chugged an entire bottle of water.

'Great show, everyone,' Joey said, shaking hands and patting backs all around. 'David, I'm so happy you're doing better after that scare you had. I had no idea until today.'

'Yes, well, it's thanks to Laura that I could play for you,' David said. 'She paid for my operation.'

Joey gave Laura a firm handshake of gratitude. 'I have good news and bad,' he said. 'My producer and musical director loved your performance, but

454

they both feel we need to go with a headliner. What we'd like to do is use your band both on-camera and off, but we're going to book a Norah Jones or Diana Krall to sing lead.'

Laura wanted to spontaneously combust. They chose the band but not me? she thought. How could that be? I put out all the right energy to attract the job. I followed *The Secret* to the letter. I broke up with the man I was falling in love with to put my career first. This can't be happening.

David stepped forward and shook Joey's hand. 'Sir, we thank you for the opportunity, but we play with Laura Moon or we don't play at all.' Behind him, Stan and John nodded their assent. Laura couldn't believe anyone would do that for her.

'Your loyalty is admirable,' Joey said. 'But this is a big opportunity. It pays well, and you'd get royalties from the CD.'

'Lord knows we could use the bread,' David said. 'But Laura is family to us, and we won't enjoy the success if she's not part of it.' He stood behind her and put his large hands on her shoulders.

Laura was sorely disappointed that Joey Martin had rejected her, but that was no reason for the band to suffer, she thought. They needed this break. 'Guys, you *have* to do this. It'll be huge for you. Then later, when we play together, more people will want to see us because you were in the movie.'

'That's right,' Joey said. 'Your success will rub off on Laura in your future gigs.'

'I don't see why you can't use her,' David said. 'Give our girl a break. You could make her life, brother. I'm so damned decrepit, I don't know how many gigs I have ahead that might help her.'

'Yes,' John agreed. 'The public will love her. Everyone does. She's the heart and soul of our band.'

Laura was touched that John saw her as the heart and soul of the band. 'Guys, I'll be fine,' Laura said, making her special brave smile. 'I *want* you to take it. Don't you dare say no. They'll do it, Mr Martin.'

Serena had moseyed as close to them as she could without breathing directly on Joey Martin's neck. She was eavesdropping. Laura could see from the heartbroken expression on her sister's face that she knew. That made the rejection all the worse. More than anything she wanted to prove to Serena and Amanda that she could make it on her own.

'This is my musical director's call,' Joey said, 'but what's the point of being the director if I can't make a few decisions of my own? Laura, I promise we'll use you in one song. I don't know where in the film or what it'll be, but you'll get a song. Does that work for you, boys?'

'I guess it'll have to,' David said. He put his arm around Laura and gave her a squeeze. 'I'm only saying yes because it's what you want for the band.'

Laura's face took on a resigned expression. 'Of course it is.' In time, I'll see the perfection in this, she told herself. I have to trust the universe.

LAURA

'As we drive along this road called life, occasionally a gal will find herself a little lost. And when that happens, I guess she has to let go of the coulda, shoulda, woulda, buckle up, and just keep going.'
—Carrie Bradshaw, *Sex and the City*

When Laura got home that evening, she was too crestfallen to eat. Instead, she retreated to her mother's storage room. It always centered her to sit among Sunny's things, just as it had settled her mother when she was sick.

Curling up on Mom's overstuffed chair, still in her silk emerald-green dress, Laura closed her eyes and inhaled deeply, filling her lungs with the fading remnants of Sunny's trademark scent. She was simply, utterly, and immutably exhausted. Her dream of making it big had been shattered. Sure, she would get to sing one song for the movie, but that wouldn't be life-changing. She felt like an idiot for sending Charles packing. Careers were cold and cruel and no substitute for love. Her eyes filled and a lump formed in her throat. She blinked hard to stave off the waterworks. Then she thought, no, it's okay to grieve. She let go, and hot tears tumbled down her face, wetting her cheeks and spilling into her mouth and onto her dress.

Laura wiped her face with the back of her hand. She had no choice but to deliver what she promised to Misters Kinky Billionaire and Creepy Pilot. At eight the next morning, she was due at Teterboro Airport to start the ten-day shift for which she had already been paid. Maybe she'd get lucky and he'd be more in the mood for karaoke than kinky sex. Would Tamara be there? No one had told her. She closed her eyes and drifted into lala land, dreaming of the dirty deed for which she had been hired. As she slept, she saw herself serving Mr Kinky Billionaire a glass of red wine in his library. He pressed a button and called his pilot to the master bedroom suite. Laura joined the two of them there.

Slowly, Laura stripped out of her uniform as Captain Bing watched. First her skirt, then her jacket and crisp white shirt. She stood in her cream-colored lace panties and bra. Captain Bing unhooked her bra. Laura slipped it off and stepped out of her panties. Releasing her cloud of blond curls from her tortoiseshell clip, she shook her hair loose. Mr Kinky Billionaire wandered into the room. He was sitting on the white stuffed chair, reading his *Wall Street Journal*. The captain removed his belt and unzipped his pants. His protuberance popped up like a piece of toast. Laura got on her knees and took him into her mouth, licking and sucking and moaning as if she were turned on. Mr Kinky Billionaire, the revered genius whom the president regularly called to opine on world economic issues, peeped naughtily over his newspaper.

Captain Bing removed his member from Laura's mouth and quickly stripped naked. For an older guy, he was in remarkably good shape – arm and leg muscles hard and defined, ripped abs. He lay Laura out on the king-sized bed and began to kiss her neck, her breasts, her nipples, her belly. Soon his mouth was between her legs while Laura writhed and moaned. It was all make-believe. Laura observed that Mr Kinky Billionaire had unzipped his own pants and was rubbing himself slowly and then faster, his eyes rolling back in his head. It was disconcerting to see this master of the universe, whose recent hardcover biography Oprah had picked for her book club, pounding and pulling on his penis. The captain finished faux-pleasuring Laura and stopped to put on a rubber. Even in her dreams, she practiced safe sex. He entered her, tenderly at first and then harder. Laura saw Mr Kinky Billionaire slapping his salami behind his newspaper to the same rhythm. While Laura faked the Star Spangled Banner of orgasms, she heard Mr Kinky Billionaire moaning as he spread his fourteen-karat seed all over the white chair. She wondered if, as the stewardess on duty, she would be expected to clean up after him.

The captain reversed thrust and took Laura from a new angle. As he jackhammered away at her, Mr Kinky Billionaire left the room. Laura pushed the captain off. 'But wait, I'm not finished,' he said.

'Finish yourself,' Laura says. 'Show's over.'

'I hired you and I can fire you,' the captain said. He pushed Laura back on the bed and tried to take her even though she resisted.

Suddenly, from the bathroom, out popped Charles with Violet in tow, warning the captain to leave Laura alone. The captain refused, and Charles stabbed him through the heart with a pair of scissors that Violet had pulled out of her pink Hello Kitty back-pack. Laura grabbed a throw blanket and covered her naked self, feeling humiliated that Charles and Violet knew her secret. If the jet weren't cruising at thirty-six thousand feet, she would have run out the door in shame.

Laura opened her eyes and shook her head vigorously. What a nightmare, she thought. 'I can't do it. I can't,' she said aloud. 'Who cares about my *Behind the Music* episode? This is too weird even for me. Mama, I need some help here!' She scrolled through her BlackBerry, searching for the captain's number. That's it; I'm quitting. But then she remembered they had already paid her for ten days. She had spent the money and had no way of making it back. The time had come to face the music.

SERENA

*'The mildest, drowsiest sister has been known
to turn tiger if her sibling is in trouble.'*
— Clara Ortega

Serena and Amanda slouched down in the taxi to be sure Laura wouldn't see them. 'Follow that cab, but not too close,' Serena told the driver. 'They're going to Teterboro Airport.'

When Laura didn't get the movie gig, Serena knew that she would report to work the next day for her flight attendant job. Laura was a woman of her word. If she'd taken that billionaire's money, she would do whatever he asked of her. Laura was naïve and generous to a fault. Obviously, the man wanted her to do something illegal, immoral, indecent, or all of the above. Otherwise, why would he have paid so much? Serena guessed he expected Laura to sleep with him. I won't allow it, Serena thought. Not only could this damage her little sister's psyche forever, but she would be sullying the Skank name. Not that Laura was a Skank herself, but she was related to one.

461

Serena considered going to the airport before Laura arrived and confronting the billionaire, but realized that she didn't know the man's name and would have no idea on whom to use her matchless skills at public humiliation.

The day before, Serena had called Amanda to see if she knew anything about the captain of industry who had hired their sister. Amanda didn't.

'Do you want to apologize to me for stealing Jed?' Amanda asked.

'Not unless you want to apologize to me for leaving me imprisoned all night,' Serena said.

'If you're not apologizing, then I'm not,' Amanda said.

'Well, I'm not apologizing because you really should apologize first,' Serena said. 'But I'm calling a truce, because I think Laura's in way over her head.' She went on to explain what she feared their younger sister was about to do. 'I'm following her to the airport tomorrow morning to stop her. You in?'

'Have I ever shirked an opportunity to save one of my sisters?' Amanda said.

'Ooh, ooh, stop, they're pulling over,' Serena told the driver, throwing two twenty-dollar bills at him. 'Let us out here.'

Serena and Amanda, both dressed in head-to-toe black for camouflage purposes, hung back but kept Laura within their sights as she entered the small terminal building. She was wearing a navy miniskirt and a white silk blouse. 'A bit risqué for your traditional flight attendant, don't you think?' Serena whispered.

Inside, a pilot was introducing Laura to one of the most recognizable men in the world. He had graced the covers of every financial magazine, starred in his own bestselling biography, and made the news regularly. 'Can you believe someone that respected would take advantage of our baby sister?' Amanda said. 'Despicable swine!'

Amanda and Serena stood by a pillar about ten feet away from their sister. Look at him, leering at Laura, undressing her with his eyes, Serena thought. She could no longer hide her feelings. 'Stop, you lecherous goat!' She shouted so that everyone in the terminal could hear. 'That creep wants to bed my underage sister and, and, and feed her illegal drugs and make her launder money for him.'

'Laura's not underage,' Amanda said.

'He doesn't know that,' Serena whispered.

Laura spotted her sisters. Her mouth dropped open and her face turned bright red.

All activity in the building froze. People turned and stared. The billionaire maintained a cool expression as though none of this had anything to do with him. Laura glared at Serena and Amanda, begging them with her eyes to leave her alone.

'Laura,' Amanda cried, 'If that plane leaves the ground and you're on it with that pervert, you're gonna regret it.'

'Maybe not today, maybe not tomorrow, but soon and for the rest of your life,' Serena added.

'For God's sake, Serena,' Amanda said. 'Is this a joke to you?'

'No!' Serena said. 'You started it with that line.' Then she remembered that she had vowed to stop making excuses and blaming others. 'Sorry. Not your fault. But she *will* regret it for the rest of her life. We both know she will.'

Two large men with biceps of steroidal proportions emerged out of nowhere and grabbed Serena and Amanda. Security, no doubt. 'Unhand us, you lugs!' Serena screamed, thrashing her arms and legs to no avail.

Another set of gargantuan bodybuilder-slash-bodyguards whisked the billionaire away from the fracas. Serena realized that legends like His Hominess pay big bucks to be insulated from the ugly consequences of their sordid actions.

'Laura Moon, I *forbid* you to go on that jet!' Amanda screamed.

The captain had clenched his jaw so tight that the pulsating blue vein on his neck looked about to explode.

'Let my sister go or I'll publicize this, I swear! I did PR for Versace for years!' Serena shouted. 'My next-door neighbor's sister's children go to private school with Rupert Murdoch's kids from his second marriage! I can make your boss's kinky proclivities front-page news with one phone call!'

'Who *are* those nuts?' Captain Bing demanded.

464

Laura shrugged. 'Never saw them before in my life.'

'Laura, dammit, we're here to save you! Can't you see these people are up to no good?' Serena screamed and struggled with her captors. 'Let me go, you repugnant bovine!'

The captain nodded his head toward the goons holding Serena and Amanda. 'Big Mike, Hammer, let them go. What's this about? Who are you?'

Laura held her head in her hands. Clearly she was embarassed, although Serena couldn't see why. It was those criminal pervert employers who should be ashamed of themselves.

'We're Laura's big sisters and she is not going to work for you. If she does, your boss's face and lascivious intentions will be plastered across every newspaper tomorrow morning for all your share-holders and his wife and children to see,' Serena said. 'Got that, Bub!'

Captain Bing's eyes flashed with anger. He turned to Laura. 'You breached your confidentiality agreement. We'll be back in New York in ten days. Big Mike and Hammer will be in touch to pick up the twenty grand you owe us. Don't think we won't collect.' With that, he turned on his heels and marched toward the tarmac.

'Laura, are you okay?' Serena said. 'Thank God we got here in time.'

'Don't be mad at us,' Amanda said. 'We were afraid for you.'

Laura's cheeks were mottled with red spots of

rage. 'How could you do that to me? What makes you think I need your protection? I was about to quit. But I would have been calm and apologetic, not raving like a lunatic. I could have talked them into forgiving my debt, or at least giving me time to pay it back.'

Serena shrank back. 'Oh. Really? Never mind.' No one ever appreciates me, she thought.

'We're sorry,' Amanda said. 'If we'd known . . .'

'C'mon, let's get out of here,' Laura snarled in a very un-Laura-like manner.

'Wait, Elliott sent something for you,' Serena said. She reached into her bag and pulled out a silver necklace with two half-heart charms hanging from it. 'Some man named Charles wanted you to have this.'

LAURA

'All that I am or ever hope to be, I owe to my angel Mother.'

—Abraham Lincoln

Laura took refuge in her mother's storage room as soon as she got home, slamming the door behind her. Damn Serena and Amanda for interfering, she thought. I know I could have worked it out myself. Now what? She paced back and forth, thinking. In ten days she would have to return twenty thousand dollars she didn't have.

Glancing around the room, Laura thought there *had* to be something among all this junk that she could sell to raise cash. The envelope containing the inventory of her mother's stuff sat on top of the vanity. Laura pulled out the list. What could it possibly include? Mom's old green sweater from Macy's? Her pressboard night table from the Sixth Avenue flea market? The TV with the broken volume button? She scanned the list and chuckled:

Inventory of Sunny Moon's belongings:

1. *Clothes that need to go to Goodwill.*
2. *Flea-market furniture you can toss.*
3. *Old books that have gathered dust. Read whatever interests you and donate the rest.*
4. *My vanity table and bench. I'd like to think you'll watch yourself put on makeup in the same mirror that I always used.*
5. *The armoire my mother left me. The key is in the top drawer of the vanity. There's a surprise for you inside.*

Kisses and hugs, Mom

Laura eyed the armoire. She'd meant to call an appraiser to take a look at it, but hadn't had time. It must be an antique if it came from Grandma, she thought. Laura drifted over to the massive piece. If I'd known there was a surprise inside, I would have opened it months ago, she thought. After retrieving the key, she stood in front of the armoire, removing the hairpin that was stuck in the lock from the day she had started to pick it. Gently, she inserted the key and turned it until she felt a click.

Opening the armoire doors, Laura noticed that there was very little inside. An old pair of tennis shoes and a shopping bag from Klein's, a store on Union Square that went out of business years before. Behind it was a roll of wallpaper, probably from Mom's bedroom.

Laura took the bag out of the armoire and sifted through it. Inside, there were a long rope, a sandy pair of jeans, a crumpled shirt, socks, underwear, and an old watch. Taped to the front of the bag were two envelopes, one with Laura's name on it, the other with the names of all three girls. 'What do you know? More messages from Mom on the other side. Oh Mom, you devil dog, you . . .' she giggled as she tore hers open.

My Dearest Laura,

It's about time you opened the armoire! Let me guess, Sam gave you the inventory list months ago and you're just now reading it. Do I know my baby girl or what? Unlike your sisters, you always take your sweet time. I love that about you.

This letter will answer a lot of questions that I know you and your sisters must have. I am writing it to you before I can no longer remember who I am or the events of my life. How I wish I was brave enough to tell you this in person, but I can't seem to form the words.

Darling. If you'll reach into the back of the armoire, you will see a rolled-up painting that Daniel Lassiter gave your father the day he took Serena to his home to try to leave her there. I have never unwrapped it, but I suspect it's valuable.

You may wonder why I didn't sell it in all

these years. We certainly could have used the money. But that painting represents a tragic point in my life and I refused to benefit from the biggest mistake I ever made. You may recall that, years ago, I worked for Daniel Lassiter as a cook. He and I became friends, and when I left his employ, he gave me two pictures. One we sold and the other we kept at home.

After I returned to the city that summer, your father and I ran into a big patch of trouble. I discovered that while I was away, he had had an affair with a woman he had worked with for years. When I confronted him, he denied it, but I knew it was true because she called me in an effort to break up our marriage. I was so angry with your father that I claimed to have had an affair with Daniel Lassiter. It wasn't true. We were good friends that summer, but never lovers.

Serena was born about nine months after I returned from the Hamptons. Because of the timing, your father always believed she was Daniel's daughter. At first, I did nothing to dissuade him of the notion. I was so hurt by his betrayal that I wanted him to suffer. Later, when things got better between us, I told him the truth. He never believed me. I know I did a terrible thing to let him think even for a short while that Serena wasn't his. Whenever we disagreed, he would bring it up. Somehow, in his mind, his affair was forgivable because a child never came of it, but mine wasn't. Serena was a constant reminder to him of my supposed infidelity.

Years later, your father and I had a bitter fight over money. He had lost his job and we were in dire financial straits. In a fit of anger, he took Serena to Daniel's studio and tried to leave her with him. I called and warned Daniel that your father was on his way. I told him about our struggles and how your father thought Serena was his child so he wouldn't be blindsided. Daniel, God bless him, gave your father a painting that we could sell and told him to go away and never come back. He was trying to help me with our money problems.

Unfortunately, the gift backfired. Your father told Daniel that by giving him that painting, Daniel had confirmed his suspicions about Serena. Why would he do that unless Serena was his child?

You know what happened next. I have always felt I had blood on my hands for your father's death. When the police delivered his clothes and the painting Daniel had given him, I stuck everything away in the armoire and never touched it again.

Laura, I have left you and your sisters each something that I particularly want you to have. In your case, besides my lovely clothes and used furniture (I'm joking!), you are inheriting my personal effects. The painting in the armoire is part of my personal effects and it is yours. Please do not hang it up as it represents a terrible time in our lives. Sell it and do something extraordinary with the money. I leave it to you to decide what that is.

Love always,

Mom

P.S. I am attaching another letter addressed to the three of you. After you share this note with Amanda and Serena, please read the other letter together.

Laura's eyes welled as she folded the letter back up. She could hardly believe the story her mother had told. She would need time to process it all. In her mind, she pictured Sunny standing next to her and realized that she had delivered the painting at the absolute perfect moment.

Thank you, Mom, she thought. How did you know?

SERENA

'Love endures only when lovers love many things together and not merely each other.'
—Walter Lippman

S erena and Elliott met with Kenny Grover, the contractor the Bullocks swore by for all their S&M needs. Kenny was bald with a body shaped like a peanut on steroids – a thick chest and pumped arms separated from two tree-trunk thighs by a cinched waist. His firm specialized in creating fantasy home bondage environments. Their motto: If you can imagine being whipped in it, we can whip it up!

Behind Serena's master bedroom were two walk-in closets that she and Elliott used for storage. Over time, they had become perfectly organized junk receptacles, full of everything they couldn't find a place for but couldn't bear throwing away.

Serena, her hair pulled into a tight brown bun, wore skinny black jeans, a tight black turtleneck sweater, and spiky leather stilettos to the meeting, a look that said 'S&M' without screaming it.

473

'Do me a favor,' she said to Kenny, 'toss everything. I don't even want to know what we're getting rid of.'

'I can do that,' Kenny said. 'No problem.' He knocked on the wall that separated the two closets. 'You see? It's hollow, no structural beams. We can take it down and combine the two spaces. That'll give you plenty of room to store your paraphernalia and put in four to five pieces of equipment. It depends on the size of what you choose.'

'Can you provide the equipment?' Elliott asked.

'Oh yes, we're a full-service dungeon builder,' Kenny said. 'My great-grandfather started the business in 1912.' He opened his briefcase and pulled out a catalogue. 'Browse through this. Plus, if you go to our website, you can see all the custom pieces we've designed that aren't in the book.'

'When can you start?' Serena asked. 'We're anxious to get it built.'

Kenny checked his watch. 'If you can give me a deposit for half, I can get a Dumpster here right away and a crew of two to empty the junk and start taking down the wall. My guess is we could have the whole thing constructed in two weeks, three at the most.'

'Two weeks!' Serena said. 'Really? Okay, let's do it.' She had heard horror stories about New York contractors not finishing jobs on time, stealing money, delivering shoddy construction. But Mrs Bullock could not have recommended Kenny more highly. Maybe S&M contractors are more reliable than regular ones because they're afraid their clients might hurt them if they don't deliver, she thought.

'I'll take the kids to the park now, before work,' Elliott said. 'But promise you'll wait for me to look through the catalogue?'

'I promise,' Serena said. 'You go on.'

Elliott gave her a long smooch on the lips. 'Mmmm, I'll miss you, Baby,' he murmured. There was nothing like building a home dungeon to infuse a marriage with new vitality.

LAURA

'What's the good news if you haven't a sister to share it?'

—Jenny DeVries

As Laura rode uptown on the number-four train, she decided it probably hadn't been smart to take the subway to Christie's. The painting had to be worth a million dollars, maybe more. Anyone could have snatched it out of her hands. It was large and bulky, like a rolled-up rug. She had purposefully dressed down in torn jeans and a vintage CBGB T-shirt so potential thieves would think she was poor.

At Christie's, she met with a thirty-something, tall, impeccably dressed woman named Oceana Gilbert-de los Santos. Her head of thick silver hair was incongruous with her young, unlined face. Oceana was as cordial and reserved as the hushed over-air-conditioned halls of the famed auction house. Laura noticed that she spoke like an announcer on public radio – slow, deep, and whispery. It was obvious Oceana didn't believe her when she claimed to be holding a never-before-seen Daniel Lassiter. Laura lay the butcher-paper-covered painting on a table and unwrapped it, then slowly unrolled the canvas to show Oceana what lay inside. It was the first time she had seen it as well.

Oceana gasped when the artwork was revealed. 'Ohmigod! Ohmigod! Ohmigod!' she screamed, losing her cool public-radio persona. 'This can't be. I don't believe it!'

'What?' Laura asked. 'What is it?'

Oceana was already on her phone calling her colleagues to come see what Laura had brought them. Two young women, Oceana clones, came running in. When they saw what lay on the table, their mouths dropped open in unison.

'What is it?' Laura said.

Oceana managed to compose herself. 'Can't you see? It's . . . it's the lost portrait of Jackie Kennedy.'

Once Oceana said it, Laura immediately got it. There was the dark hair, the pink pillbox hat, the big brown eyes, poufy red lips, the slim body – but it was all painted as if in a big rush. Arms were suggested, breasts were swirls, stray black lines were abundant. The figure was painted wearing the iconic pink suit, and there were splotches of red on it. There was nothing realistic about it, but it distinctly suggested Jackie Kennedy on that infamous November day.

'This painting was mentioned in the artist's

archives along with a faded Polaroid snapshot, but no one remembers seeing it,' Oceana said. 'There was a notation that it had been gifted to a friend, but there was no name to go by. Supposedly he painted it the year after JFK was assassinated.'

'That's incredible,' Laura said. 'Then it must be worth a lot of money, right?'

Oceana donned a pair of magnifying glasses, the kind jewelers wear, and inspected the painting. She glanced up. 'If authenticated, it could go for a hundred million.'

'At least,' Oceana Two said.

'In better economic times, a hundred and fifty,' Oceana Three added.

'Dollars?' Laura said, her eyes goggling.

'We don't deal in pesos at Christies, Ms Moon. Here's what we're going to do,' Oceana said, reverting to her efficient, professional curator self. 'You will leave the painting here to be authenticated. I will give you a receipt and warrant its safety. Don't worry. I'm calling Lloyds of London as soon as you leave. You need to bring us proof of ownership. I take it you want to sell it?'

'Yes, I do.' Laura explained how she had acquired the piece. 'I can only show you the will and the letter from my mother,' she said. 'Is that enough to prove ownership?'

'It should be,' Oceana said. 'We can confirm the story about your mother working there through the Lassiter family. The East Hampton police should have a record of your father's suicide and the items they inventoried and returned to your mother. There's a Polaroid of the painting in the artist's archives. If this is what it appears to be, it will be huge news in the art world.'

'Huge!' Oceana Two said.

'The biggest story of the year,' emphasized Oceana Three.

'How soon can you sell it?' Laura asked. The sooner the better, she thought. Big Mike and Hammer would be paying her a visit in nine days.

'Our largest auction of the year is a week from today,' Oceana said. 'You're too late for that. I'd like to make this the centerpiece of our spring auction.'

Laura groaned. She needed the money now, not in the spring. 'Why can't I get into the sale that's coming right up?' Laura said. 'How hard can it be to add one more piece?' She hoped she didn't sound too whiny.

'Have you noticed there's a global recession going on?' Oceana said. 'The art market is completely unpredictable right now. Lately, paintings we thought would fetch millions haven't even sold. I wouldn't want to present a piece this important without doing heavy advertising, you know, putting it in our catalog, previewing it in major markets. It's imperative that we have the right collectors in the audience so you can get the best price.'

'Although, if I may,' Oceana Two interrupted. 'We *are* auctioning another Lassiter that evening, so his collectors are already coming.'

'Plus, in this depressed market, we could use the addition of this piece to generate buzz,' Oceana Three said. 'The last-minute acquisition of an unknown work by a major artist will be big news. Collectors and museums that weren't planning to come will be begging for seats.'

'Grovelling,' Oceana Two said.

Oceana raised her eyebrows and clucked her tongue in thought. 'I suppose. Yes, *yes*! It's brilliant. As soon as we establish provenance and confirm the painting's authenticity, we'll put out a press release. No! We'll have a press conference.'

'How about a cocktail party for press, museums *and* collectors?' Oceana Two said.

'I'll call the caterer,' Oceana Three said.

'Then we're set,' Laura said, relieved to be selling the piece quickly. 'I'll get you what you need from me to prove ownership of the painting this afternoon.'

Laura couldn't wait to tell her sisters. Even though her mother said she should sell it and do something extraordinary with the money, she wanted to split the proceeds with Amanda and Serena. Her mother couldn't have known how valuable the painting would be when she wrote that letter. If she had, Laura was sure she would have wanted all three of her daughters to share equally in whatever it sold for.

When she got to Serena's apartment, Amanda was sitting in her kitchen having a cup of tea. A toy firetruck, Chinese-letter flashcards, and an abacus lay on the floor – highly unusual; Serena was obsessively neat.

'I have something big to tell you,' Laura said, clutching the receipt she had gotten from Christie's in her fist.

'I have something important to tell both of you,' Serena said. 'But you first.'

'No, you go ahead,' Laura said. 'Hey, where are the kids?' 'Elliott took them to the park before work,' she said. 'He'll drop them off soon.'

'Wow,' Laura said, 'he's really behaving himself. So tell us, what's your news?'

Serena took a piece of paper out of a white envelope. 'We got the results of the DNA testing. It's confirmed,' she said, 'Daniel Lassiter *is* my real father.'

'Oh my God! I can't believe it. I guess Serena gets everything,' Amanda said. 'That's what we agreed to, right Laura?'

'*What?*' Laura said. 'How is that possible? Are you sure there's no mistake?'

'Positive,' Serena said. 'Read the results yourself.'

Laura scanned the paper and there it was in black and white – the two subjects whose DNA was tested had a common parent. But this made no sense, given their mother's letter. She said there was never an affair with Lassiter. Why would she lie about that? According to the medical examiner on *Law and Order*, DNA testing was extremely accurate. Laura didn't know what to make of it. Something was screwy here.

'So what is *your* big news,' Serena said, changing the subject quickly.

'What? My big news?' Laura said. 'Oh, it's nothing compared to this. I . . . I wanted to tell you Joey Martin asked me to sing 'Pennies from Heaven' for his movie.'

SERENA

'Beautiful, beautiful, beautiful, beautiful boy.'
— John Lennon

B y four o'clock that afternoon, most of the junk was gone. Kenny's crew – Vladimir, a tall, lanky Eastern European with spindly arms and hands that could pass for shovels, and Jose, his older, rounder, and shorter assistant, were throwing everything into plastic bags and then sliding them down a chute from Serena's bedroom window to the Dumpster on the street below. Serena asked them to let her know when the wall was being demolished so Sebastian could watch.

Vladimir moseyed into the kitchen and whistled when he spotted Laura, whose bright smile, long shimmering blond hair, and shapely legs were too much for any man to ignore. Serena was giving her a glass of NanoGreens juice, which was equal to six servings of vegetables and five servings of fruit. Amanda had just left to view a loft on Franklin Street and Broadway that Mariah Carey was selling. Sebastian was constructing an elaborate fort with Lincoln Logs while Valentina cut a tooth on her Barack Obama action figure.

Vladimir cleared his throat. 'We're about to break through the wall,' he reported. 'Kenny says I need to get a check for half the job.'

'Oh, yes,' Serena said. 'Come, Sebastian. Maybe you can help.'

'Excuse me, what did you say?' Vladimir asked. He only had one ear and Serena had been talking to his earless side.

'I'm sorry,' she said, moving over. 'Sebastian would like to watch, if that's okay. Laura, would you mind running up to my desk and bringing the checkbook?'

Laura dashed to the family's home office while Serena and Sebastian followed Vladimir to the master bedroom to see the wall come down.

Vladimir handed out dust masks and hard hats for Serena and Sebastian to wear. 'Young man, would you like to make the first hole in the wall?'

'Me? Yippee!' Sebastian said, jumping up and down. 'I want to be a construction worker when I grow up, too.'

'No, you don't,' Serena said, rolling her eyes. 'That would be a complete waste of your Harvard education.' She took a step back so as not to get white dust on her black pants and cotton turtleneck.

'Come,' Vladimir said. He gave Sebastian a sledgehammer and positioned himself behind the boy. Then he wrapped his hands around Sebastian's. 'Ready? One, two, three!' On three, they whacked the wall, leaving an indentation. 'Let's do it again. Ready? One, two, *three*!' This time, Vladimir put more muscle into the swing and a hole magically appeared.

'You are a strong boy,' Jose said, rearranging his testicles.

'Yay me!' Sebastian said. 'Let's do it again.'

'Wait!' Serena said, panicked. 'Oh my God. Stop. I forgot to ask. Did you check for asbestos?'

'This place was built years before they used that,' Vladimir said.

'I knew that,' she said quickly. 'Sebastian, stand by the hole. Let me take your picture.' Sebastian did as he was told, posing with the heavy sledge-hammer in his arms like a fireman while Serena snapped a cell phone photo and sent it to Elliott.

She made herself comfortable on the floor as the demolition droned on before her eyes. Sebastian was fascinated by every new hole appearing in the wall, but she was bored, as was often the case when she shared an experience her son couldn't get enough of – visiting construction sites, watching jets take off, assembling bird skeletons. It was lucky for her that Sebastian appreciated so many of the same things Serena loved – opera, theater, Gilbert and Sullivan, Shakespeare in the Park, art museums. She checked her watch. 'Jose, my older sister is due back any minute. Can Sebastian stay, or should I take him with me?'

'Please can I watch?' Sebastian said. 'I want to do what you do when I grow up.'

Serena chuckled. Over my dead body, she thought.

LAURA

'More than Santa Claus, your sister knows when you've been bad or good.'
                    —Linda Sunshine

Laura shuffled through the papers on Serena's desk in her large, sunlit office. What a mess, she thought. Everything in Serena's house was obsessively neat except for her desk. This was nothing new. Growing up, Serena had kept her bedroom spotless, her closet perfectly organized by color and type of clothing, and her perfume bottles lined up from smallest to largest, but her desk was always piled high with junk and she could never find anything she needed. They used to call it the black hole.

Laura opened the middle drawer. It was filled with office supplies – staples, glue sticks, scissors, Post-its, stamps, and the like. The two side drawers were deeper. One was stuffed with files, newspaper and magazine clippings, random CDs. The other contained packs of American Spirits. There had to be two dozen at least. Laura knew that

487

Serena hid cigarettes all over the house so she'd be covered whenever her oral fixation reared its sucky face. 'How can you smoke when you have two children depending on you?' Laura said to no one in particular. She gathered up all the packs from the drawer and stuffed them behind the heavy bookshelves, where Serena wouldn't find them.

Wait, what am I supposed to be looking for? Laura thought. The checkbook, right. Is it one of those big business checkbooks, or a little one? Serena didn't say. Laura lifted up various piles of paper and files on top of the desk and *voilà*, there it was, a small checkbook in a blue fake-leather case right under a Xerox copy of a piece of paper with 'Agreement' written at the top in Amanda's handwriting.

What kind of agreement would Amanda have with Serena that didn't include her? Laura wondered, feeling left out. Curious, she read on:

Inasmuch as Serena Skank admits to coercing Sunny Moon to leave her entire estate to Serena Skank, and

Inasmuch as Laura Moon, Amanda Moon, and Serena Skank agreed that Serena Skank would keep their mother's entire estate if it is discovered that Daniel Lassiter is Serena's father, and

Inasmuch as Amanda Moon will make sure that DNA evidence shows that Daniel Lassiter is indeed Serena Skank's father, and

Inasmuch as Serena Skank will then be entitled to inherit Sunny Moon's entire estate,

Now, therefore, in consideration of Amanda Moon *never* telling Laura Moon how Serena Skank unduly influenced their mother into leaving her entire estate to Serena Skank,

Serena Skank will sign over half of said estate to Amanda Moon after 'DNA evidence' confirms that Serena Skank is entitled to it.

Both Serena and Amanda had signed the agreement.

'What!' Laura said out loud. How could her sisters conspire against her like that? When they had told her that the DNA showed that Daniel Lassiter was Serena's father, Laura had known something was wrong, but she'd never imagined they were in cahoots against her. Why would they do that? Hadn't she always been a loyal sister to them?

Quickly, Laura stuck the agreement in her pocket. There has to be a reasonable explanation for this, she thought. I just can't imagine what it is.

SEBASTIAN AND SERENA

'The heart of a mother is a deep abyss at the bottom of which you will always find forgiveness.'

—Honoré de Balzac

Jose let Sebastian take a few more swings and then told him to stand back. He and Vladimir took crowbars and began pulling off the drywall, exposing the wooden frame of the house. As pieces of wall fell, Sebastian picked them up and dropped them down the chute.

'This is more fun than the playground,' Sebastian said.

'Huh?' Vladimir said. 'You have to talk to the ear.' He pointed to it.

Sebastian examined Vladimir's face. It was red and pock-marked. His chocolate brown hair was long and stringy, which made his missing ear less obvious. 'What happened to your ear?'

Vladimir touched the spot where his ear used to be. 'It's very sad,' he said. 'Long story short, I told my mother a big lie and she cut off my ear

490

with a butcher knife to punish me. She tried to cut off my tongue but I begged her not to because I needed that to eat.'

Sebastian's eyes grew wide as coat buttons. 'Your mother cut off your ear?'

'Yes, *for lying*.' Vladimir said, flashing his black eyes when he spoke, making a face like a bogey-monster.

Sebastian gasped. He threw off his dust mask and hard hat and ran to find his mother. That was it. Enough was enough. He had been living a lie for too long and it had to stop here and now. Mommy had given him life. He owed her the truth.

'Mommy, Mommy,' Sebastian cried.

Serena and Laura had their heads together in the kitchen studying Jessica Seinfeld's cookbook. Amanda was in a gold St John Knit suit, her red hair piled loosely on top of her head, jabbering on her cell phone about a buyer she might have for Mariah Carey's loft. Valentina was removing the pieces from her human-body model and chewing on a pair of lungs.

'Sebastian, are you finished helping?' Serena said. 'Aunt Laura and I are going to make grilled-cheese sandwiches with squash puree instead of cheese!'

'Mmm, yum,' Aunt Laura said, smacking her lips.

'You're lying, Aunt Laura, you don't think that sounds yummy at all, do you?'

'Busted,' Laura admitted. 'No, it sounds gross.'

'You better say you're sorry for telling a lie or Mommy's gonna cut off your ear.'

'What?' Serena said. 'Cut off her ear? I wouldn't hurt any of God's creatures, not even an ant. You know that.'

'Mommy, I'm sorry I lied to you,' Sebastian said, throwing himself at his mother's feet, clinging desperately to her leg. Hot tears were streaming down his face and clear snot was running from his nose. He reached into his pants and pulled out one, two, three, then seven dummies. He ran to Valentina's swing and dug another one out from behind the seat. From inside the sofa cushions, he rescued two dusty, hairy ones. 'I'm a bad boy,' he cried. 'Punish me, Mommy. But don't cut off my ear.'

'Honey, I wouldn't cut off your ear. But you shouldn't lie to me. It's wrong to be dishonest,' Serena said.

'I know,' Sebastian said. 'But I'm only four.'

'It's okay,' Amanda said, snapping her cell phone shut. 'Your Mommy forgives you. What does she forgive him for?'

'Lying about his dummies,' Laura explained.

'I'll get you the rest, Mommy,' Sebastian said, running downstairs toward his bedroom.

'What brought that on?' Laura said.

'I have no idea,' Serena said. 'It's so hard to be a mother. Especially when it comes to teaching your children right from wrong.'

Laura flashed a wry smile. 'You're an honest

person. Sebastian and Valentina will learn morality by watching you. Sorry I lied about the grilled-squash sandwich.'

'Don't worry,' Serena said. 'Although I think you should be more open-minded about tasting healthy foods.'

'Let's always be honest with each other, okay?' Laura said.

'Of course,' Serena said, 'we already are.' Why did Laura bring that up? she wondered. It goes without saying that I wouldn't lie to her . . . except if I absolutely had to.

Amanda's eyes darted around the room like she was expecting a visiting dignitary to arrive any second.

Serena took two white cards out of her tote and handed them to Amanda and Laura.

'What's this?' Laura asked.

'It's an invitation to Christie's. I've decided to sell the Daniel Lassiter sketch at auction,' Serena said.

'I thought you wanted to keep it for sentimental reasons,' Laura said. 'It's the last thing you have of your father.'

'I changed my mind,' Serena said. 'Elliott and I are renovating and we can use the money. Will you come?'

'Sure,' Laura said. 'How much do you think you'll get for it?'

'I'm told a few hundred thousand,' Serena said. 'The art market is soft right now.'

'The art market follows the real estate market,' Amanda said knowingly.

'Yes, but apparently they're also selling a van Gogh watercolor and a Lassiter oil at this auction, so several important collectors will be there, which can only help my sale,' Serena said. 'Oops, that reminds me, I have to pay my contractor. Laura, did you find the checkbook?'

Laura handed it to her. 'I've never been to an auction. Do they know you're Lassiter's illegitimate daughter?'

'Um, no,' Serena said. 'I didn't think it was relevant. Can you hand me that blue pen?'

Laura passed it over. 'It might make for a better story in the auction catalogue. I actually know someone at Christie's. Let me call her for you.'

'No,' Serena shouted. 'I mean . . . Kate Lassiter doesn't even know.'

'But surely you've reached out to her?' Laura asked.

'I will soon,' Serena lied, but only because she absolutely *had* to since Amanda had lied about Daniel Lassiter being her father. Although, for all she knew, he *could* be her father, since Amanda had faked the results of the DNA test they'd shown Laura. Oh, what tangled webs we weave, she thought. 'I . . . I just need time to get used to the fact that I have another sister.'

'You've been thinking about this your whole life,' Laura said. 'Anyway, I'd think you'd want to meet her right away, wouldn't *you*, Amanda?'

'Leave her alone. Let her do it on her own timetable,' Amanda said, wringing her hands in her lap.

Sebastian rushed into the kitchen, his arms piled high with dummies. 'Mommy, here are the ones from downstairs. I got more in the den, okay?' He dropped the rubbery mess on the floor and ran off.

'My God,' Amanda said, eying the massive collection of pacifiers on the floor. 'Did you buy him that many?'

'I guess so,' Serena said, 'through the years.'

'He was sure hiding a lot from you,' Laura said. 'I'll bet he's relieved to come clean and know you still love him.'

'He's my son,' Serena said. 'I'll love him no matter what he does.'

'And you're my sisters,' Laura said. 'I'll love you both no matter what you do.' Laura looked each of them in the eye.

Amanda's face turned crimson. 'What do you mean by that? Did we do something to you?'

'You tell me,' Laura said, cocking her head.

Sebastian came back into the room with two more handfuls of dummies. 'That's it, Mommy. There's more in the car, but I'm not allowed outside without my leash.' He dropped them into Serena's lap. 'Do you forgive me?'

Serena nodded. 'Of course I do.'

'Yay,' Sebastian said, doing his wiggly-worm dance. 'Mommy forgives me. I'm free! Free at last.

Thank God-and-Mommy I'm free at last!' He skipped over to Valentina, who was sticking her human-body model's spleen into her nose. 'And I forgive you, Tina.'

'What do you forgive *her* for?' Serena asked, grabbing the spleen from Valentina's tiny fingers.

'For being born,' Sebastian said, skipping to the door.

LAURA

'God could not be everywhere so he created mothers.'

—Jewish proverb

The next afternoon, Laura hustled down Greenwich Street towards P.S. two thirty-four. She checked her watch and slowed down when she realized that the talent show wouldn't start for twenty minutes. A stream of parents and caregivers were making their way to the event, many carrying video cameras and bouquets of flowers from the local Korean grocers and Morgan's Market.

Laura had taken her time getting dressed for this moment. She wore her favorite form-fitting yellow-and-white V-neck wrap dress, a Diane von Furstenberg she had picked up for fifty cents at a yard sale at Grace Church with the tag still on it. Her wild golden hair bounced with curls, framing her radiant skin and bright emerald eyes. Laura held her head high, feeling confident about what she planned to do.

She followed as the crowd moved like a school of fish toward the auditorium. There, Laura scanned the audience for Charles. Sure enough, he had staked out a prime aisle seat in the second row. Violet, wearing a purple Hello Kitty dress, sat slouching next to him, yawning like she was bored.

Her stomach flipped as she scuttled toward their seats. She couldn't wait to surprise them. Charles gasped and then erupted into a devastating smile when Laura tapped him on the shoulder. 'Hi, you two,' she said.

Charles gave her a hug and kiss. Violet stayed seated, facing forward, her arms crossed. She glanced up. 'Oh, hello Laura. How marvelous to see you again.' She looked away.

Laura knelt down and gently stroked Violet's hair. 'Hey there little one, why aren't you backstage getting ready?'

'I quit,' Violet said, refusing to make eye contact. 'I'm too heartbroken to sing.'

Laura's face fell. She knew she was the source of Violet's distress. Reaching behind her neck under her hair, she removed the silver necklace Charles had sent her. 'Here,' she said, offering it to Violet. 'This necklace is magic. It heals broken hearts.'

When Violet saw what Laura had in her hand, a soft gasp escaped her. 'Where did you get that?'

'Your Daddy sent it to me,' she said. 'But I think you need it more than I do. Now here, turn around.' Violet held up her curly brown hair as Laura hung the chain around her neck.

Violet turned so Charles and Laura could see her wearing the necklace. She squealed with delight.

'Okay, now break a leg,' Laura said, motioning toward the stage.

Violet shook her head emphatically. 'No, I dropped out. I'm not on the list. And anyway, I stopped practicing.'

'What are you talking about?' Laura said. 'Let's get you back on the list. If you forget the words, I'll sing it with you.'

Violet's eyes grew wide. 'No! Once you're off the list you can't get back on. That's the rule. And *you* can't sing with me. It's not allowed.'

Laura reached over and took Violet's hand. 'Come. There's no time like the present for you to learn that in life, you have to break a few rules.'

'Daddy,' Violet said urgently. 'Tell her I'll get in trouble.'

Charles shrugged. 'Personally, I'd rob a bank with Laura if she told me to.'

'Daddy!' Violet said. 'You wouldn't dare!'

'Wouldn't I? Now shoo,' Charles said, waving her off.

Violet, her face bright with embarrassment, tailed Laura to the stage. She watched with fascination as Laura sweet-talked Mr Oglefeld into putting Violet back on the list in the very first position.

'I don't believe it,' Violet whispered to Laura. 'Mr Ogrefeld never does anything nice for anyone. He's the school grump.'

'My mama always told me you catch more flies with honey than vinegar,' Laura said. 'Come on.' Laura motioned for Violet to join her behind the curtain. 'Let's do it.'

'But there's no piano,' Violet whined. 'I can't sing without accompaniment.'

Laura reached into her bag and pulled out her trusty kazoo. 'Ta-da! Backup!' she said brightly. 'I'll play behind you, very lightly, okay?'

'Ohoooh,' Violet groaned.

'And now, singing the perennial favorite, 'Que Sera, Sera,' is Violet Shine and her friend, Laura Loon,' Mr Oglefeld said.

'That's Moon,' Violet shouted as the curtain opened.

'Laura Moon,' Mr Oglefeld said.

'Ready,' Laura whispered, 'one, two, a-one-two-three . . .' She brought the kazoo to her lips and played. Violet's soprano voice was as clear as church bells on Sunday morning. '*When I was just a little girl, I asked my mother what will I be. Will I be pretty, will I be rich, here's what she said to me . . .*'

Que sera, sera, Laura sang, putting her kazoo down. She took Violet's hand, gave it a light kiss, and improvised a minuet with her while singing the mother's part. Violet performed the second verse and Laura serenaded her with the chorus. '*Now I have children of my own, they ask their mother*

500

what will I be? . . .' Violet sang. It was as if they had spent a lifetime practicing for this moment. Laura sensed with all her heart that the spirits of Sunny and Violet's mother were accompanying her *que sera seras* while dancing their own minuet together behind Violet as she sang her sweet song.

AMANDA

'Having a sister is like having a best friend you can't get rid of. You know whatever you do, they'll still be there.'

—Amy Li

'Yoo-hoo,' Serena called to Laura, motioning for her to come sit down. Serena was dressed for business in a tailored black pantsuit, cream-colored blouse, and spiky boots all purchased from Banana Republic. Naturally, Amanda wore one of her classic St John Knits. Laura was more festive, in a fitted red silk Escada she had picked up at a secondhand shop in Southampton the afternoon they visited Kimba Flick. Everyone knew the best hand-me-downs could be found in the Hamptons, where the socialites purged their closets away from the prying eyes of their Park Avenue friends. It was a fashion bonanza for the regular folk size four and under.

Laura took the empty chair next to Serena in the second row. 'Sorry I'm late,' she said. 'What's happening?'

'You were supposed to be here two hours ago,' Serena said. 'Do you know how hard it's been to hold that seat? Where were you?'

'Sorry. I had dinner with Charles. You said your piece was toward the end.'

'Yes, but you could have missed it,' Serena said. '*Then* what would you have done?'

'Committed suicide, I suppose,' Laura said.

'It's not going well at all,' Amanda said. 'There was a Damien Hirst that was supposed to sell for a million and a half and it only sold for eight hundred thousand. Then, there was a Francis Bacon that was supposed to go for fifteen million, and nobody bought it.'

'Yes, but they sold that van Gogh watercolor,' Serena said. 'For seven million!'

'They expected it to go for ten,' Amanda said, her stomach churning. They had to sell their Lassiter for at least three hundred thousand. Richie was expecting a check tomorrow. It would take a hundred and fifty grand to cover her principal and interest. She'd figure out the taxes later. This was her last hope for raising the money she needed.

'Ooh, it's time! She's carrying our picture,' Serena cried.

Amanda watched as the Christie's representative displayed the framed Lassiter sketch of the voluptuous woman that had graced their home for as long as she could remember. She glanced at Laura, who flashed her a bright smile. Please God, forgive me for betraying my sister, she prayed. I promise I'll make it up to her.

'Ladies and gentlemen, here we have lot number forty, a graphite sketch by Daniel Lassiter circa 1952.' The auctioneer was slim, with short, blunt, jet-black hair and Lina Wertmüller glasses. She wore a tailored suit, spoke in a rapid public-radio voice, and presented with a businesslike demeanor. Amanda noticed that everyone who worked at Christie's gave off the same impression.

'In the nineteen-forties and fifties, Daniel Lassiter produced a series of paintings on the theme of woman as goddess. The piece we are presenting tonight is a study for the oil-on-canvas *Goddess II* that last sold for $110.5 million from Richard Branson's collection to George Soros through a private dealer. *Goddess II* is one of six *Goddess* paintings Lassiter created and is the only one of the six in private hands. Through the years, eight studies for this particular painting have been sold. This is the ninth and last known preliminary drawing for *Goddess II*. It has been in private hands for well over twenty-five years.'

'That's us,' Serena squealed. 'We're the private hands.'

'Calm down,' Amanda said. 'Don't wet your pants.'

'We'll start the bidding at two hundred thousand, do I hear two hundred thousand?' The auctioneer gazed about the room, but no one raised a paddle. She glanced over to the phone bank, but the professionals manning the phones shook their heads. 'Ooh-kay,' she said. 'The reserve on this etching is one hundred and fifty thousand dollars, do I hear one hundred and fifty thousand dollars?' Once again, silence.

'My God,' Serena whispered, her cheeks a vivid scarlet. 'This is humiliating.'

'Oh, come on,' Amanda griped. 'Someone bid something.' Her heart thumped like a tom-tom. This could not be happening. After she'd violated everything she believed in to get her hands on half the estate, now no one wanted to buy the Lassiter! Was this God's idea of a joke? Sure, Serena was deeding her half of the Duane Street house, but who knew when that would sell in this crummy market? She was well and truly screwed. Richie might cut her a break, but Kneecap and his 'family' certainly wouldn't.

As a woman wearing a gray Armani suit whisked the unsold drawing off the stage, all hopes Amanda had for bringing this financial nightmare to an end vanished. A glazed look of despair spread over her face as her heart deflated in defeat.

Two men carried the next piece and placed it on a different easel. It was an oversized Jackie Kennedy oil by Daniel Lassiter. Christie's had stretched it onto a wooden frame. 'Ladies and gentlemen,' the auctioneer said, 'To tell us about lot number forty-one, we have a special guest who will give us a bit of history . . . Miss Kate Lassiter, the artist's daughter.'

A middle-aged blond woman with an open face and an inviting smile stepped up to the podium and put on a pair of multicolored reading glasses.

'Hey,' Laura said, punching Amanda's arm. 'That's not the woman I sang to at the manicure place. What's going on?'

Amanda was knocked out of her coma of despair. 'I . . . I . . . I'm not sure.'

'Ladies and gentlemen, Christie's asked if I would shed some light on the next piece, a portrait of Jacqueline Kennedy that was painted by my father in 1963. It is reminiscent of his Marilyn Monroe and Jayne Mansfield paintings from the 1950s in that it suggests the subject, but is executed in his trademark roiling grafitti-like style where the feminine form is a cross between the sensual goddess and the nurturing earth mother. As you can see, Jackie's body is outlined in thin and thick black lines, which loop and streak throughout the painting suggesting life and movement even in the sobering presence of crimson splashes of color, representing blood. Abrupt and angular strokes of pink, blue, and red have been applied using a palette knife, scraped away, and then restored, giving the subject a three-dimensional texture that is typical of the artist's daring work.' Kate stopped to take a sip of water before carrying on.

'This particular piece is one that I do not remember ever seeing in person, although my father kept a Polaroid photo of it in his records. It was given away as a gift in the late eighties and only recently surfaced in the estate of Sunny Moon, a woman who once worked for my father.'

Serena furrowed her brow. 'Did she say Sunny Moon?'

Amanda was confused. 'Laura, do you know about this?'

'Shhh,' Laura said. 'I want to hear.'

'Does *that* painting belong to us?' Serena said, hitting Laura hard on the leg. 'Why am I just learning this now?'

'It belongs to *me*, okay?' Laura said. 'Now hush, both of you.'

Serena's mouth dropped open and squeaky noises came out, her head darted this way and that as if she couldn't contain her energy. She was like a cat on a hot tin roof.

'. . . was known for giving away paintings as gifts or in trade for services during hard times,' the auctioneer said. 'It appears that this was a gift that no one knew still existed until recently. And now I'm going to start the bidding at eighty million dollars.'

Amanda gasped. Eighty million dollars! she thought. Hallelujah! I'm saved. She glanced at Laura, who was watching the proceedings with rapt attention. What does she mean; it belongs to *me*?

LAURA

'She is your mirror, shining back at you with a world of possibilities. She is your witness, who sees you at your worst and best, and loves you anyway. She is your partner in crime, your midnight companion, someone who knows when you are smiling, even in the dark. She is your teacher, your defense attorney, your personal press agent, even your shrink. Some days, she's the reason you wish you were an only child.'
—Barbara Alpert

According to Christie's, the Lassiter was estimated to sell for one hundred and ten million dollars. But after the sorry showing of the etching, Laura just hoped someone would bid something. She only needed twenty grand.

'... ninety million, do I hear one hundred, one hundred from Mr Eli Broad ... do I hear one hundred ten? One hundred ten million dollars from Mr Henry Kravis. Do I hear one hundred twenty? Excuse me?' Oceana whispered something into the auctioneer's ear. 'My, my, it seems we have a bid of one hundred *thirty* million from the gentleman who wishes to remain anonymous on telephone number six. Going once, going twice . . . oops . . . one hundred thirty-*five* from Mr Broad. Going once . . . going twice . . . *sold* for one hundred thirty-five million dollars.' The room erupted into violent applause. A few people actually stood. It was twenty-five million more than Christie's estimate, a shock given the shaky state of the economy. To Laura, these were pennies from Heaven . . . literally.

Serena erupted like a geyser. 'Oh my God,' she screamed, 'that was *our mother's* painting? We're rich! Laura, were you trying to surprise us?'

'That painting,' Laura declared, 'was *mine*. It was hidden in Mom's armoire. It's part of her personal effects, which she left to *me*.'

Amanda jumped up. 'Wait, this can't be,' she exploded. 'Mom left *you* the painting? What about *me*? Serena gets the house and the drawing and I get nothing? Laura, surely you'll share with *me*. Haven't I always been there for you?'

All activity at Christie's stopped. The audience was instantly mesmerized by the reality show taking place in its midst. It was the art world's equivalent of a hockey fight.

'What, and I haven't been there?' Serena demanded. 'Who gave you your birthday party this year? I think we should split everything three ways. I'll even throw in my inheritance, the house *and* the drawing.'

Laura shook her head and wagged her finger at

both sisters. 'Uh-uh, no, no, no, no, no.' She reached in her bag and pulled out a copy of the agreement Serena and Amanda had made to cut Laura out of the inheritance. She held it up for everyone to see. 'This is a contract between my sisters to defraud me out of my inheritance!'

Gasps could be heard throughout the room. The auctioneer banged her gavel to restore order. 'I think we should move on to the next item up for bid . . .'

The crowd shushed her. They wanted to see what would happen next.

'Both of you should be ashamed of yourselves,' Laura said. 'If you hadn't been so greedy, I would have been happy to share this money with you. But as it is, I'm keeping it myself, *all* of it.'

'What do *you* need with so much?' Serena said. 'You live like a student.'

'Not anymore I don't,' Laura said, storming out of the room.

'Wait, wait,' Amanda said, crutching after her. 'Please!'

Serena noticed that everyone in the room was staring at them. 'Sorry, folks. Show's over!' she yelled, heading for the door.

In the anteroom, Amanda grabbed Laura's shoulder just as Serena caught up with them. 'Stop. Please. I . . . I . . . at least let me explain. I wasn't being greedy. You see, last year I mortgaged the house so we could diversify our investments. I was trying to be financially smart.'

'You mortgaged the house?' Serena said. 'Without telling us?'

'I've been managing our finances for years and you never cared a bit when I tried to involve you,' Amanda said. 'Mom needed money for medical expenses so I borrowed four million against the house. I used a little bit for her and the rest I invested with Bernie Madoff.'

'You borrowed four million against the house and invested most of it with Bernie Madoff?' Serena said. 'How could you be so stupid?'

'Who's Bernie Madoff?' Laura asked.

'He's the biggest crook in the history of the world,' Serena said, shaking her head. 'We're doomed . . . doomed.'

'I'm sorry. I didn't know he was a thief when I gave him our money,' Amanda said. 'Lots of smart, sophisticated people fell for his scam.'

Serena began to whimper. 'So almost a third of what Mom left me was stolen by that creep?'

'We might be able to get five hundred thousand back through government insurance, and I've contacted a lawyer about trying to go after the rest, although he's not optimistic. But yes, the money was stolen,' Amanda said. 'That's not all. With the real estate market so soft, I fell behind on the mortgage payments, and the bank was threatening to foreclose, so I borrowed a hundred grand from a loan shark to bring the payments up to date. They're threatening bodily harm if I don't pay it back with ridiculous interest.'

511

Laura gasped. 'Did they break your leg?'

Amanda's face went red. 'No, my collector let me fake a broken leg so his employers would think he'd put the squeeze on me, but that's the last favor he'll give me. That's why I had to get Serena to give me half the estate, so I could pay him back and close out the mortgage.'

'You *faked* a broken leg?' Serena exclaimed. 'That's so . . . so dishonest!'

'Oh, there's the pot calling the kettle black. I could say a *lot* worse about you,' Amanda started.

'Excuse me.' Oceana Gilbert-de los Santos stuck her head out the door. 'Do you think you can take this outside? You're disturbing the auction.'

'Oh, sorry,' Laura said. She headed for the exit and her sisters followed. At the front door, Laura turned to her sister. 'Amanda, how could you lie to us like that?'

'I didn't lie,' she said.

'You didn't tell your own sisters the truth – you were in trouble. We would have helped,' she said as soon as they were outside. She gestured to the diner across the street. 'C'mon, let's get coffee.'

'Screw it,' Amanda said, throwing her crutches on the ground. She hobbled on her cast to the restaurant. As soon as they'd slipped into a window booth, Serena and Amanda on one side, Laura on the other, the waitress dropped off menus.

'Coffee for me,' Amanda said.

'Me too,' Laura added.

'Hot water and two lemons, please. And some

honey, too. Caffeine is so bad for you,' Serena said, clucking her tongue.

'So is nicotine,' Laura said. She turned to Amanda. 'Seriously, why didn't you come to us?'

'Because you couldn't have helped. I need a hundred and fifty grand. You didn't have that,' Amanda said. 'Besides, I've always taken care of *you*. I was ashamed of what a mess I'd made of things.'

'And well you should have been,' Serena started.

'Serena, would you shut the fuck up!' Laura said. 'Amanda's been there for you your whole life. Don't you see how pathetic it is that she didn't think she could turn to us?'

Serena shrugged. 'I suppose if you put it that way . . .'

'So that whole scene at the nail salon with Kimba and Kate Lassiter was staged?' Laura said.

Amanda blushed, then nodded. 'I had to make sure the DNA results showed that Serena was Lassiter's daughter. The women you met as Kimba and Kate were friends of mine from work who have places in the Hamptons. I was desperate to repay the loan shark. If it's any consolation, I planned to make it up to you as soon I could.'

The waitress returned with their coffee and hot water. 'Oops, I forgot the honey,' she chirped. 'I shall return.'

'But the report said Lassiter was Serena's father,' Laura said. 'I saw it myself.'

'I submitted *my* DNA with Serena's,' Amanda

said. 'The results proved that Serena and I are siblings, that's all.'

'Still, I can't believe you two would try to cheat me like that,' Laura said.

'Don't forget,' Amanda said, 'Serena started it. She convinced Mom to leave her everything. I'm not the only bad guy here.'

'Serena,' Laura said, 'what possessed you?'

'Hello! You're not so ivory-pure yourself,' Serena said. 'You and Amanda left me handcuffed and half-naked in the dungeon at the Bullocks' house. That was cruel and inhumane. I could easily have died.'

Laura almost sprayed the table with coffee. 'What?' she gasped. 'I did no such thing!'

'Here's your honey,' the waitress said, slapping a cone shaped bottle onto the table. 'And let me refresh your cup,' she added.

'No, thanks,' Laura said.

When the waitress had left, Amanda spoke up. 'I left you handcuffed and half-naked. But you deserved it.'

'I did not,' Serena said.

'You did. And anyway, it saved your marriage, so you should thank me. Laura, I'm sorry we tried to cheat you,' Amanda said. 'But it was for a good cause. If I don't pay Richie back, bones will break and blood will spill. His employers are ruthless animals.'

Serena stared at her. 'God forbid, he might hurt *us*! Or Sebastian and Valentina!'

'Let me guess,' Laura said. 'Something like that happened on *Law and Order* once, right?'

'Well, yes. It absolutely did,' Serena said. 'The loan shark's henchmen kidnapped the debtor's entire family. One of the bad guys raped the debtor's daughter just to show him they were serious.'

'As long as Richard's my collector, we'll be safe. He wouldn't hurt us. But his employers are a different . . .'

'This Richard fellow sounds like a real peach,' Serena said, rolling her eyes.

'He is. He let me fake a broken leg instead of giving me a real one,' Amanda said. 'Plus he's kind and tender . . .'

'You slept with him, didn't you?' Serena accused.

'It's not like that,' Amanda started. 'Anyway, that's not important right now. What's important is this painting. Laura, how long have you known about it? And why didn't you tell us?'

'I just learned about it,' Laura said. She pulled Sunny's letter to her out of her purse and read it to her sisters. When she finished, she caught Serena staring longingly out the window. The sadness of her posture, the slumped shoulders, the lowered chin – Laura felt sorry for her.

'So Daniel Lassiter *wasn't* my father,' Serena said softly. 'It was Dad all along, and he still never loved me.'

'Mom was sorry for the part she played in that. But there's more that she wants us to know,' Laura said, pulling out the second envelope, which was addressed to all three girls. She tore it open and took out the letter inside. 'I'll read it, okay?'

Serena and Amanda nodded.

Dear Amanda, Laura, and Serena,

By now, you know my secret. I'm sorry I hid it from you for so long, but it was the source of so much pain for all of us that I wanted to lock it away forever and hide the key (which is precisely what I did).

Serena, I pray to God you will forgive me for the terrible lie I told your father. I know you suffered all those years when he couldn't find it in his heart to love you, and after he left you on that beach. I also know that your years of illness took their toll. But you MUST put all that behind you and live a life unencumbered by these sorrows. Please, let it go and enjoy the beautiful future you have with Elliott.

Girls, I know you've asked yourselves why I didn't divide my assets into thirds and give you equal shares. As a mother, I realized early on that children have different needs. I thought long and hard about what I could leave you that would make the biggest difference in your lives. Ultimately, I believe I gave you each something of similar value, though not the same thing. Call it equality according to Mom.

Laura, you and Amanda must have wondered why your sister got the house and the drawing. Last week, Serena took me to see the lawyer and I changed my will. She told me that if I would leave her the house and the Lassiter sketch, she would make sure I was well taken care of. Please don't be angry with her for doing that. You know your sister. She's always been terrified that she'll be left alone with nothing. Whatever you girls have, Serena wants. Whatever Serena has, she clings to like a life raft. Serena's selfish act (and Serena, you know what you did was deceitful and you should be ashamed of yourself) made me realize what Serena needed most from me.

Serena, as you requested, I left you the sketch and the house. In my will, I specified that Amanda and Laura could live in our home for the next year. My hope, however, is that you rise above your terrible fear of loss and share the house with your sisters for the rest of your lives. To you, I am leaving the gift of generosity – your generosity toward those who love you most. If you take me up on this, you will find that giving doesn't make your life smaller. Instead, it makes room for the abundance that comes to those who give willingly and lovingly to others.

Laura, thank you for taking such good care of me in my last illness. Even though it is all in front of me as I write this, I know you will be my guardian angel until the bitter end. In recognition of your generosity, not just to me but to your sisters throughout your life, I have left my furniture, clothing, and personal effects, which include the painting Daniel gave your father. Laura, my hope is that you sell the painting, keep what you need to feel secure, and use what is left to create a life for yourself that nourishes your soul while making the world a better place. You, my darling, are happiest when giving to others and that's what this gift will allow you to do. Knowing that something good will come from our family's painful legacy will help me rest in peace.

Amanda, I will never forget how you sacrificed and pitched in after your father died. The family couldn't have made it without you. Don't think for a minute that because I didn't leave you the house or a painting that I love you any less than your sisters. But you are so capable of making a grand living that I don't want to insult you by suggesting that you need my money. My sincerest hope is that by making sure Serena and Laura are financially set, I am giving you the best gift I possibly could. That is the gift of freedom – freedom from having to take care of anyone but yourself for the rest of your life.

There is something else, Amanda. I have also left you my jewelry. It isn't worth much money, but I always cherished it because most of it came from Grandma. My prized possession has always been her two-karat wedding ring. Here is a wonderful secret. That ring is magical. After your great-grandmother passed it down to Grandma, she met Grandpa, fell in love, and married him. Theirs was a legendary love affair that lasted fifty-seven years. Darling, please wear this ring as a daily reminder that there is more to life than making a living. My hope is that you will make a life for yourself, a life that includes more love and less work, more following and less leading. May this ring be as magical for you as it was for Grandma!

Laura, Serena and Amanda – you are the best of me. My final wish is that you be there for one another no matter what. Girls, do you see how my stupid lie led to an irreparable breach with Daddy and so much pain for us all? Always be honest with one another. Never let anything come between the three of you no matter what. There is nothing you can do to one another that cannot be forgiven. If your father had forgiven me, think how different our lives would have been.

Love is so damn complicated. It's not about everything being perfect between each other all the time. To quote a song: 'Love hurts, love scars, love wounds, and mars any heart not strong enough to take a lot of pain.' Remember that next time you want to kill one of your sisters.

I'll love you forever,
Mom

Laura closed her eyes and a single tear spilled down her cheek. She folded up the letter and put it back into her purse. 'I guess Mom knew what she was doing.'

'She sure had my number,' Serena said, in a broken whisper.

'How could she disinherit me for being too competent?' Amanda groused. 'That's so unfair. She penalized me for taking care of you all my life. If she knew how much trouble I was in . . .'

'Mom thought you were set financially,' Laura said, putting her hand over Amanda's. 'She gave you something she believed you needed *more* than money.'

'What? *Love?*' Amanda said, as though it were a terminal disease.

'A life,' Laura said. 'And freedom.'

'Even *I* see how poignant that is,' Serena said. 'And I'm selfish and deceitful.'

Amanda's eyes brimmed with tears. 'Poignant, schmoignant. She didn't want to *insult* me by leaving me her money. I'm sick of everyone thinking I can take care of myself. Sometimes *I* need help. *Now* what am I gonna do?' She slumped forward, sighed, and took a swig of coffee.

'It'll work out,' Serena said, gently patting her sister's back. 'Laura, I know Amanda and I shouldn't have tried to cut you out of the inheritance, but now that you have the money for the painting, do you mind if I give Amanda half the house and the sketch?'

Amanda dropped her cup. Coffee spilled every-where. She grabbed a handful of napkins and tried to blot it up. 'Wait. What's the catch?'

'There's no catch,' Serena said, her voice breaking slightly. 'I never should have gotten Mom to change the will. But since I did, she gave me the chance to be generous for once in my life. Let us help *you* for a change. Besides, I don't want some loan shark to bash your head in.'

'Or kidnap your children?' Amanda said.

'That either,' Serena added. 'And it could very well happen, no matter how sensitive you think your personal collector is. *Law and Order* doesn't make those stories up out of thin air. They rip them from the headlines.'

'Say, Amanda,' Laura said. 'You know the building across the park from ours, the red brick one that's for sale?'

'The one they're asking twenty million dollars for?' Amanda said.

'Yep,' Laura said. 'I want to buy it. You can be my broker. If Serena gives you half the house and I give you the commission on the sale of the building, you should be able to pay back all the loans, right?'

'Wow!' Amanda said, staring at her sister in astonishment. 'Well, mostly, but not soon enough. The money for the loan shark is due now. I was planning to use the proceeds from the sketch to pay him. But it didn't sell. Laura, would you give me a loan from your sale? If I don't deliver a check to Richie tomorrow, there *will* be blood.'

'Loan sharks take checks?' Serena said. 'Not on *Law and Order* they don't.'

'Of *course* they take checks. You think anyone would give a loan shark a bad check?' Amanda said. 'So Laura, would you?'

Laura nodded. 'Of course. And I'll only charge twenty-percent interest a week.'

'Everyone's a comedienne,' Serena said, laughing.

'You think I'm kidding?' Laura asked, her eyes twinkling.

Amanda turned to Laura. 'Don't get me wrong. I appreciate you offering me the sale. But what do you need with a twenty million dollar building?'

'My God, that would make a spectacular home for me and Elliott and the kids,' Serena said, her eyes fraught with longing. 'Can you imagine?'

'Will you live in it?' Amanda asked Laura.

'No . . . well, maybe on the top floor.'

'Are you opening a bed-and-breakfast?' Serena asked.

'You'll see,' Laura teased, her eyes bright with excitement. 'Now, can we all please forgive one another for the hurtful things we've done since Mom died and start over?' she said. 'All I ever wanted was for us to get along.'

'Yes, absolutely,' Amanda said.

'Me too,' Serena said. 'I'm sorry for what an ass I've been. But I'll tell you what I'm not sorry about. I'm not sorry Lassiter isn't my father. Who needs another sister when I have the two of you?'

AMANDA

'The heart wants what it wants. There is no logic to these things.'
—Woody Allen

Amanda sipped hot chocolate from a bowl-sized ceramic mug at Kitchenette's back-corner table.

Across from her sat Richie, her collector and lover. It was the first time she had seen him since the night he'd saved her in more ways than one. As Amanda admired his wavy black hair, olive complexion, and thick dark lashes, she felt strangely defiant. Richie had been there for her when she needed him most. Did it really matter that he was a bill collector of nefarious persuasion, a hoodlum she couldn't introduce to Riley's crowd, her sisters, colleagues, or clients? Tough titties, she thought. Those people weren't keeping her warm at night.

'You're awfully sexy for a workday, Red,' Richie said, his eyes sweeping over her appreciatively. 'What gives?'

Amanda glanced down at her outfit, a pair of

peach silk pants and a loose cream blouse unbuttoned to show cleavage. Her flaming red hair was wild and curly. Today she felt like showing off her inner girl. 'This old thing?' she said, her eyes cast down. Then she lifted them. Richie looked adorable, almost like a little boy. Only he was a man, a man who beat up and killed people for a living. Amanda realized there was something really hot about falling for someone everyone else was afraid of, seeing his humanity when others couldn't. She didn't care what society thought. If Carmela Soprano could do it, so could she. Of course, who knew Richie's heart? He loves me, he loves me not, he loves me . . .

'What? What?' Richie said, regarding her curiously.

'Nothing. Hey, I have a surprise for you,' she said, sliding a thin envelope across the table. 'Here. A check for one hundred and fifty thousand dollars.' She smiled. Her long nightmare was finally over.

'I can't accept that, Red.' Richie said, pushing it back.

'What are you talking about? It's good.'

Richie shook his head. He reached over and took Amanda's hand. 'I haven't been altogether honest with you. You know how I told you about being a former CIA assassin and a collector for your loan shark?'

Amanda cocked her head in confusion. 'Yeah . . .'

'It was a lie.' He leaned across the table and

whispered, 'My cover story, if you will. I'm a detective. I was infiltrating the Santoriellis' loan-sharking operation. We arrested the whole crew yesterday, seized their books and all their records. There's no one left to collect your loan.'

Amanda gasped. 'You mean Kneecap and Thor are . . .'

'In the slammer, yes,' Richie said. 'This is their third felony arrest. If convicted, and I assure you they will be, they're going away for life. That's the law, you know. There are mandatory sentencing guidelines.'

Amanda could hardly process what Richie was telling her. She tried to recall all their moments together. Were there clues she'd missed? 'But . . . but . . . wait. That day you made me get in your car with Kneecap in the backseat,' Amanda said. 'What if he hadn't gone to pick up his kid? Would you have hurt me?'

'No, I would have come up with a way out,' Richie said evenly.

'But *I* thought of having you pretend to break my foot,' Amanda said. 'Not you.'

'It took you long enough, Red,' Richie said with a wry smile. 'I was afraid I'd have to suggest it myself and then you'd suspect me.'

'But why did you quit my case?' Amanda said. 'That doesn't make sense.'

'We were near the end of the operation,' Richie said. 'I figured I could do more good as your bodyguard than your collector. But when you asked me to take you back, I decided it was a wise move. The Santoriellis were becoming more violent.'

'Was that you following me?' Amanda said, her eyes narrow.

'It was me protecting you,' Richie said.

Amanda considered the man sitting across from her. This was a lot to take in. Thirty seconds ago, she saw him as a bad boy, an irresistible criminal like Butch Cassidy or the Sundance Kid. Now he was a cop, a good cop like Dirty Harry or James Bond. But he's been lying to me, she thought. Can I forgive that? *Hell yes, I can!* 'Will you need me to testify?'

'Maybe,' Richie said. 'Would you?'

'Of course,' Amanda said. 'As long as I don't have to go into the witness protection program after. But wait! What about Kneecap's brothers and cousins and fathers and partners-in-crime? What if one of them gets sprung and comes after me?'

Richie raised his eyebrows. 'Don't worry. They're all going down, every last one of them. And if any of them gets out, which they won't, they'll have to go through me to get to you.' Richie gazed at her and his features softened. 'Seriously, Red, let me protect you forever. I love you.'

Amanda's eyes dropped shyly. Then she gazed up at him. 'I love you, too, Richard. You're everything I *never* thought I wanted in a man, but I can't imagine life without you.'

Grinning, he reached into his back pocket, pulled out a wad of cash, and dropped two twenties on the table. 'Come on, Red,' he said, igniting her heart with those lethal brown eyes. 'Let's get out of here.' Richie led the way. In keeping with her mother's wishes, Amanda happily followed.

AMANDA, SERENA AND LAURA

'Sisters are different. They heard the sobbing in the darkness. They lived through all your triumphs, all your loves and losses. They have no delusions. They lived with you too long. And so, when you achieve some victory, friends are delighted – but sisters hold your hands in silence and shine with happiness. For they know the cost.'
—Pam Brown

One year later . . .

It was a crisp Autumn day in New York City, the kind of day where the blue sky seemed to go on forever and the air smelled of East River, which wasn't too pleasant but better than exhaust fumes. A crowd had gathered in front of the Sunny Moon Music Center for Seniors. The Off Our Rockers Quartet was playing in Duane Park with Norah Jones. The boys had befriended her during the filming of Joey Martin's movie and she'd offered to perform for free when she heard about Laura's new venture.

Eva, Laura's soul coach, assured Laura that her father's and mother's spirits were present. They were holding hands and glowing with white light.

Mom is so proud of me, Laura thought, giggling. I can feel it. See Mom, new life! Nourishes my soul! Just like you wanted. And I'm so glad you made up with Dad.

'Laura, the crew from VH1 is here,' Charles said. 'You should probably start the dedication.'

'Thanks, Babe,' she said, giving him a peck on the cheek. A month earlier, Charles and Violet had gotten on bended knees with two very important questions. Charles asked for Laura's hand in marriage, and Violet asked Laura to adopt her. She had said yes to both, but requested some time to think about the kind of marriage she wanted to have and mother she wanted to be. Going from Laura Moon to Laura Moon Shine would be a huge life change. She didn't want to rush into it. Charles told her to take all the time she needed to figure out the details.

Amanda, on the other hand, loved being Mrs Richard Briscoe. After Laura moved to the top floor of the senior center, the newlyweds settled into the bottom two floors of the house on Duane Street. Detective Briscoe was an old-fashioned guy who just wanted to support his wife. After the stress of the last year and a lifetime of striving to succeed and putting everyone else first, Amanda quit real estate to let her husband take care of her. For the moment, she was perfectly content.

'Hello, everyone,' Laura said to the crowd. 'Thank you for being here. Today we are dedicating the Sunny Moon Music Center for Seniors, the first facility of its kind in the country. We live in a city filled with the best musicians anywhere in the world. As they age and stop performing for their livelihood, they still yearn to make music. Now they have a place to come jam with fellow musicians and give music lessons to seniors and others who have always wanted to learn an instrument, or improve their skills.' The crowd burst into applause.

'Thank you,' Laura said, her turquoise eyes sparkling. 'My sisters and I are so proud to open this Center in the name of our mother. She used to love it when I would take her to Golden Manor to hear the Off Our Rockers Trio perform, the band you enjoyed earlier that was playing with Norah Jones. And when I joined the group and we became a quartet, well, don't get me started. This is exactly the kind of place she would have adored. We are so pleased to be able to offer it to the seniors of Manhattan at no cost to them.

'We have many plans for this Center. Vans will shuttle between nursing homes throughout the city and here. We have hired some outstanding choral leaders who will organize a number of singing groups in all different genres that seniors can join. Every afternoon there will be shows featuring various participants in our program. The performances will be here and in senior centers around the city. Each year, our top artists and choruses will be showcased at a benefit concert to be held at the Jazz Theater at the Time Warner building. This is all very exciting, and I'm thrilled to have played a part in the Center's creation.'

'You did a hell of a lot more than that, honey,' shouted Emma Schneiderstern.

'Mrs Schneiderstern, please, no smoking while you're using oxygen,' Laura said.

'But we're outside, for God's sake,' she argued.

David pulled the cigarette out of her mouth and stubbed it out on the ground.

'Another mission of our Center is to provide financial support to the elderly who reside in assisted-living communities and are having trouble paying rent. The economy is in the worst shape it has been in in years. Right now, many older people who thought they'd saved enough for retirement have seen their nest eggs depleted. They are struggling to cover their expenses. Our goal is to help them live out their lives in dignity and comfort.'

Laura noticed Marc Tannenbaum and his boyfriend in the crowd and waved at them. 'Oh, I'm so glad you came! Now if I can have my nephew, Sebastian, and my special girl, Violet, up here to help me christen the building . . .'

Sebastian cut a dapper figure in his little blue suit and tie, but he was reluctant to step forward.

'Come on,' Violet said, 'don't chicken out on me now. We're going to be on TV!'

Sebastian and Violet took Valentina's hand and climbed onto the dais to dedicate The Sunny Moon Music Center for Seniors.

Laura got on her knees behind the three children, and together they swung a bottle of champagne against the red brick exterior of the Center. It burst on the first strike, causing the crowd to cheer.

'Whoo-hoo!' Laura cried. 'We're in business.' Serena and Amanda ran over to hug their sister.

'I'm so proud of you,' Amanda said.

'If only Mom were here,' Serena added.

Laura grinned. 'She's watching us. Dad, too.'

'Oh, look, everyone, there's Richard and his mother,' Amanda said. The diamond ring Sunny had left her sparkled in the sun as she pointed to her husband. He was making his way through the crowd holding the arm of a white haired, liver-spotted woman with sparkling brown eyes. 'Laura, my mom is practically deaf, but she wants to learn to play the drums. You know, so she can feel the vibration?'

'I'm sure that can be arranged,' Laura said, taking Charles's hand and giving it a squeeze.

Elliott joined the family. 'I think we should set an episode of *Law and Order* at the Senior Center,' he said. 'That would given you national visibility.'

'Great idea,' Richie said. 'I'd like to write the script for it.'

'Since when do you want to be a TV writer?' Elliott asked.

Richie shrugged. 'Since I got a brother-in-law who works in TV. God knows I've seen it all.'

'You're on,' Elliott said. 'Write me a script I can use that takes place at the Senior Center and I'll direct it myself.'

Amanda squeezed Richard's shoulders. 'Ooh, honey, a star is born!'

'Do you think some of your talented musicians could give Sebastian saxophone lessons?' Serena said.

'For sure,' Laura said. 'That's part of what we're offering. But a saxophone would be bigger than Sebastian.'

'We'll get a special one made to size, right, Elliott?' Serena said. 'And Valentina is desperate to learn piano.'

'At two?' Laura said.

'Not even,' Serena said. 'You forget how gifted my children are.'

'Whatever you want,' Laura said. 'Come, let's go watch the concert.'

The family wandered over to Duane Park where the Off Our Rockers Quartet had started another set. When Norah Jones finished her song, she handed the mike over to Laura.

'Ladies and gentlemen, days don't get much better than this one,' she said. 'It gives me tremendous pleasure to sing our favorite number for you. A-one, a-two, a-one-two-three . . .

Out of the tree of life, I just picked me a plum
You came along and everything started to hum
Still it's a real good bet, the best is yet to come . . .'

ACKNOWLEDGMENTS

Thank you to the readers who enjoy my work and to the booksellers who sell it. Your support means the world to me.

Contact me at theivychronicles@aol.com. I love hearing from readers and I always write back. Please visit http://karenquinn.net/ and join my mailing list so I can send you my free newsletter that is guaranteed to make you laugh or your money back.

To Robin Straus and Sarah Nundy, my remarkable agents, thank you for your support, enthusiasm and for always taking my calls. Kate Lyall Grant and Libby Vernon, I am so appreciative of your editorial notes and killer book jackets. Shari Smiley, no one wheels and deals in Hollywood like you. I am so grateful to have such an exceptional team of women in my corner.

To Mark, for encouraging me to go after a career that didn't seem possible, you have my unwavering love and devotion. To Schuyler, who is perfect in every way, except for your dirty room. To Sam, my teenage boy-wonder, as much as I annoy you, that's how much I love you.

For your love and friendship, and for taking the time to read and comment on my work before it's polished and ready for the world, I want to thank Shari Nedler, Tatiana Boncompagni, Judy Levy, Anne Sherwood Nicholas, Candice Olson, Kathleen Stowers Potter, Jane Robbins, Kathleen Smith, and Brooke Stachrya.

Special appreciation to:

... Shari Nedler, Mom, for being my number one cheerleader and book tour chauffer,

... Michael and Don Nedler, my brothers, for always being there for me,

... Anne Sherwood Nicholas, for extolling me with tales of your singing telegram career, contributing Laura's singing telegrams for this book, and sharing your experience of caring for your mother, Margaret Cronn Sherwood, who suffers from Alzheimer's,

... Kathleen Stowers Potter, for your unwavering friendship and incredible book parties,

... Reba Miller, for all those Manhattan real estate war stories,

... Laura Cantor, for your Manhattan dating stories,

... Jennifer Jruska, who lived through one of the funniest episodes in this book. Thank you for letting me use it,

... Regena Thomashauer and all the goddesses at Mama Genas School of Womanly Arts. Your sisterhood means the world to me. I am especially grateful for all the support you gave me when *Holly Would Dream* was released,

. . . The Legends of Jazz & Blues with Bernie Lee, who play every week at Vines Wine Bar in Orlando, for inspiring the Off Our Rockers Quartet,

. . . Lezlie Harrison, for singing the coolest version of *Que Sera Sera* (with three *Seras*) that I've ever heard, and to Jay Livingston and Ray Evans for writing the song,

. . . Haya Leah Molnar for showing me the soul coaching journey technique,

. . . Evan Handler, whose book *Time on Fire*, gave me hope when my brother had non-Hodgkin's lymphoma. Thanks for reminding me of an experience I'd just as soon forget, but needed to remember for this story,

. . . *Law & Order*, my favorite TV show, for twenty years of brilliant storytelling,

. . . Stuart Calderwood for copy editing *The Sister Diaries*.

And finally, while space prevents me from acknowledging everyone's specific contribution to *The Sister Diaries*, I want to thank the following people who inspired, supported, and accompanied me for at least part of my extraordinary writing journey: Jim Berg, Anna Bidwell, Meris Blumstein, Buck Buchanan, Jennifer Cohen, Laura Cunningham, Alice Cullina, Catherine Cussett, Jennifer Cohen, Charlene Dupray, Amanda Filipacchi, Kathleen

Frazier, Heather Graham, Stacey Green, Shelly Griffin, Richard Hine, Scottie Iverson, Caimin Jones, Auna Jornayvaz, Kathy Kaye, Tina Koenig, Emma Lowth, Beverly Knowles, Aline Brosh McKenna, Ann Christiane Moller, Nancy Moon, Ben Neihert, Dr Christiane Northrup, Sarah Jessica Parker, Joanne Porzio, Alessandro Ricciarelli, Erika Recordon, Leslie Schnur, Barbara Silkstone, Trish Todd, Joanne Tombrakos, Linda Warner, Amanda Weil, Dr Jamie Wells, and Stan Zimmerman.